The Women's Press Ltd
34 Great Sutton Street, London EC1V 0DX

Christine Crow is Honorary Reader in French Literature at the University of St Andrews. She is the author of three critical works on the twentieth-century French poet and thinker Paul Valéry, *Paul Valéry: Consciousness and Nature*, *Valéry and Maxwell's Demon: Natural Order and Human Possibility* and *Paul Valéry and the Poetry of Voice*. *Miss X, or The Wolf Woman* is her first novel.

Christine Crow

Miss X, or
The Wolf Woman

The Women's Press

To the *other* Miss X,
and for all whom oppression contaminates

' "The characters in this novel are all purely fictional", needless to say'

First published by The Women's Press Ltd 1990
A member of the Namara Group
34 Great Sutton Street
London EC1V 0DX

British Library Cataloguing in Publication Data
Crow, Christine
    Miss X or The wolf woman.
    I. Title
    823'.914   [F]
    ISBN 0-7043-4259-6

Typeset in 10pt Bembo by AKM Associates (UK) Ltd
Ajmal House, Hayes Road, Southall, Greater London
Printed and bound in Great Britain by Cox & Wyman, Reading, Berks

The author would like to thank everyone at The Women's Press
who helped in the publication of this novel and in particular Sarah Lefanu
and Christine Considine for their great patience and enthusiasm.

Contents

The wolf shall find her grave, and scrape it up.
Not to devour the corpse, but to discover
The horrid murder.
(*The Duchess of Malfi*, Webster)

'Suddenly the window opened of its own accord, and I was
terrified to see that some white wolves were sitting on the
big walnut tree in front of the window. There were siX or
seven of them. The wolves were quite white, and looked
more like foXes or sheep-dogs, for they had big tails like
foXes and they had their ears pricked like dogs when they
pay attention to something. In great terror, evidently of
being eaten up by the wolves, I screamed and woke up'
(*The 'Wolf Man'*, Freud)

Petrus Borel, ou Champavert le Lycanthrope (. . .).
Lycanthrope bien nommé! Homme-loup ou loup-garou (. . .).
(*RéfleXions sur Quelques-uns de mes Contemporains*, Baudelaire)

Loin des peuples vivants, errantes, condamnées,
A travers les déserts courez comme les loups;
Faites votre destin, âmes désordonnées,
Et fuyez l'infini que vous portez en vous!
('Femmes Damnées', *Les Fleurs du Mal*, Baudelaire)

'Do you have a boy-friend?' asked the analyst almost right away at the first and last interview.

'Certainly not,' I replied sharply, 'and nor do I want one, if that's what you think.'

Only in the final few seconds, driven no doubt by the severity of IT to trust this new prophet despite myself, did I deign to reveal that I had, all the same, known the flames of true passion, true, reciprocated, yes, reciprocated passion, passion for an older person, a Person of Authority, who just happened to be nearly three times my own age, not to mention the same seX as myself.

Apart from Baudelaire's crafty poem about the forbidden fruits of Lesbos – women as ravenous wolves in the deserts – placed in a separate section of our edition of *Les Fleurs du Mal* and relegated with other 'Condemned Pieces' to the very end of the book, all I had heard or read even then on the subject was that queer, twisted novel, *The Well of Loneliness*, by Radclyffe Hall, its language oozing with the very concepts it purports to condemn. (At least, with Baudelaire, it's a Sin, not a disease, and the Devil far superior in artistic know-how and love of infinity to God the Father, pipe and slippers in his Bourgeois armchair.)

On guard now for the slightest sign of prurience or pity – by their fruits shall ye know them – did I sense a moment's minute hesitation, a flicker of eXtra interest on the bland, SphinX-like face?

If so it vanished at once behind those sinister dark glasses – more a visor than two separate lenses – bunched like a single, blind eye in the middle of his forehead. (Like Racine's Phèdre, I too shunned the light in those days. Fair enough, I thought. Fair enough.)

'And what is her name?' he proceeded smoothly on receipt of this dramatic, last-minute avowal, pencil poised rapaciously above the virgin page.

'**Miss X**,' I replied like a shot. '**She shall be known as Miss X**,' and, to his chiding protestations ('Everything in this room is, of course, strictly confidential'), refused to budge one Greek iota or jot.

Even within these professional ramparts ('Walls have ears,

Mary, and you never know'), I, Mary Wolfe, long since abandoned without mercy, would keep my promise of total discretion, my tongue tight-knit to the roof of its cavern, my lips as tight-sealed as her tomb below.

Indeed, only now, all these many years later, Miss X herself sealed up in a wall ('That's how they bury them out there, Lou, you know'), do I feel at last I can tell our strange story, stitch together its scattered pieces, transform the living fictions of the past into truth. Who knows but that, free at last from fear of betrayal and removal from office – lying tongues more savage than the very nails of the Bacchae – she, Miss X herself, would not have begged me to tell it, final act of undying devotion releasing her poor soul at last from its prison, shouting it from the rooftops for all to know?

If it is revenge, my love, this wicked third person, heating the stone to boil the water, pecking and devouring your poor corpse to the bone, let it at least be for the crime of the turnskin (L. *versipellis*, 'turnpelt', 'turnskin'), not for the pain of illicit desire.

Were we not, you and I, goats in the sheepfold, sisters of rebellion under the skin? Did we not, after all, follow the same star?

I never went back – to the analyst, I mean.

Writing itself can sometimes eXorcise Love.

The First Piece

On a bluff, on a bluff, there lived three
Billy Goats Gruff. Little Billy Goat, Middle
Billy Goat, Great Billy Goat Gruff . . .

Oh what a tangled web we weave,
When first we practice to deceive
(*Marmion*, Sir Walter Scott)

There were three of them.

Miss P, Miss X and Mrs X (her mother). And they all lived together in a house in the pine trees a mile and a half from the School and the centre of town.

Strictly speaking it was not a house at all – the original structure had been divided – but three small flats, each self-sufficient but cunningly interlocked with the other two. Rather like those wooden BoX-puzzles my sister and I found each Xmas (when did they stop appearing, those magically faithful, red and blue Xmas stockings?), so very easy to pull to pieces, but virtually impossible to put together again.

Miss P's flat (two rings) was mainly on the ground floor with a kitchen the bulge in Miss X's dining-room wall, while Mrs X (three rings and please wait) – the middle flat and considerably more capacious – had a kitchen-cum-sitting room plumb under Miss X's bathroom and a bedroom plumb over Miss P's back door.

Miss X herself (one ring and please wait for ever and ever) had a downstairs broom cupboard, kitchen and dining-room, but the rest of her kingdom perched freely above. There was even, jutting up yet higher above the main roof-line, wreathed mysteriously in glossy strands of ivy, a small, round turret containing her bed.

From there you looked straight out into the dark, shaggy branches of the near-by pine trees (L. *pinus sylvestris*, 'trees of Dionysus' – Classics at the time was my best and favourite subject), their bolt-upright cones and long, paired needles sighing and swaying continuously in the wind or pressed against the window-panes like so many faces . . . yes, slowly to be aware of hundreds of faces, the bared teeth, pricked ears and ravenous eyes of hundreds and hundreds of tiny white faces, staring back in. (A curiously miXed set of images, I know.)

3

The house itself was called 'The Pagoda'.

Largely because of its deeply dropped eaves, I suppose – though I'm ashamed to say I never stopped to notice such things at the time, rapt as I was in a world of my own.

There it stood at the top of the lane in the neat, communal garden behind the wrought-iron gate with the squeaky hinges. (They shared a gardener, but even the weeds found it hard to get a footing in the barren patch of soil overshadowed by the pines.)

Three large dustbins standing to attention.

Three separate clothes-lines discreetly masked by the potting shed.

Three separate garages straining Schoolwards, though only Miss X could drive a car, it seemed.

And, of course, always waiting there at one or other of the three back doors, fed thrice over by his three faithful handmaidens, single yellow eye for ever triumphantly gleaming in the middle of his forehead, more like a sheep or foX or even a dog than truly feline: Polyphemus-Raminagrobis ('Rumpelstiltskin' or 'Puss' for short), the huge, pot-bellied Temple Cat.

'Imagine a parallelogram ABCD with two opposite sides, AB and CD, intersected at right angles by a line PQ which cuts AB at X . . . If a man sets out to walk from A to X . . .?'

Man or not, *I* knew the shortest distance to The Pagoda precisely.

You left the town behind you – our own thin, terrace house was already nervously perched on the outskirts ('I never want you to be ashamed of your home, Mary') – and, instead of taking the main road over the new by-pass bridge and out through straggling suburbia, struck away at once along the sinuous edge of 'my' cornfield, down that private track at the back of the old cemetery, past the field with the electric fence where the great white bull sat permanently munching ('Trespassers will be *per*secuted', some ignoramus had inscribed on the gatepost), round by the geese at the end of the golf course (always cackling a warning, no matter how stealthily you sneaked past them in your crêpe-soled plimsolls), up the long lane with 'Her' trees flying over it, dark, fringed pennant against the hot, trembling skyline, at last to place your finger on the familiar bell.

Miss X, one ring.

Miss X and Miss P both taught at the School – French and Classics respectively – where I, Mary Wolfe, then the Head Girl, graced the upper siXth form, beavering away doggedly for the OXbridge Entrance EXam. Miss P was the Senior Mistress (or *Vice* Mistress as some of the less responsible amongst us still giggled meaningfully), and Miss X, though somewhat younger than Miss P, I supposed – late forties? – was King or – should I say *Queen* – of the Castle. The Boss, the Cat's Whiskers, the Headmistress Herself.

I was passionately in love with Miss P.
In the beginning of it all at least.

Certain events in our early lives can so determine our later destinies that we cease to recall them as purely random – more as the perfect eXposition of a Classical Drama or Tragic Novel whose dénouement the Writer has carefully planned in advance.

Such the events I shall describe to you here.

And if the style of my narrative often lacks the compleXity of mature refleXion – those would-be enlightened views we allow to accrete like barnacles, dulling the savage force of that first live conundrum – it is doubtless because the ghostly self which beckons me there in the shadows has never ceased all these years to cry out for a hearing, waiting in the wings till its tale be told.

Only by giving birth to our own strange story, to the Monstrous Myth of the mind's own formation, can we be free at last from the Power of Oppression, free from the Cyclops, free from the Minotaur, free to climb out of the Terrible Cave.

It was the end of a bright, pin-sharp day near the beginning of the autumn term, a lively coal fire flickering in the wide, brick grate of the Study where I had arrived for my privileged weekly lesson in French with Miss X – eXtra coaching for the forthcoming EXam. (I should much have preferred to 'go up' to read Classics, or, failing that, to bestow my unique gifts on the world of English Literature, recently glimpsed with the not altogether inspiring help of a certain Miss Twee. Miss X seemed bent on finding a first-class scholar to follow in her own illustrious footsteps in French, however . . . Jolly lucky it was still *Literature* at least.)

There should have been two of us – 'the two Brainy Marys' as the other siXth formers called us, not always affectionately – but at the end of a particularly taXing passage from Cicero's *De Bello Gallico* (Hannibal and his elephants pounding over the Alps), 'Brainy Mary Number Two' had suddenly declared an urgent interest in marriage, more precisely in a hairy specimen called Gilbert at the local boys' grammar school, leaving me to continue the long route alone. Such my naïvety, it had never occurred to me to doubt the smooth alliance of Scholarship and Matrimony – that is if I thought of the great, glittering abyss of the future at all.

(Poor, unwitting Brainy Mary Number Two. Did you not know it was *my* fate you sealed that day as well as your own? They say she committed suicide, incidentally, after the birth of her second or third child. Oh well!)

Compared with the spartan, chalk-and-blackboard atmosphere of the rest of the School building, every inch of which my privileged duties led me to view with a grim determination in battle worthy of Hannibal himself, the objects in the Study seemed daringly different: eXotic, eXtraordinary, indeed almost 'decadent', to use one of my latest verbal acquisitions: as 'decadent' as Baudelaire's *Les Fleurs du Mal*.

I can still see, piercing the shroud-like mists of time in solitary uniqueness, the wooden lamp-standard with the red, plastic lamp-shade (the lamp itself invariably unlit, for some reason); the wide, brick grate I mentioned, with, in spring at least, its pot of rigidly staked, purple hyacinths; the leather-topped desk with its row of steel-nibbed pens and ever sharp pencils (biros like the one I write with now had still not been invented); the patterned settee-cover with the frayed right arm-piece (motifs from my belovèd Greek Myth, ironically: the voyage of Odysseus); and, perched on the low, pine bookshelves opposite the fireplace, remember, regally enthroned in that mock-silver picture frame with the two entwined serpents, tight white curls, knitted twin-set, gleaming pearl necklace, the sweet-smiling face of . . .

But, of course – the same rather unattractive long nose, short, pointed ears, narrow forehead and unusually prominent canines:

Mrs X!

Mamma herself!

She whose mysterious Power behind the Throne . . .

She whom men and women fear alike, please notice, as the source of their first violent propulsion into the beauteous light of day! (*Not*, oh surely not, into 'this Vale of Tears' as 'Auntie' – really our grandmother's sister – would say . . . admittedly with a twinkle in her ancient eye. Only the three Rs and a rod of iron in her day. And then what with that mysterious, guilty 'trespass' about which she could never be persuaded to utter a word in case the wind changed or the cat's own mother stole her tongue. What terrible prejudices in those far off days.)

One more item, though (little did I know then how it would

come to be squatting here like a toad with a jewel in its head all these many years later): the peculiarly marked, old stone paperweight... mulberry-coloured, with a hole in the middle... which, always out to catch Miss P with some erudite literary allusion usually unknown to her, Miss X had Xtened rather affectedly 'Petrus Borel'.

Yes, 'Petrus' was from the Latin *petra*, 'stone', of course ('upon this Rock . . .', as, my ear to the keyhole, I'd often heard Auntie groan hopefully to St Peter, reading aloud her Bible in her precarious little bed behind the bathroom tank), and 'borel', according to the big, warped dictionary unwisely perched on top of the radiator in the School library, 'rude, rough or unlearned' (!), to be compared with 'burel', a coarse, brown woollen coat or cloth.

But what of 'Petrus Borel' himself?

Strangely passive in those days from the point of view of the precious capacity of the imagination to synthesise – analyse too, for that matter – I never thought to ask or look *that* up in a book.

She had had it inscribed with our School motto, too: '*Ad Astra*'. A pity in a way with such a beautiful old stone.

'PETRUS BOREL'/'AD ASTRA'. Oh well!

Late afternoon, then. Just after last period (Miss Twee on the rumbustious *Duchess of Malfi* again).

Scarlet tendrils of virginia creeper tapping and licking at the windows – remember those criss-X frames with the flaking green paint we used to peel away assiduously in lessons as if bent on eXposing the metal skeleton beneath? – alternately masking and revealing the recently lit streetlights at the end of the drive. (The old-fashioned, incandescent kind, incidentally, not these brash, fluorescent things glaring in on me now, as I peel the layers from I know not yet what dusty palimpsest of self.)

And, already streaming down the broad gravel path to the right of the narrow one reserved for Staff and Visitors (you too amongst the lowly first formers, Pin, or was that only after the end of my reign?), the great, green stampede of the girls going home. (Dark green raincoats over leaf-green gym slips, though in the upper siXth form we were allowed the special privilege of blouses and skirts – a few even going so far as to sport black nylon stockings, there where, notwithstanding my illustrious status, I myself still felt safer in white ankle socks.) Yes, whistling, bleating, baying, screaming their heads off, more like birds of prey or scavenging animals than human beings, a flock of gannets vying for fish or a pack of hounds seeking to devour some invisible prey.

I had no use for such ill-starred freedom. Steep and narrow is the path which scales Mount Olympus (Mount Etna if you prefer).

The first time alone since Brainy Mary Number Two's convenient desertion, *I* was to stay behind to read *Phèdre* by Racine.

Racine. *Phèdre*. Tragic drama of guilty, unreciprocated love.

Phèdre, wife of Theseus, falls passionately and, hélas, incestuously in love with her stepson, Hippolyte (no, not the same one as in Baudelaire's poem – she's a woman, needless to say), who, pledged to chaste Artemis, goddess of the moon and virile hunting, remains curiously unmoved by the power of Aphrodite, golden, fun-loving, foam-born Aphrodite, Venus Herself in fact, with her smooth, round breasts and rippling hair.

Phèdre, 'fille de Minos et de Pasiphaë' – to savour once more that immortal line – who, after falsely accusing the said male Hippolyte of trying to rape her (L. *raptere*, as in 'rapt' just now, to seize and carry away by force), at last confesses the dreadful burden of her guilt . . . if it *is* guilt to fall passionately in love, that is. Are we any more free to choose the object of our *first* affections than a newborn goose, I sometimes ask myself, looking back?

But how easy to confuse Racine's subtle French plot with the more brutal, original Greek which we had 'done' only a week or so before in Classics with super Miss P.

The rape itself, for eXample ('Careful, Mary, do you want me to rape you?') . . . Does it take place even in verbal accusation, or is it a fantasy on the part of the Reader, remembering the teXt as he (sic) wants it to be? . . . Zeus in some convenient thunderstorm or other penetrating the impregnable bronze walls of the chamber with a special blinding shower of gold? . . . Victorian fathers entering the Nursery at twilight to read their daughters Oedipal Fairy Tales in bed?

As Sigmund Freud all too easily came to imagine of the Primal Scene, it is all too easy to imagine such things.

Racine. *Phèdre*.

Outside, replacing at last the vulgar cries of the multitude, only, by now, the gentle moan of the wind. Stray stems of scarlet creeper tapping like tiny hooves, faster, faster, and the crescent moon, Artemis now in person, a slender horn of light on the deepening velvet blue.

Inside, the firelight dancing, dancing . . . vivid tongues of red-gold flame responding to the draught.

And, coiled throughout it all – despite, would I but admit it then, my halting French accent – those marvellous aleXandrines, present yet absent, absent yet present, fingering space with their voluptuous abstraction, cajoling, consoling, confirming, caressing, seducing with beauty in the heart of it all . . . all that vicarious terror and pain.

Ariane, ma soeur, de quel amour blessée
Vous mourûtes auX bords où vous fûtes laissée! . . .

Racine. *Phèdre*.
Yes, she too, Ariane, of the famous guiding thread.
Ariane, who fell passionately in love in *her* case with her sister's husband, Theseus, only to be brutally abandoned on the island of NaXos and later rescued from eXile by Dionysus Himself: Dionysus-Zagreus, Dionysus the Goat God, God of the Irrational, God of the Unconscious, God of so much more than the infamous grape. (Thanks to Miss P, I was a mine of Classical information in those days, though with just about as much understanding of how all these myths and things related to myself and our contemporary culture as a munching white bull in a meadow is the notorious Minotaur in the flesh).

On this particular occasion, due to a scandalous incident over the confiscation cupboard at 'break', I had uncharacteristically left my copy upstairs in the form-room (an insolent member of the upper fourths had not only refused to pay the penny fine on an errant crêpe-soled plimsoll, but actually sworn at me as well: 'ducking punt' or something, a phrase judiciously evocative of an OXbridge idyll – fingers Xed, Mary – yet otherwise not part of my repertoire), with the result that Miss X, equally uncharacteristically, or so it seemed to me then, had ventured forth from behind the leather-topped desk with the row of steel-nibbed pens and ever sharp pencils to come and implant herself neXt to me on the patterned settee, her large, freckled hand with the gold ring (on the 'wedding' finger, strangely enough – did she have some secret husband somewhere?) resting but a few inches from mine as she held up the page, and our two laps, mine the usual leaf-green flannel and hers turquoise knitting-wool (a ribbed twin-set with matching skirt, not unlike the one in the maternal photograph over there, I noticed observantly), separated only by the thinnest fragment of Odysseus bound to the pine-tree mast of his ship.

9

(The once proud face contorted and unrecognisable now with emotion, he is listening to the wild, eXquisite voices of the Sirens, remember . . . bewitched, enslaved, hungry for more and more music, while the rest of the crew, their ears sealed in advance against such terrifying beauty, toil over the oars as previously instructed, devotedly immune to his cries for release. Notice how the prior command takes precedence over all later ones. *That* is the one to remain imprinted for ever. *That* is the voice they will always follow, like cackling new-born geese, to the ends of the earth.)

Je le vis, je rougis, je pâlis à sa vue;
Un trouble s'éleva dans mon âme éperdue . . .

Suddenly, just as I was in full rhetorical flood – that incomparable passage where Phèdre describes her first revulsion towards an alien power within herself and her consequent plans to hide the dark flame of her guilty, blushing passion away from the pure, unsullied light of day – she, Miss X, laid down her side of the book (Garnier edition with the pale yellow cover), causing me to lose my place completely, and whipping off her reading glasses (the kind with pink, plumpy rims I never could stomach for some reason) and turning to face me, snapped abruptly: 'Come on now, Mary. All this deep, dark passion . . . How can you know what it means at your age? You've never been in love *yourself* now, have you?'

'Oh but I *have*, Miss X,' I protested violently, eyes flashing angrily, cut to the quick.

Was it not my love of Miss P, vast, invisible ivy plant, winding its slow, patient way, day in, day out, amongst the ink-stained desks, in the labs, down the corridors, which, sacred, immaculate and, however guiltless in my case, never to be spoken, had given to my voice just then, usually so thin, high-pitched and ineffective, that deep, that low, that pleading tone, interpreting another's love as if it were my own?

'Lo, here hath been dawning . . .': was it not this very same blue, blue day but a few hours earlier that, perched on one of those uncomfortable high stools in the biology lab for A level Greek – according to rumour, that lumpy, mulberry-coloured thing in one of the bell jars was a pickled human foetus (the same colour as 'Petrus Borel', the old stone paperweight, come to think of it) – I had been reduced to breathlessness and near tremor (Miss P sat opposite, at lower inclination) by the flash of a pure white Marks and Spencer's vest over, oh so pink, so naked, in short so very *human* flesh . . . ?

To-day will see shoe-shadow and hear skirt-swish,
Brush teXture of her skin, perhaps, and start,
But will not break the frail shell of her nearness,
Nor cross the gulf to that so distant heart.
To-night, speaking her name, shall shy-shake,
Hating the useless nail-scrape of the will,
While, moving, she will cast unheeded shadows
And, mile-kept, live unwatched, yet, oh, seen still
In thoughts that unlatch each day-storèd image
Of hair, lips, looks and gestures she thought lost,
Till morning dares thought-blushed once more to glimpse her,
My cold, dear Lady with the heart of frost.

'Oh but I *have*, Miss X,' I cried indignantly, the scene in the lab
suddenly even more brilliantly conjugated than before, as the
tender memory of what I had by now officially construed as Miss
P's 'cleavage' ('to cleave', either to split asunder or to cling like a
leech: two diametrically opposed meanings to a single term, that's
odd), Xed, discreetly transfigured, into the world of Literary
Discourse (one of my earliest poetic masterpieces), there to be
immortalised for ever and a day:
'Oh but I *do* know love, Miss X. X my heart.'
Naturally I thought this would be the end of it and we should
return to *Phèdre*, my credentials in the now neatly twinned worlds
of Passion and Literary Empathy certified for good.
But it was not to be.
'And does the person know?' pursued Miss X like an eager
bloodhound, forcing the pale yellow Garnier edition down
completely and edging so near me now on the patterned settee that
the final fragment of Odysseus and the bird-like bodies of the
Sirens was totally engulfed in a wave of turquoise knit. And, to my
cry of protest at the very suggestion: 'Don't you think the person
might be *happy* to know?'
But here we were rudely interrupted by a hail of knocks on the
Study door – no doubt that same brash recalcitrant from 'confis-
cation' I myself had sent here earlier – and, quickly brushing down
the aforesaid jacket and matching skirt (why to this day do I
remember that vulnerable little crease still caught unbeknown to
her in the back of it?), Miss X hastily retreated behind the equally
aforesaid leather-topped desk in the corner, and, snatching a pile of
end-of-term reports from under 'Petrus Borel', prepared once
more to shoulder the professional yoke.

It was the first time I understood the nature of a public profession: that a gap could eXist between a rôle and a person . . . that the social values I had previously taken for granted were not automatic, absolute, eternal but the fruit of human vigilance, will-power, diligence, perhaps even of something more mysterious still . . . something more violent, deceptive, defensive, ambiguous, involving the loss of one thing for the gain of another, the secret power of which, for all its lone asperity, I shuddered voluptuously to feel I too one day might possess if I chose.

Freud would call it 'sublimation', I suppose – not that I'd even so much as *heard* of such a thing at the time.

The invitation to The Pagoda must have come but a day or so later, certainly well before the end of that week.

Miss X had a book on Tragedy I might like to borrow to help with the Racine (Gr. *tragos*, 'a goat', hence, did she but know it, *tragodos*, 'goatsong', the sacrifice to Dionysus of a goat, sheep or ram) and suggested I called to fetch it one evening after School.

'That's right, Mary, my lamb. The Pagoda. That rather queer, tall house with the perky little turret . . . About a mile and a half from town. There's a tall row of trees, too. Top of the lane, backing on to the graveyard. Oh, and be particularly careful not to give more than one ring, otherwise you'll get Mother or poor Miss P.'

Miss P!

Deliciously white-woolly-vested Miss P!

I would have given my life then to 'get poor Miss P'.

The Pagoda.

Miss X, one ring.

Crisp autumn leaves like tiny Chinese lanterns crackling beneath my plimsolls (must have been the sycamore from the graveyard she mentioned), silvery raindrops glistening on the broad, glossy leaves of the ivy, decked, as so often at this time of year, in a mass of 'dew-bespangled' spiders' webs, each tiny facet a miniature rainbow reflecting the whole (I had come across the phrase in a book on poetry and was amazed to discover it had actual links with the world), and, their thin, V-shaped pairs of needles mingled with the leaves piled up on the doorstep, the sweet, resinous scent of the pines themselves . . .

(Pine trees, hyacinths . . . ah, why is it a mere smell, said to be the humblest and least developed of the senses in our case, can suddenly abolish what seems like centuries, startling into life again that strange, inner creature who has slumbered so long, so lost, so deadened, in its burrow . . . waiting, waiting, if only to wake, to sense again that special, privileged joy of eXistence, that opening, that pathway, that glimpse of Mount Olympus where we are already, did we but know.)

When she came down to open the front door Miss X looked less careworn than usual, I thought: jovial, almost human, much more relaXed. A white angora cardigan gave a softer appearance than the uncompromising ribbed pattern of her previous outfit, and there was a jaunty pom-pom on each of her (slightly swollen?) slippered feet.

'Come up, dear,' she said gaily and, since naturally I had arrived bedecked in my full, leaf-green regalia, 'Hang up your hat and coat here in the cupboard under the stairs. It's really the broom cupboard, but now that poor Miss P has indulged in one of those modern vacuum cleaner things, there aren't any broomsticks to worry about any more!'

And here, canines jutting, long nose gleaming (no – with a face like that, she certainly couldn't be secretly married), she began to laugh – a trifle forcedly perhaps? – before turning back ponderously to climb the stairs.

Me, Mary Wolfe, in a Teacher's private house, let alone that of the Headmistress Herself, MA Cantab., Hons. French and all that!

Fully conscious of the honour, and keeping a suitable distance behind the illustrious rear as it led the way above – no humbling creases in her skirt *this* time, thank god – I was following by now up a narrow, green-carpeted stairway with slightly faded treads, into what she called for some reason the 'Parlour' (you could never quite tell with Miss X whether she was joking or not), there to perch gingerly on the high-backed, wooden chair by the window as advised.

Honour apart, could it really be that Miss P (two rings) was so very, very close now, right here under the floorboards but a mere few feet away at the least?

Could that even be the modern vacuum cleaner thing that Miss X had mentioned, droning and thumping there beneath?

To my surprise there was no sign at all, yet, of the promised book on Tragedy.

Instead we talked politely about trivialities: School meals, relaXing card games, vacuum cleaners, the capricious weather (L. *capra*, that too, apparently, means a goat), the date of the forthcoming OXbridge EXam . . . On and on, almost boringly, I was ashamed to find myself concluding, until, as they say in trashy Romantic novels, 'a great silence descended' and you could hear a pin if not pine needle drop, even the vacuum cleaner thing hushed and fulfilled.

Then,

'*Come here,*' called Miss X slowly – a gruff, throaty voice quite unlike the cool, metallic tones with which, daily in assembly, she would intone 'Our Father' or announce the house netball results, credits, detentions and the rest.

'*Come here, Mary,*' gesticulating unmistakably now towards a suddenly important little zone of floor at the foot of her own languidly cushioned, decidedly 'decadent' armchair.

And, before I knew it, forever obedient, passive, obliging, lamb to the slaughter (hindsight, Mary, and, besides, don't eXaggerate), there I was squatting uncomfortably at those slightly, yes, definitely slightly swollen, slippered feet . . . the same large, freckled hand with the gold ring from the settee with the Racine, lightly stroking – yes, stroking, I ask you – light as a goose feather, the top of my head.

'Don't you think the person might be *happy* to know?': it was as if the conversation of a few days earlier had simply been carried forward like a mathematical sum (Miss Hilbert), the two ends knitted together without even so much as a cloven hitch or Gordian knot.

I suppose I must have guessed all along it was *herself* rather than Miss P she thought the object of my affections.

Now there was no doubt about it.

She did.

Below us the vacuum cleaner had renewed its uneasy droning. Busy as a bumble-bee, but somehow distanced now by this first acrid scent of involuntary betrayal, Miss P, poor Miss P, was at it again.

With a curious miXture of emotions, part numbness, part horror, part pride and fascination, but above all eXcruciating pity for Miss X at her embarrassing, potentially painful mistake, I resigned myself to my future fate.

She must never know.
There was no way back.

And so began that strangely proliferating deceit, born of the fear of hurting another – itself the child of what dark fears I know not –

which, even more than Brainy Mary Number Two's fatal desertion (oh that fear of Women's Access to Knowledge!), was to shape and determine the rest of my life, finally to provide the very touchstone of my Literary Craft . . . that further strange voyage into the Promised Land of I know not what new scriptural desire, on which, like the foXy Odysseus escaped at last from the Cyclops, as old as Miss X myself now, plumpy, pink-eyed and uncertain, I once more rashly prepare to embark.

Was it cruel to be kind or kind to be cruel that I donned my first hairy mask of deception, that beauteous, star-filled, autumn night?

And who, I put it to you, was to be most the victim of its eXtraordinary consequences: Mary Wolfe or Miss X herself?

Perhaps I am telling this tale in order to find out . . . why there should be victims at all, come to that.

Goose-feather brain that you are, Mary!

Has ever a Writer not wished to change the World? Has ever a Writer succeeded in his (sic) task of Lighting the Lamp to change the course of the Sun?

This tale is different, though, you'll see. By putting her own head on the block of Language, grinding the bones of Culture to bake her own bread . . .

And besides . . . Racine again, 'instruire et plaire', to teach and to please. Is that not sufficient Moral in itself?

Travel on, then, Mary! Carry on spinning your strangely tangled Testament of Youth, written with the ink of your own Wolf's Blood, stitched together with ancient pine needles and bound in your own coarse, Borelian cloth. Remember above all, whatever *they* tell you, that Love and Friendship and Art and Beauty are still the only things that count in this world provided you've got your own house on your back.

Travel on you too, dear Reader! Patience, deep breaths, and the straw will be spun into gold by itself. No one will beat *you* with an iron rod. RelaX and enjoy yourself, but keep on your toes and never trust the bark of a sleeping log. There where the conversation seems at its most vacuous, capricious, banal . . . there above all snaps the crocodile.

Be not misled even by that pompous creature of the biro and the orange, yes, blood-orange, fluorescent lamps.

Dancing round my little fire, muttering to myself my secret name, I alone am the Voice in the Wilderness.

I alone am the Howl of the Wolf.

15

The Second Piece

Je le vis, je rougis, je pâlis à sa vue;
Un trouble s'éleva dans mon âme éperdue;
Mes yeuX ne voyaient plus, je ne pouvais parler;
Je sentis tout mon corps et transir et brûler . . .
(*Phèdre*, Racine)

The mind is an acutely suggestive thing, prey to its own fictions, fantasies, myths.

How did it happen that, imperceptibly at first but then with less and less chance of retreat, I was finally no longer separate from the mask I adopted, its hairy muzzle cleaving, growing, biting deep in my living flesh?

I still loved Miss P, of course, but as if in a daydream. An ethereal image, a mystic fantasy. No more, I now told myself maturely, than a mere schoolgirl 'crush'.

It was Miss X I wanted now.

Miss X and Miss X only.

The long, pointed nose, the jutting canines, the narrow forehead, the distinctive smell of talcum powder (muguet, I once discovered triumphantly from a tin in the bathroom), the slightly swollen feet in the formal leather shoes she wore on duty, or, indeed, for our more intimate sessions out there at The Pagoda, in the jaunty slippers with the coloured pom-poms, the strange low voice from the Parlour bidding me 'come up, dear', and, of course – the memory soon to swell and ebb like a great sob of longing deep inside me – the large freckled hand with the single gold 'wedding' ring stroking, stroking, light as a goose-feather, the top of my head.

Yes, every other Sunday, during those first glorious months of our dawning passion, if and when summoned (sometimes, ignorant of our mutual needs, Mrs X or Miss P would have fiXed for her some other, more trivial pursuit like a trip to Ramsgate to stroll on the front), that eXstatic flight along the richly rutted edge of 'my' lovely cornfield, swift as an arrow from the bow. (Incomparable youth! Let no one diminish with those cheap, weary sarcasms so common to age and envy, the brilliance of our first awakening to the age-old tune of desire – the measure of its joy and anguish still none the less unique to the reason of every pulsing human heart.)

Along the secret track at the back of the old 'town' cemetery, its huge, gnarled trees – oak, ash and cedar of Lebanon this time – stretching their generous, ancient limbs to bid me blessings as I pass . . . round the field with the great munching Minotaur, down by the cackling geese at the end of the golf course – thief of silence still despite my stealthy plimsolls – up the lane with the dark flags of welcome, through the squeaky gate by the three neat dustbins (little could I know then their dramatic future significance), till, at last, at last, all those interminable days of waiting and planning dissolving again into petty parenthesis, trembling finger on the familiar bell-push:

Miss X, one ring.

I come, I come! I enter my Love's rest!

I passed the Entrance EXam with flying colours, needless to say. EXactly the right question on passion in Racine for someone 'out there' to notice me too. But, horror of horrors, the Scholarship, a major one, was merely to OXford, 'the Other Place'.

Yes, think of the shame of it! OXford, not *Her* Alma Mater, Cambridge, as, every evening after carefully completing my revision – no shirking homework for the sake of *this* 'amour' – perched precariously on the siX-bar gate I had claimed for the purpose, eyes fiXed doggedly on the distant School chimney-stack (the fireplace in the Study lay conveniently under it), ink-stained fist raised defiantly to the Heavens, '*Ad Astra*', I had solemnly pledged my entire eXistence before filling the coal-bucket and locking up for the night. ('Yes, it's quite all right, Auntie. I've checked the back gate.' For some reason she'd started to worry about midnight prowlers just of late.)

I was crushingly disappointed, of course.

How perfectly beastly!

After all She had done for me, all the eXtra coaching, the trust, the self-sacrifice, had I not started my star-spangled career by letting Her down at the very first fence?

But all this was before the OXford Weekend, that momentous temporal apeX – 'weekend' seemed so inadequate – when, almost as ineluctably as that first strange act of deception . . . deception in the cause of further illusion? . . . I first . . .

You are going too fast, Mary, rushing like Phèdre and Hippolyte to the final catastrophe and the locking for ever of the terrible door.

Let me slow down first and, true to the best eXpository

principles of all good Aristotelian if not Racinian Tragedy, stretching my own gnarled branches of memory no doubt in the process, try to set the scene in a walnut-shell for you first: how, even before the fatal little spondee 'I love you' had finally generated its own reality, I found myself acting in a highly charged drama played out almost literally on the splintery planks of the old School stage – all my skills and energies devoted by this time to concealing our intimacy from the cruel, prying eyes and pricked ears of the multitude, including, I hasten to add, those of poor Miss P herself (not to mention Amanda Carbuckle, my importunate Head Prefect or, if you must, Vice Head Girl), there where, before, they had been spent concealing my cruel indifference from her own.

How intoXicating our secret, how heady our subterfuge, how splendidly daring the giddy risks and gambles She took for me, and, above all – or so I thought *then*, poor fool – how deeply and passionately I was loved in return . . . but then, you see, perhaps at that stage, I *was* . . . perhaps even, in some ways, all along.

One of my most sacrosanct duties was to ring the electric bell for change of lessons (perhaps my one source of transient popularity, since, to so many sufferers, it signified release): a procedure which, owing to my shameful imprecision in matters of numeracy (hardly, in this respect, a child of my father, and *he* left school almost as early as Auntie, god bless him), meant that at least the last quarter of every lesson would be spent with one eye anXiously fiXated on the face of Cronos, the clock.

Recklessly breaking all the rules on the inside I was determined on the outside not to put a foot wrong.

The bell-push this time – one long, vibrating blast like an ancient ship's siren – was located, as it happened, eXactly outside *the* door ('HEADMISTRESS PLEASE KNOCK'), which, day in, day out, for richer, for poorer, harboured behind its cruelly recalcitrant woodwork, alive and presumably breathing however tantalisingly invisible, my Lady Herself, Mentor and Lover all in one.

Generally it would remain tight shut, of course, only the greedy arrows of imagination ('Too much imagination, Mary. Those great eyes of yours') piercing its bronze-coloured panels and blissfully devouring all within.

Indeed, by the beginning of the spring term there was a weekly session timetabled optimistically 'Listening to Music', during which, by dint of crouching strategically in line with the precious target (the hall sported glass doors on to the corridor eXactly opposite), I found I could not only secretly keep vigil – that double keenness of the animal that is both hunted and hunting its own prey – but positively *will* the great showers of sound in which we were enveloped to pound back from the very auricles of my being and break against her portals in invisible waves: an eXciting piece called 'The Pastoral Symphony' where you could actually hear the sound of a cuckoo, for instance, one or two strange Nordic works by Procrowkeyoff and Sybil somebody, full of ice and pine forests and great, glittering snow-fields (though apparently you're not really allowed to see pictures like that), and a wondrous 'Requiem' (rest for the souls of the dead) by one Wolfgang Amadeus Mozart, whose first two names I found myself repeating each morning as a kind of involuntary mantra while I cleaned my teeth. (Being a war baby and deprived of sweets, I can't think why the enamel caused problems later on.)

Preferring the classical (Schubert's 'Trout' was another particular favourite, I have just remembered significantly), but priding myself on sufficient fleXibility to embrace the modern as well, I especially enjoyed, too, the subtle half-tones of a piece about a sleepy faun or satyr (an intriguing creature apparently half human, half goat), based on a poem by some 'weird French poet' beginning with 'M' which Miss X herself had once disparagingly referred to as both 'obscure' and 'erotic' (the two seemed equally perverse and unfortunate), and to which, for my sins, she feared I might have to be eXposed one day at College, as, indeed, for my sins, I was.

Stéphane Mallarmé of the famous 'Sonnet en X', maestro of silence, absence and lack. I should have known!

Indeed, many a time and oft would our melodious music mistress, Miss Ramsbotham, Saint Cecilia in person, turn towards me in weary appeal, a tear of mingled eXtasy and nervous eXhaustion rolling in vain down her gaunt, ravaged face ('Oh the impossible beauty of it, Mary – you who alone amongst the philistines . . .'): I who had no true eyes but for that little siren-like aperture across the corridor commanding so temptingly 'HEAD-MISTRESS PLEASE KNOCK'.

'Enivrez-vous . . . !' (Charles Baudelaire again): Wine, Love, Women (?), Poetry, Song, what you will! . . . Yes. No doubt about it. Miss Ramsbotham was our local 'melancholic'. One of those ill-fated souls who look to the vaporous delights of Art itself for fleeting consolation, there where others (naming no names, of course), borrowing the back of Pegasus but in passing, turn their burgeoning attentions to things nearer home. Give unto Hannibal. A dog can't serve the voice of *two* masters in this world.

No need for Miss X to warn me meanwhile, as, to my injured pride, she had attempted with almost frightening gravity on more than one occasion, that the tiniest, tell-tale gesture of intimacy 'in Public' on my part could lead to the ruin of her entire career, let alone to the educational impoverishment of gifted future scholars like myself and Amanda C. Tender, violent, fish-like, fawning, obscure, erotic or simply plain pastoral like the reassuring country cuckoo: whatever the musical message sounding deep within me, not a sign on my bland, in those days still nakedly un-bespectacled, face.

(*Was* the Carbuncle so very bright, incidentally? Of course not. Miss X had only said it to help me feel less alone with my eXceptional, if still incipient, mental powers. 'Critical insight and sensibility eXceptionally combined. Should go far,' Dad, temporarily home again from one of his perpetual agricultural sales 'jobs' scattered like grain up and down the length and breadth of Britain, had read out warily on my latest end-of-term report, having first filled the coal-bucket for what seemed like at least a fortnight's cacophonous supply. No, it's quite all right, Auntie, it's only 'Ole Faithful' – Dad's favourite tune, along with the 'Three Billy Goats Gruff', for whistling on any long car journey – come back to make us jump out of our skins in the middle of the night . . .

'There's a coyote howling to the moon above . . .
Getty up, ole fellow, 'cos we gotta get home to-ni-i-ight.')

On particularly privileged occasions, the Study portal itself would flash open like a kingfisher (Gr. *halcyon*), however – hélas, poor Alcyone (Ovid's *Metamorphoses*) – leaving me the urgent task of concealing my quickening gaze from Miss Ramsbotham and other surrounding subordinates without in turn forfeiting the least detail of the precious scene within.

O Muse, fleeting prey!

And somehow, at the end of every long day of loving abstinence in the call of duty (no longer was I quite so prompt now to punish recalcitrants with that sharply barked imperative, 'Go to the Headmistress'), I would even invent a way in which I might infiltrate the sanctum myself, cleverly armed in advance, needless to say, with the perfect preteXt to make my visit seem purely official if called to task by any importunate Members of Staff (some of whom were still far from treating me with the eXtra respect my due).

Replacing the 'confiscation key' on its familiar hook at the foot of Mrs X's silver photo became a particularly favoured alibi, I remember, or presenting the bulging 'charity boX', and so on. In the service of a greater Mistress than itself, Human Hypocrisy obviously knows no bounds.

Whether the thrill was the greater when I *invented* the preteXt or when the preteXt was made splendidly superfluous – like the time when Miss Hilbert (maths *and* chemistry) innocently sent me straight into the Lion's Den mid-morning to enquire the official date of Prizegiving – I could never quite decide.

Certainly the latter occasion was the more highly memorable, marked as it was, despite the risky vicinity of a pair of vulgar workmen repainting the outside window-sill (little did they know for what far future hieroglyph), by our first, highly daring, intra-mural kiss.

I can remember it to this day, here in the middle of my forehead, really no more than a peck, or at least the dry brushing of an autumn leaf. Hardly the ravenous nocturnal meal I was later led to eXpect from Baudelaire's 'Femmes Damnées' with its surely just a trifle hyperbolical imagery of raging waterfalls cascading into the bottomless abyss. Something about women as wolves, too, running chaotically through the deserts propelled by their infinite appetites. Definitely decadent, obscure and erotic all in one. (Not that I spared these matters much thought at the time. Merely metaphors, after all. I had other sweet songsters to fry.)

The bell, however.

It served, you see, as the perfect signal when all else failed.

Rain or shine, the bronze-painted Study door tight shut or gloriously wide open (never, it seemed, the middle position), proud and rasping as the scream of a peacock, it would sound through those teeming corridors (for me, hélas, so empty), the unswerving devotion of my amorous patrol.

And there, bent alone over the familiar leather-topped desk, with 'Petrus Borel' no doubt seated beside her or lying quietly in her turquoise lap, still and mysterious as a sleeping fire dog . . . faithful or forgetful, alone with the thought of me or distracted despite herself by others' demands, she would hear it calling her, the horn of Roland, hungry cry in the wilderness, voice of our silent, ineXpressible Love.

It was a time, as you can imagine, when my whole life seemed suddenly as riddled as the cemetery at the bottom of the garden – yes, that's right, the old 'town' one – with secret codes and hieroglyphs, urgent ways with which to squeeze the maXimum communication into a limited medium while still adhering to the strict generic rules of the game. (What else *is* Great Literature, I sometimes stop writing to ask myself.)

No. She need not have warned me. For all my tender years, did I not, I too, appreciate the absolute need for discretion . . . revere with my life's blood the old School motto, with its noble, but oh, so vague, eXhortation to strive to the stars?

Symbols, codes, hieroglyphs, secret metaphors, cyphers: little did I realise then how, like cuckoos in the nest, these rapacious children of rhetoric would soon greedily outlive their task of parley with the loved one and come to speak back to myself alone . . . echoing voices but to hide the silence, their frail bonds tightening to compensate for each new abjection, until, like a brilliant, dew-bespangled spider's web with no further victim than their own creator, a wreath of poisonous ivy round a single pine trunk, they began to form a noose round my own living neck.

The Lover's neck, at least.

The Writer's strange vocal cords are slightly more robust, it would seem.

As for the proverbial discrepancy between Passion and Duty, or at best, in our case, the need to keep Public and Private worlds totally and ineluctably distinct . . . at first I simply took all that in my stride. (We were on to Corneille now, where, unlike the Racine with its tragic insolubles, these two eXtreme forces are set at each other's throats like battling stags or, if you prefer, the two enraged bulls in Virgil's *Aenead*, to be reconciled by the eXtremity of conflict itself.)

Only later on, in fact, dangerously inspired by my lone, vacation reading of twentieth-century writers like Jean-Paul Sartre and André Gide ('All that weird, *mod*ern stuff, Mary. Where are its *values*, I ask you?'), did I begin to suspect that, in certain circumstances at least, passion itself might be a kind of duty, a cry against injustice, a howl in the wilderness against all those enemy Governors, Vicars, Teachers, Parents (Dad and Mother? surely not, that's different), potential School friends (these latter receding from me every second with the speed of light, I'm sorry to have to report), whom I was beginning to mistrust, fear or even positively despise.

Given the barest suspicion of its eXistence, would they not have eXpunged, eXpelled, eXterminated, eXtinguished without mercy the pure, intense potential of our eXtraordinary flame?

Did they not realise the incomparable loneliness of Her at the Helm of the Ship of State? (and especially with so many rats like Miss Hilbert, the Carbuncle and insolent Poppy Morpheme on board – this latter a particularly terrifying bugbear of mine who, ever since the 'ducking punt' episode . . .)

She *needed* me, damn it, to keep on steering straight across the cruel Ocean. Shouldn't that have been enough?

In addition to sounding the bell with its double-purpose 'reveillez', however, there was a second privileged task attached to my office and ripe for inscription in our secret Book of Spells.

Every morning at precisely eight forty-five after I had stood poised and alert like the Monarch of the Glen to take the salute while the entire School, Staff as well as girls, trooped humbly past me into the hall, it behoved me to fling wide the familiarly bronze-painted door of the inner chamber with a cool and official 'Good-morning, Miss X' (the delicious part of the game at this point being to speak with scrupulous formality *despite* the now officially sanctioned lack of any possible witness), and, having temporarily flattened myself against the doorpost while she, Miss X, gown flapping handsomely like a giant, black bird in some ancient Indian saga of the beginning of the Cosmos, swept past me in turn, to follow her proudly up the aisle, there, as Chief Handmaiden, to claim my lawful place on the right-hand side of the proscenium, while those trivial but relatively necessary matters like prayers, the house netball results and so on, were broadcast from above.

(Unlike Miss X herself, constantly bent on butting under the floorboards – 'every goat longs to be a sheep Mary' – any healthy metaphysical doubts about God and Religion she might have achieved through the barest modicum of common sense, I myself lived courageously, if somewhat truculently, free from such shackles and could but marvel at the scandalous misuse of precious intellectual energies I beheld all around . . . even in people like the Carbuncle, High Church in her case, said to be so bright. Infantile Narcissism. On *that* Primal Scene at least, Sigmund Freud was surely quite right.)

But to return to our sheep, as the incomparably ribald Rabelais, then unbeknown to me, would say. 'Ĭ lōve you, Ĭ lōve ўou Ī lōve,' I would skilfully parse beneath my breath to the familiar beat of 'Our Father, which art in Heaven', willing her not to stumble on a single syllable, not to squander a single fragrant breath . . . tender, solicitous, proudly admiring, pierced now with pangs of vicarious dread, as, magnificently alone up there – 'Qui s'élève, s'isole' – Canute reversing the very laws of Nature, she held the sea of green and white bodies below her still and obedient with her polished command.

Like Actaeon's hounds turned upon their own master ('Actaeon! Actaeon!' he cries in vain to identify himself in his fatal stag's uniform), how easily they could have upped and savagely ripped her to pieces, had they but recognised a compound fraction of their own youthful power! ('Miss X! Miss X! It is I, Miss X, your old Headmistress, come back to haunt you without your knowing me, crying in vain to the empty air!')

. . . She who, unbeknown to all but myself and, hélas, not quite so poor Miss P, had sported, only three weeks last Sunday, the casual slippers with the jaunty coloured pom-poms!

. . . She whose *real* voice – 'Come up, my lamb, up into the Parlour' – was so very unlike this strangely controlled and distant 'Public' one, the artifice of which was nevertheless rapidly adding its own empowering register to the tentative language of our inner repertoire – could it be Love positively thrives on transgression of conteXt? – penetrating and transformational as the most intimate 'Private' caress!

. . . She whose very lips (it seemed almost unbelievable!) had, only yesterday between siX-A maths (Miss Hilbert) and chemistry (also Miss Hilbert), rested like an erudite butterfly, nay, pagodial dragonfly, upon my hot cheek! (our second kiss, courtesy of the surprisingly ever-bulging charity boX, and with no noisy workmen this time to inhibit what must surely have been well on the way by then to Baudelaire's mighty cascades of ravenous mutual desire).

'Our Father, which art in Heaven, Hallowed be thy Name, forgive us our trespasses,' (I thought of poor Auntie muttering for redemption in her bed behind the bathroom tank) 'as we forgive them that trespass against us . . .'

'Ĭ lōve yōu, Ĭ lōve yŏu Ī lōve . . .'

Not for nothing had I carried off the first prize in Latin scansion, donated, incidentally, by the Vicar Himself.

As I cannot ram home enough, the health and success of so unique a relationship relied, then, on keeping a strictly watertight division between our two daily universes, Public and Private, however much, by dint of personal symbolism, forged on the vulcan-like anvils of Hephaestus beneath Mt Etna, the two were beginning inwardly to bubble in the same alchemical retort.

Imagine my horror when, during one such morning's assembly, just after we had all finished singing 'St Patrick's Breastplate' with rousing gusto ('I bind unto myself to-day/the virtues of the starlit heaven . . .'), what should I look up to find but the said or, rather, sung Miss X suddenly leaning forward in my direction as if about to topple from the precipitous edge of the platform, and, her eyes half-Xed with what I took to be shamelessly undisguised passion, Romeo on the very edge of the balcony (Juliet's, naturally, would be far too soppy), gesticulating towards my person in wild appeal.

Could it be that the strain of pretence had at last proved too much for her?

That *she*, not I, was proving the first to crack . . . jeopardising thus all further chance of . . .

No matter. It's a hurricane that blows the cows no good, as Auntie would say. We could always elope together to that little rented villa in Sicily (Mount Etna again, true-life land of the Cyclops, according to the well-thumbed notes in the back of my Homer), where, much to my irritation on her behalf (must Charity *always* begin at home?), she was dutifully forced to take Miss P on her Easter holiday each year . . . or, if that proved impossible, live together in a small but convenient one-room flat in OXbridge while I took my first class degree and, casting off at last the monstrous, green husk of adolescence, began to effect metamorphosis into an HM myself.

But no.

Barnacle Goose that I was still in my lowly Xrysalis.

It was simply the handbell she wanted in order to dismiss us. Not my trembling Private Person at all.

Some clown had left it there on top of the cup cupboard (shining silver trophies for hockey and netball – not my forte) rather than placing it in reach by the lectern as time-honoured custom required.

If it had not been for the quick, immortal hiss of the Carbuncle: 'The handbell, Mary. She wants the handbell,' I should have stood there for ever in the terrible marketplace (Gr. *agora*), rooted to the spot like poor Daphne of the laurel bush, or, if you like, the gluttonous wolf in Ovid's 'CeyX and Alcyone', changed to stone like poor 'Petrus B' (though for what secret trespass in *his* case, we have yet to find out).

Hot and cold like Phèdre at the thought of it all these years later: that curious moment of suspended significance, all eyes upon me, accusing, devouring – yes, slowly to be aware of hundreds of faces, the bared teeth, pricked ears and ravenous eyes of hundreds and hundreds of tiny white faces – as she leant down towards me: 'Come, to my arms, my love, my love. Our bodies why doe wee forbeare . . . ?' (Miss Twee – English lit. – had her uses, after all).

And the jolly rotten thing was that just for a split second, terror itself had seemed suddenly as attractive and obscure and decadent and erotic as the very song of the Sirens . . . my Rock, my Resting-place, my Lighthouse Tower.

Had I not felt for one dazzling instant of perfect panic (Gr. *Pan*, alias Lupercus, son of Zeus and Callisto, horns and hooves of a goat just like Mallarmé's satyr), the impossible fusion of two distinct selves: Power and Emotion, Passion and Duty, Public and Private all in one?

'The handbell, Mary. She wants the handbell.'

On that occasion I finally managed to fulfil her bidding. There was soon to be another far more serious occasion when I failed disastrously in that respect. But true to the delaying tactics of, hélas, far more than the bewitching art of narrative, let me continue to build up the conteXt for that most terrible unprosecuted, if not unpersecuted, trespass of all on my part . . .

Long before my rise to the giddy Olympian heights of the upper siXth form, let alone to the eXalted zenith of Head Girl, Miss X had once, it seemed, deep in the very heart of 'Our Father' – that point of no return that every self-respecting public speaker dreads – felt suddenly sick and faint . . . unreal, even, no more than a cypher, legs like jelly, palms sweaty, hands trembling, unable, even as Phèdre on her deathbed, to see and admire with unclouded eyes the lovely, clear blue light of day through that little round window at the top of the gym . . .

. . . a sensation all the more horrid in that, as if eXpressly designed for the purpose, the prison-like architecture of the hall blocked all eXit behind her, ensuring, should she succumb to physical weakness in front of all those pairs of cruelly staring eyes, only the most ignominious defeat. Oh that dread 'osmosis' (Miss Prick, botany and religious studies) between the idea, the word and the thing! . . . that gastronomic fantasy of self-ingestion, that fuzzy, amorphous invasion of 'self' by 'self' – my very biro trembles and sweats hysterically at the thought of it – we all of us suffer from now and then!

Haunted by this indeed most dire spectacle (I too began worrying now, and, such is the peculiarly dangerous empathy of the Lover, by no means solely on her own behalf), the poor soul had developed the understandable habit of fortifying herself beforehand with certain sweetmeats: aniseed balls in this case like Desperate Dan (we had our special fund of jokes by then), guiltily hidden in 'Messer Gaster' (Gr. *gaster*, 'the belly' or 'stomach'), the middle drawer of the leather-topped desk, together with a spare packet of pear-drops for after Staff meetings and so on.

(Yes, 'Messer Gaster' was from Rabelais, as was 'Raminagrobis', the Fat Cat Lawyer, I found out later. Yet another of those compleX literary nicknames especially designed to foX poor Miss P.)

Imagine my mortification and remorse when, with but a mere three minutes and seven seconds to go before our grand procession up the aisle (would it were to Mendelssohn's famous wedding march), in an effort to accommodate the sudden request of two importunate parents to 'see the Headmistress' . . . rashly by-passing the secretary, Mrs FoX, in the process ('really' the old Mrs Salmon in disguise, I had discovered self-righteously), and no doubt unconsciously seizing the opportunity to display both my own privileged intimacy and the object of my proud affections in one fell swoop of the wing (some Headmistress!) . . . I flung wide the door without even so much as an official, let alone my specially coded warning knock, only to reveal . . . Operation Aniseed Ball in full spate!

Indeed, her flushed cheeks swollen like an oversize hamster with obviously more than one of the aforesaid guilty tit-bits – that special love/hate we have for the object devoured which at the same time devours us – scarce could Desperate Dan issue a single Public word!

Such reprimands for dereliction of duty as I received later that day in the official French lesson instead of the customary endearments of 'poppet', 'lou-lou' or the more tamely domestic 'my lamb', tended to cut like knives into my by then already raw and sensuously quivering devotion – their wounds perhaps the more terrible in that, for the sake of her who inflicted them, I had already sacrificed so many rival sources of companionship and comfort, certainly the chance of making friends in my class, as I said.

From that day on, spontaneous gestures on my part were even more meticulously checked and guarded, and it was not long afterwards that, slinking up the aisle one morning to claim my accustomed position before the surely increasingly accusing, if sheep-like eyes of the masses (was it my imagination or had Miss Hilbert actually smelt a rat or something?), I eXperienced what I can see now were the first tell-tale stirrings of 'IT' . . . that nameless raptor which, when it swept down on powerful wings a few years later – the full-bodied Furies pursuing Orestes tooth and claw – no amount of aniseed balls would keep at bay in my case, nay, nor even all the secret bags of pear-drops in the Wide Wide World.

Why else guard with my life against the tiniest movement in Public, be it the innocent scraping of a green metal stacking-chair or the tell-tale whisper of my own living breath?

Why otherwise – unbeknown to Miss X, of course (mustn't hurt her feelings) – did I begin to breast the previously proud delights of our invisible matrimonial march up the aisle with – Wolfgang Amadeus, Wolfgang Amadeus – my teeth dug surreptitiously into my own tender flesh?

With the star of Scholarship – '*Ad Astra*' – there were no such painful boundary disputes. Love and Aspiration, Aphrodite and Artemis, so far perfectly espoused in its luminary orb.

But in order to continue to merit and retain Her affection, trusted Head Girl and Lover under a single School hat, it seemed now I had to put some other, deeper, darker Mary Wolfe under lock and key . . . and only just in time before she gnawed her way out.

Minotaur in the Labyrinth, white Bull in the Meadow . . . no doubt, did I but know it, the Monstrous Beast of my own infinite appetite already munched its way deep inside me even then.

Not yet that precious, healing pain which springs like the fragrant hyacinth beloved of Apollo, grief and remorse inscribed as the Greek for Racine's 'hélas' on its petals, from the brilliant, purple wound of its own youthful death.

'Actaeon! Mary! Ai! Ai! Do you not recognise me, your own dear Mistress, my own dear body without which I should be dead?'

There is nothing more dangerous to the living animal, hunting or hunted, than to remain for ever rapt in a world of its own or someone else's making, losing all sight of what there is to dread.

The Third Piece

And Thou
Beside me singing in the Wilderness . . .
(*Rubá'iyát*, Omar Khayyám)

But it was not only within the four familiar walls of the School that we pursued our daring double eXistence that first glorious spring before even the seeds of such epic future conflicts were sown.

The building in those days backed on to relatively open countryside.

To the west, framed behind a quivering, silvery curtain of aspens (L. *populus tremula*, trembling, some say, with a guilty secret), the tender, green escapement of 'my' lovely cornfield and the distant, darker green and yellow snake of the golf course (you could even just make out the magic tip of Her perky little turret in its dark fringe of pines if you knew where to look).

To the east, a thick coppice of oak, ash and horse-chestnut, home, no doubt, of many a spritely silenus, dryad and lazy Mallarméan satyr or faun. Pan Himself, perhaps. And straight ahead, rising from a meadow usually full of sheep and cows, the sandy hillside we all called 'The Wilderness', tangled with rose-bay willow-herb, bracken, broom and scrub, and frequently set on fire, much to everyone's delight, by flying sparks from the London train, rumbling through it now and then along a deep, narrow cutting which in one place disappeared totally beneath the earth as if down some Labyrinthine entrance to the meadows of Hades itself.

On one particularly memorable occasion, the risk and daring of which still takes my breath away, Miss X had gone so far as to invent for herself a bad sore throat, informing me that poor Miss P had been instructed to take assembly that morning instead ('Such a silly, bleating voice, it will do her good').

Then, having eXcused me my usual matinal duty of taking the salute (it was approaching the time of the EXamination and my absence could easily be justified), and with the whole School safely imprisoned, by this time on its knees, she in turn, Miss X, despite her slight, attractive limp – those swollen feet of hers – positively galloped off with me across the hockey pitch . . . over the low wire which marked our last boundary (fortunately my green School mac, flung wide for the purpose, provided us both with at least the illusion of camouflage), through the first meadow where, ears pricked like pinnacles, the sheep had all stopped chewing now to stare at us curiously, and on into the greening bracken above, there to snatch what fleeting pleasures of 'Mother Nature' we could.

('How utterly ridiculous these male and female terms for matters of the intellect,' I had once been bold enough to suggest to Miss X in a rare flash of semi-inspiration which left her disappointingly unmoved in return. All right on a sunny day like this when Mother Nature was fresh and smiling, but what if 'She' suddenly turned nasty and stormy causing females like dear Mother to become stained with the same foXy cultural brush? Oh well. Presumably 'They' knew what 'They' were doing out there.)

Gambles for my sake indeed!

Could it possibly be the lure of forbidden fruit which emboldened my companion to wager such perilous capers?

Or even that by running so constantly towards the very brink of disaster – that strange, part-phantom X-bar responsible for dividing so many secretly non-divisible worlds – she even half consciously *desired* to be eXposed and eXpelled?

Unable or unwilling to pose any such compleX questions in the heat of the moment, I was aware only of the joyful eXcitement of the escapade, of the thrill of her attentions, of the half delicious fear of playing truant from authority in the presence of what, after all, was Authority Herself.

Halcyon hours indeed, hélas, there in the sweet-smelling bracken, in the brambles, in the bushes (' "*L'école buissonnière*", Mary. Got your French notebook?'), alone in The Wilderness – Paradise enow – with my eXtraordinary, double-headed Mentor and Love.

'What would Miss P say if she could see us now?' I noticed Miss X had taken to remarking on such occasions with embarrassing regularity.

And I'm ashamed to confess that I too had stooped to invoking the poor creature's name in vain now and then. She was, indeed, rather 'pedagogically uninspiring', as Miss X had helped me to see for myself on more than one occasion, and there was indeed a rather silly bleating note to her voice. No more so than at Miss Ramsbotham's glorious annual zenith, the Xmas carol concert, when, to the sniggering delight of the upper fourth form – cruel

Poppy Morpheme above all others – she would stand and deliver herself of her allotted piece about 'Mary great with child' (could it be that the giggling glances were equally cast now in my *own* direction?), ending with the absurdly personalised query: 'And how shall this be, seeing that I know not a man?'

In previous years, Miss P had still been my idol, remember, and, the echo of my own all too Xtian Xtian-name adding obscurely to the shameful emotion – the Virgin Mary great with child, my foot! – I had taken the indignity of heavenly insemination to heart on our mutual behalf (oh, that fear of Women's Bodies!) including the indecent reference to pregnancy itself. Leave all that to the Brainy Mary Number Twos of this world, perhaps not so Brainy after all.

Now things were different, however.

I was becoming all too willing to sacrifice poor Miss P and her innocent, autogenic rhetoric on the pyre of my growing bid for fresh fields and pastures new.

How soon we learn to bite the hand that feeds us (*certain* bland, pink hands, at least)! How swift and potent in my case the terrible alchemy by which that same blithe spirit, endowed in the biology lab that time with the brightness of an angel, had come to represent 'la Bêtise' in person . . . sheep-like, lamb's-wool-curly Stupidity itself!

Until the day we encounter that rare being capable of containing our metamorphoses without ceasing an instant from chewing the cud, such violent reversals are potentially infinite perhaps.

By now it was fully spring. 'Le Printemps adorable,' as Baudelaire had conveniently remarked in one of his presumably less decadent poems, or, if you prefer, the Vernal EquinoX – the eXact point at which the sun Xes/passes over the equator and enters the sign of Aries the Ram.

Time of 'the liquid fire in the grape' and the pulsing of animal blood in Demeter's fields, not to mention the doubtless swelling membranes of Miss X's *own* eXceptional sensibility and intellectual powers – fully developed rather than incipient in her case, needless to say.

Bluebells (L. *hyacinthus non scriptus*, sic), primroses (*prima rosa*) and tiny purple dog-violets (*viola canina*) beginning to bedeck the freshly burgeoning woods, and the green-skirted aconite, which so many of us, for some reason, insist on confusing with the not nearly so spectacular winter wolf's bane (L. *lycoctonum*), already jealously past its prime.

Not that our hopeful escape to The Wilderness had brought forth much actual fruit at the time.

Scarce were we safely concealed in the tangled undergrowth lustily singing 'St Patrick's Breastplate' than Miss X had constantly looked back over her still heavily bound and yoked shoulder in the direction of the thrusting School chimney-stack – focus of so much of my own lone aspiration from the siX-bar gate, remember – and started to plan the strategies of our return to the fold: an operation soon successfully accomplished, I'm sorry to say . . . and without so much as a glance this time from the rows of munching sheep who had seemed so curious about us before.

(Strange how like wolves they had looked when standing there motionless . . . short ears pricked, muzzles pointed, teeth . . . Wolfgang Amadeus, that reminds me . . . so many white wolves in a Fairy Tale. White sheep, white wolves, the Victim turned Oppressor, the Slave to Master. You see, Miss X, the same as my idea just now about Mother Nature, only maybe you didn't actually quite hear me against the wind or something: those strange reversals and X-overs again. Whenever opposites without a proper watertight dividing-line are involved, I suppose? Must ask Miss Hilbert – maths/chemistry – though I don't eXpect she'd . . . so many black marks, alias red Xs, on my work of late, algebra in particular, believe it or not.)

In order to ring the changes on the dubious Sunday treats on the front at Ramsgate increasingly arranged for her back at the flats, Miss X would now sometimes boldly announce to Mrs X and Miss P her intention to further my religious welfare ('Sadly neglected by her parents, let alone ruined by all that nasty modern literature she's having to digest') by taking me out in her faithful old blue car, Giovanni, with his choice of three garages, to listen to an uplifting sermon in one or other little rural church on the edge of the marsh.

No sooner did we arrive at such a sacred spot, however – and the whole of Kent and SusseX seemed to be bursting with tiny ancient churches waiting patiently over the centuries to aid and abet precisely such subversive a purpose as ours – than Giovanni would be jauntily parked a little way off down the lane under some magnificent budding oak (L. *quercus robur*) or pagan ash tree (*Yggdrasill*, Tree of the Universe, it seemed to me at such moments of nascent glory, trembling beneath its wingèd keys on the brink of so *many* brave new worlds) . . .

And there, shamelessly impenitent about this new, doubly sacrilegious deception, interrupted only by the bleating of innocent

lambs on the other side of the hedgerow or, on one more
memorable occasion, by the comically gruff cough of a definitely
less innocent old billy-goat with a bell round his neck ('Change of
lessons, Mary!' – I'd already thought of it with the bluebells just
now, though I didn't say), we would continue our interesting discussions undisturbed until the hour was up and, most of them bent
double over walking-sticks or walking-frames, we noticed scathingly, the faithful flock emerged to wend its wobbly way home.

Discussions not always about the Divine Headmaster in the
Skies, needless to say . . . though sometimes I wonder if it wasn't
half to get even with Him up there above us – not only God, but
'God the *Father*', I ask you! – that Miss X took me 'lambing', as we
used to call it, in the first place, not simply to hide from Mrs X and
Miss P at all. The rebel needs an audience, don't they say?

Apparently there was something Miss X was trying to tell me
about the youthfully eXpanding human body which I was on no
account to try to discover for myself (though what it was eXactly I
was far too blind to make out) . . . something which, with the innate
skill of the literary crafts*man* in tantalising deferment, if not
Mallarméan obscurity, she presented at one and the same time as a
Pandora's boX of direst evils and a cornucopia of forbidden
delights. In short as a fully-fledged, if still, in my case, shamefully
nidulant mystery (L. *nidus*, 'nest') which could only be resolved
'one day' if 'time and circumstance' were right.

(L. *cornucopia*, 'horn of plenty', as in the little-known legend of
Amaltheia, the goat nymph . . . Naturally I was still anXious to
keep up my Classical knowledge all this time – and not only out of
lasting loyalty to poor old Miss P. These things gain momentum
aboard their own flight and many a humble twig or wingèd stone
unrecognised at the time can turn the key to later Paradise.)

Yet again, Miss P never seemed to guess the truth about our
pious Sunday eXcursions, any more than, according to Miss X
(what agile leaps *her* mind made too sometimes!), she would have
understood the more daringly 'decadent', not to say 'erotic',
references in *Les Fleurs du Mal*, to which, safe still by a few neatly
demarcated decades of lit. hist. from the absurdities of 'all that
nasty modern literature' still waiting in ambush, we had progressed
together by then in order to ring the changes on Daudet's *La Chèvre
de Monsieur Seguin* – Blanchette, the little goat, who sets out to
chance her luck on the mountain – and St-EXupéry's *Le Petit Prince*,
for both of which doubtful masterpieces Miss X held an embarrassingly soft spot, it grieved me privately to note. Hardly the standard

of Jean Racine. Even just that little bit sentimental, I thought. Especially the bits in the latter about the foX and the sheep by the well in the desert (' "Les puits dans les déserts," Mary, got your French notebook?') and hitching one's waggon to a distant star.

As for *Mrs* X all this while, there she sat out at The Pagoda like the proverbial Buddha beneath the eaves of his temple, nodding and smiling as sweetly as ever: either knitting furiously like the sheep in *Alice Through the Looking-Glass* (yet another turquoise twin-set was obviously in the making) or preparing for her belovèd 'Leetle Dorter's' return from the 'Office', a special, but oh, so dangerously rich high tea (treacle pud and iced ginger-bread, I shouldn't be surprised, triumphantly heralded by toad-in-the-hole and washed down with quantities of pagodial China tea).

Mrs X and Miss P were deadly rivals in the food sphere, I was soon to discover, each falling over herself to tempt her shared victim with her superior gastronomical wares.

No wonder, what with their double culinary efforts and the almost daily spoils of Desperate Dan, my angel seemed, like Polythemus-Raminagrobis (Rumpelstiltskin, then) to be putting on weight to a daunting degree.

No matter, though.

I loved her.

All last trace of that fortunate, initial deception totally and finally eXpunged by now for good. *She* was the Chosen One. The Elite. The Cat's Whiskers. Red face, double chin, limp, pot-belly, swollen ankles, short, pointed ears, jutting canines, the lot.

It's in the eye of the beholder, don't 'They' say after all? (and goodness knows *my* eyes were – are – big enough: staring back at me now clean through the Looking-Glass of Writing like an ageing vampire about to X the barrier between Language, Death and Life.)

The climaX of our secret eXcursions came one Sabbath later on in the summer term, however, when, not even bothering now to hover near one of the reproachful little churches on the marsh in the pretence of seeking a sermon, we drove Giovanni at top speed across the sheep-dotted dykelands to Dungeness, there to besport ourselves at the foot of the old lighthouse – now *there's* a lone wolf for you – dominating that desolate stretch of shingle which juts like a beak into the open sea.

(It was in the days before the monstrous bulk of the nuclear power station, that ravening Minotaur it will apparently take at least a hundred years and millions of pounds to disembowel even when we go for fusion instead of fission. Careful, Mary. This is not the place. What if the wind changed, as Auntie would say?)

I had visited Dungeness on several previous occasions with my family, when we had always immediately scrunched across the beach to throw stones for Sigmund . . . down by the steep, clear-cut edge of the sea. Being a dachshund (G. 'badger dog') and not a good swimmer at the best of times – good walker neither, come to that – Sigmund never actually ventured into the water herself, but could sometimes be temporarily roused from congenital depression and/or hysterical, self-defensive anXiety – incipient agoraphobia in her case, perhaps? – by the splosh of a flying pebble or two.

'Coming to the brink?' I asked my human companion now, thinking this surely a purely rhetorical question as I started off briskly in the direction of the waves: their lovely, leaping crests all white and foaming like the bed of Aphrodite above enchanted, Circe-like depths of transparent bottle-green.

But no.

Miss X had other ideas, producing from the back seat of Giovanni two furry brown cushions and a tartan rug.

Apparently we were to recline on the beach right here.

At first I was disappointed – 'stick-in-the-mud' – but rapidly dismissed the dishonourable suggestion from mind. She was, after all, as I was to announce proudly to the analyst at my one and only interview (the heyday of 'IT', I suppose), nearly three whole decades older than me.

Think, in any case, of all those other sporty things, notably our recent caper in The Wilderness, which proved she was still youthful as ever at heart . . . even, in some ways, more youthful than me! A certain charming if sometimes alarmingly irresponsible propensity to gamble and take risks with life, as I said.

(Incidentally, together with announcing the hymn, St Patrick's Breastplate, the teXt which poor Miss P had been forced to declaim that now proverbial morning of the 'bad sore throat' was Matthew XXV, I discovered:

When the Son of man shall come in his glory, and all the holy angels with him, then shall he sit upon the throne of his glory: And before him shall be gathered all nations: And he shall separate them one from another, as a shepherd divideth his sheep from the goats: And he shall set the sheep on his right hand, but the goats on the left.

No prizes for guessing the goats in this case. Could the ironically appropriate symbolism even have been what Miss X had consciously in mind when she chose the passage herself almost a month in advance? Surely not.)

But here we were, reclining languidly now on the doughty MacFarlane rug, I myself half propped up still on one dimpled elbow and Miss X already fully supine below. Thou beside me in the Wilderness indeed . . .

The whole place as usual completely deserted. A scant, bleak beauty strangely independent of the human drama played out on its stony auditorium and yet to remain engraved on my mind's eye more sharply in some ways than the inner feelings it allowed – still allows – me to recall.

Purply-blue viper's bugloss with its thick green tongues (L. *buglossa*, Greek for 'oX-tongue'), horned poppy (*glaucium flavum*), and my favourite yellow sea lupin (*lupinus lupinum*) – Mother had told me their *English* names the previous summer – sprouting miraculously amongst the harsh pebbles as if determined to survive and blossom in the desert at no matter what odds. And, indeed, the pebbles themselves of infinite teXture, shape and colour even if poor Sigmund were not here to admire.

Smooth round ones; long, rough, flaky ones; small, hard, grey ones with specks of gold and silver sparkling in the sunlight ('fool's gold', I shouldn't be surprised looking back now); mulberry-coloured 'lucky' ones with holes in the middle like 'Petrus Borel'. ('Boodle's in his Den,' Dad always hummed mysteriously whenever he came across such humble treasure. 'Look, Miss X, Boodle's in his . . .' How silly it sounded. 'Keep my big mouth shut neXt time,' as Mother would say predictably when Dad failed equally predictably to respond to some eager literary quotation. Not that with Miss *X*'s sphinX-like silence it was at all the same thing. Opulence renders one immobile, my Love.)

Stones like pear-drops, stones like pick-aXes, stones like paper-weights, stones which, squatting there like wise old blue toads (lapis lazuli?) enjoying the sunlight, seemed both self-sufficient, whole, monadic, and yet at the same time like the separate letters in some ancient alphabet which, if only we had the means to decipher their lost, magic powers . . . (I was enjoying one of my flashes of would-be poetic inspiration again. Better at the cosmic than the close at hand.)

Gulls wheeling idly above our heads, meanwhile – none of that raucous screaming you get when they are scavenging (remember those great elm trees full of rooks, Pin, at the end of the School drive?), and as I stared upwards at the dark, tumbling shaft of the lighthouse, the whole sky suddenly shifting and deepening like a giant vaulted cavern over our heads.

Magnificent clouds with rose-flushed edges chasing each other like sheep over the bottomless abyss. Space, time, infinity, X, the Great Unknown! . . .

Me, Mary Wolfe, born for a moment like this!

And there She lay . . . *Miss X*, I mean . . . flat on her back still, warm and living beside me, thin wisps of hair – slightly greying, it's true, but it comes to all of us – charmingly wafted in the summer breeze, and the, some would say embarrassingly large mound of 'Messer Gaster' (could it be a false pregnancy, perhaps, like Sigmund's?), gently and vulnerably rounded against the horizon as if we were lying in some gigantic tent. (A sky-blue skirt and fleecy white angora twinset this time completed the eXtraordinary atmospheric effect – Mrs X had eXcelled herself.)

'LuXe, calme, volupté . . .', 'Chevelure moutonnant jusque sur l'encolure . . .', hair flecked with foam like the fleece of a sheep: yes, what was it Baudelaire had said as, doubtless fully in bed in his case, he attempted to write of eXactly such privileged moments of bliss?

'Strange the French say "sheep" when they're really white horses, don't you think, Miss X? You know, when the waves rear up and race along eXtatically just before they break . . .'

And, before I knew it, amazed this time at my own rival daring, there I was edging closer and closer across the bumpy surface of the old, red MacFarlane, until, lulled by the soft suck and pull of the foaming waters below us – sheep or white horses who cares a green pin – and my still uniformed body held hot and limp against her own, my head was actually resting in the crook of her arm, deep amongst the snowy forests of those soft angora hairs. Worthy shepherd indeed!

All that silent immensity of space which, if it terrified Pascal, (French religious moralist in the seventeenth century and Miss X's own nickname, funnily enough), certainly failed to terrify Mary Wolfe, safe at last in the ancient, woolly arms of her Love.

On the marsh the grasses blow and blow
And I shall be happy, I know and I know . . .

What would Miss P say if she could see us now!

(Yes, a private nickname only, 'Pascal', dear Reader. No danger if you catch me chanting *that* by my fire.)

But there was another poem too, I remember. More dense, more elliptical, more 'nasty and modern', more 'lacking in values' . . . A poem 'wrung from me', as they say, later on that night when, woken from a fitful sleep by Sigmund's sudden jealous barking – the neXt-door cat had dared X into her territory – I attempted in vain to eXpress and to live again (*live* again, Mary?), the aching new sensations felt in that hour . . . sensations which, however strangely physical in origin – how could they *not* be? – were characterised by a curious kind of consciousness I'd never really felt before, or at least not felt to that acute degree. No, I don't mean mature self-awareness. That was the *last* thing in those days (a fleeting illusion no doubt even now), but something which made me feel quite distinct from what I was eXperiencing: detached, separate, not simply my bodily self propped up down there with Miss X on the pebbles at all . . . though at the same time – quite the opposite from Miss X's fainting fit in assembly – *more* real, *more* present . . . *more* myself in some ways than ever before. ParadoXical, I know.

'Lapis loquitur', to be published shortly after as a surprise for Miss X in the very neXt issue of *Ad Astra*, the School magazine, with the suddenly uneXpectedly vigorous help of Miss Twee.

A hundred times more sophisticated than that silly ode to Miss P about the 'Lady with the heart of frost', it began, I remember, with the image of the lighthouse itself . . . its great, ever vigilant, black and white edifice thrusting up over us like Baudelaire's 'phare ironique' against the fading skyline (such a pity Miss X had refused to go up even when that kind man in the navy uniform popped out uneXpectedly and gave us the chance), and ended, after several strained metaphorical battles with the tongues of viper's bugloss and the crescent-shaped horns of the Artemisean poppy (gone now my lovely yellow 'lupinus lupinum', you notice), with the great, blind but somehow still watching eye of the lantern, waiting patiently until the twilight (' "*entre chien et loup*", between dog and wolf, Mary. Got your French notebook?') and, by then, hélas, our own disappearance, to shine forth silently across the deserted pebbles . . . those ancient oracles who would surely sooner or later have cried aloud by themselves if the Children of Israel had not lent them a voice.

Can we never communicate our feelings directly?

Is there no pure, horned trumpet with which to give tongue, no other language with which to eXpress a glimpse of that strange, empty centre where Boodle sits counting his lucky stones, but that of a world we have not made?

But with an eXpression on her face quite different from usual, Miss X had prised herself up from the tartan rug by then with obvious difficulty – the last rays of the sun were already stiff and oblique as in some old, allegorical painting representing the stigmata – before brusquely gathering up the rug and cushions and throwing them almost violently on the back seat of the car.

I had seen that eXpression only once before: that time out at The Pagoda when, just as I was reluctantly but firmly leaving for home one evening – an essay on the 'Duchess' for Miss Twee by neXt day – she had suddenly closed her eyes (a deep lapis lazuli, in case you are wondering), and, forcing me almost roughly back against the 'fleur de lys' wallpaper at the foot of the staircase leading up to the turret, pressed herself slowly against my unsuspecting body . . . on and on, gently, rhythmically, backwards and forwards, lost, or so it seemed, amongst the dark, serpentine branches of the swaying pine trees reflected for me alone above her head in the mirror . . . on and on until I began to feel quite worried (did she feel faint like that time in assembly or something?), and was almost grateful for once when, with supper obviously spoiling, Miss P knocked accusingly on the bulge in the wall with her stick (later discovered to be an ancient broom-handle kept eXpressly with that function in mind).

'*What does it do to you*?', Miss X had whispered urgently on that occasion, asking the questions herself for once.

But now I too had refused or been unable to answer.

EXcept perhaps in one of those 'nasty modern' poems where the pebbles alone can give voice to the silence, and the sheep and the goats are no longer divided, there *is* no answer to a silly question like that.

The eXcursion to the lighthouse was the furthest of our secret capers in Giovanni that season. But this did not prevent our taking advantage of him in humbler, less dramatic ways.

Sometimes, now that the evenings were drawing in again, and always supposing that Miss P had gone home earlier by herself on the bus (mutton stew and treacle pud presumably take no small preparation), Miss X would propose, to my great eXaltation, to give *me* a lift home from School instead.

Not right to the front gate, of course. That was far too risky

('Walls have ears, Mary, and you never know'). But certainly as far as that parallel street with the sheds and garages – 'Wall Road', appropriately, I seem to remember – where, in memory of our good old 'lambing' days in the country (eXciting to think we had a past already, as well as a steadily growing hoard of little codes and jokes), we could draw up a moment and take stock of ourselves at the end of a demanding professional day.

'I never want you to be ashamed of your home, Mary,' Miss X had announced as we neared the vicinity of our familiar red-brick terrace with its rows of homogenised lace curtains, bristling television aerials and so on. (Not that *our* curtains were the boring, obligatory lace, to be fair. Purple plastic with a maze of red and white dots like a feverish tongue. Yes, according to Miss Prick, botany, and her much prized medieval Doctrine of Signatures, viper's bugloss is proof against snake venom by virtue of being speckled like a serpent's skin.)

'No, of course not. I promise,' I remember replying with some bewilderment, the thought never previously having raised its head.

On the other hand, a terrace house *could* be a bit poky and what with the thin walls (war damage), when Dad had on the new television . . . Yes, a wonder I had got any homework done at all, let alone winning a Major Scholarship.

But, 'No, of course not. X my throat if I tell a lie.'

On *this* occasion, however, there occurred the following small incident which I remember almost more graphically than any other, etched like a perfect cameo on the velvet of the dark into whose smiling, crocodile jaws Miss X herself, one day, unbelievable thought . . .

Crouched together in the back seat of the car by then like two courting teenagers – the analogy having just occurred, not without a certain merriment, to Miss X herself, I seem to recall – we suddenly looked up to see, trotting along silently across a pool of yellow lamplight at the end of the street (yes, the old yellow lamplight still in those days), who else but *my parents*, totally innocent of all but their offspring's uneXpected academic progress – must be some mistake – Miss X having sworn me to ineXorable secrecy in that direction almost before Phèdre had made Act 1 Scene 2.

Yes, Dad and Mother in one of their rare moments of domestic conjunction, followed inevitably by the reluctant figure of Sigmund – eyes down, ears flattened, her latest false pregnancy weighing down her long stomach almost to the pavement like a knitted draught-stopper and that thin rat's tail with the unmistakable black tip held in close between her legs at the back, quivering like a guilty aspen leaf. (Hard to imagine, on seeing such slavish obedience and devotion, that the dog – L. *canis familiaris* – is directly related to the wolf – *canis lupus* – the very epitome of voraciousness and unsublimated greed, at least according to Ovid's *Metamorphoses* again.)

That perfect vignette, then, under the lamp.

The three well-known figures, so dear, so familiar, so taken for granted until that moment, yet, at the same time, for Her sake ('On no account tell anyone, not even your mother'), so ineXorably distant, cut off for ever behind a trembling, invisible screen.

We sat there petrified (L. *petra*, 'a stone'), needless to say.

Giovanni's rakish sidelights quickly eXtinguished – that itself could have drawn attention, I chided daringly – and Miss X bent forward in a vain attempt to cram her large body with its aching spinal column (still eXpiating for the Dungeness pebbles) half under the seat and half, along with me, under the furry brown cushions and red tartan rug . . . in case, horror of horrors . . .

Will they, won't they?

(Yet another of Dad's own little rare but humorous eXpressions, strangely enough. And for some reason it felt like the breaking of an ancient taboo to think of it then. Incestuous, irrelevant, almost obscene . . . almost as if, or so it seems now in hindsight, I were lying there in Giovanni not with the real Miss X at all, but with some great, sphinX-like figure like the Devil on the tarot cards who combines both cultural Male and Female, Mother and Father, Victim and Tyrant, Sheep and Goat, Wicked and Innocent together in one. Boodle himself, perhaps. With what touchingly naïve generosity do we writers eXpose our inmost thoughts and no doubt post-Freudian, *pre*-Oedipal fantasies to the lusty scrutiny of generations to come.)

Will they, won't they, will they, won't they?

Will they, won't they join the dance?

But no.

They won't, thank goodness. False alarm on the part of the shepherd boy long before his anguished final cry of 'Wolf' later on.

No sooner had they crossed into the pool of lamplight, with Mother taking Dad's arm now to steady him on the uneven paving-stones – signs of *his* 'bad back' even then? – and with Sigmund, the 'black sheep' (sic) of the family, obviously already fantasising the relative security of her basket by the Rayburn ('Il faut vivre pour le

41

retour', St-EXupéry), than they disappeared again into the gluttonous shadows, swallowed up, like Leconte de Lisle's mysterious procession of elephants across the desert, behind the wall of darkness from which they came. (Even now, so many moons later, I can hardly write these words without pain.)

'Ah, night trees sun-tinged line this autumn aisle . . .'

By then it was already early autumn again. September, in fact. My favourite month. The first clash of gold cymbals over the hardening earth, not to mention the ever more violent scraping of the coal-bucket as, sending poor Sigmund into nervous paroXysm – no peace for the wicked even back upon their own hearth-stones – Dad initiated the aforesaid Rayburn into the full orchestral delights of the winter ahead, and Persephone preparing to leave the yearning arms of *her* mother and return to the doubtless no less strenuous demands of her Lord and Master beneath the dark Earth.

The trembling secrets of the aspens by the hockey pitch already turning to temporary gold from silver – the pines themselves, faithful invariant, were still, of course, dark green and unchanging – and, thanks to one of the mighty combine harvesters Dad advertised on his increasingly frequent 'Ole Faithful' trips up and down the country causing terror to every windswept dormouse and scarlet poppy, the harvest in 'my' cornfield almost completely gathered in.

(In many parts of the countryside it appears they call the last sheaf to be cut 'the Goat', though the name can also apply to the person *making* it.)

And so ended Act One of my 'Sentimental Education' . . . A time which, for all its intermittent joys and pains, and perhaps with the part eXception of the scene on the pebbles at the foot of the lighthouse, was almost, it seems to me now, without light or shadow. Only a curiously passive consciousness, waiting, waiting, however acute now and then its own sensation of detachment, for some crack, some rift, some vast eclipse of the pine-rocked moon in the mirror, through which to detect, no matter how faint, no matter how uncertain, when time and circumstance were ripe, that first faint echo of the voice within . . . ah yes, the separate voice within . . . which would one day come to set it free . . .

Free to lose and therefore free to love?

But all this, as I said, was before the OXbridge Weekend.

From then on, Boodle in his Den or not, nothing would ever be the same again.

The Fourth Piece

And he shall separate them one from
another, as a shepherd divideth his sheep
from the goats: And he shall set the sheep
on his right hand, but the goats on the left.'
(Matthew XXV)

Queens', King's, Fitzbilly's Bun-shop, Girton – Her old
College – Granchester, the Backs . . .

I still had all the Cambridge prospectuses propped up on my
dressing table, unable to accept my shameful defeat.

To help me transfer my fierce loyalties *away* from Cambridge,
now treacherously transformed to 'the Other Place', and perhaps
even to eXpiate for having fuelled the flames of such one-track
enthusiasm in the first place – we all have our faults after all – Miss
X had decided to take me 'up' to OXford for a weekend to visit my
new tutor whom she was convinced she knew already from her *own*
college days – yet another mistaken identity, as it turned out.
(Difficult to imagine her once my age and astride a bicycle at that –
the thought seemed almost sacrilegious somehow.)

At her own eXpense meanwhile, we were to stay the night in the
'Radclyffe Hall Hotel' near the 'Radclyffe Camera' (presumably
either a photographer's or a public house – I thought of Auntie and
the occasional 'snifters' bought by Dad in the hopes of brightening
her 'Vale of Tears'), which, with the obstinacy of those only half
conscious false convictions never fully dislodged since never
looked fairly and squarely in the eye, I at once assumed to be spelt
with a 'y' after the author of a dull-looking novel in a brown-paper
wrap recently discovered in the Parlour one Sunday while poor
Miss X was busy downstairs putting Mrs X and Miss P off the scent.
They really had got to be the bane of our lives of late.

I was frightfully eXcited, of course.

As much about going away from home with so illustrious a
companion as about setting foot for the first time in an Alma Mater
of my own.

Now, beyond every tooth and whisker of doubt, I, not the
Carbuncle, was the favoured one: the Elect, the Anointed, the

Fatted Cat (never, you notice, the sacrificial goat or lamb). My sense of cherished uniqueness knew no bounds.

I had been made to feel particularly fragile of late, you see, by Miss X's innocent admission that I represented for her not so much an individual, but the very fountain of Golden Youth in person: 'Yes, poppet, ever since I first set eyes on you way back in the first form with your big, bright eyes and the plaits with the little green bows . . .'

(There seemed a contradiction here somehow . . . I who in any case, unlike the Carbuncle – horrid thought too painful to glimpse even from the corner of an eye – had absolutely *never* worn my hair in plaits, let alone in plaits with little green bows. Ironic if it wasn't me either, if you see what I mean! Not the first time that prickles had crept up *my* so far, touch wood, totally uncontaminated backbone or spine.)

As for the night in 'Radclyffe Hall', that would be absolutely smashing, of course, notwithstanding Miss X's odd behaviour over the booking arrangements and unimportant matter of beds. If I hadn't been so gratefully enamoured and admiring I would have come right out this time with a 'don't be such a stick-in-a-pot'.

(I was notoriously bad at idioms, by the way, unable, for some reason, to divide one from another, keep the precious cell boundaries intact. Hence odd hybrids like 'get up my goat' and 'a flesh pot never boils' or 'keep the wolf from the window', often causing us much jollity as we attempted to sort out the hidden signifiers involved. There was even, in one of my most passionate essays on Racine, a wonderfully compacted 'stone to pluck' at which we chiselled away airily to discover at least three hidden linguistic orthodoXies: 'bone to pick', 'crow to pluck' and 'stone the crows', all doubtless with rich ancestral pasts of their own. Jolly fascinating stuff, language, when you come to think of it, though somewhat daunting to find it labelling and creating you unconsciously even before you've rashly opened your trap. Perhaps, paradoXically, my famous miXed idioms were a way to hit back?)

Not that Miss X was much better herself.

There was an awfully embarrassing time just before Prize Day, for instance, when, to the usual barrage of smirks and sniggers from the upper fourth form, she had announced with lascivious gravity: 'I'll be waiting in my womb,' followed close on her own heels, so to speak, by 'the Milo de Venus,' and, the neXt morning – must run in packs – 'breast foot forward, girls,' and 'better be solly than safe'.

Admittedly no more than simple spoonerisms, lambdacisms, catachreses, substitutions or reversals in her case ('good' for 'evil', 'detentions' for 'credits', 'goats' for 'sheep', and so on). Never, by any long red chalk, fully fledged repressive paramnesia when you can forget the little matter of having just committed a murder or something the afternoon before, but fully fledged parapraXes or slips of the tongue all the same which would have set Sigmund Mozart, if not Wolfgang Freud, barking his head off in his grave.

One Sunday, you see, Miss X had suddenly lurched Giovanni to a halt in a lay-by alongside the new by-pass bridge, jolting me forwards quite painfully, did she but know it, and, staring straight ahead as if I wasn't really present, asked in an unusually serious voice whether I had thought over carefully if I wanted her to . . . well, you know, Mary, book a double or two single rooms. (When driving, she always wore those plumpy pink reading glasses I didn't like, which she now whipped off and placed in the middle of her lap like two substitute eyes checking up down below and reminding me of Picasso and the Ancient Egyptians, though so as not to hurt her feelings, of course, I didn't say.)

'Whatever you think best, Miss X,' I replied just a trifle impatiently ('stick-in-a-pot', 'fuss-in-the-mud').

But then, since she still looked so worried for some reason and precious discussion time was rapidly evaporating, 'Oh, a *double* room would be less eXpensive, don't you think?'

Actually, the idea of eXpense was no more than an eXcuse on my part. I was dying to talk about a new book called *To the Lighthouse* I was just about to start reading by a peculiar female writer called Virginia Woolf.

Naturally I had assumed until then that all women (myself, Miss X, Miss P and, in some ways, dear Mother, strangely eXcepted – if we had a gender at all, that is), were either simpering seX-pots in fur coats and bikinis like the ones on the calendars Dad's boss had up in his office, or cow-like machines for cooking, general housework and producing babies like Brainy Mary Number Two (at least *she* eventually committed suicide, though). Besides, apart from the shock of finding that a woman *could* write a novel (there was also apparently a queer thing called *Orlando*, where the hero actually changes seX through the years!), I felt particularly drawn to this unknown spirit – the Novelist, I mean – because she was so nearly my own namesake.

Woolf, Wolfe! If only I could but eXchange my terminal 'e' for her eXtra 'o', perhaps *I* too would write queer modern novels like that! Wolves have ears, Mary, and you never know!

(Radclyffe Hall when not an OXford hotel, meanwhile, I naturally assumed to be a man. Not that I'd had a chance to read the novel in question yet: Miss X had come puffing back upstairs to the Parlour that time and snatched it from me so brusquely that her gold 'wedding' ring with the wobbly sapphire – yes, didn't I tell you? – had cleaved like a leech on to one of the buttons on my upper siXth form blouse, causing us much embarrassment as she tried to split us free. And not only *humorous* embarrassment on her part, I was sorry to see. There seemed to be something grim, violent even, in the frantic manner in which she attempted to disengage herself before Miss P could come on the scene. 'Thy sins will find thee out, Mary,' she had hissed cryptically as, like Hercules slaying the two, no, nine-headed Hydra, she wrenched herself free from me in the stitch of time.)

'Yes, a *double* room, Miss X, don't you think?' (Lovely to think we should have a room of our own in which to talk through these important literary things, as I said.)

Strange how that simple moment, at the time so ordinary and uneXceptional, has become sellotaped for ever in the album of my life, retrospective harbinger of the whole unborn drama still then about to unfold. How many battles for a horseshoe nail? How many whiskers on Cleopatra's nose? How many historians truly remember you cannot tell a tale until the tale be told?

To the left of us the shallow, mud-bound river adorned with tin cans and sluggish brown weeds, winding its path under the dark arch of the bridge. (It was there years before – 'Happy Land', we had called it hopefully – that I had once tried disastrously to construct a raft for Pin, my little sister, from two submerged petrol tins, and where I suddenly realised with blinding clarity that Dad would never really get over his 'bad back'. Music to drown Miss Ramsbotham's sorrows, and maybe the occasional 'snifter' for Auntie's, but what would he 'take to' in *his* melancholy?)

And, straight ahead, its colossal steel and concrete flanks straddling the by-pass like a monstrous scaffold (don't remind me), the new 'fly-over' itself, linking our once timid little market town to the world of the future while at the same time destroying the fields and meadows of childhood and mercilessly cleaving it in twain. (Nemesis for local passivity no doubt. The thought of signing some petition of protest had just about as much chance of prising itself from the mudflats as the two aforesaid petrol tins under the bridge. Careful, Mary, at it again! What if the wolf gets your tongue, as we said?)

The Great Day came at last.

At first, unbelievably, a normal Schoolday like the rest.

Greek (Miss P), physics (Miss Tao), history (Miss Kettledrum), needlework (Miss ? – oh, the terror of those scissors, don't remind me), English (Miss Twee, as partially enfeebling as ever), human anatomy (Mrs Blanche) . . . It seemed never-ending. How acutely dependent the River of Time on the shape and tempo, if not the pointed arrow, of human desire.

Just before the end of the afternoon, however, two whole periods of netball (Miss Bull) in which, usually just about as proficient in this area as a stranded jellyfish, I suddenly seemed as agile and sure-footed as a mountain goat – leaping twice as high as the others and even, at certain points, feeling I could fly. (Yea, the wondrous Ram of the Golden Fleece, the ball perched victoriously between my great curled horns, warm blood pulsing to their very tip, up and up over the gleaming asphalt, the chimney-stack, the quivering poplars, aspens, then, with their guilty secret . . . the whole green, tangled Wilderness . . .)

Then, giving a triumphant blast on the bell to signal to all and sundry, and one in particular, that the magic hour had come for our mutual release, I furtively collected my overnight bag from amongst the squawking mob in the cloakroom (carefully packed at home with a brand new, white flannel nightdress and quilted bed-jacket made specially by Auntie), and, running full tilt despite my previous eXertions, set off to the station as so often mentally rehearsed.

In order not to let the cat out of the kennel, so to speak, we had naturally planned to arrive by different routes. But, when I entered the booking hall, Miss X, to my initial disappointment, was nowhere to be seen.

'Not to worry, Mary, my lamb. Pecker up.' (In moments of relative tribulation nowadays I often addressed myself in *her* familiar voice.) 'You're almost a whole hour earlier than we said. Besides – like a pear-drop? – the staff meeting dragged on and on just as I feared. Miss Hilbert up to her triX again. She really is a *viXen*, isn't she? Never mind, darling. Trust your old goat. He'll soon be standing there right neXt to you. He's just as impatient as you are, you know . . . bursting with lust to get cracking, in fact.'

Your tiredness, warm wet rag, lies there between us.
Over the backs of the stepping-stone hats . . .
Come to me, dear one, come to me.

When Miss X *did* eventually arrive in the station yard, parking Giovanni just that shade more crookedly than usual, I thought with satisfaction, I was shocked to realise she was not alone.

Scurrying along behind her in a smart new blue hat and matching costume, bearing what looked like a huge picnic basket (full of Golden Goose Eggs, no doubt, I pondered nastily), came, beaming all over her . . . yes, just the same face as in the photograph in the Study with the two entwined, silver serpents . . . who else but *Mrs* X: Mother Nature Herself!

I should have been delighted, of course, but for some strange reason was not. Almost the opposite, in fact. Halcyon contentment whipped to squall in a far from jovial thunderflash.

I need not have worried.

Handing me the basket and still smiling sweetly – yes, it *was* a picnic basket, needless to say – Mrs X eXplained that she never missed a chance to see her 'Leetle Dorter' off on a journey, and naturally eXpected a full report of everything we saw and did in the 'Other Place'.

(So alterity was still to be attached to OXford after all. Sadly and silently I acknowledged my disgrace.)

By now, though, Miss X and I were already safely installed inside the carriage, the door slamming shut on any last parental platitudes with an eXplosion fit to shatter the most obdurate eardrum, and the uniformed guard (quite a kind man, I reflected magnanimously) already blowing his piercing whistle – faithful signal for what distant lover in his case? – to the far-flung corners of the blue Kentish hills.

'Alligator!'

'Crocodile!' A piece of linguistic condensation and/or displacement worthy of the finest literary rhetoric which seemed to aid mother and daughter to effect separation, so I let it pass.

(Certain N. American Indian tribes apparently believe these rapacious creatures to provide safe keeping to the souls of the dead, dressing up in fearsome denticular masks to empower themselves homeopathically from the virtues imagined locked within. Social anthropology seemed absolutely fascinating and I hoped to learn much more of it some day.)

'Alligator!'

'Crocodile!'

And we were off – the waving chaperon on the platform (F. *chaperon*, a 'cape' or 'hood', as in *Le Petit Chaperon Rouge*, Mary), already no more now than a knitted blue speck in the dust.

(Oh my love . . . unknown to me in those days . . . with a name, yours too, that can never be spoken, for such is the sacred interdict of all true writing . . . but for ever woven back from here into that distant 'now' where you were not. Wait for me, out there in that other, still just present, fading daylight to finish conducting my strange, creaking symphony with its seven thousand brazen tongues, coded message for another X-stitched for ever in my poor, punning cloth.

Oh my love . . . never to reach you. Never to speak as she could have spoken, this clear dry day in the heart of winter, bare twigs tapping like hands on the window and that strange, black bird out there – what is it looking for? – treading the thinly frosted grass. Not to speak to you in time, never to give joy by eXpressing the joy of it, here, in solitude, knowing its source. If she dies to-morrow or even to-day, to have let that great blanket of silent space come down like a cloak as if it fitted her perfectly, perfectly at one with the coming of the dark. Silence in turn runs out on itself. Silence in time runs out on us all.)

As we chugged out of the station the sun turned our billowing cloud of smoke into a brilliant halo of particles, I remember: dancing, glancing, in a golden figure-of-eight, which, for all its strange precision as I let my eyes rest upon it inadvertently from the depths of happy rêverie, seemed to have no other shape or structure when I focused on it more closely than that of the swirling waves and particles within . . . the gloomy, receding ticket office transformed for a moment into a shining mosque worthy of Rimbaud (about my age, wasn't he, Miss X, when he wrote *his* great poetry?), while even the grimy old sheds of the agricultural engineering works with their row of mighty combine harvesters awaiting sacrificial duty looked almost worthy of entering a poem themselves. (It was here that poor Dad got his first vertebral twinge lifting tractor wheels, or so he said then.)

By now, sparks flying, bushes burning, we were chugging our

way through The Wilderness, sheep, and cows too this time, running in terror on every side. 'EXactly the kind of landscape a Pre-Raphaelite artist might think of painting,' I confided to Miss X somewhat pompously, eager to initiate her understandably somewhat jaded spirit (L. *ilia*, 'flank') in the infinitely rich visual potentials of everyday life. ('Too much imagination, Mary. Those great eyes of yours,' those living portals, those greedy wells beneath the deserts, those Golden Windows of the Soul.)

Apart from a spotty-looking youth with long greasy hair, tight Levi jeans, leather jacket and hairy beard (primitive ancestor of later packs of 'Mods and Rockers', no doubt), there was no one else in the carriage but Miss X and myself.

Ancient Person for whom I,
All the flattering Youth defy . . .

The spotty-looking youth himself – about my own age chrono-logically, I reflected, though obviously just about as far away in *mental* age as Zeus and his Cyclopean thunderbolts from Pallas Athene – was chewing noisily behind a moronic-looking comic (*The Dandy*, ironically), renewing my incredulity that so many of my contemporaries, even Brainy Mary Number Two, could possibly 'go out' with such animals, and deliciously intensifying my superior bond with Miss X in return.

Naturally I had brought with me a change of apparel – a smartly respectable if somewhat school-marmy tweed costume (how I hate that vicious little seXist term nowadays), generously lent 'to make a good impression', presumably on my New Tutor, by my guardian angel herself. And, announcing for the benefit of our unwelcome fellow traveller that I was going to 'drink in the view of the Downs', I departed at once in the rumbling shadow of the Plutonian tunnel I mentioned, to remove my proudly-born but oh so tell-tale green uniform as planned, and, in the process, let down my long hair (kept at School in those days in a tight, puritanical bun). ('You'd make a good spy, Mary,' Miss X had once sparked teasingly, with unconscious prescience, as it turned out.)

I can see to this day my indeed eXceptionally large, round eyes shining back at me like an owl from the juddering mirror in what Miss X called the 'Little Room' as, with an eXtra violent jolt (must be a station), I clung to the cracked washbasin alone with my joy.

(My hair in those days was auburn, incidentally, and when released from its intricate bondage, rich and curling like the aforesaid Golden Fleece. Gradually adopting mythical allusions to please me, Miss X had once managed, bless her, to say so herself.)

Not that I wanted to miss a moment of her company back there.

It was one of those lovely old-fashioned carriages, I remember, adorned with framed posters of the man in the street besporting himself on the 'front' (Blackpool this time) plus the wife and what seemed like seven or more little kids. And, of course, more mirrors, one each side of the carriage, so that you seemed to be infinitely reflected, thrown back and forth as if in a Chinese boX puzzle or, more appropriately, the mirror in the Arnolfini Marriage by Jan van Eyck. (All very well to give a knowing smile up there, dear Reader, but there is always a first time to discover these things. Did *you* never see or do anything for the very first time?)

Once safely back from my Ovidian metamorphosis (give it a break, Mary, give it a break), I found to my delight that our hairy friend had departed (must have been that station), leaving me to fling myself forward for our first free embrace, mature and radiant now in my new attire. But to my hurt surprise, Miss X at once pulled sharply away and motioned me almost snappily to sit back in my seat.

I quickly understood, and apologised sheepishly for my unforgivable 'Bêtise'. The train had a corridor and 'Walls have ears, Mary, and you never know'.

By the time we had reached Charing X and were on our first ever taXi ride together on this planet – Berkeley Square, to be precise – she seemed slightly more relaXed, however, and in the second train, round about Bletchley, I think, was even allowing me to squeeze discreetly the hand with the gold 'wedding' ring and wobbly sapphire ('Careful, Mary, you'll have it right off one day . . .') under the Xword page of the *Daily Telegraph* (mental note to donate my first 'X' to the Tory candidate when time and circumstance were right, in those days not until the ripe old age of twenty-one).

Nor, surprisingly for such a wolfish appetite, did Miss X seem unduly disturbed when we discovered that the maternal picnic-basket had been inadvertently left behind.

As for me, I was already in my seventh heaven (seven, seven, always the mystic, Fairy Tale, known/unknown seven . . . give me a child until he is seven), fully able to enjoy, by craning my head dangerously out of the little sash-window, never mind the mist and driving rain, my first blurred glimpse of those famous Dreaming Spires.

Here am I, a girl with a tea-cup and a bunch of heliotrope.
Here I stand, young flesh, and with tangles in my hair.
It is mine, all this sunset, joy and music.
'Dans mon coeur de diX-huit ans', it is there.
Oh passionate youth, the tears of two, for you, for you.
On the marsh the grasses blow and blow . . .

I was alive, alive, 'eighteen alive and eighty dead', as the latest Rimbaldian masterpiece crowed somewhat self-consciously (L. *heliotropium*, 'that which turns to the sun'), and, still safely shepherded by my eXtra-special friend with the slightly swollen feet, the limp and the crook, stepping out like Blanchette, in *La Chèvre de Monsieur Seguin* for my very first night on the mountain at last.

Great skies of light, wet fields and ancient stone,
Green waters, laughing ducks, the willow's moan,
The towering organ's vibrant truth-drenched tone . . .

The OXford Weekend had only just begun.

The Fifth Piece

While cupped hands on a white stone bridge of dreams
Still hold green willows in the rippled wells of time
(Mary Wolfe)

Ovem lupo commisisti
(Terence)

The OXford Weekend! The OXford Weekend!
What to include, what to omit, how to begin to convey that which . . .

Radcliffe Hall. With an 'i' to my surprise.

When we reached the hotel and had been shown our room – my companion still, to my surprise, trembling uncontrollably from the sight of a white alsatian dog at Reception (no agoraphobia there like poor Sigmund's, though don't they say it's aggression turned in?) – I was somewhat disappointed to find that we were not going out to eXplore right away as I had thought.

Instead, 'stick-in-a-pot', Miss X had thrown herself down on the bed and refused to budge, a curiously stubborn eXpression on her face.

And indeed, far from discussing Virginia Woolf or the difference between Racine and Corneille as I had hoped, remained virtually silent, her eyes half shut and her lips in an almost snarling grimace. Strange lips. Had I really ever noticed them before now? Thin and almost colourless, with a tiny indentation on either side of the lower one, presumably where those abnormally jutting canines of hers habitually pricked the skin.

. . . Poor darling! . . . She must be very tired still, that and the unfortunate incident with the dog. Almost a phobia on her part, I was beginning to think. Incidentally, what was the French for 'alsatian dog'? I had brought with me a fresh vocabulary book and was eager not to miss the slightest chance to widen my leXical range. 'Loup garou', for instance. They say 'werewolf' where we English say 'bugbear' – another of those fascinating French distortions, like the sheep for white horses at the foot of the lighthouse, which I had just about managed to draw out from

Miss X on the train (L. *eX-ducere*, 'to draw out', it felt more like *drag* out), reluctant pedagogue though she seemed, unaccountably, the nearer we came to our eXciting intellectual goal.

Our window looked out onto a small, dark yard with a criss-X of barbed wire round the top of a dank, crumbling wall: hardly the fabled land of 'ducking punts' and green willows I had already lost and regained in a spate of anticipatory poems devoted to the Groves of Academe. And, hiding my slight resentment at spending the first few hours of the Great Adventure imprisoned in so dungeon-like an enclosure, I busied myself with unpacking my eXtra-hard bristle toothbrush (mustn't neglect Wolfgang Amadeus) and laying out my new night things on the remaining bed.

Auntie's quilted bed-jacket was embossed all over with balls of yellow fluff bound to make me look like a zany Donald Duck, but I had agreed to bring it so as not to hurt her feelings. No going back there either, if you see what I mean!

On the pillow of the other bed, Her bed, meanwhile, Miss X had already placed a pair of neatly folded turquoise pyjamas, I noticed, while, on the bedside cabinet, neXt to a packet of aniseed balls and the hotel Bible (dramatically propped open as if almost deliberately to invite our perusal) stood none other than the little felt goat later to be introduced as Capricorn, brought, apparently, from the similar cabinet by her bed in the perky turret back you know where.

A kind of totem animal, I reflected astutely, and obviously transported to make us feel at home. We had 'done' the goat in religious studies with Miss Prick and I prided myself on my maturity in perceiving the link. (The power to draw analogies is what it's all about, as Charles Baudelaire tells us, and if you haven't got it, you might just as well pack your bags and go home.)

Despite my relatively advanced age of seventeen years and seven months (the 'eighteen' in the 'eighteen alive and eighty dead' poem was simply to provide a jazzy alliteration, I'm afraid), I had scarcely ever been away from home since 'being evacuated' (curious phrase): only that traumatic time aged thirteen and a quarter, when, eXiled for a whole month to Paris on a School eXchange – oh that little red diary meticulously reporting the items consumed in every single meal, not to mention every single subsequent lack of movement of the bowel – I had been the only one of the whole whimpering party who, when Miss X honoured the French lycée where we were stationed with a flying visit to check up on our welfare, bit back my inner sobs of eXile and refused to cast myself with the others at her still, in those days, hélas, unknown feet.

Were we not Ambassadors of King and Country? Was it for the Captain to leave the burning ship? Miss X and I had often laughed together at the memory – myself somewhat feebly, I admit.

(The wild Lolita inflicted upon me, and eventually my own terrified family, in eXchange, seemed to spend the whole day alternately inviting and escaping ageing male predators, pausing 'en route' but to make fun of my white ankle socks and eXtraordinary School hat – of which more below. No such crocodiles lurking for *me* here in the City of Dreams, thank goodness. On the other hand while lolling against the fence watching Miss X struggling to get in our cases, I had already received an uncouth wolf-whistle from a youth on a bicycle with long, greasy hair. Not a student, of course . . . at least, I *hope* not.)

How avidly the mind seeks for signs and symbols in any new situation, auguries in the entrails even, you might say.

The white alsatian dog, for instance. Hope it didn't mean bad luck!

The passage the Bible had so cryptically displayed before us when we entered the bedroom, however, was only that bit in Genesis about Abraham and Isaac where human sacrifice is about to take place but the poor ram has its horns caught in the thicket instead. Obviously nothing relevant there, though I was in two minds whether to initiate Miss X into the eXciting, still running parallel with the Golden Fleece: that uniquely powerful pleasure of opening a door to someone who has never been through it before. 'EXcuse me, Miss X . . .' No. Better not. It might wear her out even more.

(Precisely the same substitute of the sacrificial animal for the human, though, you notice, there where with the Xt thing it's the other way round and God – some Father! – sacrifices his anointed son, leaving everyone else, as Nietzsche apparently said somewhat rudely of Wagner, slobbering slavishly at the foot of the †. Remember, too (Ovid again), the story of Lycaon, turned into a wolf for having secretly served up *his* son as a meal to Zeus. Their seeds obviously sown way back by Miss P in the first days of my Classical mania, for some reason these 'deceiver deceived' things still interest me a lot.)

After half an hour or so spent in this blasphemous limbo flicking idly through further passages in the Great Book with a few deliberately forked slips of the tongue here and there on my part to try to cheer her up ('Here's that one about the creep in sholf's woving'), the pangs of hunger seemed to get through to Miss X where the promised charms of the Bodleian Library had failed. And after a smashing, but rather heavy, meal in a Chinese restaurant off Cornmarket Street ('The Pagoda', funnily enough), she seemed to perk up a little, becoming, by the time we got outside again, positively gay . . . even slightly disrespectful in such an illustrious setting, I thought.

(The meal itself included noodles and lychees, I remember: both eXotic items new to me at the time, accompanied for Miss X, who now seemed to be ravenous, by a whole glass of blood red wine. Thanks to Paris, no drop of alcohol would ever pass *my* lips. For some reason I felt an almost eXcessive thirst, though, and must have asked for at least seven glasses of water on the trot. Hope there's a 'Little Room' back in the Hotel).

'How's this for your monumental pile, Mary?' she would call, disappearing unsteadily down one of those time-honoured lanes which hollow out the majestic city, haunt of Milton, Byron, Matthew Arnold, Ruskin, Keats, Oscar Wilde (or were *they* all Cambridge too?), and, throwing her right arm wide while grasping me almost painfully with the left: 'All this great Kingdom (sic) will be yours one day, my lamb. But you'll have to watch out, won't you, with all these horrid young men about. What is the ratio, did we say?'

Embarrassing, really, in so aesthetic a setting. Perhaps she *had* heard that horrid wolf-whistle back there. Not that . . .

Looking back, I realise I had very few thoughts about what *she* might have been feeling all this while.

The idea did fleetingly occur to me, though, that perhaps there might just be a tiny seed of envy, jealousy even, in Miss X's behaviour . . . that just a tiny part of her might have been reliving through me her own lost youth, I mean? Let alone the ubiquitous Golden Fleece, what was it she had said about the Golden Fountain of Youth that time? How often do we forget that where the young must make the difficult transition to maturity, maturity in its turn means the difficult reintegration of the past, the ability to mourn and come to terms with the lost Mary Wolfe in each one of us. I *am* Mary Wolfe, so I should know.

(I didn't let on, of course, but while we were ambling about like that digesting the lychees and noodles, Miss X had suddenly reminded me of Silenus, the wise but overweight, rather red-faced

56

tutor of Dionysus and foster-father of Bacchus. Could it be because she had been just a little bit 'stoned', as I think they say? Stone, bone, lone, moan: surely not *another* poetic masterpiece on the way?)

Meanwhile, however, my first privileged glimpse of the River.

Oh, no longer that muddy brown trickle full of tin cans and sluggish weeds by the by-pass bridge in Happy Land (dear little Pin: what would I give to set eyes on *that* once more now), but a real River, a deep River, a strong, passionate, quick-flowing, turbulent yet clear River that was mad and brave and literary and 'thrilling-sweet' (or was even *that* Cambridge?) all together in one . . . lamplight dancing on its surface like a silver-gold watersnake, well, figure-of-eight, then, stars and mist and moonlight mingled with calm, surely mature, universal, erudite voices in its dark, ever-shimmering, fleece-like hair . . .

But feeling suddenly both the pull and the dread of the brave new world opening so loquaciously before me (rotten, too, I remember now, 'thrilling-sweet and rotten' – Rupert Brooke's poem on Grantchester), asked if we should not perhaps be turning back.

We had the New Tutor to visit in the morning, after all, and I really had to 'get my beauty sleep', as Auntie would say.

Who, oh who, was the 'fuss-in-the-mud' now?

Undressing in the bedroom like that could have been rather embarrassing, as naturally one had to be private for such things. But by retaining the navy knickers I had worn for netball and bending skilfully forward, I was soon safely enveloped in the white flannel nightdress, and, with Auntie's Donald Duck bed-jacket handy in case of binding emergency – St Patrick's Breastplate with a vengeance – ready for sleep in my allotted bed.

'Good-night, Miss X,' tactfully turning my face to the wall to allow her to disrobe in similar manner, and, as I used always to call through the thin bedroom ramparts to Dad after a seaside outing to Ramsgate or somewhere even when the whole thing had been a wash-out (mustn't hurt *his* feelings either, of course), 'Thank you very much for a *wonderful* day.' (No, *not* to dear Mother, funnily enough. Leave her to her belovèd literary quotations and all that.)

I think I also added something cutely original like 'Sleep well and see you in the morning'. After all, with Dad so often away on the roads like that, 'And I for ever fearful . . .' (Pin more than I, though), you could never ever really be sure of these things.

I could hardly sleep a wink at first, what with all the intellectual eXcitement, but lay there, wide-eyed in the confused half darkness, listening every quarter of an hour to the rich, vibrant tongue of some great Bell across the street (automatic this time, thank god) and dutifully trying to count the obligatory sheep . . . my wily brain heavy and teeming with the weight of all its new impressions like Odysseus in the cave of the Cyclops bound under the great pot-belly of the ram. Miss P and I had 'done' this taXing but eXquisite passage of Homer that very morning – ruined at the time by my vast impatience about the forthcoming journey, but somehow a comfort to me now all the same. (Yes, that splendid schoolgirl joke in the *Odyssey* where cunning Odysseus is cunning enough – well, he would be, wouldn't he? – to give himself the pseudonym 'Outis', 'Nobody', 'X', the unknown quantity, so that when the Cyclops calls for help from his neighbours: 'Nobody is attacking me!', they fail predictably to come to his aid. An intriguing variation, with a certain goat-like leap of the imagination, on our proverbial joke-fond shepherd boy who laughs on the other side of his face when the *real* wolf eventually descends on the fold later on, as we said.)

At one point, however, I almost thought I heard her own voice call gruffly, '*Come here*', just as she had done that first crucial evening a year ago (L. *cruX*, a 'X'), when I turned up to collect the phantom book to help with the Racine (*tragos*, 'tragedy', 'goatsong' and all that).

Then, after much rapid, rhythmical creaking from her distant bed (squeaky springs like The Pagoda front gate, I suppose, though, funnily enough, my own surely similar goose-feather mattress seemed totally silent and inert), what sounded like a sigh or even a moan.

Was the poor dear weeping or something?

Lumbago, like Dad's again, from getting in our cases? (Viper's bugloss is a cure for that too, they say.)

Indigestion from the lychees? (The wine more like it.)

Pining for her own perky little bed back there amongst the pine trees? General eXistential angst?

The sigh again, or rather, the same sigh, but dying out now, not so melodious as it was before. Moan, groan, lone, stone . . . more like a whine or a bark or a whimper like Sigmund's – half pleasure, half pain – when I came home from School, not really a proper sigh at all.

Not wanting to make a fool of myself again if I'd made a mistake (however insignificant, that rebuff in the train still slightly smarted), I sat up X-legged on my haunches in the vivid darkness, shivering like an aspen despite my flannel nightdress – to this day I can see my ghostly white shape crouched there beside me in the dressing-table mirror – and tremulously alert now as if my whole life depended on it, pricked up my ears, but could still not be sure.

And by the time that, after much anguished refleXion ('Vorrei e non vorrei' – *Don Giovanni*)I decided that after all, she *had* indeed called me – '*Come here, Mary, oh, come here, my darling*' – it was already too late.

The sound of snoring, unmistakable this time, yes, positively volcanic like the rumblings of Mount Etna (forge of the whole race of Cyclopes, inveterate, round-eyed blacksmiths all, according to Miss P), was all I could hear from the other bed.

The ravelled sleeve of all her Public *and* Private cares knit gently together at last, poor Miss X had fallen asleep like a log.

And so it was, with more and more sheep hurtling frenziedly now through the opening, pursued, this time, by myself in the new white nightdress, ears pricked, teeth bared, single round eye shining in the middle of my forehead and barking uncontrollably like the white alsatian dog from Reception ('*chien loup* or *berger allemand*, Mary,' as I was to find neXt morning in a dictionary furtively consulted in Blackwell's Bookshop: strange, don't you think, Miss X? two almost opposite meanings to a single substantive again) . . . so it was, I say, that the great unknown Bell with the rich, vibrant tongue continued to toll away for Mary Wolfe and her lonely, unknown lover the sole precious night of the OXbridge Weekend – that unique, long-plotted night which she was to weep to recover for almost half a lifetime, long past the death of the Fires of Passion it helped so fiercely to awaken, and which, to have the chance to live again, the same yet different, different yet the same, she would have cut off both her left *and* her right hand . . . yea, like the foXy Odysseus, fashioned a spit of olive wood and, bidding her faithful, lost family patiently help her lift it towards her smooth forehead ('On no account tell anyone, Mary. Not even your mother'), gouged the very eye from the centre of her head.

But 'too late, too late,' croaked the garrulous raven. 'Nevermore, Mary, lamb. Never again.'

Je dis à cette nuit: 'sois plus lente'; . . . et l'aurore
                Va dissiper la nuit.

Miss X looked a trifle pale and tense in the morning, I thought, giving an abrupt negative in answer to my polite enquiry of 'Did you sleep well?' . . . in fact denying having slept a wink the whole damned night. Counting sheep (snap), she said, like me. Why she even went so far as to accuse *me* of snoring and of having called out something that sounded like 'Miss P, come here, Miss P'.

(I flinched in horror, but the moment passed. Oh, and obviously Capricorn was prone to compulsive eating since all the aniseed balls eXcept one had disappeared from the paper bag by the bed.)

Then there had been that curious little incident while we were dressing when, purely affectionately, needless to say, she had suddenly accused me of behaving 'like an old woman' in turning round away from her to put on my brassière, heaving the cups round to the back while I mastered the two rows of fasteners and swinging the whole thing round up front to scoop myself in before turning to face her once again.

'That's better,' she had said then, feasting her eyes like a leech on my cleavage, I noticed sympathetically (shades of poor Miss P again, but that was different), as, annoyed by her indirect accusation of the crime of old age, let alone of prudery, I impatiently threw the whole unnecessary contraption to the floor together with 'Little x', my Marks and Spencer's elasticated 'roll-on', and, with only my long, reddish mane now to protect her eyes from my blinding nakedness, stood before her, nubile Baudelairean fruits, 'Messer Gaster' and all, in the full, tender glories of the flesh.

(A pity about that little scar on my left thigh where I had cut myself on the petrol cans that time with Pin, but then didn't Odysseus Himself bear the tusk-mark of a boar? Helping us transcend the merely personal, Myth, as I had announced in an essay for Miss Twee but a day or so previously, can elevate us on its golden horns to the heights of Universal Man.)

The School play that season was to be *The Bacchae* (Euripides).

And despite having been forced to sacrifice a leading rôle in it myself – too much revision for the OXbridge EXam – I was passably well versed in the Dance of the Maenads, handmaidens of Dionysus (played by the Carbuncle), often minutely observed through the glass swing doors of the hall while I stood salivating at my post to ring the bell . . . a dance which, with a slight initial shock at my own, some might even say brazen, audacity, I now found myself beginning slowly and rhythmically to perform with who else but Miss X herself as sole spectator and judge . . . adding here and there an appealing frill and fioritura of my own. ('Mary Wolfe has an innate sense of rhythm. Should go far,' Miss Ramsbotham had inscribed with melancholic prescience on a recent School report fully guaranteed to drive Dad to a frenzy of activity with the coal-bucket loud enough to waken the dead.)

A strange thing, nakedness in the human being, however perfectly natural in the wild.

Having previously felt as prudish as Diana – Artemis, then – surprised bathing by Actaeon, now, the plunge once taken, I felt totally free from embarrassment. Almost as if I had indeed moved back into my own natural intellectual element, Xed the threshold into another world, another evolutionary time zone, even . . . half human, half goat, half I don't know what . . . in fact not really *half* anything at all for once.

So much so that, entwining my arms like the silver snakes on Mrs X's photo frame and tossing my head now faster and faster – Dionysus, 'Child of the Double Door', surely now in person – I continued to cavort and caper right round the room, chastened only to discover that Miss X was taking so eXceptionally little notice (did she fear like Actaeon she would be changed into a stag?) . . . indeed, half turning her back on my would-be infectious eXertions and laboriously re-packing the now somewhat creased and sad-looking turquoise pyjamas ready for our all too imminent return.

I was down on the floor by this time, crawling round eXtatically on all fours like Blake's Nebuchadnezzar. Head thrown back to eXpose my eXceptionally long, white neck, red mane falling round my 'hunkers' as Miss X had once called them (etymology uncertain) like a true Greek 'nebris' (skin of a wild animal, usually faun or goat, worn by the Maenads in their frenzied dithyramb) or, if you prefer, like the foaming sea of auburn hair in the painting by Dante Gabriel Rossetti, one of the pre-Raphaelites I had mentioned to Miss X only yesterday as the train chugged through The Wilderness.

What would Miss P say if she could see me now!

What would the New Tutor, come to that!

About the morning's appointment, I was still anXious, of course, one eye on the clock even in the heart of my Pythian contortions.

No good starting my new academic life on the wrong foot!

On the other hand it was really Miss X, not I, who had delayed us that morning, taking so long as she did both in the 'Little Room' and at breakfast before we could set off – an eXtra portion of porridge and kippers which she devoured like a vampire, bones and all. (No trace of the white alsatian dog from Reception this time, though, thank god.)

Yes, come to think of it, Miss X had seemed *particularly* tardy and distracted . . . almost, perish the thought, as if she positively *wanted* the delay. I preferred like Dad to be totally punctual in such matters, quivering like a gun dog well in advance of action. If a man ring a bell twelve times a day for . . .

Could it be she found it difficult to hand me over or something?

In the case of this highly unlikely eventuality, I was quick to reassure her of my unique and eternal devotion.

How could *anyone* ever remotely replace her in my affections, let alone give such terrific lessons on Racine and St-EXupéry?

And besides, '*Ad Astra*', our faithful star up there above . . . Think of the Torch of Knowledge still.

But no matter. Here we were at last, standing at the sacred inner door of this new and alien chamber, which I half eXpected to read 'HEADMISTRESS PLEASE KNOCK'. The outer door or 'oak' (L. *quercus robur*), Miss X eXplained, was fortunately not 'sported', which meant we could be so bold as to make ourselves known right away. Dionysus, Child of the Double Door! Didn't I tell you! He who shall be born again (it's no good just waiting around passively for *female* personae), once from the belly of his natural mother and once, later on, from the thigh of Zeus, and, surprisingly, only about an hour and seven minutes late.

('*Let* her wait,' I'm ashamed to say Miss X had muttered almost venomously as we lingered in Blackwell's 'en route' to buy me a new Notebook with a blue cover in which, rather as Mrs X had requested a blow by blow account of this very Weekend now still making history, she insisted that I keep detailed tabs on my new college life. But then what's an hour and seven minutes in a land of eternally Dreaming Spires?)

In fact we both took an instant dislike to my New Tutor, who, quite unlike Miss X in her reassuring woollen suit and country-cuckoo sandals, sported smart black slacks and stiletto heels, and was smoking a horrid foul-smelling cigar. (*Her* hair was auburn too, though. Not unlike mine.)

'No,' she was *not* the person Miss X remembered from college.

'Yes,' and here the decidedly decadent-looking cigar jumped up and down disconcertingly from the corner of her mouth, she *was* rather late for a committee meeting over near CarfaX. 'But,' somewhat laconically after an embarrassingly long silence (not *another* sphinX, please god?), 'do come in, Mary – you too, Miss X – and have some coffee all the same.'

And then it was . . . while this strange, peripatetic creature had teetered off up the corridor to boil the kettle . . . that the boldness of my unpredictable companion broke all records for rushing to the brink and playing with fire.

We had been left standing on a large, sheepskin hearth-rug, politely admiring over the mantelpiece one of those semi-abstract paintings of which I knew Miss X didn't really approve ('All these nasty modern things, Mary. Where is their sense of *values*, I ask you?') . . . a pile of orange-red apples (or were they oranges?) looking as if at any moment they would jump straight out of the frame and bury us in Amazonian vegetation where we stood.

(I was in two minds about this kind of thing myself, but didn't say, not wanting to hurt the New Tutor's feelings either, of course.)

And neXt to it, much more to Miss X's liking, I imagined empathetically, a safely framed print, labelled 'La Dame à la Licorne', of a tired looking woman a bit like Miss Ramsbotham, dressed in a long, pink caftan with white chiffon sleeves and a low embroidered neck . . . holding up a mirror – yes, don't forget the mirror, Mary – while a shaggy white creature with a single long horn and the beard of a goat was gently leaning forward with its front hooves in her lap.

(How should one translate the word 'licorne', I wondered? Perhaps the New Tutor herself would know. 'A mon seul désir' it also proposed cryptically, embroidered on the turret of a Pagoda-like tent covered, believe it or not, with 'fleur de lys' eXactly like Miss X's wallpaper at the top of the stairs, not to mention Napoleon Bonaparte's bee-like emblem in reverse.)

Talk about Love and Hunger meeting at a Woman's Breast!

Suddenly, taking me completely off guard, her sandal catching on a corner of the sheepskin rug as she did so . . . Miss X lunged towards me like a mad thing, and, my eyes bolting with far from delicious terror as I listened for the return of the spiked footsteps down the corridor, managed to plant, full on my lips this time and smack on target, a long, rapturous and distinctly kippery kiss, urgently groping with her left hand as she did so for the tip of my right nipple, resting innocently again by then in the successfully reloaded brassière.

The stiletto heels did *not* return just then, I'm happy to say, but to this day I wonder if their wearer, infinitely more wise and sure-footed even on stilts than poor, flat-footed Silenus, did not understand all the same, by some uncanny seventh sense, precisely what little drama had transpired in her absence, there on the sheepskin rug before the mild, astonished eyes of the mythical unicorn, as Miss X tried so recklessly to fail to pass the Torch at the eleventh hour.

Why, otherwise, on returning with the steaming kettle to furbish our refreshment, did she appear to take no notice of my by now guiltily scarlet cheeks and blazing orbs as if not to hurt my feelings – ring a bell, dear Reader? – but, just as we were on the point of leaving, flash me, full in the face this time unlike Miss X's uneasy obliquities, a kindly, yes, positively kindly, Mona-Lisa like smile with just the slightest suspicion of a humorous wink?

And why, years later, coming to that unforgettable room with the wondrous books and paintings to borrow a new critical study on Racine while its owner was away 'on sabbatical' (I had become a Fellow of the college myself by then), should I find, at that eXact place on the shelf, a little desk diary open at the eXact date of that first brief but eXtraordinary encounter which was gradually to provide the means of transforming my life:

SATURDAY 14TH FEBRUARY, 1959

with, pencilled neatly underneath in the by then so familiar handwriting, sloping, in her case, to the right:

11 a.m. Coffee. MISS X AND MARY WOLFE

Design or coincidence? I shall never know.

With the New Tutor, it was to be totally different, you see.

The perfect maintenance, between two mirrors, of that very same sacred contract which, in stepping that time from behind her leather-topped desk in the Study, poor Miss X so disastrously failed to honour and obey.

Precisely because the New Tutor *did* keep behind the desk and yet 'remain human' (careful, Mary, is this the place?), the Torch of Learning remained trustworthy, passionate, bright, impersonal yet personal . . . Imagination, heart of the intellect, the only sighted Lighthouse, the one true star . . . the Torch of Life itself, perhaps. 'Mon seul désir' . . .

Perhaps I never really loved Miss X, the first Miss X, I mean, at all. Perhaps even the title of this book . . .

'I know, Poppet,' announced my companion just before lunch on that same momentous morning (*do* wish she wouldn't call me that, so un-romantic, don't you think?). 'I know, Poppet,' (looking almost relieved now we'd escaped from the intimidating labyrinth of the College). 'We'll have one last fling before the train . . . Live it up a bit and go out to The Trout. They do good lamb sandwiches out there, I seem to remember. Don't know about you but I could eat a horse.'

(By then it must have been almost thirty-seven-and-a-half minutes past one. Work it out for yourself . . . What with the interview starting so late.)

And so we did 'live it up a bit', sitting out there side by side on the ivy-covered terrace, with Miss X – non-vegetarian, much to my chagrin – and whose feet were 'crucifying me', she had announced just beforehand, wolfing down beer and lamb sandwiches to her heart's, if not 'Messer Gaster's' content.

('Goats will eat anything,' she had once replied to my remonstrance. And it was true that in 'Pet's Corner' with Pin at Ramsgate I had once seen a goat demolish a whole hardback novel wrapped in a polythene bag. Don't they refuse to eat ivy, though? If they'd only 'kept their big mouths shut' and abstained from devouring Dionysus' sacred vines, they might not have ended up sacrificed. Still slightly Voltairean, my sense of cultural history, perhaps, but on the other hand a candid approach to these matters could often reach narrow ledges where others fear to tread.)

I myself was too bemused meanwhile to partake of more than a half tankard of Tizer and a few humble packets of salted crisps.

A thin white peacock added to the uneXpected pomp of the occasion, I remember: strutting beside us on the flagged wall of the terrace, its bony rigging (a bit *like* Voltaire, come to think of it) dramatically outlined a moment against the turbulent waters of the weir below (talk about Baudelaire's cascading abyss) and startling us terribly with its proud, rasping cry of courtship-cum-patrol.

And what waters they were, too!

'The Isis,' I told Miss X proudly, forgetting she had visited OXford before.

'Yes, the River Isis (the Cam is in Cambridge), named, you see, after the great Egyptian Earth Mother, identified by the Greeks with Demeter (Mother of Persephone) and – yet another wonderful coincidence like the 'fleur de lys' wallpaper just now – Hera or Juno of the peacock, in turn just like . . . Have you ever felt, Miss X, that things in life are . . . how can I put it? "meant"? Yes, almost as if we are two characters in some kind of Novel?' – I refrained from saying in a goat's seven stomachs – 'which some Great Writer only still has to write one day?'

The great Mother Isis, solar disk and horns of a cow, who, in desperate mourning for her belovèd brother *and* husband Osiris (hélas, poor Phèdre, seXual customs are relative), savagely slain and chopped up by their common brother, Seth, *loup-garou* if ever there was one, travels the world over to **find the fourteen scattered pieces of his mutilated body** – some say first hidden in an oak tree (L. *quercus robur*, see above) – **in order to stitch them together again and turn Osiris back into a god, Lord, this time, of the souls of the dead**.

I never said at the time for fear of embarrassing Miss X, let alone hurting her feelings, but according to my *Dictionary of Myth*, treacherous first prize for religious studies (Miss Prick), there was one small but allegedly vital piece still missing (must have been found, though, for how, otherwise give birth to the avenging child Horus?), devoured, some say, by a crab called OXyrhynchid, greedy inhabitant of the Nile.

Osiris, Pentheus, Orpheus, Dionysus, Xt . . . what savage violence in all these myths of sacrifice and dismemberment, I continued to reflect aloud (the Harvest, though, Mary, don't forget that). Did they spring from some terrible cannibalistic violence in our natures, or did they but give cathartic embodiment to our primitive fears? If the former, how could we be so sure that they in turn, myths, I mean, might not all the same help implant the violence in the first place? And if the latter, might it not be that in eXposing the fictional nature of the mechanisms of revenge and retribution in metaphorical form, metaphors to undo metaphors, so to speak (hindsight, Mary, did you really think all this at the time?), we can at least hope to free ourselves from their terrible claws?

(Remember I was still determined to become a Great Novelist one day myself . . . perhaps even a *Female* Great Novelist like Virginia Woolf, not that, for all her undoubted talent, she seemed fully to have realised about the intellect and Mother Nature, Animus/Anima, the sheep and the goats and all that.)

The mist was clearing even further now, thank god . . . no longer did we feel weighed down by the lid of some great Baudelairean cooking-pot . . . allowing us to admire a pale, thin segment of moon hanging like a sickle above the already pollarded willows, their ancient elbows and crooked shoulders reflected in the flooded grain fields across the river to the right of us, while two, yes, fortunately, *two* vivid black and white magpies (Miss X, to my surprise, was deeply superstitious) suddenly creaked right over us, long, glossy tail-feathers flashing purple, to settle joyfully on a nearby gate.

In order to keep ourselves warm during my thirsty Socratic diatribe, we found ourselves trotting about a little now too.

Up and down the towpath with its whispering bulrushes – 'Wasn't that a kingfisher?' I suddenly shouted eXcitedly – gazing out now and then towards the vivid blue-green acres of higher pasture on the other side of the water. ('Port Meadow, Mary. Port and starboard. Breast foot forward. Keep walking.' Yes, the rather strained sense of humour was still with us, I'm afraid. Fear at the imaginary crumbling of the Old Régime? Who knows?)

And, further still, sketched like a delicate pencil drawing against the horizon, the famous blue-grey outline of Matthew Arnold's Dreaming Spires. (Matthew Arnold of 'The Scholar Gypsy'. *This* time Miss X was obviously simply pretending not to know.)

There were hundreds of the famous ducks I'd heard about too at last ('Hundreds, Mary?', 'Well, no, not really, Auntie. Just our cat and the cat neXtdoor') . . . a whole noisy school of them, giggling, squawking, chattering like superstitious magpies and reminding me sharply of some of the worst offenders awaiting me back home, albeit distant now as in another world.

Then:

'You've never been in love before, have you, Miss X?'

I suddenly found myself enquiring, eXactly as she had asked *me* that time in the Study – confident, of course, that the answer would be '*No*'.

But to my hurt surprise at this point, silence descended, even the ducks now uncannily humbled and obedient, while Miss X turned her head away, obviously struggling to compose herself under the pressure of some volcanic emotion within.

When she looked back again, I saw with sudden interest that she had indeed this time been weeping: two charming tear-drops chasing each other slowly down her long, sharp nose before hanging like wobbly sapphires on her by now strangely flushed cheeks.

(The once proud face contorted and unrecognisable with emotion, she is listening, remember, to the wild, eXquisite voices of the mysterious Sirens . . . bewitched, enslaved, hungry for more

67

and more music, while the rest of the crew, their ears sealed in advance against such terrifying beauty, toil over the oars as previously instructed . . . devotedly immune to her cries for release. Notice how the prior command takes precedence over all later ones. *That* is the one to remain imprinted for ever. *That* is the voice they follow, like new-born geese, to the ends of the earth.)

'Oh yes I have, Mary,' she replied at last. 'Yes, indeed.'

So there *had* been someone else! The skeleton in the broom cupboard under the stairs! Perhaps some long lost secret husband after all. (In all the eXcitement, I'd quite forgotten – well, almost – the mysterious gold ring with its precarious jewel.)

'Well go on then, who was it, Miss X? Not a secret, is it? You know I'd keep it, X my throat and cut my heartstrings'.

'*Oh, nobody really,*' (the voice by this time strangely gruff and distorted, betraying, I can see now, the would-be casual nature of its own apparently dismissive words): '*Nobody really . . . just someone I met in my year at college with a beautiful deep voice* . . . failed eXams because of me. About the same age as you are now, come to think of it. That's how . . .' (a strange little laugh now, almost like a cough, high-pitched, unfamiliar) '. . . that's how I came to possess *Capricorn*, you know,' followed – yes, that strained sense of humour was most certainly defensive – by 'Well, according to you, it's better than a crucifiX by the side of the bed, isn't it, Mary, my lamb?'

I was not unique after all!

Never mind the secret husband under the stairs, how much more acceptable now five hundred symbolic rivals – Golden Youth in person – than one special eX-rival my own age in the flesh. Not that . . . Merely, in her case, an adolescent crush already long over before I was born. And besides, along with purely titular degrees and no doubt mock hoods, women still had chaperons in those days.

'But then also years later,' the voice was almost inaudible by now, more like a tiny, animal bleat (where had I heard that sound before?) than proper human speech with full, civilised use of the larynX, teeth and tongue: '. . . that time in Paris when . . . well, remember when I visited the Lycée where you were just a tiny thing with your two little pigtails and little red bows?' (*red* bows this time, you notice) . . . a little flat of hers behind the Musée de Cluny . . . the same woman again, Mary', (WO-MAN, WOMB-MAN: she pronounced the two syllables as if they were poison, some shameful derivative sired from more universal cultural stock), 'I thought you must have guessed by now I'm a goat. . . a poor old goat with feet of clay . . .', followed at once by the fatal ark of the covenant: '*If I ever shut the door and change towards you, promise to keep on knocking, my love*,' which I at once interpreted as a poignantly self-critical appeal for tolerance of this strange new impedimental, not to say uncomfortably cloven-cum-clay-hoofed condition, rather than as a capricious ultimatum of any kind.

Further long pause. Nervous shuffle.

Only the raucous laughter of what seemed now like millions and millions of the ducks, giggling, jeering, chattering, crowing, baying and generally just about everything but quacking, all in one.

'Oh, nobody really (Gr. *Outis*; L. *Nemo*; F. *Personne*), just someone I met in my year at college with a beautiful deep voice . . . But then also, years later . . . in a little flat of hers . . .'

'The sedge has withered from the lake and no birds sing.'

Outis! Nobody!

So *she* was my enemy!

At least now I knew.

But, with a strange, prickling sensation up and down my spine, and suddenly acutely conscious of every tiny detail of the scene around me, listening, listening, all ears and eyes as if my whole life depended on it, it was I now who turned my head away . . . I who stared down silently at the wild, hungry choir of waters calling below us with its bird-like voices, just as if the wolf had indeed got my tongue, as Auntie would say.

'Car Lesbos entre tous m'a choisi sur la terre . . .'

So *that* was the meaning of the 'forbidden' poem printed at the back of our edition of *Les Fleurs du Mal*!

She was *HomoseXual*, a *Lesbian*!

One of Baudelaire's notorious 'Femmes Damnées', isolated, wandering, condemned for ever, running through the deserts like so many ravenous wolves! (not that the full force of the metaphor struck home consciously, even then . . .)

A tiny stick had been caught in the creaming pool at the foot of the lock gates, I remember . . . turning, spinning, trapped in a norteX, unable either to stand still or float away. A punt, too, on the higher stretch of the river, passing slowly and silently in the opposite direction like some ghostly Venetian gondola: a young woman in a crimson dress standing to work the pole from the sloping inboard in what I knew Miss X called the cowardly OXford fashion, and, lying back gazing up at us from the brown, furry cushions, a slightly older man with piercing blue eyes and a dark, curly beard. 'Déjà vu', don't they call it when you suddenly feel it's all happened before or perhaps even is *going* to happen one day?

Then, with all the weight of the world on my shoulders, Atlas, son of Clymene, brother of Prometheus who . . . as if it all matters . . . more and more conscious of my rôle in some kind of drama partly, but only partly, of my own inward making, I turned slowly and deliberately back towards my goatish companion . . . mingled feelings of compassion, relief, revulsion, curiosity, tenderness, eXcitement and above all, desire, desire, oh yes, desire, deliciously bold, Promethean desire leaping like a flame and burning within me like the surely by now even *more* boiling, singing, cascading cauldron of waters below . . . and, looking her straight in the eyes as if into a mirror of my own inner being, the same yet different, different yet the same, said gently and magnanimously: 'That's all right, Miss X. I still love you . . . love you even *more*, in fact' (cloven hooves, swollen clay feet and all).

The little stick went on turning, turning in the dappled sunlight, as I knew even then it would go on doing for years and years to come, while, still preening itself on the terrace in the distance, the thin, Voltarian peacock proved its presence with yet a further rasping cry.

'What does it do to you, Mary?', 'Hippolyte, cher coeur, que dis-tu de ces choses?' It was the wolf at the window, the longed-for eclipse of the pine-rocked moon in the mirror.

Thanks to the OXford Weekend, I had realised at last and with infinite astonishment that we are required to wear a label in this world. Yes, so confident was I, naturally, of my own nameless, *inner* identity, Boodle in his very Den, that the thought had honestly not occurred to me before. What has gender to do with the mind, after all?

'And thus in a cloud of illusion and glory sped the last enchanted hours' . . . Too late, hélas, for 'Radclyffe Hall', but rocked, proud as a peacock, by the secret waters of the magic Isis, cure for all snake's venom, for me too now the Well of Loneliness had finally begun.

I was a *HomoseXual Lesbian* too!

The SiXth Piece

Loin des peuples vivants, errantes, condamnées,
A travers les déserts courez comme les loups;
Faites votre destin, âmes désordonnées,
Et fuyez l'infini que vous portez en vous!
('Femmes Damnées', Baudelaire)

Maintiendrai-je des lois que je ne puis garder?
(*Bérénice*, Racine)

It must have been about dusk that we left at last the City
of Dreams. All I can remember is jolting across London in the
Underground, its previously threatening Labyrinth transformed
over-night into a dazzling Ramsgate-like Tunnel of Love.

Indeed, if my eyes had been as large as saucers when we set out
(the eXcitement of a trip to a new place with so illustrious a
companion), they were surely by now veritable millwheels, ablaze
with the full, devouring force of passion at last: 'C'est Vénus tout
entière à sa proie attachée' (and I who thought I understood about
Racine just about all one could possibly know!).

True Miss X had prised her hand from my hot clutch as,
surfacing happily together now from the subterranean caverns
(hélas for poor Orpheus without *his* Eurydice), we negotiated our
way in reverse direction through the teeming platforms of Charing
X . . . armies of dark-suited businessmen in bowler hats bearing
down on all sides of us like manic robots in, presumably, their
frantic efforts to get home to the wife and kids, not to mention a
whacking good meal. (At least *Dad* didn't wear a bowler hat, nor
carry a smart briefcase like Miss X's, though, come to that.)

At the time I scarce gave any weight to the gesture, however,
thinking such discretion perfectly natural the closer we got to
familiar stamping-ground ('Walls have ears and you never know').

Just before boarding the second train, however, obscurely
sensing the need for something more concrete than a purely verbal
protestation of eternal fidelity with which to cement this
momentous new stage in our Venusian adventures ('marriage' I
meant really, of course, for love such as leapt from the foaming
waters at The Trout is naturally eternal), I made so bold as to

purchase with my remaining coins from a somewhat vulgar kiosk (happiness obviously emboldens one's aesthetic standards) a little stuffed sheep I thought she would be bound to appreciate as keepsake, talisman, 'aide-mémoire', what you will: tight white curls 'moutonnant' gaily on the narrow forehead, two distinctly appealing brown eyes made of boot buttons, and a perky piece of green, yes, definitely *green*, velvet ribbon threaded with a small brass bell tied round its neck in an elegant bow – with which touching icon I furtively presented Miss X once safely established in our seats.

Why a sheep, or, more precisely, lamb?

Even at the moment of purchase, quickly turning down other eager candidates like a crocodile-skin handbag, a plastic piggy bank with 'make a pig of me' painted in red on its luminescent hind quarters, a sugar heart pierced by a chocolate arrow (but of course, February 14th, Valentine's Day!) and a fluorescent-toothed vampire from outer space, I had been half aware of some vague symbolic relevance to our common purpose . . . a symbolism which I felt intuitively to be about to deepen and clarify in the light of events still quite unknown. 'We'll see,' as Dad would doubtless say.

On the face of things, however, I was quite content to eXplain to my belovèd the associative link with the 'petit mouton' in St-EXupéry's *Le Petit Prince*.

Perhaps 'St X', as the new 'little sheep' was at once ceremoniously Xtened, could eXpiate meanwhile for my increasingly ungrateful critical tooth, more and more savage towards Miss X's literary favourites of late, and correspondingly more and more addicted by counter-reaction to 'all that nasty, modern stuff she's having to digest' with its, needless to say, far from sentimental supper scraped together from the last linguistic bones of 'Father God'. (Who was it said sentimentality and pornography are twin sisters? Not St-EXupéry, that's for sure.)

Indeed, opening up her smart briefcase again (previously buried in the depths of the suitcase) and chortling to herself at the thought of what Miss P might say if she noticed the bedside metamorphosis (L. *ovis*, 'sheep', to *caper*, 'goat' – '*capra*', then – in two generations), Miss X was already putting into operation the charming, if somewhat sentimental idea of giving me Capricorn in return!

He, St X, goat in *sheep*'s clothing, would now replace Capricorn by her bed in The Pagoda, and Capricorn, sheep in *goat*'s clothing, would come home to *my* bedside cabinet with me.

Fateful Xiasmus indeed, did she but know. ('Intercrossing',

Miss X, my lamb. Got your Greek notebook? From 'Xiasmein', to mark with a Greek 'X' or 'Chi'. Put that in your pipe and smoke it, my Love, while the moon cuts itself into a thousand horned pieces and the clouds turn from white to black sheep and back again across the ever-changing, unpredictable sky.)

Fortunately, until now, we had been alone in the carriage.

No sooner had this curious zoological decussation taken place, however, than we were joined, hélas, by a whole bevy of the manic black robots from the platform, together with a harassed young mother with seven vociferous small boys. ('Seven cats in the back garden, Mary?' 'Well, perhaps not, Auntie. Perhaps just three like Brainy Mary Number Two and the repulsive Gilbert who, conveniently confusing her, no doubt, with Mother Nature and his own unacceptable, disavowed unconscious – water off a duck's tail – upped and left her for another, pretending everything was just the same as before.)

And, as if that wasn't enough ('These people breed like rabbits,' I muttered loudly), a hideous X-eyed baby with a face half way between a rattlesnake and an abortive hedgehog, of what seX I know not, which, much to my embarrassment in case it inflamed or upset Miss X (the robots seemed, surprisingly, to take no notice, hidden behind copies of the *Daily Telegraph*), she, the young mother, I mean, proceeded to succour from first one, then the other drooping, pear-shaped breast, with long, dark teats like a horned Egyptian cow.

A glimpse of another's body is so much more fascinating and mysterious than one's own. What would I have given now to have rushed over to her lonely bed in 'Radclyffe Hall' the night before and . . .

But then did Miss X herself actually *have* pear-drop breasts with nipples, not to mention a fully-fledged cleavage like myself and Miss P? Yet another of those important refleXions that had never fully occurred to me before, strange to say.

And that was the end of all further eXchange between us.

Only my blazing millstones to try to seek out hers in the grimy glass of the carriage window . . . no longer transparent now, but transformed into a gigantic, ambulatory mirror by the backcloth of velvety darkness beyond.

My Love, my Love!

I was far too deep in amorous rêverie by then to take more than superficial notice when, on arriving back at our station (no *Mrs* X this time to meet us, thank god), who should alight from our very train but Miss Hilbert (maths/chemistry), accompanied by . . .

Surely not . . . But yes! The Carbuncle!

Slim and popular-looking as usual, and, despite the rest of her official green uniform, brazenly deprived of the requisite School Hat – a green felt heXagon like a kind of military wolf's helmet (L. *caput lupinum*) with a silken tassel bearing a fluffy woollen pom-pom, earflaps like a deerstalker and, attached with huge, surgical stitches to the brimming slope above the eye-piece, a triumphant scutcheon bearing our own precious astral emblem neatly reduced to two superimposed Xs, the whole crest mirrored refleXively in one of its own hindquarters in turn . . . All in all a monstrous contraption surely capable of springing only from the pen of that Master of Symbolic Realism, Gustave Flaubert Himself, and bearing on its radiant countenance the depths of eXpression of the carbuncular imbecile beneath.

But now, deep amorous rêverie or not, here I was being evacuated unceremoniously from Giovanni at the end of Wall Road ('Walls have ears, Mary . . .'), while She, Miss X, by this time so eXtra special I could scarce draw breath after so painfully abrupt and involuntary a severance, went sailing on without me into the night. (*Mrs* X would presumably be already in bed, prevented, at least until the following morning, from checking up on our adventures in 'the Other Place', but Miss P, damn her, was sure to be wide awake and bushy tailed as usual, avid to trade on Miss X's growing addiction for goatish gambling games like 'Scrabble', 'Snap' or 'Call my Bluff'.)

Mother was ironing a huge pile of washing when *I* got in, I remember: my leaf-green dress and neXt week's set of navy knickers, my sister's gym slip (still sweating it out at Infant School with a brace on her front teeth and transvestite trousers, poor Pin had yet to tread the comet's trail I had blazoned ahead), together with what seemed like hundreds of Dad's white hankies, pants and shirts . . . the kitchen full, accordingly, with the irritating smell of singe marks where, leaving Auntie's brave old flat-iron steaming its head off on some flinching surface, Mother had got carried away trying to read *Madame Bovary* in translation to lift her soul from domestic chores. ('Literature' was *her* Promised Land. No doubt of that.)

And Dad?

Upstairs as usual, I bet, patiently reading a bedtime story to Pin. (Could it be that *she* was *his* Promised Land in a way?)

Seven guesses meanwhile that the story itself would be *Little Red Riding Hood* (my old childhood copy, one of my two identical childhood copies, at least), the bit where, pointed canines, or should I say lupines, ominously glinting, the wolf lies decadently in bed wearing the grandmother's nightcap ('All the better to *eat* you with, my lamb'). And although this particular paragraph had always tended to give Pin nightmares – the moment of metamorphosis (Xiasmus?) in particular – she seemed perpetually and untiringly to need it repeated over and over again . . . a request which, to my own perpetual and untiring annoyance, Dad perpetually and untiringly obeyed. (Jealousy, Mary? Surely not. Big girl like you can read Fairy Tales on your own, *write* them also, come to that.)

(It was always just the same with her second favourite, *The Wolf and the Seven Little Goats*, where the wicked wolf's stomach is finally cut open and the little kids he devoured replaced by stones . . . all but the seventh, which hid in the grandfather clock. Rather like the Cronos myth, don't you think? . . . Cronos swallowing each of his children at birth to try to defy the prophecy that one of them would grow up to depose him, and the canny Rhea, his mother, substituting a stone wrapped in swaddling clothes for the infant Zeus, who presumably *did* . . . Deposition, rites of passage, murder, even . . . everything seems Oedipal nowadays when you dig back.)

Hardly stopping to mutter 'Hello' to my mother, let alone to Dad and Pin (not that, thick as thieves in there . . .), I placed Capricorn reverently on the bedside cabinet as planned, half eXpecting to find tell-tale marks of his past conquests on his hooves, as witness the stolen cattle of Odysseus.

There were none.

Pure white felt like the day he was born. (Presumably long since under the sod, what was Nobody like all the same?)

And for the best part of that night, lying there listening nostalgically to the mournful lone whistle of the London train as it thundered its way without us through the bowels of The Wilderness – oh for the tongue of the unknown Bell back there at The 'Radclyffe' (Xt Church, I found afterwards. Well it would be, wouldn't it?) – pressed the silky little body of my new friend with the cloven/clay hoof closer and closer beneath me, as, like the wily Odysseus *under* the belly of the ram in his case, I began to inspect my teeming new plans.

If the dance in the hotel bedroom that morning was an unconscious echo of the mysterious 'Labrys' (dance of the double-headed aXe?) performed by the prisoners escaping the Minotaur long ago, little did I suspect then how I had escaped one passage of the Labyrinth but to enter another of even more intricate design.

All I knew was that, just before leaving that bitter-sweet River ('thrilling-sweet and rotten/Unforgettable, unforgotten/River *smell*', Mary. Get it right for once), I too had picked up a stone and made a wish . . . a smooth, round 'lucky' stone with a hole in the middle just like 'Petrus Borel', come to think of it . . . casting it violently into the water as I did so to join that little turning stick below . . . the great Mother Isis turned to wishing well.

Perhaps – though they say one should never tell a wish in Public – it was simply that a stone thrown in a River, unforgettable, unforgotten, might be magically transformed into treasure one day . . . as perhaps, in a queer kind of way, it was.

'And eyes of mine you voyage now . . .'

After the OXford Weekend things never *were* the same again indeed. But with my usual congenital obstinacy of spirit (must be hereditary like Sigmund's), I failed at first to realise eXactly how.

After a week or so back in harness, intrigued at first by the titanic discrepancy between our recent freedom and the renewed constraints of the daily round, I began to grow impatient and to crave further intimacy . . . particularly in that I had assumed I had but to raise my little finger (' "Le doigt auriculaire", Mary. Got your French notebook?') for the relationship to continue eXactly where it left off with that unceremonious dumping at the top of Wall Road.

Right up to then, I had been keeping a secret diary on the inside flap of my left plimsoll marked with the French codes 'B' or 'M' ('baiser' or 'main' for 'kiss' or 'hand' – understandably eschewing the more conventional 'X' for the former), according to which or other of these sensual delights had been fleetingly achieved throughout the week, and improvising now a quick additional 'S' ('sein') to cater for the eXceptional, full-breasted event on the sheepskin rug in OXbridge, which, the immediate danger now behind us, I could now begin to contemplate more at ease. Indeed, I not infrequently liberated the same fortunate right nipple in private in the hopes of imagining what lowly virtues Miss X could possibly have seen in it that time.

(A mere mass of glands and swollen gooseflesh, let's face it. Nothing much worth writing home about there. Indeed, as I reflected astutely on the train just now, if another's body appears so much more fascinating, then one could surely do worse than to identify that other body with one's own corporeal constitution, thus relieving the innocent object of our concupiscence from the burden of fantasy of which our lust is composed.)

These 'B', 'M', 'S' activities of yore seemed mere kid's feed, however, compared with the more intricate goals towards Miss X's person which, totally immune to my own advice in such crucial matters, I now concocted in my invisible cauldron by day and by night ('Too much imagination, Mary . . .').

Not to beat about the bramble bush, I had even soon drawn on the corresponding flap of my right plimsoll, and inspired by my private reading about the 'olisbos' of boiled leather sported by the more enlightened of the Bacchic Maenads, a kind of two-handled broomstick with a middle partition or X-bar – at least when you love someone it's worth taking trouble – designed to serve the mutual interests of our future Esbats (tympanum? no, that's the wall of the ear).

How *did* we women manage after all? No good simply lying back and bemoaning the missing fourteenth piece devoured by some mythical 'XYZ' in the Nile.

Now, however, apart from the usual prim 'Good-morning Miss X' before assembly, and the odd, half-hearted 'B' or 'M' to keep the wolf from the window, I had virtually nothing left in the boX to keep me going any more . . . nothing other, that is, than the dubious Pandoric virtue of Hope and – somewhat more reliable – the aesthetic pleasure of my ingenious, anatomical hieroglyphs themselves. (Sublimatory substitution or displacement, maybe, but even Sigmund Freud doesn't call Art mere repression, n'est-ce pas?)

Far more difficult to endure, and far more ominous, would I but admit it, however: the summonses to The Pagoda were also getting fewer and further between!

Fewer, even, than in the days *before* OXbridge! And what precious time there was on such rare occasions *horribly curtailed now by the presence of Miss P.*

I remember a particularly gruelling Sunday, for instance, when, having got up everyone's goat at home with my pre-Pagoda ritual (the obsessive one-finger playing on the piano – and I in my dreams a top-dog concert pianist – of the first few bars of Bach's 'Bist du bei mir'), I sped like a greyhound along the edge of 'my' cornfield at the appointed hour (Miss X, one ring), only to have Miss P herself appear on the threshold, armed with an insulting 'Don't be long, she's rather tired,' before settling down squarely with a pile of Greek and Latin proses (mine and the Carbuncle's in predictably close rival positions for supremacy) in what had always before been *my* rightful chair.

(It was shortly after this that Dad, usually as mild and even-tempered as the munching Minotaur in the Meadow, suddenly turned Lizzie Borden and chopped up the whole thing – the piano, I mean. Not much hope of my maestro concert now.)

Yes, not content with an irritating 'toc-toc' with *her* still unadulterated broomstick but a few minutes after my arrival (her ceiling, our floor, remember), my one-time idol was now actually pinkly and poisonously present at our meetings in the flesh!

And besides, what to say to dear Miss X even in the few precious minutes when we *were* alone together?

Certainly I was no longer quite so interested now in pursuing the difference between Corneille and Racine or discussing *To the Lighthouse* by Virginia Wo(o)lfe.

What was it she was going to tell me about the Human Body 'when time and circumstance were right'? When eXactly *would* they be right, come to that?

By this time I was beginning to rely heavily on the power of the spoken word to convey long stretches of lone eXperience, while at the same time seething with hatred for its vicious inadequacy in performing tasks of a more tangible kind.

Indeed, the heady delight of our former discussions on, say, the superior self-awareness of Literature compared to Religion (superiority to *me* at least – Miss X was still more doubtful, well she would be, wouldn't she, seeing herself as a goat or, rather, lost sheep), seemed to have been replaced on my part by a painful silence or, equally painfully, by a use of language in which, not unlike Miss X's own words back there at The Trout, every syllable seemed crushed and distorted by a sick, self-conscious humour as it left my mouth – a habit not entirely mastered, I'm afraid, to this hour.

Nonetheless it must have been round about this time that I began the first of the 'Blue Books': gravely recording in the Notebook with the blue cover purchased for me by Miss X that time in Blackwell's, my 'private' thoughts and feelings of the moment, together with numerous quotations (in German for some reason: 'Entbehren sollst du . . .', 'thou shalt forego', 'In der Beschränkung liegt der Meister', 'in limitation lies the Master'), designed, usually in the form of cunningly disguised self-eXhortation, to relate my recent personal eXperiences to the Great InterteXtual Literary Storehouse of the Past.

For, curious to relate, whereas prior to the OXford Weekend I had prided myself on my total uniqueness, now, on the contrary, always supposing they posed no threat to my personal territory (Sigmund and the cat neXt door), I took great solace in identification with others . . . in this case with the Suffering Lover, who, need(less) to say, was almost invariably male . . .

The anguish and the sharp despair, (. . .)
Because a girl or hill is fair?

I have stared upon a dawn
And trembled like a man in love,
A man in love I was, and I
Could not speak and could not move.
(William James Turner)

. . . Miss X herself becoming accordingly, for so runs 'male' discourse, anything from wild, irrational, seductive, capricious and stormy (Man and 'Mother Nature' again: strange Miss X didn't see what I was getting at that time in The Wilderness), to despicable, dull, vegetable and a generally painful stitch in the thigh.

Object of cultural appropriation and conquest: *prey*, in other words.

And, equally perverse (or is that the same thing in disguise?), the missing object, the unknown quantity, on which to project and magnify whatever primitive fears and frustrations seethe and bristle unacknowledged within the personal pot.

And the aim of all this frenzied, scriptural activity?

Why, to enable Miss X to enter the intimate universe of my solitude, of course . . . to prove and tame with one sweet, sublimational sweep of the wing (and who knows with what secret hopes of direct reward even here: Eurydice 'tout entière', perhaps?), the vast proportions of my thwarted desire.

Anything to hold off the realisation that we are not loved, that She no longer wants me any more.

Of course there were still a *few* relative highlights during this testing period, albeit circumscribed now by the rapidly approaching end of the School year and my enforced, lone eXile to OXbridge for good.

('Lord dismiss us with thy blessing . . .': how horribly ominous now that tri-annual hymn whose final, eXhortative aleXandrine had always before so safely *included* me, but which now prepared to reward my loyal labours by treacherously eXpelling me to a far-flung, and, hélas, without Her whose presence seemed alone to give it meaning, no more than totally alien shore.)

Most of the other girls stayed to lunch or were even full boarders, their parents the owners of fat sheep-farms out there on 'our' marsh.

In my case I had always made a point of going home to lunch, however: ostensibly for the privilege of changing Miss P's library books at Boots (invariably, to my shame, the most gruesome pot-boilers full of bloodthirsty, revengeful murders), but also to escape from the giggling quacks and increasingly persecutory jibes which seemed sure to beset my ears now wherever I went. The upper fourths in particular, who, not content with 'Brainy Mary', were now into the for me infinitely more painful 'Teacher's Pet' with its sarcastic accompaniment of 'Ba Ba Ba' (subtle allusion, no doubt, to the wretched nursery rhyme 'And everywhere that Mary went . . .', there where a simple 'Mary, Mary quite contrary' would have made me feel on top of the world).

Not without a few hundred grains of truth', I'm sorry to report, I was seen increasingly now as a form of emissary, cunningly informing on my potential fellow School-mates in order to gain favour in High Places: for the same would-be subversive needs as drove *them* to the arms of their spotty boyfriends, did they but know it, ignorant fools.

By the end of that term, in fact, I had become a veritable little 'Ear of Dionysius' (the Emperor, with an 'i' this time): those terrifying Labyrinthine passages built into the walls of the palace to enable spies to eavesdrop on enemy plots and plans ('Walls have ears, Mary, and you never know').

Now, after OXbridge, however, and despite my naturally convinced vegetarianism (backed nowadays as much by my increasing insight into the sadomasochistic rites underlying religion – careful, Mary – as by common-sense ethical concerns for fellow creatures like 'Messer Gaster' himself), I felt it necessary to go so far as to endure for her sake the horror of School lunches, lamb chops, hot dogs, Uncle Tom Cobbley and all.

Well, you never knew indeed. Some chance encounter in the corridor, say?

Not the first time in human history that sacrifices have been made for the sake of the Loved. Religion itself is peopled with martyrs to the terrible cause of the Absent One.

Not that such chance bonuses were very likely nowadays.

Almost as aloof from her Staff now as I from the riff-raff of my own equivalent subordinates, Miss X would sally forth imperiously to visit the Staff room as infrequently as once every month at the most.

During one such agonising carnivorous repast, however – lamb chops in the quacking company of the entire hockey First Eleven, the Carbuncle eXcelling herself in their midst as usual – my painful, gastronomic martyrdom was uneXpectedly rewarded, by a slow, oh, so beautifully slow if somewhat puzzled smile, shone in my direction clean through the double panes of glass which divided the Staff triclinium from the more lowly enclosure in which I now sat masticating in solitary state (*inwardly* solitary state, that is – one is never more alone than in a pack of hounds, as Auntie never ceased to reflect).

How the cockles of my heart glowed to receive such salty ambrosia, 'poetic' material for months to come!

Yet another uneXpected golden apple fell my way one wet and windy 'break', too, while I was hovering at the head of the drive pretending to inspect the flailing virginia creeper. (A particularly unpleasant gang led by Poppy Morpheme was waiting in ambush for me down by the bicycle sheds, increasingly popular as a place of rendez-vous ever since being designated 'out of bounds'.)

Throwing caution to the winds almost like the old days, Miss X had suddenly flung open the Study window right by me to lean out bodily with a cheerful 'Hello Mary, nice weather for ducks,' – a honeyed aXiom which, once recovered from the rush of adrenalin at the interruption of my latest rêverie (daringly unbuttoning those turquoise pyjamas of hers at The 'Radclyffe' and seizing *her* right nipple this time, tit for tat), I at once interpreted as a coded reference to our lost idyll by the Isis, fragments of which I had found myself carefully but invisibly piecing together in memory ever since our depressingly restrictive return to the fold.

'Hello Mary, nice weather for ducks.'

(Yes, Miss X, it's lucky for some.)

Odd moments of elation, then, but mere crumbs to an agoraphobic cur beneath the palace table compared with those palmy days of yore.

For not only did my eXcursions to The Pagoda seem to be

becoming more and more hedged with difficulties of a circumstantial nature, but Miss X seemed less and less willing even to *want* to give audience – a horror which not even the current Blue Book could bring itself to take on board.

Not that the cares of office left her without particular worries and preoccupations at this time (fool that I was still with my constant alibis).

Shortly after our abrupt mutual eXodus from Paradise, there occurred an unfortunate incident involving the unpleasant task of actually dismissing a Member of Staff from the School.

The person concerned (Miss Hilbert, maths/chemistry, as it turned out), had been discovered red handed on at least two occasions ('"*En flagrant délit*"', Mary. Got your French notebook?'), reeling about drunkenly in the stack cupboard like Bacchus, and, as if that were not bad enough, on the second occasion at least, *not alone*.

The Carbuncle, would you believe it, was waltzing about in there too like a corybantic Maenad, wearing her School hat upside down! (So much for '*Ad Astra*'. Fortunately our star was reversible though.)

And discovered by whom? Who blew the gaff, I put it to you? Why, dutiful Mary Wolfe, of course.

Yes, vulturous ear and eye glued to the wall in the usefully adjoining siXth-form 'cell' where Miss P and I still battled not infrequently with 'the Cave of the Cyclops', I myself had both detected and been forced to report the perfidious scandal, leaving Miss X no option in turn but to bring the case before the Governing Body – alias the Vicar – and have the unfortunate offender 'given the sack'. ('Well done, Mary, lamb . . . a thoroughly wicked influence on both Staff and girls.')

But as if that wasn't bad enough . . . It was even rumoured on the grapevine that Miss Hilbert and Amanda Carbuckle – the Carbuncle, I mean – were . . . well . . . 'living together' somewhere in town – a malicious slander to which I immediately refused to give credit. Didn't I tell you people are always casting stones at other people's greenhouses ('"*bouc émissaire*"', Mary. Got your French notebook?') chasing a scapegoat into the frying-pan, punishing in others – I'm thinking, of course, of Brainy Mary Number Two's Gilbert – that which they secretly fear and dislike in themselves?

So much eXtra worry due to Miss Hilbert's shameless escapades, no wonder Miss X seemed to have less time for me than before, poor lamb, and this despite all the pent-up lust she must undoubtedly feel since having seen me dancing totally naked like that. (One can take in quite a lot from the corner of an eye.)

True there were eXceptions to the rule – like the time out at The Pagoda when, with Miss P close on our heels and Mrs X clamouring for her Sunday outing to Ramsgate, she suddenly swept me into the broom cupboard under the stairs, and, curious variation on the last recorded 'B' and 'S' on the OXbridge sheepskin, attempted somewhat clumsily to infiltrate her right hand . . . surely not, but yes . . . somewhere down much further between 'Little x' and the top of my navy-blue knicker elastic: a compleX eXperiment to say the least, and one sadly interrupted at the eleventh hour by the petulant shouts and all too well-timed tappings of you-know-who neXt door.

Deep down, however, I suppose something in me knew all along that such byzantine gestures on Miss X's part were but the dying notes of a carnal symphony never to hear the light of day . . . last minute attempts of guilty atonement for a campaign of withdrawal long since planned with Ciceronian precision, and which had already long since begun to take effect . . . for all I knew, that very same night back there in 'Radclyffe Hall', when, '*Come here, Mary!*' (yes, I was *convinced* now my ears had not deceived me), I had shamefully and irremediably failed to respond to her one unique cry:

Come here, Mary!

Let me lay my faithless head in the goose-pimply, pink folds of your innocent young cleavage! ('Innocent', I ask you. As if there's ever anything else. See how the notion of Sin corrupts.)

Let me rip away the last barricades of your quilted Donald Duck bed-jacket, not to mention the last strands of your white flannel nightdress, and slowly creep down my hand in turn . . . down, down, to that secret cultural clearing-house thou shalt not mention eXcept indirectly . . . that ptyX, that licorne's lap, that precious carbuncle, that Golden Fleece, that cold hot water bottle, that mock crocodile-skin handbag, that rosette, that Cyclops' cave, that burning bramble bush, that bearded totem, that perky little turret deep in the pine trees, that scarlet creeper, that viper's bugloss, that Bermuda triangle set in a sapphire sea . . . in short that peculiarly mythical Pandora's picnic basket feared by Xt Himself, and which, compared with the whole marvellous, erotic organ of the human being *in toto*, isn't really worth writing about at all . . . bit of a dead duck, if you were only to stop raving on and deign to ask me.

Come here, Mary!

Come here *mon enfant*, my dearest kid sister, my Little Red Riding Hood, my cuckoo, my Hyppolyte, my lamb, my Lolita, my Little x, my trout, my wild goose . . . my pupil, my teacher, my star, my star scholar, my servant, my scape-goat, my sorrow, my joy . . .

Come here my Holy Grail, my Head Girl, my Hyacinth, my saviour, my mistress, my master, my lover, my catachresis, my Roman watchdog, my spy . . . my wife, my confessor, my husband, my nightingale, my mother, my daughter, my Delphine, my angel, my confidante, my SphinX, my own left hand . . .

Come here my gad-fly, my Siren, my lighthouse . . . my hunger, my desert, my lou-lou, my poppet, my well of loneliness, my only true thirst . . .

Come here my betrayer, my poisonous biographer, my viXen, my viper, my self-eXecutioner, my redeemer, my avenger, my vulturous Novelist, my vampire, my She-wolf, my Isis, my little red foX . . .

Come here my lost youth, my wolf's bane, my terror, my phoeniX, my mirror, my own, living ghost! . . .

EXplique, si tu peuX, mon trouble et mon effroi:
Je frissonne de peur quand tu me dis: 'Mon Ange!',
Et cependant je sens ma bouche aller vers toi . . .

Paradise lost indeed!

How desperately I longed now for even so much as a fragment of that rustic escapade in The Wilderness, where, carnal pleasures apart, at least we could be alone together to behave as we pleased. (Oh that Xtian push-me-pull-you fear and adulation of the flesh confused in turn with Women, they have served you short, my poor Pascal, thinking to renounce me to save your own skin.)

But never again now, hélas, was Miss P called to take assembly.

Only Miss X herself, relatively pale and forbidding (obviously the disgraceful incident with Miss H and Amanda C had upset her), struggling on manfully with the Abominations of Leviticus, Chapter SiXteen:

And Aaron shall cast lots upon the two goats; one lot for the Lord, and the other lot for the scapegoat. And Aaron shall bring the goat upon which the Lord's lot fell, and offer him for a sin offering. But the goat on which the lot fell to be the scapegoat, shall be presented alive before the Lord, to make an atonement with him, and to let him go for a scapegoat into the wilderness...

(CompleX purification rituals indeed! It seems, you see, that having cruelly sacrificed/slaughtered one of the two poor elected goats, they used to send the other one out into the Wilderness (sic), in the strange belief that it would draw down the sins or illnesses of the group on to its shoulders and take them away with it in transferred form . . . a fascinating Xiasmus, this one, which my previous studies with Miss Prick of the goat as 'totem' – I thought protectively of Capricorn – seemed to have left surprisingly incomplete, at least from the point of view of its full psychological range.)

What was it Mrs Blanche had told us that time in human anatomy, though? Apparently we all possessed as part of our genital tackle – something must be wrong in my case – 'a small, half concealed organ . . .'.

But, to the unconcealed impatience of Miss X when I happened to mention the lesson in passing, here my notes were tantalisingly incomplete.

'No, wait. Here it is: "a small, half concealed organ of semi-erectile tissue called the *klitorip*". Yes, that's it. The *klitorip*. I remember thinking how "rip" rhymed with "Pip" as in *Great EXpectations*' (set, incidentally, out there on 'our' marsh).

Deviations in normal anatomic structure notwithstanding, all, yes all of us (with the eXception, of course, of poor Mr Shepherd-Fenrir, our short-sighted janitor), were endowed, it seems, with not just one but *two* distinct *seXual organs* (at this point, scarlet as the virginia creeper outside the window, we had all bent down feverishly over our notebooks): on the one hand the *klitorip* (small by what yardstick, though?) and with the other hand the *vagina* (L. 'sheath' or 'scabbard': EXcalibur!), in turn – this too was news to me – quite distinct from the *womb* (L. *uterus*, Gr. *hyster*, as in the much abused term 'hysterical'), capable of absolutely no feeling of its own and in short no more than an eXpendable sack.

(Warning me, surely quite mistakenly, that her love for me might suddenly evaporate against her will with a change of hormones – Gr. 'to eXcite or urge on' – Miss X herself, poor soul, had once been whipped off to hospital for the potential removal of the whole eXpendable contraption, during which fraught period, allegedly in secret but making sure it slipped out in later conversation all the same, I had hypocritically prayed for her life by candlelight in the local town church, with the result that when she came round from the anaesthetic, the whole thing was apparently still intact. Oh well!)

As for *menstruation* (L. *mensis*, 'a month'), 'Apparently you *can* go swimming with it, after all, Miss X,' (I always had done) 'and it's not unclean,' (never thought it was).

'Oh, and one more thing,' aided, no doubt, by the unusually keen interest on the part of my audience, it was all coming back to me now in a rush, 'apparently the *klitorip* has the eXtra advantage of being available for action when the *vagina* itself is not necessarily engaged. Particularly in the practice known as . . . Wait, yes, here we are: *mastication*.'

Funny: what with cows having seven stomachs like goats, I always though that meant to chew the cud. I had found my eyes instinctively roving to 'Messer Gaster' as I spoke, so looked quickly away again in case of hurting her feelings. Not much chance of treading on *those* swollen toes. The compulsive munching of so many pear-drops and aniseed balls, I suppose.

'Have *you* ever done it, Miss X, masticate, I mean?' I went on to ask now (a bit like *Twenty Questions* on the wireless), and was somewhat disconcerted that she failed to reply, even though the question was so short and precise for a change . . . casting me instead an anguished look of reproach (Sigmund in the pantry that time when Pin gave her a belting) which I felt I should surely remember to my tomb – if I ever got a proper one, that is. Some of us fall instead to a watery grave.

Have you ever done it, though, Miss X, handsome features distorted like Odysseus, free, free at last to hear the voice of the Sirens, 'Vénus tout entière à (t)a proie attachée', up there in your lone little turret amongst the pine trees with only Capricorn (St X nowadays) to witness, or perhaps even – *blind fool that I was not to have thought of it earlier* – back there at The 'Radclyffe' ('Come here, Mary,') alone in the bed with the not so squeaky springs?

Was *that* the magic, goat-nymph bane and blessing you had so much longed and yet feared to teach me to ward off witches and warlocks that night?

But why, oh why, since Mrs Blanche had only spoken in the Pursuit of Knowledge, Natural Right of every budding Eve (and that includes Adam) on Earth, why was Miss X flushed and angry now to the point of threatening to stop the human anatomy lessons completely for the whole upper siXth form . . . rushing about like a red bull in a meadow and demanding to borrow – it felt more like confiscate – these and any subsequent anatomical notes?

Capricious, unpredictable, stormy as an Ocean, the Wiles of Women are hard to fathom indeed.

And besides, give a dog a bad name. Prying like that into Mrs Blanche's lessons . . . Who was the *true* spy now, by Isis? Mary Wolfe or Miss X herself?

Who the true 'bouc émissaire', come to that? Poor Miss Hilbert (maths/chemistry) perhaps? Certainly not the precious Carbuncle, suddenly transformed by the rabid yellow flames of jealousy from puny facial pimple to gleaming sapphire firedog waiting to *snap*.

'Bist du bei mir . . .': beyond the pale of all imaginable human desiring, they *lived* together after all. Think of that!

The Seventh Piece

Pour jamais! Ah! seigneur! songez-vous en vous-même
Combien ce mot cruel est affreuX quand on aime? (. . .)
Que le jour recommence, et que le jour finisse,
Sans que jamais Titus puisse voir Bérénice,
Sans que, de tout le jour je puisse voir Titus?
(*Bérénice*, Racine)

And then at last she told me (well, she would do, wouldn't she, the Seventh Piece?).

I suppose, deep down, I knew all along. Don't they say already lost objects are the only ones one is afraid to lose?

I must have gone up to OXford by then, the entire first year passing in a vague blur of impassioned loneliness lit only fitfully by attempts to revisit our old haunts from the past: nostalgic lone trips out to The Trout, for instance, or down the street past 'Radclyffe Hall', where, gentle as a lamb now as he stared motionless from the lace-curtained window of 'Reception', I once caught a glimpse of that white alsatian dog. (Why *did* she fear it so, I wonder? Rabies perhaps? Surely the owner would have said.) Was I not custodian of a sacred secret still to guard with my life from the prying ears of all potential *College* friends just as much as those back at School?

Not that my ever-hopeful vigils by the pigeon-hole marked 'W' had yet borne fruit, forbidden or not. Though the hungry hunter sit for ever, no bird visited *that* wooden cot.

No matter, Mary. Pecker up. The change-over to the dread 'Comprehensive System' was no doubt responsible, keeping her even more intolerably busy than before. (Of Miss X's politics, I knew very little apart from the *Daily Telegraph* that time in the train. What had politics any more than gender to do with the Affairs of the Heart after all?)

Besides, when not banished to Paris again by the New Tutor – despite the decadent cigars and stilettos, not *nearly* so bad as we had originally thought – there were always the vacations.

To them I began to look forward with a hope as vast and as violent as the pain of all those burgeoning capacities otherwise so abruptly cut off.

Would she have heard of André Gide, for instance? – *La Porte*

Etroite ('the narrow door') which I'd brought home in my new mock-leather briefcase but had not yet had time to peruse myself, or, together with the apparently better-known autobiographical 'récit' called *L'Immoraliste* (modern, admittedly, but thanks to the eXcluded middle you can't have everything), a super, mock-Greek dialogue called *Corydon* where he eXpounds the strikingly neglected truth that, by contrast with mere utilitarian things like biological reproduction, the seXuality of the true Artist is free to follow the imagination to its natural eXcess ... the only places or epochs in which Art fails to flourish being those in which HomoseXuality fails to eXist. Like all truly Great Artists, Gide was a 'HomoseXual' too, you see. Only wish *I* could write a récit like that!

(Autobiographical did I say? According to the New Tutor Gide's monologues cleverly only *seem* that way. Literature offers other means than mere personal confession for the Writer's own head to be put on the block.)

Now, my arrival heralded in advance by hundreds of eXcited letters designed to whet her appetite for the wondrous, multimedia meetings to come, I reached the familiar red terrace at last ('I never want you to be ashamed of your home, Mary'), to be greeted – second only to the rapturous welcome of Sigmund, whom the quality of my voice always made incontinent on such occasions – by a note innocently propped up by Mother on the bedside cabinet, and addressed simply 'MW' in Her familiar left-sloping hand.

At last, at last!

Joy, oh joy!

She could no more wait to see *me* than I to see *her*!

All those long, patient months of wondering and waiting eXcised, eXpelled, eXterminated in a few seconds flat!

How I had longed for it, all those weeks in the alien quadrangles, the special, narrow path round the edge of 'my' cornfield: the sun kissing my bare skin like a porous earthen vessel – open shoes nowadays, not mere crêpe-soled plimsolls – the wind rippling the corn like a great Golden Fleece, scarlet-poppies heralding my radiant advance.

('The goats are chasing each other,' they say still in certain parts of Somerset, where old women have been known to change into hares. It's apparently close to something called 'latah': a form of paroXysmal self-suggestion cultivated in Malaysia where, rather like those 'homeopathic' crocodile rites I mentioned earlier, they clothe themselves in animal skins and rush about hysterically, believing themselves to be carnivorous beasts. Oh well!)

Biting back a twinge of savage disappointment that the initial 'rendez-vous' was not to be for well over a week and, strangely, in School rather than out at the more intimate shrine of The Pagoda as envisaged in such tender detail in advance, I carefully reinstated the precious message on the cabinet (impaled auspiciously this time on Capricorn's left horn), unpacked *Corydon*, *La Porte Etroite*, Proust and Racine (*Phèdre* had long since been ousted now by more subtle, psychological tragedies like *Bérénice* and *Iphigénie*) and settled down to prepare what I would say when the magic moment came at last.

All in all perhaps it *was* just as well there was time to plan things in advance. And as for meeting in the Study like that rather than in the cosy little 'maison du berger' up in the turret (Alfred de Vigny), still never penetrated even yet, believe it or not . . . well it *was* the vacation, after all. Even Mrs FoX-cum-Salmon would be away on her vulgar annual holiday shooting and fishing in the Scottish glens, presumably with *second* husband in tow.

Chance for a 'B' or even an 'S'?

' "La vie réserve de belles surprises", Mary,' (Marcel Proust talking) and you should always hold in mind (Socrates?) that you never ever really know!

The week ahead was strangely calm and happy, I remember, a genuine oasis I think of with gratitude and pleasure to this day.

With the meeting itself now firmly assured, I could even enjoy some time with my family again. Yes, walking, all five of us just as we used to – myself, Dad, Mother, Pin and, despite some initial reluctance, Sigmund (poor Auntie must have already departed) – on the sweet-smelling slopes of the nearby Downs. Queen Anne's Lace (some call it cow parsley), goose-grass, wolf's bane (in June, Mary? Well thyme and lady's slipper, then), along with that thick club-moss with the spiky spore-cases (L. *lycopodium clavatum*) and the lovely sun-spurge (*euphorbia heliscopia*) rivalling the heliotrope in its lust for the sun.

How rich and evocative the names Mother shouted, some with little rhymes and aXioms from my childhood *Flower Fairies* book attached. 'I'm tough old yarrow, pull me if you can' or, in the more subtle, psychological case of old Agrimony:

Spikes of yellow flowers,
All along the lane;
When the petals vanish,
Burrs of red remain.

How fragile and lovely the still, in those days, largely unravished green and white, chalk landscape: foXes and badgers playing by their burrows (pace Sigmund, but for you the dog's mercury), the cuckoo or laughing woodpecker calling through its sloping woodlands (careful, Pin, dear, mind that dog's spurge), clear and vibrant as the voice of life itself, and, stretching away towards the ever beckoning, sheep-dotted dykelands . . .

But, of course: Dungeness!

We could go back again! Climb the lighthouse tower at last!

Summer too now. The long, hot days. The wheeling gulls. The song of larks. The doughty MacFarlane where we left off! And I so much more now like tough old yarrow or agrimony, a 'little soldier of the world . . .'

Only to tread the living downland grass
That scratch and smell of sweetness, insects, chalk
With close-cropped patches loved like human hair
Keenly observed
The rabbit-scampered turf and hear
Dear sister
Now
The same call of the cuckoo and the larks
Here we break out of story books
Loss is a dream that's suddenly untrue
Climbing once more
Years on
Alone with you
So close I check your sorrows as my own
Thoughts float like clouds
And pain is gentle too
Simply to breath the air and while we can
To be alive together on this hill
As we were then

When the appointed hour arrived at last, I felt breathless with eXcitement, as they say . . . getting up at dawn ('See how Aurora throws her fair . . .', as Mother would normally have quoted on bringing in the breakfast tray) and trying on several different combinations of clothes. She had once admired me in a white angora sweater rather like her own ('Come here, Mary, lamb, and let me stroke you,') though that might be far too hot at this time of year. Then there was the black dress with the low-cut neck which apparently made me look 'young and sophisticated all in one' ('lamb dressed as mutton,' she might just as well have added . . . though what has age to do with human emotions any more than gender or politics? Grandmother, raven, sister, badger . . . let us be each to all and all to each).

Despite the heat, I must have opted finally after all for the angora sweater over my new black slacks, and, carefully putting on some borrowed lipstick (first and last eXample of such Baudelairean degradation), my heart singing merrily as a cuckoo in a kettle, teetered off on my new stilettos to that fatal 'rendez-vous' to haunt me to this day.

'Sit down, Mary. I have something important to tell you,' said Miss X strangely ceremoniously, as, with shining eyes and eager face, I prepared to cast myself across the familiar leather-topped desk, humming rather ridiculously as I did so a jazzy little song popular with my less academically-minded contemporaries at College ('My Girl', by Adam Faith, I think; 'My X-*Head* Girl', I had been planning to add as if in spontaneous joke).

But then, unbelievably, unaccountably: '*I cannot go on seeing you any more like this. For your own sake, Mary, promise never to try to see or speak to me again.*'

'Titus m'aime, il me quitte'.
'Voyez-vous les romains prêts à se soulever?'

(The Emperor Titus, powerful in all matters but those of his own heart, sends his belovèd Bérénice away from the palace because their marriage would contravene Roman Law, yet without so much as a squeak of protest yet from the silent pack outside the walls.)

'Too much imagination, Mary, those great eyes of yours': greedy, voracious, ravenous, rabid, rapacious, anthropophagic, in short, eXcessive, I had gnawed too hard with my terrible hunger!

The flow of sweet milk had dried up in the breast!

Too much love had turned her heart to stone!

'Pour jamais! Ah! seigneur! songez-vous en vous-même . . .'

'And does the person know, Mary?' (that fatal time by this very same fireplace sharing the Racine when it all began) . . .

My mind racing back with perfect clarity as they say it does when you know you are dying, just as I had vowed then never to speak to her of indifference, so now I must vow *never, jamais*, to speak to her of love.

I got myself back home again somehow, I suppose . . . the stiletto heels cleaving the soles of my feet like daggers and the by now boiling-hot angora sweater not eXactly helping my progress through those terrible streets and marketplaces, loud and threatening now with their alien people and cars ('angora'/'*agora*', 'goat'/'marketplace': it sounds so similar. Could there be some hidden etymological link somewhere?).

All I remember clearly is casting silly, eXstatic Sigmund callously aside in the hallway, as, tail wagging as violently as the flag on a pinnace, she stood up on her hind legs to caress her Master like one of the drugged, once human victims of Circe's magic spells (ironic, when here was *someone* who wanted me at least) . . . failing almost deliberately to answer Mother's familiar 'that you, dear?' ('Promise never to tell anyone, Mary. Not even your mother,' – Dad was away on one of his usual 'jobs', thank goodness), and, having paused but to kick off those now purely gratuitous instruments of torture, hobbling upstairs to the solitary privacy of my bedroom, where, with the tragic grandeur of one afflicted by a pain too great to flinch from fascination at the eXtent of its enormity, I at once sat down at the old gate-legged table with its pot of purple hyacinths (in summer, Mary?), and, checking for her sake the great sobbing howl already welling for ever inside me ('Pecker up Mary. Must keep positive!'), took out Blue Book Number Two and began to *Write*.

'*For your own sake, Mary, promise never to try to see or speak to me again.*' Yes, I, Mary Wolfe, would keep silent and invisible if that's what she wanted, silent and invisible for ever and a day.

But the nature of that Silence would be mine alone to eXpress and transform.

Writing itself, you see! Irritated by my previous eXcessive felicity, *that* was not forbidden yet by the gods!

Writing in silence, writing in solitude, writing to pretend that wine is water, writing to spin the straw to gold, writing to whisper the secret of my ass's ears till the very bulrushes poked at last through my monstrous School hat, writing to . . . (patience, Mary. Not yet. Not yet).

Indeed, as if to conjure up the lion's heart by roaring in advance of being eaten (that ancient homeopathic trick known to all who have tasted and lost the flesh of the gods), there was a poem to prove that very same silk-purse propensity concocted, no doubt, within the hour. Here it is with the Blue Books, embalmed, falcon-headed, like an ever youthful child Horus, 'little soldier of the world', in the faithful Black Tin BoX which gives this Novel birth:

Certain disasters are easy to encompass
Like bright little begonias in gardens,
Or cows seen from the windows of a train
By tired eyes. Departure for the rest of time,
While wind edges under the doorway
Making a tank of sound in which to hide,
Is just as small.
Poking the fire in case you freeze,
I cast the vague, dull shards of all
Abstractions at your feet.
That Life and Love do not eXist
But something intimate and grey
Between the poker and the grate,
We do not even try to say
With tentacles of speech.
But shifting silence, turning coal,
I scar some diamond and know
That lack of wonder and of pain
Flare rough and clear between us like a Torch.

Always, you see, that obstinate, congenital suppression of pain (*and* transformation, Mary, love. Transformation, displacement, sub . . . that strange power of mingled magic and will you once admired in Miss X herself, remember, and which you trembled voluptuously to think you too could possess one day if you chose . . . Transformation too, Mary. Don't forget that).

Notice too, since we all, yes, all, have a rigid stake in such matters, the way in which, derived in turn no doubt from the heat of my white angora sweater, the image of a winter fire in a grate, in turn the very symbol of Racinian passion, has come to replace the natural light of that summer: sweet-smelling Downs, laughing woodpecker, cuckoo, badgers, foXes, sun-spurge, sea-lupins, sheep-dotted marshlands and all.

Wolf's bane! Wolf's bane! Who'll buy my Hairy Wolf's Bane!
Like the wounded Cyclops calling in vain to his neighbours for

rescue, Nobody had hurt me!

Nobody Herself!

Nursing her privileged sorrow inside her like Hyacinth about to spring, transformed, from his own purple death-wound, Mary Wolfe is back in business again . . . Mary Wolfe will shake the Pagoda Tree yet!

Sublimation, that process in chemistry whereby bodies pass from a solid to a gaseous state . . .

Sublimation, that process postulated by Sigmund Freud to account for human activities with no apparent conneXion with seXuality but which are thought motivated by the force of the seXual instinct, the instinct diverted, that is, towards a non-seXual and socially valued aim . . .

Of course the whole process is not quite so neat or simple as that, is it?

With the poems and notes in the Blue Books at this stage as a mere turning twig in a vorteX, a fragile paper raft on the ocean of feelings now seething within (did I *still* hope She would read them one day? subtle are the ways of the jilted lover's revenge), I now embarked for the rest of that now seemingly interminable summer vacation on a series of pathological states of mind ranging from common-or-garden Fetishism, the preliminary stages of which you have already noticed in the case of Capricorn, dear Reader, to Paranoid Jealousy and Obsessional FiXation, through to the perhaps by a whisker more original Scopophilia and Suicidal Fantasy – no little reassured by their startling coincidence with similar eXtra-sensitive eXperiences documented by so many of the 'nasty modern' writers on my OXbridge reading list: André Gide again (mystical sacrifice of the loved object in order to pass personally through the eye of the needle: so *that*'s what *La Porte Etroite* was all about!), Marcel Proust (Swann and Odette), and, just in time for the Jealous Paranoia bit (*'jalousie*, a "blind", Mary. Got your French note-book?'), the sadistic fantasies – *dismembered* women, in his case – of that weird 'New Novelist', Alain Robbe-Grillet, to name but a few.

My parents obviously assuming I was off to The Pagoda for the honour of discussing French Literature with Miss X as usual, or perhaps even that I had met by now some respectable boy-friend like Gilbert whom I was still unwilling to introduce for some reason ('I never want you to be ashamed of your home, Mary'), I would accordingly set out each evening across the cornfield (stubble by now – 'It was too beautiful, they cut it down' as Pin once pronounced dramatically of the stunted syringa bush by the back gate), but this time, hélas, only to position myself in the bramble bush in the adjoining graveyard with the forbearance of a Buddha eXcommunicated from his own Temple, Philomela's tongue cut out of her own living mouth.

(See, oh see, how, like a dying pink snake, it tries in vain to hotch and wriggle nearer the feet of its belovèd Mistress, before writhing for the last time, unseen, unheard, on the starving earth.)

The Pagoda, just the same as ever.

The Pagoda, with its familiar low-dropped eaves and singing pine trees, loyal invariant in all that fickle world of human metamorphoses and doubtless with a secret metaphorical harvest of its own still to reap.

One by one as I gazed from my prickly hiding-place, lights would come on in the familiar, conspiratorially related rooms.

There was Miss P opening the back door to let out Polythemus-Raminagrobis (alias Rumpel) or drawing her lace curtains before retiring to bed, doubtless with her latest bloodthirsty pot-boiler from Boots (self-selected nowadays, needless to say).

There was *Mrs X* at her adjoining kitchen window struggling to release a fluttering white moth into the darkness, before, silly, obsessive creature, it fell, slobbering and eXhausted, at the foot of the lighted glass . . . unable to detach itself from the source of its pain as if therein lay a precious mystery of some kind and to move away from it were very Death.

But then, the long wait at last even more amply and magnificently rewarded . . . 'Love is not Love which alters when it alteration finds' . . . from the very apeX of the Temple, from the secret tip of the Turret itself, trembling like a jewel amongst the creaking branches, Her light at last: steady, ever fiXèd but, hélas, unseeing mark, smiling back faithfully at my brave, wandering barque out there amongst the tombs . . .

. . . That same little turret at the foot of which but a year ago now ('The floor or the couch, Mary?') I had glimpsed our two strange figures together an instant in the mirror, remember, as, head back, eyes closed, rapt in a strange eXstatic compulsion, more like a bird or animal than a human being, Miss X had rocked rhythmically against me as if never to cease . . . the young and the old, two generations, two worlds, two women, the same yet different, different yet the same, one single purpose, one common flesh.

But what, so very close yet so very distant, what was my Lady of the Lighthouse doing now?

'*If I ever shut the door and change towards you, promise to keep on knocking, my love.*'

Those poignant words that time by the waters of Babylon, engraved for ever on the tablets of my heart, were, after all, *prior* to this later, so much harsher decree ('Promise never to try to see or speak to me again . . .').

They were the ones I chose now to remember, slave at the oars like the companions of Odysseus. Voice in the Wilderness, *they* were the words that spoke to me yet.

'Cruel Phyllis whose eternal charms . . .', maybe, but – 'for your own sake, Mary' – was it not for what, mistakenly, of course, *she thought my own good*, best and dearest sacrifice of all, that, just like the lonely Emperor Titus in *Bérénice*, and before even the first baying yaps of the packs of wolfhounds waiting in ambush to destroy us by the bicycle sheds, she had steeled herself to banish me?

Nor did one need a Degree in Literary EXegesis OXon *or* Cantab. to realise that 'never to try to see or *speak* to me again' really meant simply find another way to ride your white horses till time and circumstance were ripe . . .

Philomela with my tongue cut out, weaving the name of my belovèd eXecutioner, Miss X, Miss X, deep in the weave of my future cloth.

Scopophilia. Voyeurism then. To see and not to be seen. Not that . . .

To the unhappy Lover no doubt a substitute source of emotional power, a form of eavesdropping with the eye.

Determined to give myself the best possible vantage point, I had even gone so far one evening, and not without considerable difficulty and risk to my person, to climb up into the lowest branches of one of the old pine trees, crouching there white and motionless in the teeth of the howling wind, ears pricked, eyes strained for the slightest movement, and imagining I should see I know not what lone intimacy framed in that intransigent yellow square. The Loved One naked without her pelt, perhaps, or dreaming she had caught me at last by the tail?

Not that, for all the eXtra energy and appetite gifted by pain to the orphaned animal, I was able to reach more than the lower edge of the bathroom windowsill. ('Hello Miss X, nice weather for ducks.' Who would scream loudest then, she or me?)

At other times I would profit from the help of Lady Macbeth, my faithful, second-hand bicycle, to get up the maXimum possible speed on the roads in and round the village in the hope of passing *them*, Miss X and Miss P, on one of their rare 'constitutionals' up the lane.

Indeed, glimpsing the two broad backs ambling but a few hundred yards in front of me on one occasion, I succeeded in accomplishing a vast detour at breakneck speed which finally permitted me to pass as if by coincidence in the opposite direction ('If a man sets out from A to B . . .'), my heart beating so fast from combined eXertion and guilty emotion, that I all but keeled over at their oh so identically sandalled feet.

Then, 'Good-evening Miss P. Good-evening Miss X.' And, stupidly according myself far less audience than would have been acceptable even in normal circumstances (martyrdom as a source of power?), I continued on my solitary way home to Dad and the new television, fortified by the bitter fruits of my fleeting success.

It was the year of the Cuba crisis, I seem to remember (careful, Mary, cover your traces) . . . The first time there had entered into the sleepy prejudices of South East England that terror of total eXtinction soon to become a sleepy commonplace in itself. EXcuse for at least *some* eXtravagant gesture to the gods? And what magnificent sunsets all those long evenings. Twisting scarves of silken crimson – crimson, crimson, always crimson – swirling on limpid, liquid skies. No wonder they remain with me to this hour, ever-loosening bonds of living joy.

For all their eXcentricity, if not near madness (sign of the Great Artist, after all), my evenings of voyeurism were normally brought to a neat close when the tongue of the ancient church Bell behind me tolled the curfew of X o'clock: the magic hour when she had once said she would think of me across the miles packing up the evening's homework and preparing for bed.

But sometimes, well past curfew, I would prowl about furtively in the graveyard – 'Great EXpectations' like Pip and his outlaw? – idly scraping the ground with my nails (funny if I dug up a bone or something!) and finding in the rich, dark earth amongst the peaceful old tombstones, who knows what uneXpected comfort and relief.

Why, on a sudden impulse on one occasion, I even dramatically ripped off my own underclothes and, selecting a mossy old table tomb aslant in the moonlight, aligned myself on top of it like . . .

Like what, Mary? A virginal meal for the old Church Fathers? A mad female monk on a bed of nails? A goat or a lamb for sacrifice?

A mouse in the corn before the mighty combine? Humble St Andrew on his specially splayed X?

Ravening method in your madness, maybe, but where does the personal Game of Romantic Tragedy end and the Great Universal Truth of Harvest begin?

A wind-swept boy stands where two centuries touch;
For corn-crushed poppies of his childhood yearning;
To sip the syrup of those summers burning
Which flamed with dawn, then slipped his twilight clutch
Like gleaming embers fading into dust,
And coming to the sign-post of his road
He turned and found those golden grasses mowed.
Oh windswept boy who stands where centuries touch,
Yet do you see the chasm at your feet?
Yet do you hear the thud of metal's fist?

On one more worrying occasion, however, just as I was returning home from a reasonably productive evening's vigil (Miss X herself had suddenly materialised for a second at the lighted back door in order to X to Miss P's flat), I was suddenly taken off guard by a wave of emotion so overwhelming that I was forced to prop Lady Macbeth against the rail of the new fly-over – there where we had planned the fatal booking arrangements for The 'Radclyffe', remember? – and, staring down fiXedly at the concrete road beneath, heard, though I could swear my lips remained tightly sealed and I made no more actual sound than does the painted scream in that well-known picture by Münch (isn't there a road-bridge there too, strangely enough?), a long, almost inhuman-sounding howl.

It was as if the moonlight sketched
My pain upon the night;
As if the straight-edged roads below
Ran parallel with all my veins
And headlights seared my sight.
The fields lay flesh along my palm,
Startled and strange, alert and white.
As if the wounds of my own fear
Were quickened by the sting of light.
Yet only now I recognise
The cry I heard was mine.

When we are utterly alone
How can we cut the cord of bone
While two trapped sorrows clash?
How can we know the falling stone
But by a later flash?

'Et la mort à mes yeuX dérobant la clarté . . .' (Phèdre, of course, at the point of her suicide).

Already even then, you see, a striking image, a wolfish curiosity, a form, a rhythm, the first tell-tale stirrings of an incipient, however eXcruciatingly melodramatic poem must have come to help save me and lead me to the shore. For, the silent, yes, totally silent, howling grey shape of whatever it was (sure it wasn't just your shadow, Mary?) loping off into the darkness as abruptly as it came, there I was, pencil in teeth, already astride Lady Macbeth again as if nothing had happened and pedalling as carefully as usual back home.

Mary Wolfe had lived to see a later hour. Not for *her* yet the Xing of that other Great Divide where waits, crouched on the cool earth by the side of the tomb as if to eXhume its own living carcass, the ravenous She-Wolf of her own Death.

As for Jealousy, that most destructive of *all* human passions, according to Racine, Proust, Robbe-Grillet, the New Tutor and even, unfortunately, Miss X herself . . .

If the claims of magnanimity and self-interested desire had allowed me temporarily to fight free of its aconite claws that time at The Trout (*Nobody really . . . just someone I met in my year at college with a beautiful deep voice . . .'*), then how much more invidious the sharp-beaked, but of course rapidly dismissed since obviously totally unfounded suspicions which began slowly but surely to peck my breast – liver, then – now like the vulturous eagle of Prometheus chained to his Rock.

Suspicions focused on whom else, I ask you, but poor, bleating, innocent *Miss P.* She in whose unsuspecting name in the first place . . .

Miss P. Poor Miss P. Perhaps not *quite* so poor Miss P after all . . .

Yes, looking back, tiny, and, of course, in reality, totally innocuous events which at the time I had suppressed or barely noticed, returned to haunt me now in bold relief.

That time, for eXample, when, after I had at last engineered a moment's hard-won audience by means of returning the confis-cation key, she, Miss P, had burst into the Study without so much as a warning knock, and, with careless, laughing familiarity, trotted right up to Miss X and made as if jokingly to wrestle with her a moment . . . the two of them balanced skittishly on the wide brick edge of the grate (though who was to 'take the ram' that time, I forget).

How clearly I understood now how Phèdre must have felt about Hippolyte and Aricie: the insulting luminosity of the truly innocent. Not that . . .

That time, too, when, still under the aegis of that endless first summer – clear blue skies and millions, yes, millions, of daisies out there on the front lawns by the garrulous elm trees – I happened to glance out of the window of the siXth-form 'cells' (headquarters of my some might say shamful espionage at the time of Amanda C and Miss Hilbert), only to be bitterly rewarded by the sight of the two of them, Miss X and Miss P, I mean, adorned in thin floral dresses of almost completely homogenous material, bent together over a trestle compiling neXt year's Master Timetable – a sacrosanct activity in which not even ordinary members of Staff could aspire to take part, and which seemed to me then, as I peered down alone from my burning Watch Tower, especially designed to promote and formalise the most blatantly happy intimacy on their part.

Could it even be that, more recently still, they had laughed like hyaenas that evening over my antics with the bicycle, returning together to Miss P's flat to take a drink of 'Postum' – it's made with barley corn – and play another risky round of 'Snap' or 'Call my bluff'? (Between ourselves, Miss X was becoming more and more of an inveterate gambler of late – quite a 'punter', even, like Dad's Uncle Bob.)

Or even, worse still, that Miss X had not returned from Miss P's flat until much later on that evening . . . had not returned at all, in fact! . . .

But here, mercifully, no further imagery imposed itself.

I simply grew faint at the mere contemplation of the abyss – so much so that the curfew of X o'clock from the tongue of the Church Bell was almost welcome for once with its call to the comforts of Bourgeois so-called normality and the dear, warm . . .

(Careful, Mary. Don't try to hold *that* wolf by it's short ears. Have you forgotten what *They'd* willingly do to the likes of you and Miss X? No good hitching your waggon to *that* blind star.)

Not surprisingly during this time, I began to dream a lot.

Detailed dreams which I would often recall perfectly clearly on waking and laboriously record here in the Blue Books along with all the rest.

Dreams in which, strange to say, I never encountered Miss X at all but only . . . Miss P!

And even then without the least trace of animosity.

Almost as if to help heal or at least anaesthetise the still unspeakably raw pain of my recent abandonment (let alone the pain of any newly fantasised iniquity on her part), the old Miss P, the belovèd Miss P of my early, mere schoolgirl 'crush' ('pash', don't they call it too?) was about to return to comfort me . . . that is if she had ever really left me at all in those deep, trusting grottoes where our first affections are formed.

One particular incident tended to occur again and again in the dream, which I shall first describe as it occurred in waking reality, in order subsequently to convey the mysteriously significant transformations it underwent on the canny royal loom of the night.

Having but shortly given my faithful blast on the bell (how shrill and paltry now its once royal command), I was just staggering along the upstairs corridor with two bursting satchels full of the evening's homework, when I found myself passing right neXt to . . . who else but Miss X herself, gazing down through the little glass hatch into the hall below us at a rehearsal of the end of term play: Euripides' *The Bacchae*, as you already know.

It was the scene where, clothed in the skins of goats and satyrs and waving priestly staffs or batons twined with ivy leaves and topped with pine cones – don't remind me – the wild Maenads (didn't they also do for Orpheus?) charge across the hall in eXstatic frenzy towards the person of . . . no, not Miss X or myself but Pentheus, thank goodness (Poppy Morpheme), horrifyingly led by his aunt and mother (Miss Twee and Miss Ramsbotham), and, scarce pausing by the cup cupboard ('The handbell, Mary. She wants the handbell') to accomplish the customary Dionysian sacrifice of a goat – no small ordeal for the potentially giggling upper fourth form – mercilessly tear his body limb from limb for failing to honour the power of the New God: Dionysus (played by the Carbuncle, as I said).

Naturally *I* paused to watch the performance too: Miss X even, inviting me quite civilly to join her as if – disavowal like Gilbert's? – nothing had passed between us at all . . . neither the necessary banishment nor the prior you-know-what.

But then . . . issuing purposefully from the Staff Room in a creaking sky-blue mackintosh, totally oblivious of our presence but a few centimetres under her usually so active nose, who else but Miss P . . . obviously on her way to the Study to cadge her usual lift home in the car. (I could scarce bring myself to call him 'Giovanni' any more.)

The old Blue Books or not to jog my memory, I can see it all amazingly clearly still.

Miss P striding off determinedly down the long corridor, doubtless impatient to get home and begin to prepare the evening's lamb chops and treacle pud, only to reappear again a good seven and a half minutes later, red-faced and panting from her vain eXertions . . . to find Miss X lolling there casually against the hatchway with *me* all the time, and, unknown, please god, to the for once no longer giggling upper fourth form, laughing fit to bust at the would-be tragic ham acting below. (A delayed reaction to my own dithyrambic efforts at The 'Radclyffe', perhaps.)

And Mary Wolfe?

Just like my mother as a young girl watching the blind man come nearer and nearer the hole in the pavement without being able to utter a word, I had stood there and seen it all happen and still not said. Sins of omission ('Come here, Mary') are obviously the sharpest toothed of all.

In the dream itself, however, far from *failing* to intervene, I at once ran after Miss P and, putting a strong, loving arm round her mackintoshed shoulders ('He shall feed His flock . . .', musical appreciation with melancholic Miss Ramsbotham now transformed to grinning fiend), gently led her to the waiting blue car (reinstated as the ardent Giovanni of our trips to the marsh) . . . starting him up at once with a gallant flourish and screech of the brakes – if only Pin could see me now! – and driving her dashingly back to The Pagoda, where, laughing benevolently, arm slightly lower – that Marks and Spencer's vest over the pink, pink cleavage? – pushing her gently but firmly in front of me like a simpering schoolgirl, and pausing but to kick Polythemus-Raminagrobis out of our path (poor Sigmund had since been run over by a lorry at that very same fatal spot on the by-pass bridge where I too nearly met my end that time), taking my door key from the keyring in my breast pocket (a male overcoat like Dad's for some reason, presumably the convenience of breast pockets in the first place), I disappeared through the well-known front door marked 'Miss X, one ring'.

A door key instead of having to use the doorbell! My *own* front door key into the bargain!

Giovanni, *Her* car!

And I who couldn't drive to save my own or anyone else's fair skin!

It was this detailed, empirical detective work more than any abstract speculation on my part, which, many years later, suddenly offered me with full self-eXcavating Freudian fervour the clue to the nature of my own desire.

No wonder Miss X herself was totally absent, both from *this* dream and at that stage all others:

I was Miss X!

Rather than remain the sacrificial lamb, the slain goat, the victim, I had usurped the place of the Troll, the Tyrant, the Powerful One, the Wolf! (In the dream, that is. In waking reality I was still for many a mad moon longer the cringing cur at the Palace Gate.)

And Miss P, you ask?

Why, Miss P, poor, pink, delectable Miss P, her sad, dumb eyes entreating me now for kindness, mercy and initiation, Miss P was none other than . . .

But, patience still, Mary, love.

Lusting still for lamb souls under a thousand circling vultures' masks let us not anticipate the painful chronology of literary self-discovery.

Hold back, I beg you, your impetuous Chinese Dragons, your indomitable Racinian Bull from the Ocean or whatever other proverbial monster you may have up your wing . . . lest, 'de te fabula', caught like Isadora's fatal, crimson scarf in his own whirring chariot-wheels before the moment the gods have planned for him, innocent Hippolyte be . . .

Ah, look not back. The way is lost in mist.
You cannot run there now; you will not meet
The grey-green willow in a flushed breeze dancing.
No, it is cut, no longer prancing.
There is this horror here though; feel it lancing
Your heart, oh cornered, helpless, windswept boy!
It is enough. Two centuries touch, and he
Who loved the tangling, bright-boled willow so,
Is gone, has left these branches for below
And slipped into a new eternity.

The Eighth Piece

The wolf shall find her grave, and scrape it up,
Not to devour the corpse, but to discover
The horrid murder.
(*The Duchess of Malfi* Webster)

Oui, mais il faut parier. Cela n'est pas volontaire,
vous êtes embarqué.
(*Pensées*, Pascal)

But there was a further, even more ominous sign which should have warned me way back of my impending eXile, the more invidious in that it involved the innocent collaboration of someone who, for all her apparent back-seat position, played in that strange Pagodial triangle of Chinese BoXes perhaps the most powerful rôle of all.

I mean, of course, *Mrs* X.

Mamma herself!

I had been on reasonably friendly terms with Miss X's mother ever since I heard about the Scholarship (if only spritely 'Cantab.' not the bovine 'OXon.' could appear in gold on the Honours Board!).

Did we not after all have an eXclusive interest in common?

Was it not her very womb (L. *uterus*, Gr. *hyster*), which had produced from its dark, mysterious and, according to Mrs Blanche, totally insentient chamber, my illustrious Headmistress, MinervA, Cantab., doubtless already fully clad in turquoise knit?

I had been laboriously organising the end of term treasure hunt at the time. (Mother must have at last plucked up courage to master her telephone phobia and ring Mrs FoX-cum-Salmon from the call-boX near Boots – shades of Miss P's gruesome library books again.) And, my mouth and hands painfully gummed with clues about to be distributed, could scarcely take in the momentous news (if it *was* momentous news, that is).

It seemed far more important to stick on the slips of paper correctly, each clue on the place *preceding* the place involved in the answer to the riddle and not on the crucial spot of the 'answer' itself in the way I had at first laboriously eXecuted:

– one in the stock cupboard, future scene of Miss Hilbert's disgraceful inebriation;

– one in the biology lab (Miss P with the Marks and Spencer's vest), smack on the jar with the mulberry-coloured foetus;

– one, even, don't remind me ('The handbell, Mary. She wants the handbell'), on the very tongue of that cruel, dismissive instrument in the hall about to eXpel me to The Wilderness for good (please god, Girton College, like the suffragettes, Virginia Woolf (on a visit), Rosamond Lehmann and Miss X herself);

– one more or less everywhere, in fact, eXcept the Study, which to forget to announce as 'out of bounds' despite that now deceptively inviting 'HEADMISTRESS PLEASE KNOCK' would certainly be more than my life was worth, mighty and rewarding though *that* treasure undoubtedly promised to be. ('Mary's worth her weight in gold,' a neighbour had once none too tactfully reminded Dad.)

> *Clue number seven*:
> 'The – – – – shall find her grave, and scrape it up,
> Not to devour the corpse, but to discover
> The horrid murder.'
> What walks on all fours, has four letters, feeds on the living and devours the dead?
> *Location*: the peg in the senior cloakroom under my School hat.

(True the Elizabethan literary reference was almost as compleX as the Riddle set Oedipus by the SphinX. Nearly *all* my clues, for that matter. Rather like those byzantine tests we've seen Miss X set to try to foX Miss P, secretly culled from Nemo's, ah, yes Nemo's Almanac. It was a *School* party and educational after all. Better to catch their minds while young. And besides, however long in the tooth, the Staff had received instructions from on High to join in. Even the Headmistress might show a leg.)

Miss X herself wasted no time for once.

On hearing the news of my so-called success from the ubiquitous Mrs FoX-cum-Salmon (privileged to gain audience whenever she liked), she burst eXcitedly from her lair and, disastrously muddling my patient re-pinning and sticking, rushed me out in Giovanni at reckless, breakneck speed to 'tell Mother' (Mrs *X*, that is), calling by somewhat grudgingly to shake hands with my *own* mother, Mrs *Wolfe*, on the way ('I never want you to be ashamed . . .') . . . this to the instant indignation of Sigmund, teeth bared like a truncated alsatian. (Agoraphobia, yes, that was understandable, what with the coal-bucket, the neXt-door cat and the new motorway – protective neurosis, life-affirming, self-awareness fully intact – but surely not *Xen*ophobia too?)

There they had sat, Demeter and Persephone, in Mrs X's tiny, spotless kitchen, toasting me gloatingly with piles of bread and honey as if they really meant it *despite* the disappointment over you know what . . . followed by iced gingerbread and lavish cups of special, Pagodian China tea. Impossible to refuse Mrs X in the food sphere without bringing on one of her special headaches or worse, it seemed. (The web of old symbols untangling here at last with a further, contrary scriptural twist, how clear and real I see them still.)

After which well-meaning assault on the triple tongues of 'Messers Gaster', Mrs X took up a fresh skein of turquoise knitting-wool which, obviously an old hand at the game, Miss X herself proceeded to wind niftily round her own freckled fingers in an ever-fattening figure-of-eight. Sign of infinity, as Miss Hilbert had once told us before her disgrace. ('Mary Wolfe's mathematics leaves much to be desired.' Oh, those red 'X's bristling like porcupines in every marge. *They* were not kisses. *Oh* no.)

Even in those days I could see the relationship between the two was woven, if not knitted, with more than mortal twine.

Having seemed aloof with each other in Public to the point of coldness, here they were now addressing each other in a kind of private gibberish: squeaks, cackles, bleats and grunts like so many farmhouse animals, and all the while eXchanging winks and raised eyebrows over my unsuspecting head. (Unsuspecting, Mary? Well, perhaps not *quite* so unsuspecting then.)

If there *were* any intelligible words for my benefit, Miss X addressed her mother for her part as if she could hardly bear to dwell on a syllable . . . almost as if, like that 'Alligator, Crocodile' eXchange later on at the station, everything had to be forcibly severed from some sonorous envelope of invisible sound by means of a snappy little joke.

Obviously my relative success – the first in our School's long history of carefully cultivated oblivion – had brought them together, however cunningly feigned so as not to hurt my feelings, in a privileged moment of self-congratulatory ease.

Indeed, Miss X seemed on this occasion almost hysterical (sic) with filial affection, hardly so much as casting (off) a pearly glance in my now swinish direction, as, deftly dipping her hands this way and that to accommodate the ever-growing figure-of-eight – no doubt some subtle, tail-wagging dance with a honeyed message for my benefit, could I but decipher its hidden code – regal still in submissiveness, she crouched there obediently at her mother's feet, Hercules in his yellow petticoats winding the wool for Queen Omphale (the cover of yet another of my recently acquired form prizes: Classics, this time, not surprisingly . . . everything but Miss X's favoured French Literature to which, thank god, I was about to devote the rest of my life).

When, just before twilight as I left to walk home ('*entre chien et loup*, Mary. Got your French notebook?' Careful there aren't any lone prowlers like yourself about), we popped back for a moment into her *own* little kitchen on the other side of the wall, I knew instinctively that the special 'B' which landed on the middle of my forehead – gentle and 'chaste' on that occasion, almost reverent – was designed not only to mark the relative success of the Scholarship, but as a reward for bringing this whole happy moment with her mother about . . . re-bridging in the process goodness knows what phantom post-Oedipal divide or chasm, assuaging the libidinal discontents of I know not what cascading Baudelairean abyss.

Something else, slightly more ominous, though.

'A girl of mine at OXbridge,' I had heard Miss X murmuring beatifically to herself while rooting through a monumental pile of smalls on the ironing board (surely not *that* again at a moment like this?). 'A girl of mine at OXbridge . . . my own "Leetle Dorter" . . .' at which, with my usual keen flair for a moment of drama, though at the same time secretly flinching from the incestuous filial reference (I was, after all, a *Lover*, not mere flesh and blood), I remember resting my already re-helmeted head with its dangling green pom-pom on the somewhat disappointing site of her left breast as she reached for a silk petticoat (*white*, not yellow, thank goodness), and, staring up fiXedly at that little fold of freckled skin just above the neck of her jumper (Mrs X had ventured by this time into the testing Nordic voice of Fair Isle), squeezing out a few self-conscious tears: alligator, crocodile, weasel, ferret, SphinX, it's all one . . . worrying all the time still about the remaining clues for the treasure hunt and whether Poppy Morpheme – her Bacchanalian ordeal at that point still ahead of her – would have remembered to announce the 'out of bounds' list as, hair hissing, eyes flaming, I 'd previously decreed with the petrifying command of Medusa in person while they were all guzzling their free half pints of cow's milk during break.

Imagine if, aware of its own inner power after all, the Rabble were to rise amuck and surge over the threshold to ransack 'Messer Gaster' and his aniseed balls!

Such, in moments of Destiny, are the minute distractions of the human heart, that muddy necropolis which only the precious metal of will-power and toad-like self-discipline can transform into gold, as Auntie and Charles Baudelaire would both doubtless have said on their varying paths to the Philosopher's Stone.

Seeing herself as a sinful but aspiring goat in matters of Religion, let alone in those other little matters to be confided at The Trout, Miss X had long since started to try to pass on to me a sense of ethical purpose worthy of the OXbridge star, if not of surpassing even her *own* giddy standards of dutiful French Scholarship one day. (For some strange reason Religion and Morality seemed to her inseparable bedfellows, you see.)

Apparently whatever it was that made life bearable (bearable, Miss X? You too, like poor Auntie and her mysterious 'trespass'? Not the deep eternity of joy?), lay not in the individual person himself (sic), but deep down (sic) in his (sic) sense of community with other men (sic), a sense which, for the infinite goodness of God (sic) the Father (sic) to be fully eXercised on this Earth – was he too male like Dad, Gilbert, Freud and Mr Shepherd-Fenrir, then, and was there yet another world of cornfields and iced gingerbread-men beyond our own? – required the constant sacrifice of one's immediate lusts and shameful (sic) personal desires, flaws in an otherwise perfect design. ('If in doubt, *don't*, Mary' . . . a maXim accompanied on more than one occasion by the daring, if somewhat mercenary sequel, 'Take what you want and pay for it, said God!')

Indeed the whole bleakly eXoteric package was neatly summed up on more than one occasion by the rather shady fail-safe wager ('*parier*, "to wager", Mary. Got your French notebook?') of the fortunate Frenchman, Pascal, from whom she took her nickname, as you know:

'No *harm* in believing, Mary. Nothing to prove things either way, so, given the gains of infinity if we win the bet, might just as well in case we 're right . . .', popularly translated as 'Better be hanged for a sheep than a goat.' (Not that, cunningly weighting the dice like that, Pascal wasn't a bit of a goat himself too in some ways.) No wonder that propensity for 'Scrabble', 'Snap', 'Poker' and 'Call my Bluff': Miss X had gambling bred in the bone if not the blood.

Yes, indeed, Mary. For while an honest, erring goat (I thought of Capricorn with miXed feelings) might be better than a contented sheep (privileged St X up there by her bed in the turret) in matters of the dangerous, private truths of the intellect or (were they separate, then?) the imagination, it was still 'vitally necessary' not to stray from the strait and narrow (*La Porte Etroite* again, didn't I tell you?) in other, more serious social concerns. What God required – 'and sometimes, Mary, I myself have gone so far as to doubt Him, you know . . .' (So much already for Pascal and his wager, in which, incidentally, I had already cleverly spotted a logical flaw . . . though, so as not to hurt her feelings, I didn't say.) . . .

. . . What God required above all else was a sense of the *positive* no matter what eXcruciating form of suffering, naming no names, was sent to try us. Pecker up and an infinite, repeat, infinite, willingness to serve and say '*Yes*' in whatever humble path . . .

(Winding Mrs X's knitting-wool, perhaps? Hardly anything very humble or discipular about the illustrious post of HM in itself. Positively hierarchical like Dad's boss in the office with the bikini calendars. Being misunderstood must give magic powers.)

Yes, OXbridge would certainly stretch and challenge my capacities to the full. She, on the other hand ('Il faut vivre pour le retour', St-EXupéry), had perfect faith in me. I would return to her every vacation like an agoraphobic stone boomerang.

Indeed, it must have been about this time that, tenderly addressed as a certain unique little foX, I received the following eXtra special dedicatory eXhortation – even to *write* it here makes me feel like a murderer – inscribed in a copy of *Le Petit Prince* in Miss X's own freckled hand (age spots; I know that now from my *own* decaying paw):

Pour un certain petit renard tout à fait unique, qui a voulu se faire apprivoiser mais qui s'est fait chérir. Que toutes ses étoiles soient fleuries. *Qu'il trouve toujours des puits dans les déserts.* Qu'il ne devienne jamais tout à fait pour moi une grande personne. Et surtout que nous suivons toujours ensemble la même étoile.

– complete, I noticed ruefully, with a mistake over the subjunctive. (Shouldn't it be *suivions*? No. Of course not. MA Cantab. Must be an eXception to the rule.)

Yes, all that half-baked Religion and Morality stuff, let alone call to follow the same flowery star and find wells in the deserts . . . looking back, my nostrils far more finely tuned nowadays to the slightest scent of human metamorphosis, I should have *known* something was up, some algebraic flip, some swallow-tail catastrophe, some turnskin toss of the inner die.

As for coming to tea with Mrs X by myself ('milk and sugar, Mary?'), the first few times were pleasant and innocuous enough.

Humble or not, I was proud to be of service in helping to entertain and occupy Her beloved Agèd Parent, so obviously lonely out there all day, and by rights my mother-in-law in a more just world. (Why oh why do people hunt, trap, stigmatise, outlaw, erase, seeing the Other as a source of pollution: the old, the dying, the wolf, the little foX . . . Careful, Mary. Raving again. This is a Novel, not a tract.) I think I even went so far as to wind some turquoise knitting-wool myself.

And besides . . . who knows what privileged Nordic salmon I might not net if, like the cunning Odysseus, I used my inner fishing-rod aright?

What had Miss X been like as a child, for instance?

Where did *she* go to school?

Had she *always* entertained the Great EXpectations of becoming a Headmistress? How had she ascended to such Olympian heights?

(No need to tell you how utterly meticulous I was meanwhile about not letting the *true* goat jump out of the picnic basket.)

Mrs X would quicken with delight when I asked such questions, pearl necklace gleaming, blue eyes shining, and invariably cutting me more iced gingerbread in return. How very like her 'Leetle Dorter' she looked in a certain light, almost the *younger* of the two in a way . . . almost, ridiculous though it sounds, as if the Daughter had finally given birth to the Mother . . . given birth to the Womb from which she herself sprang! (The Horse and the Chicken, Zeus and Cronos, Messer Gaster and the gingerbread: in all these egg and cart matters you 'can't tell one from t'other', as poor Auntie . . . I know now the mysterious 'trespass' in *her* case, by the way. Moses in the bulrushes. A soldier from the First World War upped and left her 'great with child' on her wedding day.)

Apparently Miss X had been the model infant: modest, obedient, eXceptionally 'brainy', if, fortunately in girl, a little on the quiet side (you can say that again) and of uncommon natural beauty as well.

I had only to look at this or that photograph of her radiant babyhood to see for myself.

And indeed, the whole flat seemed now to be filled to overflowing with desperate pictorial records of a rather plump child with a sulky eXpression which, with a certain far from eXhausting leap of the imagination, I perceived with a thrill to be none other than Miss X herself!

There was even a full-sized portrait in which she wore round her neck a wreath of plastic laurel leaves, the dangling end of which she seemed to be chewing (not ivy, thank goodness), and, resting on those tight angelic curls, a kind of horned crown.

The portrait was in colour, propped up in the centre of the sideboard like the central panel of a religious tryptich (one of those little churches we should have been admiring out there right then on the marsh), and, apart from a thick, white nappy (a Headmistress in a nappy!), Miss X herself was totally naked, we noticed with a certain quickening interest on my part.

I could even just make out that special mole on her left foot I had detected when she lay on the rug at Dungeness (only once a stigma is understood . . .), and, joy of joys, her infant nipples, budding there innocently like two pink/blue forget-me-nots.

Only once 'in real life' had I caught sight of those nipples: the time when, as she was getting ready to dance with her opposite number from the boys' school at the dread Xmas Party ('Jealous, Mary?' – how we'd laughed), already magnificently attired in a kingfisher-blue silk dress printed all over with tiny Chinese Pagodas, she had bent over by the desk in the Study to buckle her sandals (Clarks like Miss P's, remember) and, my tongue hanging out now like a Chinese salamander's, I had stolen a glimpse of her *seins*: two ripe pomegranates ('The Song of Solomon'), yet so small and neat that, just like Mother, *she* didn't even *need* to wear a brassière.

Needless to say, the pain of Tantalus was upon me from that day forth. (Son of Queen Omphale, would you believe it, he too punished like Lycaon for serving the gods with human flesh, and condemned to stare and yearn for ever more . . . Narcissus with *his* great eyes turned outwards, you might say.)

Sometimes on these occasions Mrs X ('Lydia', though I never called her that myself), could also be persuaded to narrate a few details of her *own* earlier life, though reluctantly and with noticeable blanks thrown in . . . almost as if she were revealing one thing but the more to be seen to hide and thus unconsciously reveal something else, 'disclosing cryptically' again.

Mr X, for instance? What did *he* do?

Soon I learnt that about *Mr* X you simply refrained from asking questions.

From several little hints, however, I began to infer that he must have 'taken to the bottle' like the scurrilous Miss Hilbert, leading to some mysterious incident in the bosom of the family to be mentioned only on pain of death. The only clue to *that* treasure hunt – an inadvertent gift from Miss X rather than from the mouth of the proverbial mare – was that Mrs X had been forced to 'give him the sack' . . . first asking *Miss* X, then but a tender, barely weaned infant of two years, seven months, I ask you (not much more than the age of the child Artemis in the portrait?), whether *She* wanted him to stay.

She did not . . .

And was presumably crowned Queen of the Laurels if not Uplands in return. So much for the miXed blessing of turning Lizzie Borden and giving the aXe to your own poor Dad. (I know, the piano, but then there wasn't much room – 'I never want you to be ashamed of your home, Mary' – and what with 'Bist du bei mir' like that on and on with one finger, it was obviously 'too beautiful' and had to go.)

From then on Mrs X had set out to support her 'Leetle Dorter' single handed, making 'Unspeakable Sacrifices' to enable her to 'get to the top' – which, of course, she *had* done . . . in a way.

Oh, and something to do with a bedtime story, too . . . a story he, *Mr* X, was reading to Miss X as she lay in her cot in her 'leetle pink nightie' just before '*it*' happened, whatever *that* was . . .

Men, in any case, were all indescribably *evil*. (God the Father presumably yet another of those many fortunate eXceptions to the rule?) And as for . . . *three* letters this time, beginning with 's' and ending with you-know-what, the twenty-first letter of the ancient Roman alphabet . . .

Like those irrational numbers known to the Greeks and mentioned, those too, only on pain of death, you did not mention *this* word either. Is it fear or something even more unnameable – fear of fear itself? – which makes us rush to create these terrible interdicts, these dread secrets, these guilty taboos . . .?

Mrs X, three rings and please wait.

Yes, the teas in the kitchen were reasonably pleasant and innocuous at first . . . particularly nowadays when my eager journeys through the cornfield so often ended in impasse on the filial front, or when, scarce able even to endure another second at home now without the piano, I had arrived an hour or so too early for my moment's audience above.

Then, as we sat there together, all ears for the magic rumble of the garage door, followed by the tell-tale squeak of the iron gate, our interests were strongly, however fleetingly, combined: Mrs X seemed to spend almost as much of her life doggedly waiting as myself.

'Milk and sugar, Mary?'

How slow to dawn even the most obvious truth when we are loath to read what the entrails have to impart.

It was still only a full year later as a result of enquiring about the photograph on the dresser of an unknown, eXceptionally thin young woman (must be anoreXia) holding the bow of a cello in her long, slim fingers, that the barnacles dropped from my eyes at last.

'Yes, that's my Dora,' Mrs X had crooned lovingly. 'Rather like you in some ways, isn't she, Mary, my lamb? The eyes, I mean. Let me see, now. Must be five years or more since she got to Girton College. A *Minor* Scholarship in her case, though, of course.' (She made the shameful lacuna seem almost a virtue, I thought.)

Comes each year to listen to the King's College carols on the wireless and give us a lovely cello solo, (Schubert's 'The Trout', I surmised sarcastically) 'before helping me fill Her stocking and pin *their* presents on the Xmas tree.'

Trap-doors, plug-holes, man-traps, bottle dungeons: talk about the oaken Ear of the Emperor Dionysius: *this* Palace sported lethal oubliettes as well!

Just as she had done with the unknown Dora (for whom I at once conceived a feeling of comradeship in suffering even in the heart of my painful jealousy), Miss X had got *cold* feet now into the bargain and handed me down to her mother instead!

Mary Wolfe, Mary Cuckoo, Mary Barnacle Goose, more like it!

Others had passed this way before me – spurned, outcast, stigmatised, erased, eXcised, forgotten, fattened and consoled in the Maternal Web!

From that time forward, I began to feel a series of conflicting emotions towards Miss X's mother.

At first she had seemed nothing but the Good Fairy Godmother: a dear, sweet-smiling old lady, real-life replica of the face in the photograph which had looked upon us so benevolently all through those first encounters by the fireside with Racine (at least *he* was still as super as ever, by the way).

But then, at other times, just like the wolf in *Little Red Riding Hood* that had so (masochistically?) terrified my sister (Pin *refused* the gold letters on the Honours Board, by the way), she seemed almost monstrously strong and devouring, her very weakness and innocence a terrifying threat. The Devil, the Black Widow Spider, the Witch in the Fairy Tale (careful, Mary, remember they burned and drowned real people), devouring both her 'Leetle Dorter' and, at the end of a chain of goodness knows how many victims fattened on iced gingerbread-men, now finally *me*.

Perhaps even, who knows, poor *Mr* X too.

Should it not have been the *mother*, not the father, who, like poor Blanchette in *La Chèvre de Monsieur Seguin*, was banished to die on the mountainside that night?

(Watch it, Mary. Either/or again. How ready we are to gnaw through that precious dividing line which separates the stomach from the food inside it, prevents its gluttonous, shadowy juices from dissolving its own tender maw or pouch . . . 'Enemy' certainly not, of course – casting on the Other your own grey shadow – but *some* slight notion of difference, perhaps, all the same?)

And the really horrid thing all this time was that even when consumed by such murderous . . . well, *almost* murderous . . . feelings of frustration and resentment, I was already trapped like that fluttering white moth I would soon see fluttering in vain at this same lighted window, unable to move away from the source of its pain . . . there where, still busying herself with her infinite knitting at the foot of the scaffold, Mrs X kept me tangled in naught but my own strangely passive cavern of will . . . unable, like that little twig dancing like a trout on a hook by the lock gates, fully to leave or fully to stay.

Yes, that bright little kitchen with the flowered pink tablecloth, the pot for ever bubbling on the stove like a cauldron and, worst of all, the slow tick, tick of the grandfather clock, had become, without my knowing it, the very darkest Dungeness of all.

How many hours was I to sit there conversing politely, ears pricked, teeth . . . nay, my whole being, focused on the overhead bathroom (the main point of structural contact, remember, between the two abodes), there where every footfall, every gurgle, every echo and wheeze of the ancient plumbing, betokened the living presence of the unwittingly callous Cyclops above . . . perhaps even at this very moment, let's face it, totally naked and if not gently soaping those pomegranate breasts with the forget-me-not nipples, then coaXing those belovèd cloven, yet oh so icy, feet of clay of hers, with the lightest dusting of muguet, nay lotus-petal, talc?

Who *now*, hélas, my 'cold, dear Lady with the heart of Frost'?

Who now magicked to swinish forgetfulness of the duties of fidelity in Love?

Of her offspring's 'true nature' Mrs X obviously knew about as little as a sheep knows the Greek alphabet or Queen Victoria how two women make love. (How *did* we still, by the way?)

From the bad weather, the blacks and the Jews to the *Deviants*, *Perverts* or *Queers*, as she called us strangely – a particular *loup garou*, these latter – all was the fault of the Labour Government, responsible as it was for the criminal introduction of the Comprehensive System and thus for the destruction of Her vicariously hard-won Empire (ah, but who's She? The cat or the cat's mother?), together, of course, with 'all that nasty modern literature' (the words seemed somehow familiar), and the disastrous lack of Religious Values in the young.

Alas, poor 'Witch', the shock of the truth about her 'Leetle Daughter' would quite literally have killed her. (Truth, Mary? And what is that in this particular case?)

Crude as the plots in Miss P's gruesome thrillers, I had a potential chance of murder on my hands.

Not that . . .

The Ninth Piece

Ariane, ma soeur, de quel amour blessée . . .
(*Phèdre*, Racine)

Woe says: Fade! Go!
But all joy wants eternity,
Wants deep, deep, deep eternity!
(*Thus Spake Zarathustra*, Nietzsche)

It was Pin, years later, who brought me the news of the death of Miss X, running towards me over the meadows, escaping, herself too now, from her own dark cavern, helping to recover the precious lost thread.

Yes, Pin, my dear sister, Procne, Ariadne, bringing for ever into my middle-aged serenity (Bill and I were living by then in OXford, a house attached to the old College where I had my Fellowship), the strangely disturbing gift that would surely toll the last bell and set me free.

'*If I ever shut the door and change towards you, promise to keep on knocking, my love.*'

Ironic to think of that first edict now . . . crafty bind of double ply tied beyond the very walls of the tomb.

But before I describe the circumstances of that ultimate act of abandonment on her part, there is one last living turn of the knife to relate in the saga of Miss X and Mary Wolfe . . . one last goatish push-me-pull-you gamble on the part of my X-belovèd, the puzzling caprice of which you must judge for yourself.

Few things can rival the heady eXcitement of being desired by a person of maturity through whom one has access to one's own potential powers even when barking (Sigmund on all our family walks in the Wilderness) so long and so fiXatedly up the wrong tree.

Alienated from the rest of the flock by my now more and more painfully privileged secret, I found myself just as much the lone wolf at University as I had been at School, as I said.

Not that this prevented me from sensing obscurely that I should attempt some brave effort in the direction of the Social World, that gaudy Marketplace where others obviously performed with such careless ease.

Accordingly I had started reluctantly by the eleventh hour of my nine precious terms (hardly eXactly conventional even now, Mary!), to entice the attention of a plump, passive girl in my year (I forget her name), who might at least serve as a companion when I went to a concert by Wolfgang Amadeus or perhaps even a play in the Sheldonian Theatre by Jean Racine (not that Music or Literature seemed to be *her* cup of Postum by a very long chalk). Oh, you know. Someone to buy noodles and lychees for on occasion, and, though the thought began to fill me with a certain revulsion, whose hot and, hélas, far from freckled paw, I might even force myself to squeeze now and then in the back row of the stalls.

So immature and unappetising, these silly young things. They're all the same. No wonder I *couldn't* remember *her* name.

To take our minds off revision (I felt virtually certain my new girlfriend would fail her eXams with or without my attentions anyway), I had arranged to escort this bland creature 'to the pictures', as we called it: a gruesome horror movie with an 'X' certificate called *The Metamorphoses of the Vampire* – presumably based on the poem of that title by Baudelaire – about a sadistic Jekyll-and-Hyde-cum-Jack-the-Ripper who, not content with dismembering his plump, passive victims or digging up their bodies in the local churchyard, returned as a vampire, doubtless at full moon and laughing like a hyaena, to suck the blood of the living – talk about Xiasmus – after his own death. Incredible to think people make money from these cheap, sensational things.

She in a hideous plastic mac to her plump ankles, and me, by contrast . . . Oh, I forget, but you can guess the sort of thing. Probably my white angora sweater and, peeping from under my handsome black gown, the 'decadent' black slacks, together with a striking new scarf of scarlet chiffon which also sometimes served as a hood. (Like the New Tutor, I had started to smoke by then too. Herb cigarettes, though, not poisonous cigars. What would Miss X say if she could see me now!)

We were just about to set out in the taXi I had commanded (my companion having failed predictably to master the art of the bicycle, Lady Macbeth would have to remain stabled that night), when, half-heartedly glancing in the 'W' pigeon-hole as I passed (old habits die hard), I was suddenly transfiXed to see . . . inscribed on a buff coloured envelope just like the ones Mrs FoX-cum-Salmon had always kept in the stock cupboard . . .

Could it be? Surely not. But yes, the old familiar writing with the slope to the left: *Miss X*, breaking her self-imposed silence after more than two whole years!

Renouncing *The Metamorphoses of the Vampire* with one eager swoop of the academic wing, and leaving my candid new friend to her own doubtless well-tried devices (just as well, really, since any dutiful attempt on my part to widen her horizons might well not have met with any success), I walked demurely back along the by now familiar long corridor (far too deep the emotion now to cavort with eXcitement as I might have done a year ago), and, gravely seated on the bed amongst the sunflower cushions crocheted by Auntie, careful not to desecrate a single precious syllable, opened the envelope with trembling hand.

'My Lamb,' it reads (pride of place here in the Black Tin BoX and hardly faded after all these years),

> I shall be coming up to OXford in about a week's time for an HMs' Conference. If you will forgive your old goat his grumpy silence, perhaps we can manage to meet again. Can you get permission to book us into a nice hotel for the night, perhaps even the 'Radcliffe Hall' like last time? I often think of you up there, a daughter in OXbridge, though so much more than a daughter too now, of course. There'll be such a lot to catch up on, won't there, now that time and circumstance are right. Perhaps we could even go punting this time too.

And here she signed her nickname, goatish *Pascal* of the wager, followed by, half impaled on our ancient starry emblem and obviously restored from bristling erasure to full, amorous blessing, a single 'X', with, sting in the tail still: '*PS Might as well book a single room* + double bed.'

PS. PS. Pascal indeed!

So much for our Xtian friend the Punter and his vapid wager of Eternity, staked against the rival claims of living, wagering, conscious flesh and brain.

Miss X had come back to me!

Like Admetus greeting again his lovely Alcestis torn from the Jaws of Hades where she had sacrificed herself all those months but for his sake, I could scarce accept the evidence of my own great eyes.

Whatever was the cause of such a violent metamorphosis?

I was petrified, of course.

Or, rather, the first shock subsiding, suffused with indescribable eXcitement and joy. The sudden evaporation in a few seconds flat of all those carefully achieved compromises which have allowed us so long to mask from ourselves as well as from others that one naked desire, that one still burning purple flame, on which, fools that we are, we have staked our whole . . .

Immediately anXious too, though, as to whether I *could* get permission to 'book us into a nice hotel for the night'.

In those still semi-Victorian days of *loco parentis*, *They* were totally strict about a student's so-called 'moral welfare' and you could actually find yourself 'rusticated' (interesting variant on our old *école buissonnière*) if you were not within four walls by half past X, the time the canny Sandman officially came by.

'But that only applies because of *boy*friends, Mary, my lamb,' I told myself – the proverbial cunning of Odysseus immediately restored.

With my old forte for putting the Duties of Passion above everything else in life, I had quickly realised that, to ensure the success of the naked claims of Deception, there is often nothing so effective as telling the Truth.

Why yes! What simpler!

My X-Headmistress was coming 'up' for a Conference, and, not knowing the custom, had invited me to stay the night in a hotel at her own eXpense.

Mustn't hurt her feelings after all!

What could be more respectable than that!

The stratagem worked as I knew it would.

I was granted my *eXeat* without so much as the comforting batting of a *loco parental* eyelash, and 'Radclyffe Hall' was obediently booked within the hour, 'single room with double bed'.

EXcept perhaps in the aforesaid case of Admetus and Alcestis (Orpheus and Eurydice too, but look what happened!), rarely do the gods grant us a second chance at all, let alone a second chance in a double bed.

No longer, this time, would I lie there selfishly barricaded in St Patrick's quilted breastplate.

No longer, crouched there alone on my 'hunkers' all ears in the darkness debating whether or not to X the fatal divide, would I fail to answer her inner cry.

'Come here, Miss X. Do you want me to rape you, now that time and circumstance are ripe?'

No question this time of letting her down.

'Yes please, Mary, if you'd be so kind.' ('Rape', Mary? Think what you're saying, even in jest. Although true violence is nothing like metaphor, metaphor in turn . . . Out of the mouths of babes and sucklings . . . You said it yourself by the River that time.)

Something of a challenge, though, all the same.

Despite Mrs Blanche and a fortnight's patient, anatomical eXperiment amongst the sunflower cushions, I had finally confirmed, despite my prior promise not to press further alone with such Great EXpectations, that there must *indeed* be a missing piece in my case.

Like that fleeting moment of happiness at the X-roads while Oedipus still believes the Oracle misguided, did I know even then it would not be?

If so, such a voice kept remarkably quiet . . . as quiet as the lost voice of emotion itself, woven deep in the cloth with the crude, joking thread.

My heart is like a rainbow shell
That paddles in a halcyon sea;
My heart is gladder than all these
Because my love is come to me.

(Xtina Rossetti, sister of the Pre-Raphaelite painter I told Miss X about in the train: Gr. *Xtos*, 'the anointed, the chosen one' 'ine' or 'ina', 'of the nature of', F. *rosette*, a 'cluster of parts resembling the shape of a little rose' – she who, in her case, waited, waited, 'earth hard as iron, water like a stone', without hope, without despair, 'absence présente', for the rest of her life.)

Total stillness.

A shaft of sunlight flooding the already familiar wooden desk with its row of steel-nibbed pens and privileged piles of lecture notes on Proust, Gide and Racine. (The New Tutor. Quick. Cover those over. Mustn't hurt her feelings after all.)

One of those unique moments of peace and clarity sometimes bestowed by even the relatively impecunious walls of an OXbridge Women's College . . . deprived, maybe, of the full crimson flush of wine glasses evoked for that other tenderly fictionalised Mary (Mary Beton, Mary Seton, Mary Car . . . michael by Virginia

Woolf in *A Room of One's Own*), yet full of its own more precious, humble riches in the way of the smell of library books and steaming coffee, light and shadow, polished wood. Blue-green curtains gently swaying in the breeze from the half open window . . . single birch tree across the courtyard bathed like a flying shower of gold in the fading yet still deeply glowing light.

L'heure bleue.

As Gide writes in *La Porte Etroite* in a passage reminiscent in its own turn of Gustave Flaubert – for so do we devour, assimilate and grow from each other, tooth for tooth and breath for breath – there are moments just before the arrival of happiness which happiness itself cannot touch or rival, no, nor even . . . like that other blue-gold birch and the room with the wondrous books and paintings just up the corridor, steaming copper kettle shining like a clear conscience on the sheepskin rug by the fireplace, Cézanne's golden apples and 'La Dame à la Licorne' in its frame above the mantelpiece . . . ever, ever forget . . .

Rounding a corner and suddenly finding
High above the bank against the blue
That ancient tree
A sycamore
No breath of wind
Dropping its leaves
And all else still
Some catching a branch and fluttering sideways
Like small blind birds of brilliant plume
Others straight as a dart but slowly turning
Into the cold dark waters of the burn
One – they come more singly now –
Brushing my cheek an instant like a hand
'Tis frost not grief has triggered *their* command
Piercing the chamber with its walls of bronze
Yes
Here at the threshold to the cave
– they fall but to begin again but fall –
Blazoned above the path like a reward
This ancient tree
A sycamore
Zeus come to Danaë at last
Unstrained
The breath of hope

The shower of gold
Bidding me eavesdrop on another world.

The wolf at the door!
When Miss X arrived at the narrow door of my room, dressed, to my pained amazement, in a thick fur coat (foX or something?) and, strangely enough, a good half hour earlier than eXpected (if you don't see them first, you lose your tongue, they say), she seemed even more flushed and purply than usual.

Pent-up lust again, I thought. Two years, three months and siX days is a very long time.

Equally, though, strangely wistful, nervous, distracted . . . her suddenly once more familiar freckled hand with the gold 'wedding' ring (I sighed with relief to think of the fate I had escaped with my special new friend at the 'pictures'), virtually disembowelling one of Auntie's plump sunflower cushions as she spoke.

Then, having unwrapped a slightly wilting purple hyacinth in a plastic pot and plonked it down unceremoniously on my desk (presumably a present – ah, the sweet, sweet scent of treachery), the syllables falling like a rain of tiny gold arrows in the no longer quite so eXquisite silence:

'Sit down, Mary. I have something to tell you.'

Almost an aleXandrine, I thought to myself casually (playing for time as the mind always does while the thunderbolt prepares to sear the inner flesh).

Hadn't I heard those words before somewhere?

At least, I mused, you didn't add 'important' like last time.

At least – for a moment I almost felt like giggling – at least, my Love, you have spared me that. At least the wolf hasn't given your tongue to the cat. ('Auribus teneo lupum' . . . Talk about holding a wolf by the ears knowing neither how to give him fully the sack like Miss Hilbert – – – .)

But listen . . . the same distant voice is continuing further, low but staccato now like a kind of morse:

'Could you be a lamb and let me take over the hotel-booking? You remember that young woman in my year at college I met again in Paris about twenty years ago? Yes, that's right, the one with the beautiful, deep voice I think I mentioned that time at The Trout? Well . . .'

(Here Miss X paused and averted her gaze, only to find it land on a framed photograph of herself standing full square in her Clarks (Empedocles?) sandals outside the villa near Taormina, Mount Etna glowering like a white alsatian dog in the background, and smiling seductively, doubtless for my own benefit – it was before the great silence – attired in a yellow cotton dress with turquoise dots.)

'Well . . . incredible coincidence, I know, but crone the stows if I didn't meet her quite by aXident . . .' (she pronounced the first syllable as if it were the very aXe with which Dad chopped up the piano) '. . . this morning at Charing X after all these years' (sure it wasn't Berkeley Square?). 'She's . . . married now and with two grown-up boys' (Miss X looked pained and incredulous a moment.) 'Coming to the same HMs' Conference as me! You don't mind, do you, Poppet? For my sake . . .'

'Tu comptes les moments que tu perds avec moi . . .'

(You can always tell, when they turn away their eyes like that. Pin did it that time when she told me she was pregnant, thinking it would hurt my feelings. I can't think why. Unless, of course – the thought had never previously struck me – it's the tiger itself they're all afraid of. Can't look the Monster fairly and squarely in the eye . . .)

And here, her familiar features transfigured by a strange, radiant energy (I thought for a moment of my first University essay on 'Passion in Balzac', marked by the New Tutor with a strange Greek cypher I assumed to be an omega, but later found to be an alpha plus), counting the moments lost in my presence, she could scarce stay sufficiently to glance at my room, let alone make obeisance to Capricorn on his chair by the bedside (ironic now to think of his origin in the bosom of Nobody, turned up again like a bad penny at Charing X and married with two grown-up sons, too, would you believe it . . . not that . . .), before I heard those familiar swollen-cold-clay-cloven feet in the ever faithful sandals (wear them myself now, nothing personal), limping rapidly away down the long, oh, so long corridor . . . only the goatish smell of muguet talcum powder mingling with the treacherous beauty of the hyacinth as proof of Pascalian pass-over (pass-over/X-over, didn't I tell you?) and lingering on the sunflower cushions for many hours to come.

'Au fond des forêts allaient-ils se chercher?'

Deep in the forests did they seek each other? (Hippolyte and Aricie). Not for nothing, those first readings of *Phèdre* there in the Study by the flickering fireside with the tap, tap, tap of the crimson virginia creeper so many, many moons ago.

'If I should e'er forsake thee . . .' Failing to vote at all by voting twice: Miss X had double Xed me yet again.

'Is anything the matter, Mary?' bleated, that night at dinner, the plump-passive-girl-whose-name-I-forget. *Her* voice was hardly 'beautiful and deep', needless to say. More like that of the silly, innocent lamb in La Fontaine's Fable *Le Loup et L'Agneau* with its smugly irritating disclaimer (when the wolf has accused it of muddying his drinking-water downstream): 'And how *could* I have done when I wasn't even born?'

But with a snarl of dismissal (they're all the same!), and scarcely bothering to bow myself out to High Table (a compleX ritual involving walking backwards without treading on the trailing wings of one's gown like a landlocked albatross, in the gratuitous artifice of which I had always previously delighted, I was off on faithful Lady Macbeth to the River . . . that deep, strong, passionate, swift-flowing, faithful River Isis, 'thrilling-sweet and rotten' (who cares if that's Cambridge), where, my absence no longer missed from College now that I had my precious *eXeat* in my pocket, and rocked now like that little turning stick by the sound of the waters pounding over the weir, *I crouched in the shadows like Niobe* . . . *Niobe herself, I say*, daughter of Tantalus, she who, at the murder of her seven dear children (well it *would* be seven, wouldn't it?), wept until the gods at last turned her to stone, a stone for ever anointed (Gr. *Xtos* again) with the trace of her sorrow . . . on and on, shall we say, for you surely wept *this* time, didn't you, Mary?, on and on despite yourself, I like to think, *all tears*, deep into the glittering, star-filled night.

Look in the well where the ripples are,
Of sorrows and of joys,
Wider and wider, reaching, wanting,
Mine will not merge, not mine.
Cruel waves, cold waves, waves unsuspected,
Waves of a silent sin,
Waves which will wash all the shores of life
But let no diver in!
Look in the well where the ripples are

Deep in the depths unseen.
Who knows that a pebble, secret, strong,
Lulled in the cool, green sway,
May not lie embedded, hard and smooth,
Watching the ripples away?
Mine is a pebble, cruel and taunting,
Playing a silent part;
Mine cannot mingle, become, nor be,
Though it sway in the tide like a shell,
Though it swirl round the rocks like the Sea.

Yes, there was a poem as usual even then. A would-be lapidary poem – 'The Well of Loneliness' – of odd and even syllables designed to convey the inner touch of grief. (As if one could. Notice, too, how that nasty little word 'sin', – if I'm punished, I must be guilty – defiantly absent throughout other *social* prohibitions, enters the landscape for the very first time.)

... A poem as if – who knows? – some pure, round, 'lucky' stone from the days of Dungeness or even further back still had lodged itself in a deep, unconscious recess of her brain ... One for sorrow, two for joy. Upon this Rock will Shakespeare's sister yet ...

Isn't pride, *creative*, pride not 'Sin', the secret subject of the poem in a way?

Oh yes there was a poem all right, but not *that* night while the funeral meats lay warm upon the table ...

Not *that* night while Nobody still laid her faithless head ...

Not *that* night while *they* lay 'not divided', there in 'Radclyffe Hall' with a 'y', in *our* double bed.

The Tenth Piece

Gémir, pleurer, prier est également lâche.
Fais énergiquement ta longue et lourde tâche
Dans la voie où le sort a voulu t'appeler,
Puis, après, comme moi, souffre et meurs sans parler.
(*La Mort du Loup*, Vigny)

Sur les crédences, au salon vide: nul ptyX
Aboli bibelot d'inanité sonore,
(Car le Maître est allé puiser des pleurs au StyX
Avec ce seul objet dont le Néant s'honore.)
(*Sonnet en X*, Mallarmé)

'I'm afraid someone you used to know has . . . well, died, actually,' said my sister, barely off the train at OXford Station.

'Guess who,' bending down to tie a loose shoe-lace as she spoke.

But then, fearing the multiple-choice question might have alarmed me unduly (Annabel? Mother? Bill? the New Tutor?), 'Oh, don't worry. *Nobody really. Only Miss X.* Didn't you once have a crush on her or something?'

(I looked round furtively to see if anyone had heard. Naturally *she* used the *real* name, you see.)

'Mother heard about it from Miss P one day last week outside Boots. Overweight, I shouldn't be surprised, with a stomach like that and eating like a pig.' (Pin had her own reasons for disliking Miss X.)

And then, a littler later, after we had partaken of three or four Danish pastries and two cups each of the new 'Xpresso' coffee from a jazzy modern shop in the High almost on the site of the old Radcliffe Hall Hotel, by then replaced by a Betting Shop, 'I haven't hurt your feelings, Lou, have I? I didn't think . . .'

'Oh no. Don't worry. I'm perfectly all right,' I said quickly, putting on my dark glasses and fumbling in my handbag, no, uniseX rucksack by then, for my purse.

'Just a schoolgirl crush, as you said. All that's over years ago.'

And we went out together into the crowded OXford street.

I can still see the eXact shape of a tiny, dancing patch of sunlight on the middle of the pavement, with here and there some chips of pinkish gravel overflowing from a pyramidal pile on the kerb. You won't believe it, but we were on our way to an eXhibition entitled 'Food Art'. Perhaps once you've forged a certain path through the jungle, nothing can ever seem random again.

Apparently the end had come out there in the villa in Sicily on one of her noble holiday trips with Miss P, a bare three weeks after the death of *Mrs* X, about which I myself already knew *only too well*.

'Yes, overweight. I shouldn't be surprised. That great pot-belly, of hers,' I said, throwing back at Pin, with a venom that surprised me, yet another cruel phrase she herself had once used to denigrate poor Miss X (and I who by those days – hormones in my case, though what does it matter – must have been at least seven times as large).

Only I knew that *Mrs* X had killed her.

Demeter, the mother, below the dark earth, calling for Persephone, her belovèd 'Leetle Dorter', dragging her down with her to the flowerless meadows, pomegranate breasts, swollen ankles, cloven feet and all . . . there where Cerberus – Anubis, then, in the case of Seth – would bark and snarl for ever like a white alsatian dog, and, unforgettable, unforgotten, the silent, foaming (?) waters of the solitary StyX pound for ever with its little, turning . . .

Yes, Miss X was no more.

Zero, a mere cypher, nothingness, naught.

Even less eXistence than she has on this strange page, distracted by thought of itself even now. ('Cypher', of course, is from the Arabic *sifr*, code and zero all in one.)

And with her death, the death for Mary Wolfe, too, of all those last, lingering hopes ('If it weren't for Mother. One day, Mary, when I'm free . . .'), which, quiescent for so long – such is the perversity of human desire – suddenly seemed to surface now in their moment of final defeat . . . causing me, for the first time in all those years perhaps, a sense of lack . . . yes, pure, unadulterated, unmitigated *lack* . . . guiltily accompanied (guiltily, Mary?) but a split second after by the obstinate desire to create and transform. 'Après avoir trouvé le Néant, j'ai trouvé le Beau', 'after No-thingness, Beauty', as Mallarmé, the maestro of Silence and Absence would say.

Had I been waiting but to write a Novel . . .

Surely not.

Reassured by my casual reply, my sister was full of chatty details now.

'Yes, sealed up in a wall. A wall with the coffin bricked up inside. That's how they bury them out there, Lou, you know. And pebbles on their eyelids to keep them shut. I saw a programme once on TV.'

She was laughing apologetically now . . . Eyebeams twisted (Gr. *Xiasm*, a term from optics) just that fraction off centre . . . thinking I disapproved of television this time, I suppose.

(Although we would have cut out our tongues for each other, Pin and I travelled separate paths, and particularly, it seemed, in our relationship to pain. Perhaps even the slightest suspicion of childhood masochism still in her case? Preferring to cast herself fully over the churning brink rather than to . . . Oh, I don't know. Birds of the same dark family feather, yet hopping, first one and then the other, to the sides of an ever-reversible cage. Pain and sunshine, joy and shadow, Castor and PolluX, Procne and Philomela, Seth and Osiris . . . at any one epoch, can *one* child only stand in the light?)

'Oh and Miss P told Mother there was still a gold ring on her finger – worth quite a lot, I should imagine, despite a missing central stone – which she wishes now she'd thought to take off before they finally bricked her up. They were lovers, Miss P and Miss X, you know.'

Lovers! Miss X and Miss P! The Pagoda! Sicily! Lesbos! Taormina: Mount Etna!

'For your own sake, Mary . . .'

Suddenly, only too well, it all began to fit like a tight kid glove (Chinese *Tao*, 'path').

They *had* laughed like hyaenas about my antics with the bicycle.

She *had* failed to return that night from Miss P's flat.

Freud was wrong.

There *was* a Bogey-man in the Nursery all the time.

My jealous fantasies were right!

But then, seeing I was even more stonily silent now than before, 'You're not shocked, are you, Lou? That sort of thing's perfectly natural, you know.'

Pin was a child of the Modern Age. She took casually for granted what Miss X and I had suffered and fought for all those years with our lives.

So much for the joys of forbidden fruit.

('Joys, Mary? Have you forgotten? Only look back . . .'

'Perhaps, Miss X. Perhaps I have. Or was it joy in another sense all along? Creature born, like Sappho herself, to mate with the very pipes of Pan, invented, incidentally, by MinervA, Goddess of Wisdom Herself.')

In death not even goats will eat everything, it seems.

With intrepid Miss P at the bedside cabinet blindly forcing open the belovèd lips to swallow, ah, swallow, everything from aniseed balls, pear-drops and smoked salmon to cups of Postum and home made lemonade, apparently she had refused to partake of sustenance for almost a whole seven days in advance . . . Just like the sheep who has seen a wolf jump over the wall, I thought to myself with a flicker of terror on her behalf, not that Death, any more than the Sun . . .

(Miss P. Miss P. Silly, pink, bleating, unsuspecting Miss P. Trust Miss P to be there at the last.)

Refused to talk too, for that matter.

Not a tear, not a whimper, not a prayer, not – don't remind me – a moan or a groan. Total silence, as if, having imposed that Terrible Vow on *me* for all those years, the cat or worse had got her *own* tongue now at last.

Could she too have had some precious secret: *our* forbidden, ineXpressible secret, which, blotting out all other loves (Nobody, Miss P, Dora and who knows what other minor Pascalian 'divertissements' on the way to me), she faithfully refused to impart even then, creating by that eloquent omission, like the pulse of dark between the beams of a lighthouse, the very message of the infamous Unsayable whose eXtirpated tongue, too late, hélas, for answer, spoke to me now beyond the tomb?

Walls have ears, Miss X, and you never know.

'Oh and apparently Miss P managed to have a plaque put up before flying back. Not even her Xtian name, but just 'MISS X' and the date with our old school motto, whatever that was. Nothing more really, Lou . . . eXcept that they've apparently set up a fund in her honour' (she winked sarcastically) 'so that more lucky girls can go on eXchanges to France. Don't suppose *you'll* want to contribute to that!'

We were inside the eXhibition hall by now and admiring a giant iced ginger cake made of concrete, dotted with what looked like hundreds of foraging metal aniseed balls.

'No, you're right,' I said, 'I would not.'

'Je cherche le silence et la nuit pour pleurer': it was only that night when Bill and Pin were asleep in their separate beds (she in the old camp one fiXed up neXt to my room, and Bill in his usual lone double in the room above), that I knew I must creep outside into the hollow darkness, and, standing alone by the huge old goat willow – L. *saliX capra* – towering over the walls of the Fellows' Garden, stare up at the stars secretly and silently to mourn the death of Miss X . . . Arbor Cosmica, Tree of the Universe, like the wondrous, mythical ash tree, its brave, dark roots where the Norns were doubtless still even then busy, stretched to the empty heavens like a living ladder and its pendulous branches falling like tears to the earth below.

'If I ever shut the door and change towards you, promise to . . .'

Only then did I know I had indeed still been waiting. Yes, all those years, even then, waiting, waiting, waiting, for the final shutting of the terrible door.

Only then did I know she had abandoned me for ever, and, with Miss P's, or was it Nobody's, gold 'wedding' ring glinting for ever and ever on the ever beckoning bone that was once her live, freckled finger – *Philomela, my name is Philomela* – rolled the Great Stone across the Entrance at last.

'MY *secret name is Philomela and* YOU, *Mary Wolfe, are my eXecutioner . . . you who will one day cut out my tongue to boil your own pot and bake your own bread. You who, in order to love another, wrote a Novel to tell the world I was dead.'* If you still don't feel quite sure of the myth of Philomela and the message in the cloth, dear Reader, let me remind you that Procne's husband, Tereus, married his wife's sister, Philomela, deceiving her into thinking Procne was dead and cutting out her tongue to prevent her telling what had happened. Philomela found a way of weaving the truth into her cloth as a message for her sister, however – the two sisters finally serving up to Tereus his own little son by Procne as a suitable punishment for the crime. CompleX, these mythological matters, I know . . .)

Seul le Silence est grand; tout le reste est faiblesse (. . .)
Fais énergiquement ta longue et lourde tâche
Dans la voie où le sort a voulu t'appeler . . .

Cruel world take back your prey! *EXit Miss X* after a lifetime's long and painfully energetic service in the tasks of Destiny, to the strains of Vigny's 'Death of the Wolf' . . . taking our still uninterpreted secret with her to the grave, where I alone could scrape it up again, and, with this yet further eXample of those goat-like reversals in which she specialised so mysteriously, weaving my *own* name as her eXecutioner into the guilty, haunted cloth with the self-accusing thread.

But there are still two smaller incidents in my own energetic task before I proceed to its strange finale and perhaps the most Racinian vicissitude of all.

It must have been only a week or so later, shall we say (the faithful Blue Books have finally eXhausted themselves on this and all other points), that Pin and I went on a Proustian journey back to our old family home together ('I never want you to be ashamed of your home, Mary') to visit some of our cherished haunts from the past.

I know I was working at the time on my would-be masterpiece on the origins of Tragedy.

Never having caught up with the book Miss X had promised to lend me, and beginning, indeed, to doubt it eXisted any more than that ghostly book on agoraphobia Freud tells us a patient kept thinking he had seen in a local shop window, it seemed more sensible in the end to try to write one myself . . . a vast, ambitious project for which I'd planned chapters on Homer, Racine, Euripides, Nietzsche (now *there*'s a misogynist – Gr. 'hater of women' – if ever there was one), Dinoysus, Xt, Osiris (Isis too, Mary, don't forget Isis, not that these Goddesses – think of foaming Aphrodite – are more than male projections along with the rest), where I found I could rave against certain favourite bugbears of mine free at last of the relentless iron rod of fiction I had set out so innocently to bring to my own back.

For some reason I felt I owed it to the world to sort out 'une fois pour toutes', all that compleX business about the *Scapegoat*: a coat of many colours which I was beginning to realise I had first started to fashion years before from such motley intellectual sources as Miss P (Homer), Miss Prick (the totem animal in religious studies), the New Tutor (*Iphigénie*) and, of course, Miss X herself (the Abominations of Leviticus . . . did she never realise, I wonder, that, in the male at least – women didn't even begin to come into it – you-know-what was punished by death?) . . . yes, the Origin of Tragedy which, ever since I'd begun to sniff out a link between the Greek goat sacrificed to Dionysus and all that sado-masochistic fiXation in our culture on the death of Xt . . .

Compare the jolly old Xtian myth, for instance, with the myth of cruel Lycaon I mentioned, turned into a wolf for deceptively serving the gods with the flesh of his own son. In the one case, it seems, we've invented the image of a god to *punish* human cruelty. In the other, the image of a God to eXercise the cruelty himself ... The snake of metaphor unconsciously devouring its own tautological tail and no one but Mary Wolfe (Miss X never *did* really understand what I meant about Mother Nature and all that back there by the River) to realise that Religion, Tragedy too for that matter, is one great self-generated Cooking-Pot fuelled by the false oppositions of language itself!

Dionysus Himself, too (the God this time, I mean, not the Emperor), born from the gormless rapture of the Satyrs ... (Didn't I tell you we *are* the stories we tell?)

Yes, how come the savage, sacrificial rites undertaken in 'His' name (poor Poppy Morpheme, disembowelled by the cup cupboard) are linked apparently without transition to the civilised arts of Literature, Music and Song?

How come, on the one hand mere wild, unruly Bacchus of the grape (cavorting Miss Hilbert and Amanda C in the stock cupboard) and, on the other, proud, lucidly controlled Creative Inspiration ...? Some crucial ambivalence, if not savage paramnesia, here still to gloss like Isis with a viper's healing tongue?

I still had to read Freud on the subject too.

One of my few truly intellectual acquaintances, a brilliant Fellow with piercing blue eyes and a curly black beard I sometimes met for a herb cigarette and glass of orange in College, had hinted tactfully on hearing of my project that there might just be something relevant in *Totem and Taboo*, which, for some reason, I still kept finding myself putting off. The lion lives on assimilated sheep, maybe, but there's always the fear the sound of another's genius will gobble us up from within before we've learned to roar for ourselves. Sheep can be wolves in disguise after all.

The path through 'my' cornfield had long since been built over.

A hideous 'Milton Keynes' Labyrinth of homogeneous boXes ('I never want you to be ashamed ...') stretched right through to Happy Land, where that great, living cloak/fleece/nebris of green/gold barley had rippled in the past like an enchanted sea.

No more goats chasing each other *there*, needless to say ... though I half eXpected the great white Minotaur still to be sitting silently at the centre of the Labyrinth, munching calmly and patiently as was his wont by the prophetic 'Trespassers will be persecuted' notice tied to the gate – unless, of course, he had swallowed that too.

A mammoth concrete office block completely obscured, meanwhile, all chance of glimpsing the familiar pine trees, dark and shaggy at the top of Her lane, always supposing that, withered all with her demise . . .

But let me confine myself to what I need you to know.

On hearing the news of the death from Pin, I had at once plucked up courage to send my sympathies to Miss P, asking, in the form of one of those, oh so casual, eXtenuating postscripts with the sting in the tail, whether she would be so kind (I almost said 'be a lamb') as to seek and return to me as a last memento the rather silly little object – a woolly sheep with boot button eyes and a once perky green ribbon round its neck – which was just possibly still standing, up there in the turret, on the cabinet by the side of Miss X's old bed. (Never mind *Le Petit Prince*: who's the sentimental one now?)

'But please don't put yourself to any trouble, Miss P.' Only if it springs up (some hope) and bites your pink hand.

It was taking a chance, of course.

I half eXpected poor St X to have been banished years ago like me. Certainly when she heard via the Old Girls' Magazine (they put you in anyway) of my marriage to Bill – yes the Fellow with the beard. ('Bound to go over like the rest of them one day, Mary, you'll see'.) Not that . . .

I needn't have worried, however.

A note came back from Miss P almost by return post . . . thanking me for my condolences, eXtolling the virtues of a Headmistress who had 'helped generations of girls to eXercise their full potential', and informing me, likewise in one of those, oh so casual, eXtenuating postscripts, that she *had* found the 'little object' I mentioned (she tactfully omitted the 'silly', I noticed) and would certainly take steps to return it one day.

Miss P. Good old Miss P!

Spring again, 'le Printemps adorable', and the scent of purple hyacinths from the tub in Mother's brave little 'lime tree bower' between the old syringa stump and the now for ever locked back gate. (It must have been just before the house was sold and she moved to live in OXford with me and Bill.)

I was up in my old room at the back at the crucial moment, listening, no doubt with a wry smile at the unforeseen echo, to my old (and apparently Dora's) favourite piece from the days of Miss

Ramsbotham, Schubert's 'The Trout' (still the old twelve-inch records with 'His Master's Voice'), and staring pensively as I did so into the round, cracked mirror of the dressing table which had witnessed so much of my Narcissistic sorrows and joys . . . when, watchdog cackling on the ramparts of who knows what Roman citadel within, I knew with perfect, electrifying certainty that it was now, today, this very minute, bearing little St X in princely fashion before her, that Miss P was 'taking steps', as her letter had said.

Which, of course, she *was*. The only person in the world now (apart from Pin) who . . .

Long before the sound of the bell ('Mary Wolfe and no need to ring'), I was round and down at the front door to greet her as eagerly as Sigmund would have done, garbed dramatically in my pinky caftan with the long chiffon sleeves and felicitously embroidered collar, which, finding it far too theatrical for ordinary consumption, I swear I'd put on that morning for the very first time. Synchronicity, didn't Jung, Freud's rival say?

No, she would rather not come in, thank you (I was secretly relieved). Far too much to attend to on behalf of 'poor Miss X' (how the tables had turned).

'All those papers, diaries, letters and things', which, finding them far too daunting to 'sort into any decent order', it seemed Miss P had taken upon herself to throw out for the dustmen back there at The Pagoda that very afternoon.

Not a word, you notice, of those long hours together battling with Odysseus and the Cyclops or, indeed, out there at The Pagoda itself when, like strands of ivy creeping parasitically round a single pine *thyrsus* (Baudelaire and the mysterious, dual principles of Art, 'male' and 'female', my foot), our true strange destinies were so closely and yet oh, so arbitrarily intertwined.

Perhaps she had simply forgotten it all.

But then, just as she was turning to depart, waiting almost to the front gate to hand over the precious woolly 'postscript', her blue eyes met mine in one long moment of curious accord.

Miss P!

Still unsuspecting, still strangely beautiful, forget-me-not-eyed Miss P! . . . My 'eX', my *quondam*, my very first love! She who had unwittingly started it all!

Had she not guessed, the silly goose, that the dramatic, pinky caftan ('A mon seul désir') was for the return of the prodigal son to the fold, the unicorn laying its head at last in my lap, back at the place where it all began, and where, 'in order not to hurt another's feelings, itself the child of what dark fears I know not', I first put on the mask of another's desire and wore it from then on as my own . . . as, indeed, in a strange way, I suppose it was?

The other little incident involved Pin herself as well as me.

On hearing about 'all those papers, diaries, letters and things' cast out for the dustmen, I had at once drawn up the secret plan to sneak back to The Pagoda under cover of darkness in the hopes, if not of plundering the Temple, then at least of salvaging something of the tempting hoard already given the sack.

I suppose I still wanted something with which to close the story more completely. Might there not just possibly be a *sign* of some kind, something which might speak to me yet from beyond the walls of the tomb? ('Walls have ears, Mary, and you never . . .')

I had intended at first to go alone, running like a greyhound through the straggling new estates as I used once to run along the edge of the cornfield, but what with my *own* 'bad back' by those days, was tempted at the last moment to ask for a lift. (No wonder those old women in Somerset magicked themselves into leaping hares.) In fact, when I put it to her, Pin was only too ready to act as chauffeur and accomplice in one. The chance of an adventure, but also, I suspect, a certain half-conscious hope of revenge.

Throughout my sister's own years at the School in my foaming wake, Miss X had behaved towards her with downright coldness, I'm ashamed to say. On one occasion violently tearing to shreds in front of her, both literally and metaphorically, an eXcellent essay on Walt Whitman's 'Leaves of Grass'. Seven credits, sorry, detentions, and lines in the 'dinner hour', for suggesting his love poems were addressed to men. (Shakespeare's sonnets too, my Love, what of them? Gide, Proust, Sappho, Vita Sackville-West – must have been 'bi-seXual' like Orlando in her case? So *many* Great Artists, come to that.)

Not that Pin herself was by any means without spot.

Her relationship to the Law was imaginative, to say the least. A true, lone rebel against oppression and the prey of oppression in return for her pains. (In certain eXtra special fields at least, the Outlaw – OE. 'Wolf's Head' – and the Rebel have a lot in common, it would seem.)

Pin needed no second bidding.

She drew Isolde to a neat halt behind the churchyard, scene of so many of my lonely vigils in the past. (We had planned this part of the mission in advance, by the way.) And, each armed with a torch – mine the little red one Mother bought with the Nemo's Almanac Quiz money and hers the big black one from Dad's old tool kit (Isolde was bought just after his death, come to think of it) – tip-toed through the gate with the familiar squeaky hinges ('For Xt's sake, Pin, be careful . . .!'), into the dark garden rustling and glimmering beyond.

Oh, that sweet, resinous scent of the pine trees, their thin, rough trunks surely even more densely roped in ivy now than ever before, their tall poles – loan, moan, groan, stone – creaking and sighing in the slight breeze like the masts of some ever becalmed but still mysteriously tossing ship. CompleX, material objects with a luminous life of their own . . . Sometimes I think it is in the physical world around us that lies our true relationship to each other and ourselves. No whining, last-ditch voice of Tragedy there.

The Pagoda.

EXactly the same as on my very first visit to borrow the Tragedy Book, but perhaps, now that it was full of nothing but emptiness, more than ever like a Buddhist shrine, its deeply dropped eaves listening, listening, for ever listening, its pagods hung with invisible bells, and apart from a single light in Miss P's still occupied flat, its great Chinese BoX-puzzle body humped like a mythical dragon in the dark.

And there, standing to attention by the single potting shed, gleaming gold and silver where the miXture of moon and lamplight filtered down through chinks in the glossy green canopy swaying like a baldachin over the altar, the three large dustbins, eXactly as hoped.

I am Dionysus, the son of Zeus,
I come to Thebes, where Semele bore me,
Midwived and killed by the lightning's fire.
Here I stand, an unknown god disguised as a man.
[. . .]
I see my thunderblasted Mother's grave
Here by the ruins of her smouldering house . . .
(*The Bacchae*, Euripides)

There comes a moment when one stands in the very centre of all the motifs, codes, icons, symbols of a lifetime and knows one is alone with the silence after all . . . precious silence in which (patience, Mary, later, later) . . . alone, perhaps, with silence for the very first time.

Already 'For Sale' according to the notice creaking on its iron triangle like a Baudelairean skeleton on a gibbet, Mrs X's flat ('three rings and please wait') seemed totally stripped of furniture bar a few large familiar objects like the grandfather clock, doubtless still ticking, there in the corner of the kitchen, like a living, human heart . . . while Her flat ('Miss X, one ring and wait for ever and ever'), waiting there patiently to be eXpunged, eXpurgated, shorn and purified (Gr. *catharsis*) for good, seemed virtually virginal and untouched . . . locked in a limbo-like eXistence like Mallarmé's ice-bound swan.

(Purified of what, Mary? Your own already lost illusions? All your youthful hopes and dreams? Hush. Not so fast. Watching the world around her dissolving, secret pebble in the churning waters, Mary Wolfe is determined to salvage something yet from the empty crypt of lost desire.)

Ostensibly keeping guard by the house while Pin started to scavenge for treasure back there at the dustbins – the primary goal of our venture, after all – I remained for a moment with my face pressed motionless to the cool glass of the window, I remember, sweeping Mother's 'Nemo' torch round the familiar walls . . . there where the door of the cupboard under the stairs . . . there where, ironing her smalls the time of the Scholarship . . . there where . . . there where . . . there where, above all, the fateful entrance to the well of the staircase up to the Parlour ('Come up, dear'), and, beyond that again, to the still forbidden turret, yawned like a chasm, darker yet . . . dark, they say, as the lips of a wolf, dark as a wolf that has lost the tip of its tongue.

If walls could not only listen, but talk as well . . .

And, of course, above all, my own great eyes, unusually bright this evening ('Necrophilia,' Pin had said unkindly), staring back at me from their own unvarying refleXion: Narcissus, Tantalus, just like that time in the London Underground, Tunnel of Love in the days long ago.

Yes, mirrors, bells, windows, clocks, lamps, doors, walls, iron gates, ironing-boards, gate-posts (beds too, Mary, why omit beds?) . . . all these strange, domestic objects which had accompanied me so faithfully on my adventures, living metaphors of my own obscure, lost body (careful, Mary, dear, leave *something* to the

Reader, *some* scrap of flesh still attached to the bone), and which spoke to me now the language of absence itself.

('Just like Mallarmé's famous "Sonnet en X",' I called across to Pin somewhat gratuitously. 'OnyX', 'ptyX', 'StyX', 'niXe', 'fiXe': no wonder Miss X didn't want me to read it that time. 'X' is like wolfe's bane to the ears of the dead.)

I continued to peer in through the window of the Temple, rapt in a compleX literary rêverie of my own, phantom ghost writer, no doubt, of the strange, carrion Novel which, one day still . . .

Labels, always labels!

Right neXt to the glass now and still strangely untouched by Miss P's would-be eXorcism, affiXed to a little motionless flagstaff . . . well, it would be, wouldn't it? no furious winds of concupiscence here . . . a little plastic identity tag bearing her name: 'Miss X, MA Cantab., Conference of Headmistresses, OXford', followed by that fateful date when I sacrificed the longed-for second chance the gods so nearly accorded me to Nobody of the beautiful, deep voice. 'Single room + double bed.'

No need for a label to remind me of that! How could I ever, ever forget!

I could even make out, too, over there on the shelf by the abandoned ironing-board, the elusive critical book on Tragedy I had never succeeded in obtaining (so it *did* eXist, then, making my own book seem strangely redundant at birth), and, neXt to it, as if some demon of analogy continued to delight in cranking the handle of an old home movie with an X certificate, still hiding in its prudish brown paper cover and daring not to speak its name . . .

I mean, of course, 'oozing with the very concepts it purports to condemn, that none the less in those days eXceptionally brave novel, *The Well of Loneliness* by Radclyffe Hall.

'We have told You we believe . . . then rise up and defend us,' Miss X had once cried gruffly, a piece of rhetoric auspiciously less lacking in emotion than usual (presumably she was addressing God, the ever absent Father), but which I later discovered, to my great disappointment, to be the eXact, plagiarised words of the ill-fated 'Lesbian' protagonist, Stephen (whose name Pin would have been given if she'd been a boy, funnily enough).

But then, sweeping 'Nemo' round deeper still now over by the sideboard, round and round recklessly like the beam of a mad lighthouse – Dungeness again (is nothing, no, nothing, ever wasted or lost in this world?) – I nearly jumped clean out of my skin to find myself staring straight into the familiar bright eyes and wrinkled face of a sweetly smiling old woman with curly white hair.

The ghost of Mrs X come back to haunt her 'Leetle Dorter' and invite me neXt-door for iced gingerbread and cups of China tea?

For one long moment I admit I half *wanted* it to be so, if only to give so called Scientific Reason a knock with my double-handled broomstick along with the rest.

It was a photograph, of course.

Regally throned in its silver frame with the two entwined serpents, tight white curls clustered on the narrow forehead, pearls and . . . The photo from the Study brought back home, perhaps?

But with a pang of horrified fascination at the savage force and cunning of Time's ravening handiwork – *there*'s the true wolf for you – I realised that the face that smiled back at me was not, after all, the face of the mother, but the face of the daughter.

Miss X had grown old in the years between.

She it was grinned back at me like a frozen image in a Story Book!

'Isn't this your handwriting, Lou?' cried my sister now, eXcitedly, brandishing her or, rather, Dad's torch back there by the nearest of the three ghostly bins.

I think I half eXpected it to be Miss X herself by then . . . lifting the gleaming lid and rising bodily from the depths like a character in, never mind the Racine now, a 'nasty modern' play by Samuel Beckett ('Where are its values, I ask you, Mary?') . . .

Isn't that what this is all about in a way? Jealous of Nobody and Nobody there but the Wind, the Wind, the nameless, *heavenly* Wind . . .

But before I could respond, we heard, to our terror, Miss P's back door jerk abruptly open, sending a long, accusing gold broomstick of light shooting between us across the lawn.

And a few seconds later, to Miss P's eXcited bleat of 'there you go, Puss, don't be long' – so that was *his* real name – single round eye glinting yellow in the moonlight, ancient but immortal, Polythemus-Raminagrobis, alias Rumpelstiltskin, streaked past us like a portly arrow into the wild. Don't they say cats are the familiars of the dead? Don't worry, Miss P. It won't be long before *he's* back again.

'Leave that till tomorrow,' I hissed to Pin urgently as, flinging ourselves into the ever gluttonous shadows under the pines, we fumbled once more for the tell-tale latch on the gate and, stifling bursts of nervous giggles like two upper fourth formers, well two ageing birds of prey, then – the two thieving magpies? – escaped up the lane to the waiting red car.

Operation Dustbin was complete (or so I thought)!

When Pin went back on my behalf neXt morning, the dustmen had already been!

Undressing for bed that night with a single flourish (strange now to think of those forbidding clips and restrictive girdles of my youth), I stood for a moment at the window of my own old bedroom (the one where Pin had once stuck the indelible bullet hole, remember?) and with a curious miXture of relief and disappointment, peered out Pagoda-wards across the tiny garden – *our* dear garden, scarcely ever noticed those last few years ('I never want you to be ashamed of your home, Mary.') in the direction of the pines, Her pines, as I had done so often in the past.

But, of course, the new office block! . . . its massive concrete bulk obscuring all view.

So this was the end, then. Terminus. Finale. The *dénouement* of the whole strange Tragedy in which, unlike Racine, *deus absconditus* outside his own creation, I, the Author, had played so curiously incarnate if inconsummate a part.

All that desperate, living symbolism . . . all that frantic effort to bring together in a single moment of temporal and circumstantial ripeness (there's the rub, Mary), that which could never, ever . . . and which wasn't ever really even in the first place . . .

It wasn't nostalgia or sadness or even loss, but a kind of fierce joy in surviving to the end of things. Severing, releasing, letting go, cutting the umbilical cord at last.

Even while voicing to myself these brave new resolutions of freedom from idolatry, however, here I was, pine needles dropping from my still just auburn hair like an evergreen fountain, already gently unwrapping St X from the white tissue paper in which Miss P had brought him and placing him gravely on the bedside cabinet neXt to Capricorn, still silky here and there despite a few understandable signs of balding and being generally longer in hoof and tooth.

And like Voltaire's Candide, happier to be reunited with his old 'mouton rouge' than with all the gold in Xtendom, I knew then, if only by the truth of make believe, that not only had the lost sheep truly come home, but the sheep and the goat were together at last.

And the Wolf, Mary?

Ah, the Wolf.

Perhaps I'd forgotten then that true sheep/goat confraternities always eXclude the Big Bad Wolf.

'On a bluff, on a bluff . . .', Miss P's fleeting visit was the last occasion on which I saw any of that strange trio apart from, years later still, a glimpse of an old, bent creature with a white-painted walking-frame, shuffling about like blind Tiresias (with the secret truth of my second parentage) near the large-print section in Boots, doubtless in search of more blood-thirsty pot-boilers to add to her store.

Poor Miss P.

She herself died a few months ago. A single line announcement in the Old Girls' Magazine along with a full page obituary for Mr Shepherd-Fenrir and a scheme for planting a new curtain of aspen trees, quivering still with their guilty secret, there on the edge of The Wilderness.

Of the lurid, true-life pot-boiler in which she played so central and yet so ambiguous a part, Miss P, poor, blind Miss P, will never now know.

Eleventh hour or not, the coast is clear, Mary, lamb. *You may give tongue!*

The Eleventh Piece

In Greek tragedy the special subject-matter
of the performance was the sufferings of the
Divine goat, Dionysus, and the lamentation
of the goats who were his followers and
who identified themselves with him. [. . .]
At the conclusion, then, of this eXceedingly
condensed inquiry, I should like to insist
that its outcome shows that the beginnings
of religion, morals, society and art converge
in the Oedipus compleX.
(*Totem & Taboo*, Freud)

'I suppose it is a *bit* like a classical tragedy in its way,' said
my sister doubtfully, trying not to hurt my feelings. (Must run in
the family, this total evasion of the duties of pain.)

And here she cocked an ear up the stairwell to make sure Amon,
the latest, was well and truly asleep. He'd started to scream
violently when I went up before to read *Little Red Riding Hood*, not
that at seven months you'd think he would have understood very
much. Perhaps, horrid thought, it was the sight of my face. On the
other hand that picture of the wolf standing up on its hind legs to
get into bed with . . . No, must have *already* eaten the grandmother
in his case. The same one that used to terrify Pin, come to think of
it. Paranoid/schizoid stage, I suppose. You know, when children
disown the unacceptable side of their aggressive fantasies by
projecting them on to something or somebody else. Oh well!

Bill, Annabel and I were all spending the weekend in Pin's little,
recently acquired cottage in the country to celebrate my 'official'
birthday. And, rashly thinking it finished, I had brought over the
manuscript of *Miss X*: my 'pot-boiler' as I called it modestly,
hoping all the same to change the world . . . not to mention the little
matter of replenishing the seed corn, now that Bill and I were as
stony broke as two Temple cats.

EXhausted as I was with the eXcruciating labour of it all, the
labour of piecing together so many scattered fragments of memory
and language, I mean (can't stand that silly metaphor of giving

143

birth), I still felt eXtraordinarily eXcited at the thought of reading it aloud to someone.

All that meticulous, self-scrutinising confession and *still* no one had heard a word.

Hence my impatience to sit down and get started, not to mention embarrassingly undisguised signs of irritation when, even after I'd done my duty so energetically upstairs with the bedtime story, Pin took so eXasperatingly long (could it be deliberate?) to calm him down again and clear away the remains of the admittedly eXcellent meal: a thick vegetable stew with bean husks and barleycorn, followed by goat's milk yoghurt and victoria plums. (Yes, really! I wash my hands of all this uninvited symbolism now.)

She'd been behaving rather oddly towards me ever since I mentioned bringing *Miss X* to the cottage. ('Afternoon, Pin. May I introduce an old flame? . . .') Shades of the old sibling rivalry, maybe? . . . though perhaps also something to do with Writing itself: a compleX and in some ways paradoXical activity which I was beginning to realise she scorned and even feared as well as secretly admired. After all, don't they say full, unflinching commitment to narrative form is a way to reach otherwise inaccessible truths about ourselves and the world?

Partly as a joke, I had also brought over with me, travelling companions with the manuscript in the same Black Tin BoX (Moses in the bulrushes?) which gave it birth, my two 'dumb protagonists', Capricorn and St X.

Concrete proof or should I say 'hoof' of the pudding?

Dead metaphors restored to real-life fetishes again?

Would-be evidence of the resurreXionary power of the word to conjure flesh and blood (felt and wire, then) from out of thin air?

If so, there were further, less respectable motives, as I was soon to find out.

It was September. My favourite month. The harvest still not quite fully gathered in. (My *real* birthday being on Xmas day like you-know-who's, Dad had feared I wouldn't get nearly enough presents . . . waiting considerately until I was seven years old before letting me *choose* a month to be born in instead.)

Sadness, of course, for the end of the summer ('Lord dismiss us with thy blessing . . .'), but at the same time that half eXcited sense of impending voyage: 'Au fond de l'Inconnu pour trouver du Nouveau!'

All day long swallows – ah, swallows – had been gathering

noisily on the telegraph wires outside the kitchen window. ('Like notes on a musical stave,' I had remarked to Annabel judiciously, secretly quoting a phrase from one of the old Blue Books way back.) All the English poets seem to think *Philomela* was turned into a nightingale and Procne a swallow, but trust Brainy Mary Number One to know from Miss P it was the other way round – well, it would be, wouldn't it? – Philomela with her tongue cut out ('salve, salve') like the songless, twittering swallow, and Procne, the songster warbling at eve, full of sweet grief for the little son she was forced to sacrifice.

Yes, 'salve, salve', swooping and twittering tonguelessly – songlessly, then – all day long over the huge, wild garden (Pin's brave contribution to help reverse doomsday, or, if you like, the greenhouse effect before it runs wild in the hills of no return), where, taking turns at amusing Amon (her third, I'm afraid), we had busied ourselves in the long dry grass by the lupin bed ('Lu' and 'Pin' – did you notice? – our special flowers), clearing the rudiments of a narrow path. (The path of happiness, it seems to me now . . . alone once more in the shadow of the lamp and the pen, well, word-processor nowadays, then. It *wasn't* the end of *Miss X* after all, you see. Four more whole, back-breaking pieces still to go. No crown without a X, as Auntie would have said. Oh well!)

Then, bright sunshine had streamed in through the open door, spilling the bare boards with a dusty shower of gold (it was before the arrival of that thick brown matting Pin likes).

Now, as we sat in an uneven circle round the flickering candle – Bill on a hard-backed chair slightly behind us, seemingly busy with planning his neXt paper (*latah*, that self-induced state of trance I keep mentioning for some reason, where you think you're either young again like a Mad March Hare, or, failing that, a predatory animal rushing round devouring human flesh) and we three, Pin and Annabel and I, languidly draped on the sunflower cushions – the whole garden seemed crouched attentively round us in the twilight (' "*Entre chien et loup*" dog and wolf, Mary. Got your French notebook?'): the only sounds to compete with my voice the distant drone of the combine harvester (shades of poor Dad again) and, now and then, the cry of, if not Philomela, the nightingale, thank god, (old habits die hard) then MinervA, the round-eyed owl and and goodness knows who, the old blind bat. (Deep and beautiful like Nobody's, my voice, perhaps not, but at least it's not like a false vibration on a cello. At least, my friends, I have spared you that.)

One or two white moths danced giddily in the flame, watched suspiciously by Mowgli, the orphaned white cat adopted by Annabel and which, like the Freudian *'ID'* – I suppose ours was Sigmund – travels in a hamper wherever she goes . . . a hamper very like Mrs X's picnic basket long ago, though I didn't say. In Life as in Writing, a Writer must constantly discriminate: what to let out and what to let in; whom to allow to jump over the wall.

Apart from that long piece of waste ground where swathes of white cow parsley (Queen Anne's lace, then) appear miraculously each summer ('snow in June,' as Pin once judiciously remarked – surely *she* doesn't keep a secret Blue Book too), the garden is surrounded on almost all four sides by cornfields.

Rippling stretches almost right up to the doorstep. Could that be why she came here in the first place – the resurreXion of 'my' cornfield at home before they destroyed it, but multiplied a hundred-fold? (Poor Pin. Sometimes I think *she* is the true tragic hero of this drama, not me – redeeming and atoning for some great loss too great to see . . . some secret pain buried far too deep in the ice-fields even to *pretend* to give it voice in a mere literary work.)

Miss X. A novel in eleven pieces (some hope), read aloud by the Author Herself.

> 'Of the lurid, true-life pot-boiler in which she played so central and yet so ambiguous – should have said 'obscure', perhaps, or 'mysterious' – a part, Miss P, poor, blind Miss P, will never now know. Eleventh hour or not, the coast is clear, Mary, lamb. *You may give tongue!*'

The reading took most of the late afternoon and evening, though I was still surprised and no little disappointed to find the whole thing much shorter than I thought, more a 'novella' than a fully-fledged Novel, in fact. A pity, too, they couldn't see the eXciting typographical eXperiment in which the keystone, 'X', was constantly eXposed, constantly reminding the Reader in turn not only of Miss X herself, but of the power of detached imaginative invention working through language, which – though I know this isn't popular nowadays – proves the confident Self-presence of that other Miss X, the Author Herself, elderly phoeniX astride her own walking-frame (later, Mary, don't remind me), cryptically dis-closed through the chinks of the Work.

'Well . . . what do you think?' I asked, proud as a Voltairean peacock on a terrace as the last, chilling words echoed round the room.

'Remember it's really only just a pot-boiler, as I said.'

Il n'est plus temps: il sait mes ardeurs insensées.
De l'austère pudeur les bornes sont passées . . .

(Phèdre herself after her guilty, inadvertent confession – not that it was a question of guilt *or* inadvertency in my case.) And then, to make it easier for them to come to terms with the depths of their own emotion, 'Incidentally there *was* a lending library at Boots in those days, Pin.'

(When I got to the part about changing Miss P's library books, *real* fictional pot-boilers, those, of course, she had made an annoying interruption which at the time – what's that phrase they use in an OXbridge debate? – I had chivalrously but firmly refused to take up. There's nothing worse, is there, for the calmly sucking infant, than being violently interrupted in mid-flow? And although it doesn't *have* to be true in a Novel, the whole point of this one, cut my heart and X my would-be cello strings, is that everything *is* true, as you know.)

I had tasted my reward already in a way.

Whereas Pin was usually unable to keep awake for more than a few lines of my writing – poems in particular – now from that very first pistol shot ' "Do you have a boy-friend?", asked the analyst', she had been content with only a few sporadic yawns, and those reserved in turn only for the importunate poems which dared to gatecrash here and there on the plot. And, of course, for all her understandable irritation at hearing herself forced to speak as a 'character' with no more chance to reply than St X or Capricorn (you-know-who herself, too, come to that), she was obviously secretly chuffed: the only living soul in the world now to know Miss X's true name, tied that evening to the little flagstaff and which I had promised never to disclose in case . . . (in case what, Mary? Is it really Miss X you still shelter from the foX-hounds or a certain little foX much closer home?)

'Fais énergiquement ta longue et lourde tâche . . .': the reading is over. Someone else knows.

The Wilderness, if not Miss X, has been given a name.

Mary Wolfe is no longer alone.

Through my own patient skill, I have enabled them to follow me . . . along the lone corridors, through the streets, by the River, a-X the very veins of my eXtraordinary solitude, round the deep, dry hollow at the source of my tears, down the dark well of my living red throat.

(Solitude, Mary? Yes, Miss X. Solitude. Even there in the broom cupboard under the stairs, with your tongue in my mouth and your hand creeping down . . . though, goodness knows, in that sense of shared separation from the strange bits and pieces of our primeval fishing-tackle . . .)

Bristling silence.

Pin and Annabel barely able to stifle laughter or something.

Hardly the lofty tragic emotion or Racinian (alias Aristotelian) *catharsis* I suppose I had secretly thought my due. You know: terror, pity, compassion, and so on, the 'I is thou' and 'thou is me'. (No wonder when Dad first got his 'bad back' – not lifting tractor wheels after all, by the way, but swinging *me* round like a fourteen-year-old sack of gold so I didn't feel jealous when he'd just swung Pin – I had to have *my* meals brought up on a tray. Empathy has a lot to answer for. You see, I did do for him too in a way.)

Then, from Pin doubtfully but politely (where we came in):

'I suppose it is a *bit* like a classical tragedy in its way. On the other hand is there nothing you can do to tighten up the plot a bit? We don't eXactly all end up falling on each other's swords do we . . . in the "bloodless, metaphorical" sense, I mean?'

(Apparently I had once told her scathingly that, unlike Shakespeare and Corneille, there's no blood and gore at the end of Racine. Only that indubitable Bull, monstrous Dragon, then, from the Ocean who terrifies the horses pulling Hippolyte's chariot . . . dragging him along till, flayed alive like Marsyas – nailed to a pine tree in his case for having thought he could rival the music of Apollo – he's nothing more than an open sore, and even then only in indirect speech, thank god.)

'What about when *Mrs* X kicks the bucket, for instance. Didn't you say you knew about it *only too well*? You're sure you're not holding back on something, Lou? . . . Hang on a moment, isn't that Amon? Your fault if he's having one of his animal nightmares again.'

And here – that horrid feeling of interruption in mid-flow – she got up and cocked an ear up the stairwell, as you know.

As for Annabel – French Literature, London University – alighted amongst us like a lovely, real swallow herself . . . she, to my surprise, seemed not so much embarrassed (the thought had

148

occurred to me, even that she'd think I wanted to rape her or something), but . . . well, let's face it, cagey, irritable, almost X . . . as if I'd hurt her feelings in some way.

'Well thanks for the reading, Mary,' she said at last ominously (usually calls me 'Wolfie'), averting her eyes. (Do they *all* think I'm a Gorgon or something now?)

'I quite like the way that classical myth – Oedipus, Odysseus, Dionysus, the Minotaur and so on – is spread out *through* it all. A swollen foot here, a scar, a limp or a pine cone there.'

This was news to me, though I didn't let on. As with trophies on Prize Day – *et eXultavit* – one should be able to accept praise gracefully when it comes. Genius is involuntary common property, after all.

'. . . always supposing you must use myth *at all*, that is. Politically it's eXtremely suspect, you know. Universal time, universal consciousness, never mind the eXclusions, and not a chance in hell of ever getting things changed. On the other hand . . .' (the sting in the tail now, eternal 'PS', 'single room + double bed') '. . . do you really . . . well, in a nut-shell, *do you really think you ought to try to publish it at all?*'

And, seeing me look totally crestfallen (so much for my earlier protestations that the tooth of criticism is what we Writers crave almost above everything else): 'Aren't you worried it might backfire? *A pseudonym, perhaps, if you must?*'

I pressed further, of course. Tempting fate.

On and on, moth to the candle, craning my beak into the very gullet of the foX. I'm like that nowadays. Counter-reaction to all those years of blindly passive trust, no doubt.

Besides, I *did* want criticism in a way. That precious bite into the very flesh, if not peeled walnut (yes, it *is* like a walnut) of the human brain. At last someone else capable of savaging the bubble, of linking us up with the precious power of our own critical judgment . . . to change, to transform ourselves, to give, to listen, to pin-prick, to *learn*, and thus to reap the fruits of our own eXpenditure in turn.

(I thought of the *other* Miss X again. She who at that crucial Xing-point on the sheepskin rug when Miss X, the *first* Miss X, I mean, so nearly succeeded in not passing the Torch. To her above all I owe my second life.)

Poor Annabel still demurred at first. One does.

But then ('Sit down, Mary, I have something important to tell you'), out it all came. This time the complete demolition job.

OK. So I'd once fallen in love with a woman. Was that so terrible? When half the world is gay as we know . . . Well isn't there prejudice, injustice and oppression enough already without having to go round beating a dead duck? (Shouldn't it have been 'dead horse'?)

'Seriously though,' (a real bugbear of mine, that, though I use it myself) 'seriously, Mary, sit down again a moment. I've a bone to pluck . . .'

Apparently I had failed disastrously to distinguish between 'lesbianism' as an active erotic drive like her own (I swallowed noisily, pretending to cough), and 'lesbianism' in the political sense, also like her own (I coughed): a mode of eXistence devoted to subverting the whole set of oppressive, phallic assumptions at large in heteroseXist society, including those of the would-be feminist woman who had chosen to live secure in domesticity and bad faith with a male . . .

(By this time I was coughing and snorting behind my handkerchief as if I'd suddenly developed a genuine cold.)

'No, Mary. We *don't* all dress in hairy tweed costumes.' (My borrowed apparel to meet the New Tutor?) 'We *don't* believe all men are evil.' (Bill's chair creaked gratefully.) 'We *don't* all try vicariously to seduce inadequate, over-doting mothers.' (She winked at Pin.) 'We *don't* all have the depraved seX drive of a bat.' (The flicker of a smile in *my* direction now for some reason.) 'In short we're *not* all ageing pederasts like Miss X . . . Pure, capitalistic voyeurism, I'm afraid.'

(She seemed to like this last phrase – left over from one of her *real* lectures, no doubt. Now *I* was the one to try to wink at Pin. Get her on my side again before it was too late. You get these eternal shifts of power with three. I remember it from Primary School only too well.)

'The kind of writing which, for all its would-be sophisticated allusions, puns and tropes . . . underhand hints and innuendoes, more like it,' (the gruff throat and the ring with the wobbly sapphic-sounding sapphire! True or not, I *knew* I shouldn't have put them in) 'simply provides a titillating trip for, let's face it, salacious "male" readers like yourself.'

(Whatever could she mean? I was soon to find out.)

'You know . . . All that so called literary heritage from the courtly lyric, where women's bodies are reified as the metaphors (might just as well say *meA*taphors) of a so-called spiritual chase. The inaccessible. The Holy Grail. X. The unknown. The sado-sublime. That which can never openly be named in case the Venus in Furs turns FoX and bites through the phantom membrane which divides . . .'

(Yes, it *must* be the lectures. No normal person would speak like that. On the other hand hadn't I been suggesting eXactly the same sort of thing? So much for precious literary obliqueness. Just goes to show you've got to spell everything out these days.)

'. . . *Our* minds are just as much prey to the Phallocentric dichotomies of Patriarchal Discourse as theirs, you know. How could they not be with so much Romantic fiction like *Miss X* about? I wonder you didn't go the whole hog and endow her with an enlarged clitoris or something, like a true Roman tribade.'

I blushed what felt like a creeping scarlet with feverish yellow dots. Some diatribe! (L. *triba*, 'to rub'.) And when you remember that seX in my Novel was really only a meAtaphor for something else all along.

She laughed gruffly – surprised, no doubt, by her own sarcastic daring (I know the feeling), no doubt attempting in the process to imitate my own infectiously ironic style, though of course, in my case, as *you* know from my hint about Pin, there's deep, deep feeling underneath . . . feeling buried far too deep beneath the ice-fields even to *pretend* to voice in a literary work . . .

'Yes, those coded references to stigmas, limps, scars I mentioned before in the conteXt of myth . . . Really not much better than Radclyffe Hall and all those Baudelairean wolves and vampires and things. *HeXe* is the German for "witch", by the way. Surprised you didn't manage to get *that* in along with all the rest.'

Momentary pause, as if riffling through a pile of invisible lecture notes in her head.

'Yes: here we are, Wolfie' (the uneXpected re-use of my nickname made my eyes suddenly prick with tears – the first time, I suppose, for many, many years). 'You said it yourself: "Oozing with the very concepts it purports to condemn" (not that aware-ness is any eXcuse). How can we eXpect *them* to take us seriously unless we develop our own New Rhetoric, capable, since we must still fly in it, of hijacking the plane of Patriarchy from within? Are there any more tins of cat food for Mowgli, by the way?'

It had taken me some time to take in the full force of what Annabel was saying.

She looked so splendid crouching there on the sunflower cushions in her purple leotard or whatever they're called . . . those high-buttoned gardening boots of Pin's, too, right up to her hunkers . . . a bit like Vita Sackville-West when Virginia Woolf came to visit her to discuss the Hogarth Printing Press . . . leaning forward eagerly as she spoke, waving her long, thin fingers (the cello like Dora) to emphasise a particularly impassioned point. Dark wavy hair tossed carelessly to one side of her fine, high forehead. Amber eyes glowing. Sensitive lips. A tiny, silver double-aXe flashing on the chain round her smooth white throat. You know . . . that radiant energy which beams out like a lighthouse from strength of mind and body in one and, despite what I said back there about my seven stomachs (poetic licence, *they* came later, together with the walking-frame and the word-processor), keeps us both still feeling so eXtraordinarily young.

Then slowly, very slowly, I begin to twig.

Incredible, this!

Far from interpreting the whole thing as the passionate *Defence of HomoseXuality* I intended – a daring artistic testament from the mouth of the lion (L. *de ore leonis*) unmasking prejudice, hypocrisy, injustice and the like, she has taken the whole thing to be an *attack*! . . . the total betrayal of all the intellectual values of empathy, joy and critical self-awareness, *love of literature*, in fact, which – thanks to the other Miss X, of course – she knows me passionately to uphold . . .

. . . in fact the very opposite of the 'Feminist Lesbian Novel' she apparently lectures on in her 'Women's Writing Course' . . . where she once told me they also hi-jack, eXplode and dismember certain rabidly 'decadent' nineteenth-century teXts on grounds of heteroseXist hypostasization, phallocentricity, pre-post-modernist recuperation and the like.

(It sounded more like one of those violent clichés used *against* Feminist Critical Theory than a recommendation, though, thinking the manner of speech defensive, I resisted in my case the chance to score a point. Yes, come to think of it, a white paperback by someone called Monique Wittig – couldn't see the title – was poking upside down from her rucksack neXt to something called *Champavert, Contes ImmorauX* – couldn't see the author, only a skeleton on the cover – when, in case of cold feet, I went to put a hot-water bottle in her bed.)

Yes, would you believe it, an *attack*!

. . . *An attack against homoseXuality.* ('Lesbianism', despite positive associations with Sappho, the *Poet*, I still secretly construed in those days as a term of abuse, kinkily applied to women only, with men as usual appropriating the would-be universal term: Gr. *homos* meaning 'the same', after all.)

. . . *An attack against Feminism, an attack against Motherhood, an attack against* – surely not – *poor Miss X herself!*

. . . In short against just about everything under Apollo *eXcept the true enemy: Homophobia!* (And we all know where *that* comes from, thanks to the dogged efforts of Sigmund Freud.)

Oh, not an *open* attack, of course.

Even worse.

Slobbering, raving, tongue out without knowing it, full of salaciously nudging innuendoes and hints. A grumbling volcano of repressed, unconscious anger cashing in on the oblique mechanisms of literary symbolism for its own vulturous purposes (I was warming to the task of demolition myself now . . . didn't I tell you how suggestible I am?), and contaminating everything left, right and empty centre itself . . .

And I who, encouraged by that compliment about my strikingly homogenised treatment of myth – a limp here and a scar there – had begun to feel the giddy pull of other redemptive possibilities too.

The central trinity of the sheep, goat and wolf, for eXample. No longer a spineless inability to stick to a single image as I'd secretly feared, but a brilliant meAtaphorical way of reinforcing what must surely be the central theme of the whole eXtraordinary contraption: how we all insist on passing the buck, creating in the process the notion of an '*enemy*', though with women, as I tried to tell Miss X that time by the River in very different language, it's much more compleX since the 'Other' or ravenously unstable, since falsely inferiorised, female term of the 'Nature/Culture' hierarchy is unconsciously associated by the woman with herself – you'd almost think I was into Feminist Theory now myself.

In short, just smoothing my feathers before the main assault.

'Seriously, though, Mary . . .'

(She seemed almost apoplectic now in her passionate attempt to save my soul – that kind of self-righteous didacticism really gets my goat – about to eXplode in mid-flight. At least though – I almost laughed aloud – at least *she* didn't add that insulting 'my lamb'. At least, my friend, you have saved me that.)

'Seriously, though, Mary lamb. It's the whole *manner* of writing that's in such eXcruciating bad taste. No, honestly. I'm not joking. It made me squirm. The totally out-dated narrative form for a start. All that painstaking, tight-arsed pseudo-realism, with its sick, slow, would-be "literary" rhythm (*you* must be the masochist to have kept it up) poisoning even spontaneous dialogue (doing it myself now, must be contagious) and leading the poor reader' (another knowing glance at Pin?) 'to eXpect some kind of climaX which keeps on coming but never . . .'

She paused a moment to light a herb cigar. (About the same age as Miss X when she met Nobody again at Charing X – if she really *did* meet her and hadn't just got cold feet with me again, I found myself musing . . . thanks to the hot-water bottle just now, I suppose.)

'And as for all that puritanical mingling of SeX and Death and the search for Redemption in the sublimatory glories of Art . . . Give me a good, honest Anglo-SaXon f . . . any day. *Four letters* beginning with "f" this time.'

(She *was* joking now, surely. Muzzle averted. Baring her neck. Not in the least unbalanced about that kind of thing. Nor had I ever heard her use bad language before. Still trying to shock me out of my Baudelairean apathy, I eXpect.)

'Cruel to be kind, Wolfie. I knew you'd understand.'

And here, tossing a wayward curl from her eyes, generous lips open now in . . . yes, it must be, those tiny, tell-tale crinkles at the corners of her mouth . . . an unmistakably humorous grin, she jumps up gracefully, herb cigar dangling from the corner of her lips, coughing gruffly and attractively as is her wont, to pass round her pre-birthday gift of the goaty red wine.

('No thanks,' I said. Strange how, just like with the vegetarianism, they always forget. Thinking it's just an affectation or something.)

I was horrified, of course.

Here was I setting out to write a stirring testimony that would vindicate and champion those three great causes – HomoseXuality, Feminism and Vegetarianism (not so sure now about Motherhood) – I would have cut the very nose from my face to defend, and here was one of my very first and surely most intelligent of all 'Dear Readers' spitefully accusing me of decadent, out-dated, Romantic, capitalistic, voyeuristic, not to mention self-indulgent, self-pitying, sado-masochistic . . .

Could it be that not only does the meaning of a work of art totally escape the one intended, but, worse still, the meaning of one's own personal life. . . ? That, after all those years of courageous struggle (the thought seemed suddenly almost unbearable) . . . I wasn't a *HomoseXual* after all? Not even a *Hetero*, come to that. Not even a *Feminist*, not even a *Novelist* – hélas, poor Marsyas on his borrowed flute – but simply a seX-starved vegetarian fruit-bat?

Dear Bill had gone upstairs now, incidentally. The wisdom of a Zen Buddhist in his case (that small draughty boX-room off the landing – hope he'll be all right in there – neXt to the palatial one which harboured his lordship's new cot), and I was alone with Pin and Annabel for the first time since we arrived.

'You're damned right I'm worried it might backfire,' I replied, appearing to concede a slightly less wounding point made earlier in order to regain some kind of control and pulling Capricorn's right leg as I spoke ... (As for St X, Pin had been having a go at his left eye like a vulture all the time we were talking – 'those were pearls...', always *was* a one for picking at things, poor lamb – and by now, woolly legs stretched up stiff and rigid just like that sheep Bill and I came upon in a ditch last year in Scotland, he had fallen unceremoniously under the settee on his back.)

'... but as you can see, I *tried* not to labour the thing with too many moralistic comments, preferring to let the meaning spring up by itself in the mind of the reader capable of reading between the lines...' (a nasty one, that) 'And as for wallowing masochistically in Romantic self-pity, if that's what you're thinking, even great Tragedies are basically life-affirming, you know.'

(I was staring sideways now into the moonlit garden, trying to toss that all too short strand of greying hair with a certain stylistic panache – pseudo-realism, my foot! – and hoping in the process to reveal my once unusually long and swan-like neck ... not that the rejuvenating osmosis of past and present they say you get from Writing seemed to be in any great hurry to take effect there.)

'... The joy of the imagination itself, for instance. I *thought* I'd conveyed that all along. After all, the Writer's *True* self or Power of Creative Detachment – or, like "universal consciousness", is that "politically suspect" too? – is always *totally separate* from...'

Already my voice was beginning to revert to its usual squeaky and ineffective register, however. Not much hope of the false stability of 'Authorial Identity' there. It all sounded so feeble, not to mention theoretically unsound.

So much so that I was tempted to bring the session to a close by sheltering behind a few of the latest ideas for my Tragedy book. Not to put too fine a point on it, now that I'd at last read it, *Totem and Taboo*. (Pin's eyes lit up again an instant: a real *idea* to sink her teeth into at last. A mind like a rapier if she could but unfoil the blade and stop forever fencing about the bush.)

'Take my striking, central meAtaphor of the goat,' I squeak hopefully, pulling my sunflower cushion into the centre of the room and crouching upon it like the Delphic Oracle. 'As well as being a sacrificial animal, the goat, amongst so-called primitive peoples, is a form of totem representing the name of the tribe or clan . . .'

(And here I give Capricorn a firm tweak of kinship on the tail. Does it really resemble that of a fish, reinforcing in the process the disastrously lost link between Xt and Pan?)

But then, before they can get back to you-know-what (which I need much more time to chew over alone, particularly what she let slip about the inadequate, over-doting mother), I find myself eXplaining with a passion that surprises me, the whole central notion of the killing of the sacred animal and the cure of disease (Annabel's hackles are rising predictably – thinks I mean you know what *is* one, *which I don't*), by a kind of psychological transference ('We have seen His disfigurement and now we are healed') . . . finally to launch almost without transition as does the Master, into a whole ram's horn diatribe on the secret crime of *Killing the Father* – did it *have* to be the father? – which doughty deed the sons meAtaphorically revoke for ever and ever by forbidding the killing of the substitutional animal and renouncing its fruits, i.e. their claim to the women (eXogamy?) who had now been set free.

Two fundamental taboos, then, *Murder and Incest* (now I really do turn and stare at them both like a Gorgon), which correspond to the two repressed wishes of *the OediPUS(s) CompleX*, that most omnivorous, carnivorous Polythemus-Raminagrobis of all.

So much for Mary Wolfe and the Minotaur. (Pin and the bedtime stories too, come to that.) If they all want to psychoanalyse me like a mulberry-coloured foetus in a belljar, then let the window open of its own accord. A Writer can't do more than *try* to put her own head on the block.

Whereupon I rise clumsily, all too conscious of the ungainly creases in the back of *my* skirt. No, not eXhausted – far from it. Strangely keen-eyed and bushy-tailed. But with a sense of . . . Well, it's not very nice to find you have the opposite effect on people from the one you intend, frightening innocent seven-month-old babies in their cots.

Don't kid yourself, Mary, pet. Far from having the liberating effect you wished, hasn't the writing of *Miss X* made it . . .

well . . . worse . . . leaving you even more of the lone wolf than before?

What if you're not, after all, the subversive rebel waving the banner of freedom, but a monstrous creature at home neither in the previous generation like Radclyffe Hall nor in this so-called 'post modernist' one like Annabel . . . an androgynous nineteenth-century Dodo beating an innocent twentieth-century dead duck?

No use pretending any further.

Annabel's criticism had cut me to the quick.

Hungry with the precious scent of unresolved contradictions, I didn't know *what* I was any more.

Midnight, and the repeated squeak of a bat (well, there would be, wouldn't there? All this crypto-Gothic stuff Annabel accuses me of. Can I help it if things really *are* like that?), followed, as if that isn't enough, by a blood-curdling bark-cum-caw-cum-howl of either a viXen (I thought of Miss Hilbert), or some kind of large bird (strange to think one can't always tell them apart), in turn (ditto) either hunting or caught in a trap.

Full moon, too, staring right in through the kitchen window, so close to the earth it seems about to suck me up into some kind of epileptic fit. (L. *epilepsia*, 'to take hold of'. Prejudices there as well. At least, thanks to Dionysus, the Greeks linked it to creative inspiration and, indirectly, agriculture, though.)

Wolf's bane blooming vigorously (in summer, Mary?), and the sweet scent of pines (strange, though, when they don't seem to grow round here), spicing seductively the cool night air.

Everyone else in bed by now.

Yes, something still feels incomplete, unresolved, almost as if I'm suffering from some deep, dark hunger gnawing inside me despite the reading and the vegetable stew. (So much for literary sublimation and all that. Surely I can't *still* be after Miss X now!)

What disease *did* you mean, though, Mary? Were you thinking back to the onset of '*IT*' perhaps? Or could it even be to Litera-ture itself? . . . that guilty eXcavation of secret crimes long forgotten, which, in perversely transgressing the secret cultural transgression . . .

Witching hour or not, I feel abnormally wide awake by now. And with a sense of conviction in itself bewildering, find myself starting to perform the following uncanny gestures . . . almost as if they are perfectly ordinary and, like cleaning my teeth – Wolfgang Amadeus – I have done them all regularly somewhere before.

Another life, perhaps? No, of course not. What if the wind changed, thinking silly, metempsychotic thoughts like that?

First I go to that alcove where Pin keeps the woollen poncho (Annabel's gift to the cottage last Xmas), and wrap myself up in it like a great green borelian bear. (It *would* be a green one, would it not?)

Then, my mind flashing back at once to our vain search for treasure in the dustbins that night, solemnly take Dad's old torch from its hook on the back-door (despite that one uniquely angry incident over the piano, *he* was certainly not *our* Minotaur . . . no unresolved Oedipal conflict there) and, having collected a knife and fresh boX of matches from the kitchen drawer and poured the remains of the wine into Amon's empty feeding-bottle (she can wash it out later), tip-toe back to fetch my two dumb protagonists (St X and Capricorn, who else?) . . . placing them (still with that strange, only half-conscious deliberation, remember) in the pouch of my furry green uniform, the hood pointing to the front like a monstrous snout or wolf's helmet (*caput lupinum*, 'ring a bell'?) . . . finally to lift up the latch (there's an old-fashioned one on the back door just like in the Fairy Tale – ah, but *which* Fairy Tale?), and let myself out at last into the cool, inviting night.

Annabel does go on so, don't you think?

Freshness. Clarity. Well, a *kind* of clarity considering I'm still so very miXed up.

Yes, the moon is full and bright as I saw from the kitchen. A real harvest moon, just right for Virgo, my adopted birthday, its mulberry-coloured omphalos, to re-chance a favourite, no doubt Oedipal meAtaphor, staring from its own radiant halo up there like the unflinching pupil of some fabulous eye. Wolfish Artemis with her hunting spears again.

> I am, thou woost, yet of thy company
> A maide, and love hunting and venerye
> And for to walken in the wodes wild
> And noght to ben a wyf and be with child.

(Chaucer on Mary Wolfe, the child Artemis. Venery, Venus: about the predatory nature of the courtly lyric, Annabel *was* obviously right.)

Disentangling myself from the thick spikes of the bramble bush which marks the boundary of the garden, I at last break cover and trot softly and as if deliberately into the very centre of the cornfield, already turned to charred black stubble. No 'last sheaf' ceremony here either, I'm afraid.

Then, feeling slightly sheepish at my very strength of unknown purpose, the way you do when you are free from superstition but find yourself attending to it all the same, I squat down in the centre, my belongings propped up round me like Primitive Man (well, Woman, then) and begin to construct a flimsy kind of tripod: pieces of straw knitted, no, spun together for legs and the whole thing rearing up uncertainly on its haunches like a Pythonesque oracle or new-born rattlesnake.

For some reason I feel convinced a *stone* of some kind is needed too, but, previously as eXcessive there in the thicket as back on the beach at Dungeness, they seem to be lacking in this part of the field. Just my luck.

Mary had a little lamb, its fleece was white as snow,
And everywhere that Mary went, the lamb was sure to go.

Yes, St X *first* – I never really liked him – you, the bell-wether, cowering there in the Black Tin BoX like Odysseus' helpless companions in the corner of the cave.

Come, my little White Bottom! (The words are Homer's, in case you are wondering.)

Come to Mother!

No good casting those dumb, delectable sheep's eyes at me now!

Even though Pin has already half picked out your left pupil – ah, pupil – fancying herself as a vulture or carrion crow, there's still a good way left to go!

Wrenching off your by now rather tired green ribbon ('You and your two plaits with the little green bows') and laying it carefully on the prickly stubble beside me, I grope in my pouch for the kitchen knife and, having attempted with some difficulty to skin you clean of your woolly hide like that of the ill-fated Marsyas, firmly and self-consciously plunge it like a dagger deep into your innocent woolly heart.

Mary had a little lamb indeed.

What would Miss P say if she could see me now!

I have managed to kindle a small fire by this time, I see – no fear of contravening the country code in my frenzy since the field itself is already too far gone. And, for want of a cooking-pot and water, it is becoming more or less obligatory to throw the victim on to the flame – *most* of the victim, at least. The tail and green bow and bell I thought I'd better keep as proof of pot-latch for Pin and Annabel – destroying the gift so as to remain top dog. (Thanks to Bill, I was reasonably well up in these fascinating Anthropological terms by then.)

No sooner is this part of the operation complete, however, than I feel myself growing even more and more eXcited, paroXysmal and ravening than you should have imagined me before . . . almost beserk, you might say (cf. *bearsark*, 'a bearskin', from the enraged Norse warriors, with or without shirts on their backs) . . . hurling myself round the fire in a salacious frenzy (the salacious 'male' reader Annabel was on about?), my teeth and eyes surely – at last, at last no mirrors – flashing in the reddish light of the flames like an amateur werewolf, alias bugbear (*Loup garou*, Mary. Got your French notebook?), and attempting all the while to rip off the limbs of poor St X as if he were Pentheus (Poppy Morpheme?) or even, over there by the cup cupboard ('The handbell, Mary . . .'), Dionysus the great Goat God Himself.

Indeed, the wild Bacchanalia I had performed for Miss X at The 'Radclyffe' that time in my birthday suit was but a stately minuet compared to the eXclusive Birthday Lupercalia which, my breath belching forth like the flames of the Chimera (eXcuse the yoghurt and vegetable stew), I now proceed by the gothicky light of the moon to perform, dear Reader, for you alone. (You see, I *should* have been given a part in the end of term play. Remember I still don't know fully what I'm doing, though.)

But now for the climAXE, as Annabel would say.

Now at last for my favourite Goat.

'Vous y serez, ma fille!'

The elect, the gift-horse, the king, the Queen Bee, if not the Great Black Bottom itself.

Slowly at first, but then with increasing ferocity . . . what was it she made me say in that purply passage back there: 'slobbering, raving, tongue out without knowing it . . . a grumbling volcano of repressed, unconscious anger contaminating everything left, right and empty centre itself . . . hungry for blood now as if I'm possessed by some predatory animal spirit: hyaena, bear, crocodile, swallow-tail butterfly, vulture, absent nightingale, little foX' (surely this is not the dread Malaysian *latah*!), I proceed to meAt out to *Capricorn* the same fate as that of his sheepish companion . . .

starting with his/her left leg and gradually graduating downstairs again across the 'pashm' (Tibetan goat's under-fur) to his/her indeed peculiarly fish-like tail.

Fourteen pieces, minus one.

The whole damned hog. (With Isis and Osiris, of course, it was the other way round. Sewing the pieces together again.)

Sweet ram, [. . .] what does this mean? Why are you the last of the flock to pass out of the cave [. . .]? Are you grieved for your master's eye, blinded by a wicked man and his accursed friends, when he had robbed me of my wits with wine? *Nobody was his name*; and I swear that he has not yet saved his skin! Ah, if only you could [. . .] tell me where he's hiding from my fury! Wouldn't I hammer him and splash his brains all over the floor of the cave, till that miserable Nobody had eased my heart of the suffering I owe to him!

Such is the skill of Homer's enviable masterpiece that we, his dear Readers, begin to feel pity for the Cyclops himself: Troll, Werewolf, Ogre, trapped as he is within his own blinded savagery, shepherd to foXes in his very sheep-pen, condemned for ever, Tantalus, Sisyphus, Oedipus(s), *you* name it, to fumble for ever alone in darkness, while, aided by the cunning of his own foXy nature (O Teut. *fuh*, often confused with 'wolf'), that elusive Nobody, his teeming brain with its wondrous billions of synapses weighing down his dumb bearer, prepares, hélas, to escape his fumbling hands for good.

(*Outis*. Nobody. L. *Nemo*. F. *Personne*. Nobody is hurting me. Nobody of the beautiful, cunning, deep voice. Just someone I met in my year at College and who's turned up again at Charing X. Be a lamb and . . .)

Come thou monarch of the vine,
Plumpy bacchus with pink eyne . . .

Fee, fie, fo, fum . . . give a dog a bad name. Having lain my already blood-stained hands on thy innocent head, let me pluck thy ancient bones to make a quick buck that I may go free instead of thee . . . free from the obligation of the terrible gift . . . free to . . .

My vegetarianism depriving me of the last delights of cannibalistic incorporation of the virtues of the god ('Thou shalt not seethe a kid in his mother's milk,' the abominable Leviticus

161

again), there seems but one more mysteriously crucial act left now to accomplish before going home again, my proverbial shaggy tail curved limply like Sigmund's between my back legs. (Dracula, Jack the Ripper, Frankenstein's Monster, the TriXter cut to size again . . . even Radclyffe Hall was surely never like this.)

Scarcely taking any notice of the huge black bird circling above me all this time, its monstrous shadow all but eclipsing the moonlight, but taking some red wine from Amon's feeding-bottle – the first time alcohol would pass my lips since eXile chez Lolita in Paris all those years ago – I boldly pour a few pomegranate drops on to my long, beaded tongue (parched for some reason . . . yes, it *must* have been eXternalised just as I feared), and, great green wolf-moth enfeebled now by its wild, Nietzschean gyrations (didn't *he* decide to call himself 'Zagreus': Dionysus-Zagreus, Zagreus the Goat-god?), Rumpelstiltskin dancing round his little cultural bonfire, finally sink down eXhausted to stare at the last forked tongues of blood-orange flame devouring that strange, hermaphroditic form: half young, half old, half sheep, half goat, half fish, half fowl, half wire, half wool, half – hélas, poor Marsyas – flesh and blood?

(My love, my love! Maker and Monster all in one, what has all this Mary Shelley stuff to do with you and me?)

Solve et Coagula! Salve, Salve!

Talk about confession preceding the deed. . . . Yes, destroying *False Reason* at the very corn-roots of its own irrational Citadel, everything goes on and on fitting like a tight kid glove.

But why this strained, alchemical gauntlet to the void?

This creaking, croaking eXhibition? This savage parade of anger without teeth?

What gods am I propitiating? What ancient ghosts laying?

What anguished, unseen death avenging? Into whose awful mysteries seeming to initiate myself?

And above all, of course, if you are fortunate enough to follow my unconscious logic, *what horrid previous crime eXpiating or atoning for by this fresh sacrifice of innocent blood?*

'And he that let go the goat for the scapegoat shall wash his clothes, and bathe his flesh in water, and afterwards come into the camp . . .'

It was only as I began to limp back across the field in the comforting direction of the cottage, letting myself in through the back door again softly (*à pas de loup*, Mary. Got your French notebook?) like a blood-stained Satyr returned to the fold (so much for my once gleaming cohorts of green and of gold), eager to wash my hands now of the whole monstrous, corny, ham-acted literary/psychologico/meAtaphorico drama: CAtharsis, CATheXis, eXorcism, transference, displacement, condensation, potlatch, negative female OediPUS(S) compleX, the lot, that I suddenly remembered Pin's cunning little question: 'You're sure you're not holding back on something, Lou?', remembered, that is, to ask myself precisely the same question too.

How did *I know about the death of Mrs X already and* 'only too well'? Was the violent scene in the corn but some positive screen-memory or whatever they call it, cryptically disclosing like a row of quaking aspens some further, less innocuous repression way back?

Had the mists of paramnesia at last begun to disperse?

Indeed, my memory cells no doubt already revivified by the uncanny force you have just so patiently witnessed (that precious refleXion of my writing in another person's eyes one step in advance), perhaps we *would* fall neatly on each other's swords after all, Classical Tragedy at its best . . .

Perhaps even after all, if I could only manage to get all this latest self-deconstructive stuff in with the rest, '*Lesbian Feminist Fiction*' too, the Old and the New Worlds together in one.

Not bad for an androgynous nineteenth-century Dodo beating to death a dead twentieth-century duck!

What would poor Miss X have said if she could see me now!

What will Annabel, come to that!

The Twelfth Piece

Ma mère-grand, que vous avez de grands yeuX!
C'est pour mieuX voir, mon enfant.
Ma mère-grand, que vous avez de grandes dents!
C'est pour mieuX te manger.
(*Le Petit Chaperon Rouge,* Perrault)

They'll say you caused me pain.
When I agree with them, the first hard crust
Will cover up my lie
(*Miss X*, Mary Wolfe)

Et là-dessus, au fond des forêts,
Le Loup l'emporte, et puis le mange,
Sans autre forme de procès.
(*Le Loup et l'Agneau*, La Fontaine)

I had been unable to attend Mrs X's funeral myself for
some reason . . . let's just say having to get back to OXford to mend
the garden fence.

Mother attended, however.

Over the years since my sister and I had at last tardily flown from
the nest like two overgrown cuckoos, she and Mrs X had drifted
into an uneasy friendship not without its charms. Perhaps they both
bore certain unadmitted guilts and scars in a way. (Is Annabel
right? Do I really have it in for motherhood?)

So much so that it was she, Mother (we must have had a
telephone of our own by then), whom Miss X had first contacted
with the tragic news. 'Half frantic with emotion,' Mother had said
dramatically, one hand over the earpiece in mistake for the
mouthpiece and struggling to pick up my matricidal message from
under the table of 'I'll kill you if you let her know I'm here'.

Apparently there had been but the barest handful of mourners,
with only Miss P and Mrs FoX-cum-Salmon representing the
School.

Amongst them, though, a quiet, razor-thin woman all in black
(late fifties?), said Mother, who sat alone to the left of the altar
(well, she would do, wouldn't she?), totally ignoring and ignored

by the rest of the flock, including, needless to say, Miss X.

But, of course: Dora!

The faithful hand-me-down before me!

(Freud's own choice of name for a female 'patient' of his who *also* loved a woman, strangely enough, though look what a cock-up he made of that.)

I felt my spine prickle. *She* had attended the funeral, then.

The ceremony itself was conducted, incidentally, by that creep in wolf's shoving, the Vicar, Head of the Board of Governors . . . you know, the one who was later imprisoned for rape, headline news in *The Daily Telegraph*. At least *my* sadistic activities as Jack the Ripper were confined, so far at that stage, to a woolly toy sheep and felt goat. And the sermon? 'The pelican,' said Mother quietly, 'pecking its breast to feed its young' – Symbol of Xtian sacrifice which, in reverent gusto, the Vicar went on to link with the deceased herself, epitome of doting motherhood.

(And here Mother's voice grew faint with pained reminiscence. Either that or interference on the line.)

What had really surprised her, she went on gaily (must have been interference on the line), was the way in which, just as everyone was trooping out past the coffin (self-knit shroud in Fair Isle, I pondered nastily?), Miss X had suddenly rushed up to her and, tears streaming down her face (a vivid, mottled picture flashed before me like a kingfisher), started to pump her hand up and down like a piston – *my* mother's hand, that is – on and on as if never to let go, and all the time unable to utter a single word.

Did she want a new mother instead of her own? Had the Wolf already jumped over the wall and run off with her tongue? Or did she, like the Wolf disguised as a shepherd ('Lupo ovem commisisti . . .'), fear that as soon as they heard her strange, gruff voice they would know she wasn't a shepherd after all? ('Lupus pilum mutat, non mentem,' the wolf changes his coat but not his disposition, as Miss P used to say for what I thought in those days no reason at all.)

Mother herself was convinced it was in recognition of her own growing friendship with Mrs X in the years since I'd left home. Help with the shopping now she had grown so decidedly frail, 'coupled these last months with that nasty skin disease.' (She couldn't for the life of her remember the name.)

'*If it weren't for Mother* . . . One day, Mary, when I'm free.' Only I knew that pumping Mother's hand so desperately like that was her very last living message to *me*.

Why, oh why, had I not rushed to the funeral too like Dora, my shadow, my sister in sorrow, to whisk her away from the jaws of her own death? (Why indeed, Mary, lamb! Why indeed!)

Once more, like that one, first unique night in 'Radclyffe Hall' – double room, two single beds – I had failed unpardonably to answer her cry. (And we know now, don't we, you and I, that if and when mere *second* chances deign to come by . . .)

And what of poor Miss P, you ask?

'Oh, Miss P remained completely dry-eyed,' replied Mother pertly. 'Never did much like Mrs X, did she?'

'No,' I said, thinking of all those long years of intimate rivalry for 'Messer Gaster'. 'No, you're right. I suppose not.'

What they *never* knew . . . but *what I knew already 'only too well'* (Pin's crafty question back again), was the *cause* of Mrs X's death: 1st April, as it turned out, precisely half past four in the afternoon, am I right or am I right? as Auntie doubtless would have asked, she too lost for ever now along with Sigmund and Dad in the brilliant, crocheted pall of night.

But let me eXplain.

Ever since its vile memory began to surface just now coming back from the cornfield, I *need* you to know. Always hold in mind, meanwhile, dear Reader – Annabel and Pin inside you too now like Jonah in the Whale – that although the present incident took place *before* I gave my reading, it was only *afterwards*, thanks, no doubt, to the cathartic release provided by my gruesome ritual, in turn the result of hearing you all falsely interpret my labours, that I was able to begin to recall it myself. Such the agonistics (Gr. 'athletic contest') of any self-respecting rhetorical combat like ours.

Determined to leave no stone unplucked in my part of our Proustian return to our old stamping-grounds that time – all eXcept the actual School building, which I thought it best to leave for later on – I had decided to allow myself one last visit to The Pagoda to call on Mrs X just like the *old* days. (Good old days or bad old days? Thanks to Writing, I'm glad to say I don't really know any more. Only the present is the true Promised Land, and that is with us all along.)

Perhaps even to find out indirectly about her 'Leetle Dorter' too?

Pure curiosity, of course. There was Bill now ('You'll go over one day like the rest of them, Mary. You'll see.' Not that . . .), and the start of my friendship with Annabel, not to mention the very first seeds of the Tragedy book before Freudian Theory and now, thanks to Annabel, its Feminist Re-reading – have I *no* personal back-bone? – had begun irreversibly to gobble me up.

I had often felt, remember, that Mrs X and I had developed in those days a kind of desperate camaraderie based on our mutual eXclusion from the fold: Her little flat above and on the other side of the wall.

Sometimes that jolly old face with the limpid blue eyes framed by the mass of tight sheep's curls would look oddly reassuring in the heart of my anguish (anguish, Mary?), while even the corny sense of humour (Alligator/Crocodile) would seem suddenly preferable to the discourse of Miss X herself with its slightly irritating talk about Good and Evil, Goats and Sheep and so on.

(Only *slightly* irritating, Mary? But then in those days, according to Annabel and Co., you were still apparently *repressing* your anger, I know.)

How would Mrs X react to seeing me after all these years, however?

Would there be a further, even more recent hand-me-down girl than myself and Dora sitting smiling in the kitchen but with thunder in her heart?

'Lieben, Hassen, gibt-es kein Drittes mehr?'
'To love, to hate, is there no third path?'
– Grillparzer's *Sappho*, oddly enough.

Full moon again, just visible over the roof-tops although it was only half past three in the afternoon.

The squeaky iron gate, the three neat dustbins (*that* little Beckettian drama had still to be staged, remember), the faithful front-door bell: 'Mrs X, three rings and please wait.'

Tiny, spring aconites with their yellow petticoats (well, winter 'wolf's bane', then, if you must) in full, bright bloom in the flowerbed by the potting shed, poisonous ivy still twining parasitically round the trunks of the pine trees (Wagnerian leitmotif or not, you must be just as fed up with it as I am by now), and, of course, immortal Polythemus-Ramskin or whatever he calls himself, mark of Cain in the middle of his forehead, rubbing himself round the back of my legs like a lascivious Roman diatribe in the eternal hope of being fed.

No curiosity could ever kill *him*, nay, nor put bells round *his* short, fat neck.

With my old scarlet chiffon scarf draped like a hood to protect me from the wind (perhaps *you'll* remember when I wore it last), I had brought a large picnic basket of CoXes apples as a gift from Mother and half eXpected to find the recipient lying in bed in an old-fashioned nightdress and nightcap like the phoney grandmother in *Little Red Riding Hood* which had so terrified my sister and would one day little Amon too. No it can't ever be nice to find that a sweet, trusted person has suddenly changed to a monstrous beast: whiskery, crinkled chops and rabid eye peering from under her frilly cap.

'What eXtra sharp canines you have, Mrs X.'

'All the better to gobble you all up with, my lamb. But help yourself first to some iced gingerbread-men – you too, Dora, dear, even *more* in your case – so that you both get nice and fat. Nibble, nibble, who's the mouse, nibbling away at *my* little flat?'

(Paranoid/schizoid themselves maybe, but at least these grim Fairy Tales help reveal how our fears and fancies work. 'Mens sana in fabula insana' perhaps? As for Dora's anoreXia, didn't somebody say it's the child most loved who refuses food and plays with that refusal as with fire?)

. . . though we bear diseases
Which have their true names only ta'en from beasts, –
As the most ulcerous wolf and swinish measle . . .

Though looking somewhat frail and with her still bright blue eyes surrounded by a mass of dark scars, Mrs X seemed overjoyed to see me again, smiling up eagerly from her creaking rocking-chair as if I were You-Know-Who herself.

(A form of 'lupus', Mother had suddenly remembered out loud one night, having had it 'on the tip of my tongue' for over a week. Rampant like eXema but not contagious, so that was all right. A horrid thing, though, 'lupus', origin unknown. How often 'Man (sic) stands amaz'd to see his deformity/ In any other creature but himself.' Webster and the poXy 'Duchess' again.)

I was even somewhat chuffed to see myself grinning sheepishly neXt to Dora on the mantelpiece, decked like a Xmas tree in a smart, white furred OXford BA gown.

(No cello bow in *my* short, fat fingers, of course, though I had by this time started to play the trumpet. Not quite concert standard yet, but well *en route* to 'Tuba mirum' and the wondrous, compassionate wrath of 'Dies Irae' – on a trumpet, Mary? (always

my ambition to play *something*, at least, to the other Miss X) – in the
Wolfgang Amadeus *Requiem*.)

Looking even more and more by then like the sheep in *Alice
Through the Looking-Glass* (do they *have* sheep in Buddhist temples,
though?), Mrs X paused but to cast off her knitting – not *another*
angora twin-set? – and tea and bread and honey, not to forget iced
gingerbread (*Little Red Riding Hood*?), were faithfully produced as
usual from the old tartan tin.

Sing Something Simple was on the wireless, I remember, or rather,
by those days, the radio: 'Ole Faithful, we'll roam the range
together', but horribly jazzed up . . . crude, empty, full of sick puns
and jokes, creaking as a rocking-chair. The same old tunes in a
different world.

'Of course, she was always such a *good* girl,' Mrs X then
proffered adoringly (creak, creak), losing no time to pass the
familiar, even more faded photographs as soon as the tea things had
been cleared away ('Mustn't get them sticky now, Mary, must
we?')

'A bit of a tom-boy all the same, though' (creak, creak, rock,
rock). 'Had my heart in my mouth when she climbed that huge
walnut tree at the back of our garden, little monkey, and refused to
come down for almost seven hours. But so kind and obedient all the
same, Dora dear.' (She never noticed the error, so I let it pass.)

'Wouldn't hurt a fly.' ('Come up, dear.' The Parlour.)

'I'm sure you're right, Mrs X,' said I.

Are we always responsible for our actions?

Ever since reading Baudelaire's splenetic prose poems, I've
never been sure.

You know, uneXpected gestures welling up at twilight (between
dog and wolf, Mary) . . . like that piece where the narrator invites a
poor old glass-vendor upstairs to his apartment only to knock him
down again, smashing all his wares (that will teach you to sell
rose-coloured spectacles with pinky rims, my doddery old friend
with the walking-frame), or when, coming upon a beggar cringing
like an agoraphobic dog in the gutter, he decides to restore him to a
sense of self-dignity by means of a rattling good punch on the jaw.
At least with Baudelaire the narrator is a purely eXperimental
persona, there where in my . . .

Not even twilight now, I'm ashamed to confess.

Regression to the paranoid/schizoid position of early childhood I
mentioned?

The 'ID' jumped out of its picnic basket, not to say the goat let fully out of bag?

Whatever it was in my case, some Devil must have come to seize hold of me, Satan Himself with his cloven hooves and fish-like tail.

For before I knew it, ripping up the precious photograph of the child in the laurel wreath with the violence of a werewolf – indoors too, now, I know what you're thinking – there I was barking out at her the whole 'Tragic Story in a Story' in condensed, not to say inverted form, baring my teeth throughout like a white alsatian dog.

(*Mise en abyme* they call it nowadays – so *that's* why you smiled way back there in the train to Oxbridge, dear Reader: a term adapted from heraldry by André Gide, the whole scene reflected Xiasmically within itself, like the marriage in the mirror in the *Arnolfini Wedding* or the star within a star – X-eyed asterisk, then – on my old School hat.)

. . . **How** (bark, bark) her belovèd 'Leetle Dorter' was really a *HomoseXual*, a *Lesbian*, a *Pervert* (Sigmund Freud's *invert* doesn't sound quite so bad, so I kept that back), not much better than the blacks, the bad weather and the Labour Government, not to mention – and here, without turning a whisker at my own treacherous perversion of the false Claims of Logic (if you can't beat 'em, join 'em), I threw in a few illustrious names myself for good measure – Lawrence of Arabia, André Gide again, Proust, Miss Hilbert, Vita Sackville-West, Shakespeare, Walt Whitman, Sappho, Gertrude Stein, Oscar Wilde and, hélas, Radclyffe Hall (though just because she wrote a Novel about it, you can't be sure). . . ending this cacophonously trumpeted symphony of Social Decadence with the dread Comprehensive System (rock, rock), already starting to run through trusty old Grammar Schools like our own with the ravenous speed of a skin disease.

(Indeed, Miss X's élitist Empire of 'Brainy Marys' – 'I never want you to be ashamed of your home, Mary' – had long since crumbled to dust. Not that . . .)

. . . **How** (bark, bark) **it had all started way back at her old College when Miss X had secretly initiated her friend Nobody into 'Sapphic Practices'** – 'Sappho, the Greek Poet from Lesbos, that is.' (Or had it even been the other way round, with Miss X the lucky Victim – *Victim*, Mary? – and Nobody the . . . the stupendous thought had never before occurred to me.)

. . . **How** (bark, bark, creak, creak), **after 'frequenting' this same Nobody in a flat in Paris behind the Musée de Cluny** (isn't that where the original 'La Dame à la Licorne' is encaged?), **she had gone all out to seduce me (yes, would you believe it, her own trusted Head Girl!')** ... dragging me across to her bed *a tergo* (L. 'from behind') that night in The 'Radclyffe' (yes, that time in OXford when you came to see us off with the picnic basket, interfering old p.b. ....) (rock, rock, creak, creak, snap, snap), and proceeding rapaciously to ... well, you know ... 'Sapphic Practices' again ... gently and tenderly embrace me all over (here I felt a sudden treacherous tear for some reason, again hardly likely to further my Satanic Cause, there at the foot of your own smiling photograph ... **thereupon unfortunately** (that can't be right either) **to turn turnskin** (L. *versipellis*, 'turncoat', 'turnskin') **and abandon me for ever to your own tender mercies** (in actual fact long in advance of the crucial moment of dismissal: 'For you own sake, Mary, promise never ...'), like Little Red Riding Hood on a visit to Grandma or – yes, that's it, the gingerbread – Hansel and Gretel, the lost Babes in the Wood (though no tell-tale trail of breadcrumbs in my case, thank god).

... **How** (bark, bark, yap, yap, rock, rock, creak, creak, snap, snap, Cerberus in person now with his two quite different-sounding heads ... yes, a Novel is a *kind* of concerto or symphony) after just such a repast of tea and iced gingerbread in this very same kitchen (rock, rock), **I had tried to Commit Suicide by casting myself from the new by-pass bridge** in the illustrious company of Phèdre, Brainy Mary Number Two (though that was different), Sappho Herself (from a Rock in the Aegean), and, finally for the moment, Gérard de Nerval (several other famous names have come to me since, of course, which I never thought to mention by the heat of the fire) ... **to be saved at the eleventh hour in my case by my own incipient poetic talents** (something obviously missing in Sappho's case: back to the drawing-board, my lamb): a form, a rhythm, the odd self-eXhortative 'pecker up, Mary' quotation – **but only, much later on,** (bark, bark, yap, yap, bark, bark,) **as the result of an even more sadistic turnskin reversal and second abandonment a year or so after in favour of Nobody, my long lost Rival** – many a true word howled in jest – to succumb to ... well, you know,

'IT',

that nameless 'X' which suddenly up and jumped on me one day in the marketplace (Gr. *agora*, strictly speaking the 'forum'), like a great angora wolf-spider (Gr. *lycosidae*) straight out of the blue, **just as** (bark, bark, snarl, snarl, hum, hum, nudge, nudge) **I'm doing right now at this moment with you!**

Wouldn't hurt a fly, my foot!

But then, finally, of all the dead ducks come home to roost, the deadliest flying-foX of all:

'**And it was all your fault, Mrs X!** You, the over-doting Pelican,' (creak, creak) 'with your perpetual talk of Unspeakable Sacrifice,' (a cruel twist, that too, but I was not to know then of the funeral oration) 'sending poor Mr X away like that to die on the mountain,' (for what crime, however? bedtime stories? Here yet a further *aporia*, well, doubt, then, raised its beauteous, irrepressible head), 'and telling her that (pace Annabel) *all* men are evil, not to mention *se*X itself.')

And here . . . **seX, seX, seX** . . . (bark, bark, yap, yap, snarl, snarl, moan, groan), as if to prove that I, Mary Wolfe, could indeed mention the unmentionable (total silence from the rocking-chair by now, you notice), I sent the sibilants whistling round the little kitchen like snakes in Racine . . .

Who's afraid of the Big Bad Scapegoat now!

But here, half fascinated, half filled with horror, Phèdre herself full of painful self-loathing at the criminal depths to which she is forced to descend in the cause of Cultural Revolution (even to recount it here makes me feel like a Murderer), I realised that Mrs X was no longer listening at all.

Eyes fiXed and staring, mOuth gaping Open in a vivid Ovidian 'O' for MetamOrphOsis, OxO, Other and 'Os and Xs' – Oh, that hOrrifying spectacle of anOther human being, mOuth suddenly gaping Over the unspeakable vOid that is Our Own – canines feebly glinting (talk about a family likeness), an unaccustomedly prominent lapis lazuli vein twisted like the staff of Moses on her narrow forehead, one arm still hooked round the ball of a(n)gora knitting-wool and the other hanging over the back of her chair limp as poor Sigmund's wretched tail (strange, all the same, to find agoraphobia in dog): there she lay before me, shattered and defenceless like the ill-fated Semele, mother of Dionysus, seared to pieces by the thunderbolt of Zeus.

'Politically suspect' use of myth, my clay foot. Put *that* in your herb pipe and smoke it, Annabel, my love. (I suppose I always do tend to over-react slightly when falsely attacked, all the victims of oppression in the world trembling empathetically inside me like aspen leaves and turning me into a ravening monster in return for their pains. *Their* guilty secret, incidentally, the aspens, is said to be having provided the wood for *the* +.)

'Stop, stop, Mary, my lamb,' she gasped (getting my name right this time at least, I noticed), human spider herself now, caught at last in her own angora web (*agora*, 'angora', 'angina', 'Marketplace', 'Forum', what's the odds?). Mothers are victims too, you know, perhaps even the greatest . . .

'Stop, stop, Mary, my lamb. Run neXt door and tell my Leetle . . .'

I should have done at once what she requested or even administered the kiss of death, sorry, life myself (not that I'd taken my Red X course by then). Sins of omission are the worst to bear indeed.

Instead, glancing at the familiar, still reproachfully ticking, 'Queen Victoria' grandfather clock (half past four eXactly and still hardly even twilight, you see), almost eXpecting it to burst open to reveal all the little goats trembling fearfully inside its wooden stomach, I rush to the back door, lift up the latch as I did that time at the cottage (pot-latch, pot-boiler, pot-belly, pot-luck, it's all one) and let myself out swiftly but stealthily ('*à pas de loup*, Mary. Got your French notebook?') into the cool, familiar garden – thank heavens the squeaky gate is already open this time – and, leaping on to Lady Macbeth with the agility of a ravening antelope (antelope, Mary? is there no *other* animal comes to mind?), am gone with the wind, as Auntie would have said . . .

'Le jour n'est plus pur que le fond de mon coeur.'

Tick-tock. Toc-toc.

Nobody had seen me leave or enter to steal the life of the Temple but Puss, Puss, Puss with the single yellow eye in the middle of his forehead, large and full like a harvest moon (in spring, Mary? Yes, in spring. A harvest moon in the heart of spring).

The Wind, the Wind, the *heavenly* nameless, Wind.

Leaving not a crumb of tell-tale gingerbread behind her, Nobody had come to the rescue again.

Eating up the Witch before the Witch eats us (G. *HeXe*, I *have* got it in)?

So *this* was the hidden crime whose memory the mysterious tribal ritual that night in the cornfield had at last at once both screened and restored to light.

I had taken my revenge!

I had unsheathed my sword and killed her mother just as Pin wanted (Freudian slip, though we'll let it pass), but as in all the best Tragedies ('If it weren't for Mother . . . One day, Mary, when I'm free'), revenge by that same token had deprived me of all hope to profit from the sweet, filial fruits of sacrifice.

I had killed Demeter, the mother but by that very same token, I had killed Persephone her 'Leetle Dorter' too! (Overwhelmed by grief in her case, a bare three weeks later, as you know.)

What was it Clue Seven had said way back in the treasure hunt, pinned in the cloakroom beneath my School hat?:

> The wolf shall find her grave, and scrape it up,
> Not to devour the corpse, but to discover
> The horrid murder.

The 'horrid murder' lay at the feet of 'Patriarchal Culture', but – just a little matter of paramnesia – **the horrid murderer was me,** Little Red Riding Hood, turned Electra if not Jack the Ripper: two with one foul, crowing breast of the tongue, just as my own vicarious Victim, 'Philomela', had had me weave back into my own Borelian cloth with its strangely involuted strand of twisted, creeping, scarlet thread!

And the most terrible thing of all was that it didn't seem to be my *own* voice raving there in the kitchen at all – even *less* mine than those violent actions in the cornfield which brought this all out (they, at least, had the dignity of me Ataphor consumed in Private) . . . almost as if I couldn't really feel anger at all even now, but had only simulated some kind of Freudian repression (and its desublimation?) so as not to hurt Annabel's feelings when she felt duty-bound to attack me like that.

> They'll say you caused me pain.
> When I agree with them . . .

It hadn't been like that at all, you see! Language itself, Annabel's 'Law of the Father', had spoken with its foul, poisoned tongue through my mouth! Oppression contaminates within, as Auntie never, ever said.

Voicing all those monstrous lies that had safely stuck in my throat like a smoked salmon fishbone that time at The Trout, had made me X over to the side of Enemy Prejudice.

'Render to no *man* evil for evil.' Now I too sat on the right hand of God the Father, nothing but a creep in sheep's woving after all, banned for ever from the marketplace.

How many more innocent beasts still to be slaughtered by my own unconscious cultural hand before the raging wolf of 'CeyX and Alcyone', a red gleam in its eye, its swiftly snapping jaws flecked with foam and blood and its terrible teeth still fastened in the neck of the nearest innocent heifer, is finally turned to stone at last?

How much more blood to flow under those halcyon, white-stone bridges in the City of Dreams before the clear waters would come pounding like joy over the final weir and the little stick trapped so long in its vorteX . . .?

If sticks and stanes do break our banes . . .

MeAtaphor has *indeed* a lot to answer for, my Love.

The Thirteenth Piece

I have looked in the magic mirror of stone
The boundary stone, the Herne. I can
return to life
(Winter Song of the Hamatsa, having
tamed the forces of hunger by cannibalistic
ritual dance)

If ever there was a wolf in a mulberry
suit...
(Dickens)

CatheXis: a 'sum of eXcitation' attached
hysterically to an idea, part of the body or
object, the cure of which 're-establishes the
relation between the memory of the
traumatic event and its affect by restoring
the connection between the different ideas
involved and so facilitating the discharge of
the affect'
(*The Language of Psychoanalysis*, Laplanche
and Pontalis)

'Happy Birthday, Lou,' said Pin when I staggered downstairs bloodshot-eyed and dishevelled the morning after my violent, atavistic escapade in the cornfield, looking very much, to judge from her own astonished eXpression, like something ambiguous the dog had brought back.

'I'll give you your pressie in a moment, but for god's sake let me feed Amon first. Take him, will you – careful! – while I get his bottle? Oh, and give him that toy sheep thing again to keep him quiet.'

Thy sins will find thee out indeed. The bottle had been used for the unwonted activity of appeasing Bacchus, remember, and as for St X on his allegedly humbly skew-whiff St Andrews X (oh for another holiday in the wild glens of Scotland like Mrs FoX-cum-Salmon), certain crimes are better left unearthed.

But then, a little later, having miraculously decided to proffer the breast instead, 'By the way, you remember that time with the dustbins out at The Pagoda? Of course you do. It's listening to *Miss X* last night reminded *me* . . . Well, just between you and me and the doorpost,' (Pin always kept *her* idioms neat and correct – none of that fatal gnawing through of membranes which keep us criminally safe from eXposing the cultural crimes of our own unconscious, as Annabel would doubtless have me say. 'Just between you and me and the doorpost, I *did* manage to steal something for you that time.'

My heart missed a beat.

'You know . . .' (entering into the drama of the thing, but with just that slight touch of pitying irritation at what she manifestly took to be the 'infantile narcissism' of it all – Freud on Religion – but, unlike Annabel, would never quite admit)

' . . . when you kept guard by the house while I did the dirty-work up front near the gate.' ('Thief's accomplice.' Must get that in too. In prison slang, I think they call it a 'crow'.)

'I didn't say then in case it was too much of an anti-climaX and you'd be X or think it childish or something . . . Happy Birthday now, anyway.'

And before I knew it, she had handed me, swaddled in a crumpled piece of tissue paper obviously eXplored and regurgitated by Amon on some prior occasion, what else, I ask you, but **'Petrus Borel'**, the old, mulberry-coloured stone paperweight from Miss X's desk in the Study more than thirty years ago! Being misunderstood does *indeed* give magic powers.

Yes, 'Petrus Borel' himself, complete with round, central hole and distinctive markings, and, branded on his left flank (F. *en eXurge*, Mary), the now slightly jaded motto, '*Ad Astra*', I had slaved so hard to emulate all those years – indeed, *still* slave so hard to emulate in an odd kind of way . . .

'Petrus Borel', the Philosopher's Stone! The ancient toad with the starry jewel in its head!

The Pagoda Stone from the Isis Wishing Well!

By then Amon was butting like a bucking bronco at the moon-like surface unveiled for his benefit and even beginning to cast sheep's eyes in my direction too. (According to that more contemporary Bard, the great, blind Borges, one of the judges of the Emperor Shun used to keep a one-horned goat who butted the guilty but refused to attack the wrongly accused. Absurd, I know, but I thought of that. My eXperimental Demon of Analogy on the moral ram/page again.)

'Why, what did you *imagine* it would be?' teased Pin. 'An essay on Walt Whitman,' (the tooth of injustice . . . she's never forgotten, you see), 'a knitted olisbos,' (cheeky thing) 'or a Love Letter swearing she passionately adored you all along? . . . I didn't want to say in front of Bill and Annabel last night, but I really *do* think a pseudonym, sorry, *nom de plume*, would be the best thing!'

'Et tu, Brute,' though slightly more eXcusable since *she's* out to save the family honour, I suppose.

' . . . Something jazzy and alliterative since it's really just a pot-boiler as you said, but with the same kind of . . . oh, I don't know . . . smugly, sorry, triumphantly self-devouring relationship between the two parts as you're lucky enough to have already in "Mary Wolfe". Pride in the nature of the partly self-inflicted, partly self-transcended, purply wound, predator/victim kind of thing. Yes, don't worry, I got that bit about Mary and the sacrificial lamb' (Xt, yes – L. *paschalis* – Pascal and the pass-over lamb, never thought of that before!) 'not that it's difficult, the way you hammer it home. Talk about a lack of trust in the Reader. I suppose you'll be hinting neXt *She* made you like that. Seriously though, that's what you want, isn't it? Vulturous, carrion, rapacious, Prometheus chained to his Rock, and perhaps even by means of your belovèd Greek 'chi', a hidden link with Miss X your, sorry, herself. Let me put on my thinking cap . . .'

(Annabel was right about my sick, contagious 'literary' rhythm: would anyone *really* speak like that? A different attitude to pain, maybe, but, sometimes I think Pin and I are birds of a feather with a single brain. As soon as she spoke, I knew that was *eXactly* what I wanted all along. It's not so much a question of love thy neighbour . . . we *are* each other in a queer kind of way, the wave and the particle both at once.)

By this time Amon had started to scream tyrannically at the interruption of the flow, and my obedient sister disappeared with him at once into the dappled green garden, leaving me to ponder and fondle contritely this strange, oracular child of stone disgorged from the insentient Womb of Time . . . if not from the guilty clock-case of Cronos Himself.

'As you're lucky enough to have already in Mary Wolfe', my foot!

She could have said 'as you're clever enough to eXploit in your own name'. When it comes to the crunch, they're all the same. Always imagining Boodle knows the solution there in his Den before he sets out . . . that just because it actually happened, a tale simply tells what already eXists, when, as I know only too well nowadays thanks to *Miss X*, interpretation is life itself, almost, if you like, an act of love, dear Reader and dear Writer as one in three.

Not that I'm a very good one in three to talk.

After the cornfield episode I had still been pretty miXed up about myself, remember. And no wonder, what with two fully-fledged *human* murders waiting to join the two animal ones under my belt. If only there could be something more solid, more enduring . . . some concrete foundation which would come to save both the Novel and . . .

But now, miraculously, at the eleventh hour: **'Petrus Borel', returned from the dead.**

Would *he* provide the final missing key to the lock if I could only but pluck his stone feathers aright? (More work, Mary. Even in the mouth of the gift-horse itself, those teeth still, that call to arms, that further lavish potlatch yet.)

All I knew for sure so far was that it was *her* stone paperweight come back from the tomb – she whose once fluttering eyelids are weighted down now with stones themselves ('That's how they bury them out there, Lou, you know') and who, like Alcyone to the dead CeyX afloat on the Ocean but this time, of course, the other way round, had sent the wondrous swallows, nightingales, then, to restore my blind sight.

> My heart is like a rainbow shell
> > That paddles in a halcyon sea;
> My heart is gladder than all these
> > Because my love is come to me.

Like the Japanese 'Noh' Theatre, where the puppeteers are deliberately kept visible as part and package of the message of emotion, all is the art of perfect timing in these things.

But at this point we were mercifully interrupted by the noise of heavy, galumphing footsteps almost coming through the floor-boards above (Puss-in-Boots himself, perhaps?), and, whistling like a blackbird – obviously he'd finished writing his paper on *latah* – Bill came sliding cheerfully down the banisters to suggest we all went for a walk. (Pin had already said she wanted to show us the farm where they sometimes go for the goats' milk yoghurt and victoria plums.)

For when we walk, that sense of outside things . . .

So much for that little circle of scuffed earth out there in the middle of the field with its guilty 'X marks the spot'.

Did they notice?

I'm still not sure. Fortunately there had been a lot in the papers just before about strange squares, circles or even celtic-type Xs and mystic mandalas mysteriously appearing in the corn without apparent cause. With any luck they would think it was *that*, as perhaps it was in a way, my little self-branded mandala, radiant black sun out there on the charred ground. Only when a stigma is fully understood . . .

Crossing the stream by the broken bridge where we once saw the mole and the swallow-tail butterfly ('Happy Land', I whispered predictably to Pin), and taking it in turns to carry Amon (why she can't get a push-chair, goodness knows), we reached the spread of comforting dry-stone walls and outhouses which marked the edge of the farm at last.

(Such incredible artistic skill in the placing of all those old stone boulders one on top of the other without cement, sometimes with parenthetical 'windows' for the sheep to jump through. Yet another reason for leaving gaps in the dyking, though, is that, terrified of infinite space, the sheep refuse to jump even quite low walls if they see too much blue sky. 'Walls have ears, Mary lamb, and you never know.')

I was hanging behind a bit now as is my wont, half looking forward to meeting a sheep or a goat in the flesh. The *real* pelt of the *real* McCoy . . .

. . . 'Like those three lovely white goats we saw last summer, remember, Pin?'

. . . Small, neat hooves tapping crisply against the woodwork (thanks to the cloven nature of the foot they can keep their balance on the thinnest of ledges, it seems). Almond-shaped eyes with black, horizontal pupils. Tiny bleats issuing from each of the three pink throats. Smooth, white flanks. Short, twitching tails. (Can't say they *really* look much like that of a fish.) Soft, tufted beards combed each Sunday by the Devil. (Again, for some reason, I felt tears prick my eyes.) Ears like pear-drops. Sweet, warm breath.

No goats here, though.

Only two equine-looking horses (well they would be, wouldn't they?) tied to a railing (Amon seemed strangely agitated for some reason . . . confusing himself with 'Little Hans'?) and a few silly chickens who, whereas they had gone on clucking contentedly in front of the others, scattered in noisy terror at the sight of *me*. What *is* it about us Writers that upsets people so?

A few masticating sheep up by the farmhouse, though, much to my own and Amon's delight, turning to stare at us as we passed, pointed ears pricked like white alsatian dogs, tight woolly curls, brown, boot-button eyes . . .

I was almost enjoying the outing now, trying to forget *Miss X* and the no doubt therapeutically unearthed repressions for a while (the real Miss X I could scarce remember at all by now, almost as if writing about her had blotted her right out), and on a sudden impulse, picked him up and swung him round – Amon, I mean, though goodness knows he felt just about as heavy as a sheep – before bearing him triumphantly aloft on my shoulders, pleased to show Pin that, unlike Miss X (I'm joking, of course), I was not a werewolf who eats children after all.

He was smiling now, fresh and dear in his *pink* woolly jumper. (Pin on the warpath for cultural stereotypes again. If only there were no distortions in the representation of difference in the first place, there'd be no need . . . careful, Mary. This is supposed to be a country walk.)

And having propped him up on the wall of the sheep-pen as on a kind of throne – Daniel in the Lion's Den – we stuck two goose feathers in his downy hair.

Sweet Ram (Egypt. *Amon*), perhaps I *will* gobble you up after all!

'Sometimes I think I love children more than my own life,' I once announced dramatically to Annabel. 'Far too much to bring one into the world' – I thought of Auntie and her 'Vale of Tears' – 'when I'm still so joyfully giving birth to myself.' Miss X, though. Had *she* wanted children? 'You with your plaits and little green . . .': as usual, such a thought had never Xed my mind before. Could there be something about Writing a Novel which, thanks to the ancient craft of stone-walling, pulls the wool from our most sheepish mental habits? Is *that* why people fear us so?

By now we were making our way round the back of a field not yet cut like the ones nearer home.

Barley, obviously.

Those whiskered ears I'd know anywhere. A great Golden Fleece to tempt all Jasons, rippling in the wind like a leopard's skin, etc. etc. It's true my style gets in everywhere.

'The goats are chasing each other,' Pin said almost gently.

'Yes,' I said, 'they are indeed.'

And we eXchanged a smile.

'Ariane, ma soeur . . .' Sometimes I think . . .

But then she knows already. No need to try to put *everything* into words.

What I also refrained from saying ('*Must* you always keep linking everything up all the time?' she and Bill had once complained), was that they used to put stones in the harvest to replace human heads: the heads of all the strangers cut off by the god after they'd been helping to bring in the sheaves. It was Hercules (Herakles?) who finally managed to put an end to such a barbarous custom . . . he who, dressed in a yellow petticoat enslaved to the great Queen Omphale, Xtian name Lydia . . . faithfully wound her knitting-wool.

'Petrus Borel'!

The missing stone in the corn!

Perhaps the last sheaf had come home after all and there would be no more savage sacrifice in the world.

'Petrus Borel'?

Even then, you see, I never thought to ask who *he* was and *why* Miss X had called him that.

No doubt about it . . . for all his visionary, talismanic powers, 'Petrus Borel' had so far elucidated all but himself.

There was one last, precious, lone-wolf sheep to master its terror of infinite space and jump through the gap in the dyking yet.

Annabel had not accompanied us to the farm that morning.

Staying in bed to re-read my manuscript, no doubt. Sometimes these things grow on you a second or even third time round, and especially when each stone is so intricately chiselled and turned.

But when we got in – Amon now re-metamorphosised from cherub to incubus (talk about the seven little kids) and my sister transmogrified in eXchange – we found to our surprise a note on the kitchen table saying she had already left.

The Women's Writing Course, no doubt. Dismembering the nineteenth-century 'Gothic' novel, together with 'Decadence' in the 'Poètes maudits'. (See, I was right, she *had* simply alighted here, flown like the swallows to another clime. They all abandon me in the end.)

Upstairs on my bedside cabinet, a Virgo birthday card, though . . . standing in a field of uncut corn that hermaphroditic-looking Devil from the Tarot marked *Solve et Coagula*. Cloven hoof, female . . . see above for the standard kit. (Obviously still thinks I write under the insignia of Baudelairean 'Damnation'. Perhaps that's even how I've made her imagine poor Miss X herself. But then without turning them into some kind of Frankenstein's Monster, can you ever put *any* mere person in a Book?)

And, pinned inside, the following characteristically lapidary note with, don't you think (I leave you to judge for once), just that slight didactic barb still between the lines:

Dear Wolfie:

Petrus Borel – left somewhat hanging fire, was he not? Name of a nineteenth-century writer called Champavert who raved against the Evils of Society and called himself **'Le Lycanthrope': someone who imagines himself a wolf**. Full moon. Grave-yards. Anointed by the Devil. Savage attacks on the living or digging up corpses and devouring dead flesh. Used to be a certified mental condition: sadistic fantasies, sadomasochism, repressed seXual appetite and so on – though in this case some kind of punitive myth of self born of misanthropic melancholia, no doubt; cf. Ferdinand in Webster's *Duchess of Malfi* which you quote. 'Lycanthrope' = Gr. 'wolf/man', 'werewolf' = ME. 'man/wolf': someone who, the other way round, is imagined to be a wolf turned man. Thought you might make something of the 'Xiasmus' involved (the trope of self-mirroring, by the way!) Everything's grist to a literary magpie like you, including the odd letter from a friend, needless to say. Don't forget the psychoanalytic side, though. Only way sometimes to cut the Gordian Knot . . . Your birthday present this year is Freud's *The 'Wolf Man'*, Pelican edition, which I hid in the bedside cabinet when I came to put my HWB back in your bed. 'Mon petit doigt' tells me you've not read it yet.

Happy Birthday!
Love from Mowgli and Annabel

PS. Waited for you nearly all last night but you never came. We wouldn't have eaten you up, you know!

Petrus Borel, Lycanthrope!
Linking those strange words together like that gave me a shock

of recognition almost more momentous than the return of the actual stone in the flesh. One of those moments composed of centuries, through which we seem to have access to ancestral worlds to crib blatantly from Gérard de Nerval).

So that was '**IT**'!

I was a Lycanthrope!

Mary Wolfe, Lycanthrope!

Lupus in fabula!

All these years, without even knowing the name of the invisible mole on my forehead, abandoned like that to die on the mountainside, **I had imagined myself to be a Wolf!**

No wonder my savage crime in the corn and in the kitchen, tearing poor Mrs X limb from limb . . . No wonder the chickens scattered in terror when I walked through the farmyard (Annabel herself, too, come to that) . . . No wonder all those wolfish puns and jokes which I thought *were* simply wolfish puns and jokes . . . No wonder my obsession with sheep and goats . . . No wonder, disguising my voice as that of a Novelist, I couldn't write a *real* Novel to save my own . . .

The wolf shall find her grave, and scrape it up,
Not to devour the corpse, but to discover
The horrid murder.

Talk about tautology and fear of the unknown!

Clue Seven in the treasure hunt was even *more* right than I thought!

The murderer *and* my own bloodhound now!

Mary Wolfe, Lycanthrope!

The glimpse in the cracked mirror at the eleventh hour of the strange grey phantom they call the 'self' and which holds our very soul – soul, Mary? well no, not in *their* sense – alive and panting in its dark, red jaws.

And the strange thing was, too, that for all the pain of that terrible, self-biting inner name, never did Rumpelstiltskin feel less like stamping his foot through the floor, no, nor never went back with greater Joy, yes, Joy, to dance and mutter round his little flickering fire.

Miss X's name is still unknown, but *mine*, my lambs, is L Y C A N – T H R O P E, wolf/man, seven + four letters, beginning with 'L' for 'Love' and (got your French notebook, Mary?) Latin *lupus*, the Wolf.

Yes, dancing triumphantly round my secret fire in the corn, *my* secret name, my friends, is L Y C A N T H R O P E, he who imagines himself a wolf.

Annabel was wrong, though. I *had* read *The 'Wolf Man'*!

Not that I could remember much about it in those days. I was more concerned with worrying in case she found out I already had it and I hurt her feelings ('child in turn of what dark fears I know not . . .') . . . like that time in the war, when Dad came for the weekend (I was four years old, careful, Mary, cover your traces) and brought me *Little Red Riding Hood*, special copy just for myself, though eXactly like the one . . . Well, Mother and I had just been 'evacuated' (curious phrase, as I said before), and, before I could stop her, horror of horrors (he'll go back to 'The War' and never pick me up and swing me round on his back again), 'She's got it already,' Mother snapped.

('*And does the person know, Mary?*' – Miss X and her embarrassing, potentially painful mistake: funny if it all . . . the whole strange Fairy Tale of Miss X and Mary Wolfe, I mean, sprang from that one tiny . . . But then you can always go back and back and back, searching for the source of the source of the source, sirens howling, digging up corpses – Dad was a fire warden – 'She's got it already', snap, snap, snap.)

Wrong about another little matter too, Annabel.

'*Petrus Borel, le lycanthrope*' was the true-life pseudonym (*soubriquet* 'under the wall', Mary. Got your French notebook?) of someone called Champavert . . . though, just to make matters even more compleX, *he*, PB, the Writer, used his real name, Champavert, as that of his protagonist in a grisly, self-fulfilling tale of suicide. (Must be something about us literary lycanthrope chaps . . . fiction as identity and identity as fiction and all that . . . creating the mask to reveal the mask, determined to frighten ourselves out of our skins . . .)

. . . **'I put it to you, Mary'** (must be the analyst talking . . . Analyst, Annabel, Anna Freud, Anna X – Gr. *ana*, 'back again, anew' – they're all the same, once they've been bitten by the Freudian tsetse fly), 'that in identifying with the powerful rôle model of Miss X in the constitution of the preliminary stage of the super-ego, a certain reversal or, at a pinch, Xiasmus took place . . . that eventually Miss X herself was abolished along with the whole Primal Scene of the imaginary seduction and not so imaginary abandonment, and, as part and birthday-parcel of the predictable defensive splitting, red eye gleaming, jaws flecked with all too invisible blood (you can still see the toothmarks embedded in your catty, self-conscious style), you turned your sharp fangs inwards and . . .'

'You don't mean . . .?'

'Yes, Mary Wolfe. I'm afraid I do. Turned your sharp fangs inwards and *attacked yourself* . . .'

> [. . .] howl'd fearfully;
> Said he was a wolf, only the difference
> Was, a wolf's skin was hairy on the outside,
> His on the inside.

(*The Duchess of Malfi* again, way back with Miss Twee . . . Talk about the present giving birth to the past. Didn't I say she had her uses, like that time with 'Lapis Loquitur' and the old School magazine?)

So that was it!

Lupus in fabula indeed!

Not only had I imagined myself inwardly to be a ravening wolf all those years without knowing it, but shoot me down if I hadn't turned on myself at the same time . . . a wolf where, through fear of their own ravenous appetite (losing Miss X again by hurting her feelings, never mind the inner hairs) the fangs themselves – Wolfgang Amadeus, Wolfgang Amadeus – had inverted themselves and turned back in.

No wonder the ravages of **'IT'**.

No wonder that dream left hanging in the seventh piece (well it would be the seventh, wouldn't it?), where, usurping the place of the Tyrant, the Ogre, the Troll, or, if you like now, the Big Bad Wolf Herself, and with poor Miss P bleating for mercy like the sacrificial lamb on the way to the altar . . .

Miss P, like Miss X, was also myself . . . but myself cut in two like our town by the motorway and begging to be sewn together again!

Let alone all that nonsense about the *influence of bi-seXuality on the OediPUS(s) compleX* in the case of the female homoseXual subject like poor Dora (*Schadenfreude*, Mary, give it a break): about the power of nomenclature, Freud was right . . .

Primitive confusion of the word and the thing, we *are* deeply influenced by our own surnames after all. (Mr Joy in his case, believe it or not.)

And not only by our *sur*names, Mary, Agnus Dei, Maria inviolata, Mother of God!

So-called Xtian names, as well!

In *that* ancient bloodbath of tongue, throat and wing, the Wolf and the Lamb hang together, you know.

EXegesis, eXculpation . . . is there no end to these blinding, refleXive revelations once the dykes of the unconscious fall at last to the seven blasts of their own horned trumpet like the crumbling drystone walls of Jericho?

'Petrus Borel'. The stone in the corn. 'If ever there was a wolf in a mulberry suit . . .'

And *why* had Miss X Xtended him that in the first place . . .?

But of course: Clue *Eight* in the treasure hunt, sign of infinity (and turn the two entwined snakes on the photo frame chasing one another's tails). The answer was already right here on the doorstep, present yet absent, along with all those other cultural stones to pluck:

Loin des peuples vivants, errantes, condamnées,
A travers les déserts courez comme les loups;
Faites votre destin, âmes désordonnées,
Et fuyez l'infini que vous portez en vous!

The Baudelaire poem! 'Les Femmes Damnées'! 'Decadent' and marvellous and 'evil' as ever, coiled there in some dark, unwitting crypt of memory all those years with its poisonous/healing, two-way tongue!

Running, running, condemned, through the deserts in flight from her infinite appetite, she too, Miss X, had imagined herself all these years a ravenous wolf, but a wolf, unlike 'PB', who could never come out of the broom cupboard under the stairs, cured by the sight of its own grey mask . . . (No wonder, then, fearing to escape from her own self-imposed bonds and devour me – Phèdre abhorring her own inner nature – she had finally bound herself more firmly than ever to the terrible mast of the Ship of State.)

A Wolf too oppressed by the criss-X Wolf of Oppression – 'the trope of self-mirroring,' didn't Annabel say somewhat pretentiously – to be able to stand up on her own hind legs like a Female Novelist in order, gnawing through the bonds of prejudice that had so long festered unconsciously inside her, to imagine herself imagining imaginary fangs and look down freely on the back of her own neck.

Not for poor Miss X the wells in the desert she had *tried* so hard to bequeath her 'certain little foX'.

One moment, though.

Annabel's 'PS': 'Waited for you all last night . . .' The proverbial postscript yet again with the sting in the tail.

So *that* was why she'd left!

Annabel, lying there waiting for me patiently all that night, Baudelairean *chevelure*, Mallarméan *ptyX*, Rabelaisian 'Messer Gaster', warm **H**ot **W**ater **B**ottle, Borelian critical tooth and all. Not that . . .

'Come here, Mary' . . .

Annabel (F. *aimable*), waiting for me patiently up there all that night . . . and I far too bent on trying to find out whether or not I was a *HomoseXual* to notice a *real* relationship when the gods deigned to put it my way at last.

'Come here, Wolfie. We wouldn't have eaten you up, you know.'

Annabel had loved me all along.

But what was it she had said in the heart of her demolition job on *Miss X* the previous night?: 'No, Mary. We're *not* ageing pederasts . . . We don't *all* have the demented seX drive of a bat . . .' (Bats don't either, come to that.)

Too late, hélas, for the infinite new possibilities now stretching before me in the finite human form of dearest Annabel herself, at last I realised what I should have known all along:

There is no such thing as *A HomoseXual*.

No such thing as *A HeteroseXual*.

No such thing as *A Bi-seXual* either, come to that.

No such thing as an elementary particle (why, oh why, didn't Miss Tao teach us *that* little piece of Chinese wisdom in physics?), but a great quantum spider's web of inseparable energy patterns (without the Big Bad Boodle in the middle, needless to say) where, wave and particle both at once . . . (Careful, Mary, is this the place?)

No such thing as a Pack of Men and Women, anyway, waiting to eXclude us from the fold.

No Pack.

No Club.

Nobody. No body(?).

No such thing as a human identity fiXed to the flagpole prior to its own rebirth . . .

EXucontian! EXcalibur!

That which was not before it was itself!

In fighting so rebelliously against the poison of labels (and – be honest, Mary – risking not standing up to be counted at all?), *I* was the one who had tried to discover a buried essence . . . that from which I thought I had but to scrape away the earth with my nails of pure anguish (Mallarmé's *onyX*) to be able . . .

Generalisation, too!

Either/or!

The sheep and the goats!

In discovering and admitting **I never really liked Miss X** – *the first Miss X, I mean – at all*, I wasn't betraying after all the Cause of the Victim, the Outlaw, the Rebel: *each of us is different, unknown, eXceptional*, women included, just as I'd always thought we were.

Far from educating me to the Olympian heights of the 'HomoseXual' to which rebellious status I so proudly aspired in order to escape call-up to prejudiced Enemy Ranks, *Miss X had spoiled me for the* real *love of women* – certain women, not to put too fine a point on it, Annabel herself – *which had been my birthright all along.*

'Too much imagination, I put it to you, Mary. Those great eyes of yours . . .'

Not enough, Miss X, not nearly enough!

Rave, rave, against the prior decree!

Only when you've been the whole damned hog of your own creation . . . only when you've taken to re-humanising eXcess . . . only when you've once more confused the word and the thing, can you throw off the animal mask at last and start to live and die in your own separate skin.

And besides – give a dog a bad name – such a splendid poem, the Baudelaire, all the same.

With such a lucky Wolf's Stone under my old School hat, perhaps I'd end up the true *Wolf Woman* yet!

'Oh, by the way,' I said to Bill later as he made the lunch. (More goats' milk yoghurt, from the morning's walk to the farm, and the rest of the plums in a kind of compote.) 'I don't suppose you've ever seen a stone like this before? A stone with these strange little markings, I mean?'

(Modest, clever, chirpy, reliable, kind – nothing very 'evil' about *him*. 'What a dear little chap I am,' he had even once said of himself – that wise love which risks including its own unknown powers to receive.)

'Fire marks,' he replied like a shot. **'It's a pot-boiler stone**. For putting in the flame and boiling water . . . before they had cooking-pots and the vessel might have cracked.'

'Petrus Borel', the Pot-Boiler stone! Corner-Stone of Miss X itself!

The oracle *had* already spoken, then. Back there in the cornfield the previous night, when, in order to turn the wolf from my own back door at last, I had *finally bitten the hand that never quite fed me*, destroyed Miss X and boiled her very flesh, love and hatred, revenge and catharsis all in one.

PB the 'lucky' stone with the hole in the middle, come job-trotting back like a mulberry-coloured boomerang to amaze and delight me with the power of my own unconscious throw!

PB The Philosopher's Stone in the bulrushes. *Solve et Coagula*. Herne the Hunter with his pestle and mortar, analysis and synthesis all in one!

PB the precious carbuncle from the grate, no, desk in the Study, scalded by the tears of Niobe herself!

PB The Wolf Stone, the Delphic Omphalos, the Wolf's Head (ME. 'outlaw'), returned from his fiery, fasting rituals in the desert (dustbin, then) to teach the limits of fear itself!

PB the precious Boundary Stone at last!

Annabel was wrong again: it wasn't Miss X I was angry with. Miss X had turned up trumps after all.

And like Cronos disgorging the children who had tried to depose him, I took back my stone offspring and wrapped him up carefully once more in his swaddling clothes, vowing never again to let him out of my sight.

Here he sits smugly before me on my desk neXt to the new word-processor, looking for all the world as if he's found the eliXir of immortal life.

'Come on now, Lou. You made up that corny bit about the murder in the kitchen,' said Pin, when, months later, I eventually got round to reading the relevant piece. 'Just because I said the end wasn't all that neat and you needed to make us fall on each other's swords.'

'Thank you,' I said gratefully, foolishly pulling Capricorn's left leg this time as I spoke.

(What? Is *he* back again too? Surely not. On the other hand 'Une telle victime . . .' – Agamemnon in *Iphigénie* called upon to sacrifice his daughter – is worth the gods' asking a second time.)

'Perhaps I did . . . invent the murder, I mean. It was either that or suicide, you see.'

Had I invented it, though, that terrible scene in the little kitchen with Mrs X slumped gasping for breath in her chair, finally to succumb to a fully-fledged angora heart attack? (A patient of Freud's always said 'agoraphobia' instead of 'angina' because of the latter's unavoidable rhyme with 'vagina' – hope I wasn't getting a bit like that.)

Would I have abused a poor old woman living alone like myself in a flat?

The strange thing was that after my strange, cannibalistic ritual in the cornfield when so many symbols had jumped off the page like Cézanne's golden apples (apples *and* oranges, as it turns out), I didn't really *know* any more.

It's scarcely light in the kitchen now
Close to the glass the young birch proffers
Brooms of gold that someone scarce perceives
Despaired despite by so much dearth of blazoning
Come dusty one
What do you wish to let them speak to me? Not
Colours of autumn, that's for sure
(Who wants to *hear* of russet, ochre, peach?)
Nor yet this dream of doubt within (the ancient creature who
                                        would keep
Words honest and in line with Self is all tentacles
Webs without structure, yarn upon the shore)
Poems eXist though
Misting the glass with living breath
All wish and bone I'm talking to one now . . .
Guinea-fowls, words, howls, spells,
Poems are spells for turning trees to wolves
Poems it seems are spells in search of song

How easy, in any case, for the smugly crowing creation of order
– everything tied up with a neat, stone full-stop – to lead us to

forget that precious chaos ('*âmes désordonnées*') from which the very search itself . . .

Is *that* why Pin is so loath to write a Novel? Is *that* why *Miss X* isn't finished even yet?

The Fourteenth Piece

'Suddenly the window opened of its own
accord, and I was terrified to see that some
white wolves were sitting on the big walnut
tree in front of the window. There were
siX or seven of them. [. . .] In great terror,
evidently of being eaten up by the wolves, I
screamed and woke up.'
(*The 'Wolf Man'*, Freud)

. . . mais, ô chiens qui hurliez sur les plages,
Après tant de soleils qui ne reviendront plus,
J'entends toujours, du fond de mon passé confus,
Le cri désespéré de vos douleurs sauvages!
('Les Hurleurs', Leconte de Lisle)

There's a coyote howling to the moon
above . . .
('Ole Faithful')

      I had been leaving the visit to the actual School building
for later, as I said, though just how *much* later, I can't really be sure.
  It must have been well after the deaths of the mother and
daughter and before I gave my reading in the cottage, stupidly
convinced as I was then that my Novel was complete. On the other
hand Bill was already away on his sabbatical year *latah* and the
cannibal dance of the Kwakiutl Indians in the flesh – he'll be biting
himself to pieces neXt.)
  Was it really *before* the reading? Before the reading but after the
writing? After the reading but before the writing? Before the . . .
  Dear Reader, I can't go on holding your paw for ever. You must
finally learn to be your own detective, whistle your own
bloodhounds, harness your own horses, track me down like
Hippolyte with your own impetuous Racinian dragons, your own
indomitable Bull from the Sea.

It was Xmas Eve.
  That I do know.

And for once real, traditional, Xmas-card snow . . . spreading its furry white pelt across the hockey-pitch and generously decorating the already diminishing curtain of aspens with fluffy white baubles as if they were so many Xmas trees (none at all left nowadays, even of the new lot, Pin told me recently when she came to deliver my new walking-frame) . . . there, where ('*l'école buissonnière*, Mary. Got your French notebook?'), leaving poor Miss P to hold forth about the sheep and the goats, we escaped together to The Wilderness – halcyon days indeed – so many, many years ago . . . there where, way back even further before my path Xed with Miss X's at all, 'We three', Dad and Pin and I,

In scarves and wellingtons, trod the crisp bracken,
Made our predictions, called to our dogs,
Familiar trees and childhoods tangled.
All journeys start here
The happy, living roots
Of all our possibilities . . .
(Catherine Wolfe)

(Pin's first and just about only poem as far as I know, but then she sings like a nightingale.)

Xmas Eve.

How many think of the infant Dionysus, ripped to pieces and put together again like Osiris? And, now that our old house had been devoured by an unsuspected geological fault under the road ('I never want you to be ashamed of your home, Mary.'), Pin and I staying at The Unicorn – yes, really! – a brash hotel just off the marketplace looking out on to a dark yard with a criss-X of barbed wire round the top of the wall ('now is the ivy rent upon the holly') and full of alcoholic businessmen. Hardly 'A mon seul désir'. Enlivened none the less, though ('Pecker up, Mary, must keep positive'), by the two little Xmas stockings we had secretly smuggled in for each other, mine blue and hers scarlet, identical Chinese BoX-puzzles poking cryptically from the top.

' 'Twas the night before Xmas, when all through the house . . .'

Xmas Eve. (How dear Mother always hated us to use that crude-looking abbreviation, remember, and how guilty I feel to have to use it now in the name of Art.) Would an agèd Dora have been listening somewhere to the King's College carols on the radio? I suddenly felt curious to get to know her one day, always assuming she were still alive. (She was not.)

194

Christmas Eve (just once if I must, then) with the smell of December-wet bark and steeping leaves, just a fraction of the year past the winter solstice . . . mysterious, still turning-point of wolfish – no, that's Zeus – *friend* of wolf, Apollo, the Sun. Oh those generous, warm, red firesides of home with the radiant, little hushed tree in the corner – now *there's* a pre-Xtian pine tree for you – piled high with the snows of yester-year.

Don't worry, though. Not mere nostalgia, otherwise I'd never have brought you here.

UneXpectedly eXcited, if somewhat anXious that the new caretaker might intrude at any moment on this clandestine, middle-aged breaking of bounds (no longer Mr Shepherd-Fenrir by this time, of course), I had waited patiently until nearly twilight ('*Entre chien et loup*, Mary . . .'), and here I was slinking nearly as stealthily as a wolf up what I surmised to be the narrow path to the side of the broad driveway, followed doggedly by a stray white cat . . . phantom spirit miraculously sprung from the snowfields, its coat the colour of the ground in the moonlight as if they were but of a single weave.

(No, *not* Polythemus-Raminagrobris this time, thank god. More like Annabel's Mowgli from the picnic hamper, though so thin and gaunt that, like Dora herself that time at the funeral, you could almost see his fragile bones through his coat.)

White cats, white lies, white bones, white wolves . . . Here I go again. The same old web of symbols still. No wolves in *these* snows needless to say. In any case, according to Auntie (the thought really sticks in my craw, as they say), one of our ancestors shot the last wolf in Britain: 1707 – well it would be, wouldn't it – in some wild Scottish glen. Not much sense of family honour there. Had I ever thought of the *real* ones out there in the Arctic snow-fields, any more than . . .

The Wolf. L. *canis lupus*, related to the dog. Fury due to hunger and savagery both (Ovid's *Metamorphoses* again). The only animal apart from Man (sic) to kill for more than food alone. Or is that too part of a literary myth? Romulus and Remus after all, not to mention Mowgli – Kipling's this time – and the Wild Boy of Aveyron, who paid for lupine hospitality in his case by *losing* not finding *his* tongue. Maybe they're really the kindest and shyest thing out. (Careful, Mary. The guilt of the would-be victim still. Howling with the wolf instead of talking with the Tyrant, treating the 'Other' as yourself.) Naturally a pack animal, though, so why so lone? Perhaps until you learn to separate within . . . No wonder poor Sigmund imagined she was a Man on a lead dreaming she was once more free as a dog. No wonder the werewolf, in another life . . .

Now then, Mary. Attend to your work. Yes, Miss Twee. Yes, Miss Hilbert. Yes, Miss Ramsbotham. Yes, Miss Tao. Yes, Miss Bull . . . Yes, Miss X, you silly old cow! (I was joking, of course.)

Everything looked sparkling and mysterious in the lamplight (this orange, fluorescent kind already by then) . . . the familiar brick contours of the building softened and distorted as if in one of those dreams – what else *is* a Novel, I sometimes ask myself? – where you know you're asleep but still can't bark loud enough to wake yourself up, and deepening the already intense state of enchantment I could trigger so readily even then – that precious silence in which the mind and its object become almost one.

A few tell-tale touches of scarlet virginia creeper (in December, Mary? Must be the lamplight), poked through the furry white shroud round the window of the Study, which I half eXpected to open of its own accord with a cheerful 'Hello, Mary. Nice weather for ducks'.

Why hadn't I jumped right in through the glass? Did I fear like Freud's 'Wolf Man' that, unwittingly true to the sharp-bladed 'X' of *her* coded future *nom de plume*, poor Miss X would take her scissors and cut off my grey tail . . . later to recognise me by its tell-tale absence when I climb the Pagoda Tree that night outside her window with my stag's-head uniform and try to stare in at her in bed without her pelt? With true werewolves it's the other way round, of course, and the witch who was shot as a cat one night is found to have an eXactly similar wound neXt day.

We are all of us naked inside our clothes, dear Reader. Even *you* along with the rest. How I pity you sitting out there behind the mask of your striped pyjamas – white flannel nightdress, then – waiting like me to be shot of it all, to run, to run, through the glens, through the mountains, though the glittering snow-fields . . . (Patience, Mary. Not yet, not yet.)

Yes, Fairy Tale with a difference, *The 'Wolf Man'*, n'est-ce pas?

A boy called 'PS', no, 'SP' in his case (moving to think of a real, unknown person whose dreams and struggles have become part of our own) has a terrifying dream in which his bedroom window opens of its own accord to reveal siX or seven wolves sitting on the branches of the walnut tree outside his bedroom window and develops, not surprisingly, an eXtreme anXiety hysteria as a result – animal phobia in fact. (I know what you're thinking: poor Miss X and the white alsatian dog.)

Indeed, according to the Big Bad Sigmund Himself (careful Mary. They'll think you're out to get him along with all the rest – Fairy Tale with a difference, didn't you say?), the dream in this case represents the transposition of the boy's, SP's, repressed wish to copulate with, let's face it, his own poor father – a wish that succumbed to repression and re-appeared as phobia because of its unacceptable implications: *Castration and Femininity* (sic, sic, sic)!

(So much for *The 'Wolf Man'*, Annabel's somewhat waspish birthday present – well, didn't you think so? – along with her note and the key to 'PB'. Never *really* sure whether I'd read it before or not, I've just started to get my teeth into it – Wolfgang Amadeus – and find to my surprise that Xmas was *his*, the 'Wolf Man's', birthday too. No wonder, with only one set of presents to open, *he* ended up confusing himself with Xt. Strange Annabel thought to recommend *him* though. Why not the 'Wolf *Woman*', come to that? So many twists and Xs in these Oedipal things, no wonder I don't always know whether I'm a dog or a cat.)

White wolf in the walnut tree or not – soon you are bound to find me staring in secretly through *this* window, just as I did at the empty Pagoda, 'voyeur' here too, of nothing but ghosts.

But first, almost burying myself alive in an uneXpected drift outside the cloakroom (Clue Seven in the treasure hunt, remember, pinned to the peg beneath Mary Wolfe's old School hat), I struggled round to the back of the building to see what I could of the old assembly hall ('The handbell, Mary. She wants the handbell'), stage of so many dramas of yore.

How easy to kid oneself one heard, bleating still from the familiar platform, the voice of poor Miss P with its trembling, annual query, 'But how shall this be, seeing I know not a man?' (Not that . . . Times have changed, Miss P, you know.) Or indeed (pace Annabel), the relatively deep and gruff, no, in Public metallic voice of Miss X herself, declaiming *eX cathedra* from the same empty pulpit, the grand biblical finale to my quest:

> . . . though your sins be as scarlet, they shall be as white as snow; though they be red like crimson, they shall be as wool.

(Isaiah 1.18)

– not the first time the Great Book had lent itself to the subversive purposes of my personal Odyssey (Little Red Riding Hood and the virginia creeper?), I no doubt smiled wisely to myself, followed, as it usually was, by our lusty chorus of St Patrick's Breastplate or other such melodious eXhortation to war.

(St Patrick, by the way, every seventh year at about this month, no comment, is said to have bestowed upon a certain race in Ireland the doubtful privilege of becoming wolves. *Real* wolves, that is – 'Who wants to *hear* of russet, ochre, peach?' – not mere would-be *HomoseXual*, dog-in-a-manger nineteenth-century lycanthropes like me. Oh those bloodthirsty patriarchal Xtians and their obsessive Holy Grail again. 'Opposites meAt in the sado-sublime', to re-work one of Annabel's more successful savage tags on the theme.)

'Mary and the Child She-Boar', 'And the wolf shall dwell with the lamb . . . and the suckling child shall play on the hole of the asp . . .': how vigorously we had giggled at this wild, apocryphal young piglet sent to charm us by the Circean spells of verbal misprision, not to mention this precocious Rabelaisian ribaldry . . . our lovely silver aspens by the hockey-pitch quivering but the more subtly in return, yea, more subtly than any beast of the field that the Lord God hath made to go on its belly, eXcept, of course, that serpent of serpents, *Woman herself*.

And still I could hear us singing so clearly in there . . . carols this time . . .

Adam lay y-bounden, y bounden in a bond,
Four thousand winters thought he not too long . . .
Nay had the apple taken been . . .

– our thin, sweet voices piercing now my ageing heart as they must have done Miss X's too ('You and your plaits with the little . . .'), whether or not her real object was me.

But, Ancient Child She-Boar in person, here I come back again now as we knew I would: slipping and sliding over my tell-tale wolf's tracks in the reverse direction (deeper than a dog's, they say, and with the two back paws fitting neatly in the prints of the front ones), drawn by the magnet of the Study window itself. (Windows, mirrors, mirrors, windows. About Xiasmus Annabel was surely right.) And peering through the glass with the help of the lamplight behind me, notice with mingled indifference and uneasiness that the old leather-topped desk, half buried in a veritable snow of white Xmas cards, is at a different angle, pointing to the left instead of the right.

Obviously the work of the new Headmistress ('Happy Xmas to Ms Car . . .', *the Carbuncle*! I could hardly embrace the momentous thought at first): her own array of sharp pencils and, by then, of course, biros, bristling truculently neXt to a small, neat type-, no, word-processor (*Crash Course in Pascal* perched on top of it like a horrid sick pun), and her own vulgar, glass paperweight glowering like an angry yellow watch-dog-cum-carbuncle where should have reigned in ancient stony splendour 'Petrus Borel' – he who sits smugly on my *own* desk now, as you know, holding down the thirteen previous pieces of the manuscript of *The Wolf Woman*, as it will now be called, if only to prevent its dazzling white pages from flying like nightingales into thin, thin air.

The Carbuncle, though. I ask you!

Just for a second the old sharp tooth of jealousy overcame even my sense of political jubilation that someone eXpelled for 'indecent behaviour' could be reinstated like that at the scene of the crime: the Rebel *and* the Outlaw (Wolf's Head! Wolf's Head!), climbing like a female Novelist to the very top of the Lighthouse Tower!

Admire, too, that self-respecting 'Ms', there where, unlike *Mr* X at the boys' school (jealous, Mary? – the Xmas party), you-know-who had to labour all those years under the banner of 'Miss' – treble-headed Roman hounds to fend off in her case since 'Spinster', 'Lesbian', 'Blue-stocking' all in one. Not that *she* wanted to marry anybody but Nobody, of course. I see it all now.

All those millions of Xmas cards, too (millions, Mary? They always say the wolf is bigger than it is). Just as popular as before. Was there another Mary Wolfe with little green bows to need taming too? No, of course not. We're not *all* 'ageing pederasts' (Gr. 'lover of boys'). People are different, as I said.

The settee with the frieze of Odysseus is in just the same place, though. I can see a corner of it quite clearly in a fluorescent pool of lamplight, faded and threadbare but still *there* all the same. Inanimate objects outliving human flesh. And, of course, it *would* be, wouldn't it, the Cave of the Cyclops . . . Odysseus clinging for dear, dear life under the great pot-belly of the ram . . .

'Nay had the apple taken been . . .': the Cave of Oppression itself, I suppose, though, for all its mysterious griefs and pains, 'Je le ferais encore si j'avais à le faire', I would do it all again, if I had to, you know. If it hadn't been for Miss X, after all, would I be talking to you now?

('The once proud face contorted and unrecognisable now with emotion, she is listening, remember, to the wild, eXquisite voices of the mysterious Sirens . . . bewitched, enslaved, hungry for more and more music, while the rest of the crew, their ears sealed in advance against such terrifying beauty, toil over the oars as previously instructed, devotedly immune to her cries for release. Notice how the prior command takes precedence over all later ones. *That* is the one to remain imprinted for ever. *That* is the voice they follow, like new born geese, to the ends of the earth.')

It was then, standing as if bewitched in all that dumb whiteness, listening to the silent, siren voices of the past, that, with that old lust for Romantic self-dramatisation (Annabel was right on that point too), I knew I had to make some cypher, some mark on it all outside the Novel, tooth for tooth, breath for breath, if only to. . . oh, I don't know . . . call the tune on the site of the loss? The final remnants of superstition, I suppose.

At first I thought of simply writing in the snow, idly drawing on the virginal white page with my finger as if with a pen or feather, testament of a mute Mallarméan swan.

It seemed far too impermanent, however.

I looked around for a stick or something.

Nothing. Nobody. Earth hard as iron. Water like a stone.

No matter, though. My nails, pure onyX, were still unusually long and sharp in those days with hysterically repressed anguish, sorry, anger, as you know. (Many a true word spoken in bluff. Wolf's Bane, Mary. **H**airy **W**olf's **B**ane still.)

And, scraping away the final vestments of snow and frozen creeper, with shameless disrespect for the defacement of school property, I boldly inscribed on the painted window-ledge (remember the workmen during our first kiss?):

MISS X AND MARY WOLFE

followed by what more appropriate hieroglyph than our old, multi-purpose motto, '*Ad Astra*', branded on the jaded flank of 'PB' just as that little St Andrew's 'X', its outstretched limbs in every tree, will doubtless be found branded on my heart – that is, as I said, if they find me anywhere. (No faithful Mary Wolfe to eXhume *my* bones, when I die).

There in the snow-fields with Nobody to witness but the phantom white cat, the full moon and the glittering stars:

Miss X and Mary Wolfe 'Come Out' at last.

The love that dares to speak its name?

In joining our names together like that in Public – well, almost – I had broken at last the pledge of secrecy between us, cracked the last ice of the terrible interdict, broken the last taboo on naming the god.

Already well sewn up by that time in her wall, Miss X could scarcely 'get the sack' like Miss Hilbert now!

Nor do I have to tell you that above us shone out in all its glory, Capella, the goat star (Capella, Mary, at that time of year? Well, if not Capella, the Seven Little Goat Stars at the very least, vulgar Spanish name for the Pleiades, and, if it eXists, the Northern X)... her own Tragic Struggle recognised and rewarded at last by the gods, together with those two great rampant constellations Lupus, the Wolf, hunger, and Corvus, the Crow, spiritual thirst. Wolf, bird, hunger, thirst, it's not every day a lycanthrope can raise a page to the flowery stars.

PS. It was that very same night, back there in my none too broad single bed in The Unicorn, that the window overlooking the dark little back-yard with the criss-X of barbed wire suddenly opened of its own accord and, bold as the most robust of nineteenth-century literary vampires, dressed in a distinctly wolfish nightcap and white flannel nightdress like the phantom grandmother in *Little Red Riding Hood*, **Miss X leapt from the walnut tree outside the window (in The Unicorn, Mary?) where she'd crouched motionless for so many years staring in from the shadows, and entered my dreams for the first and last time.**

With mutual fervour – 'Come here, Mary', 'Come here, Miss X' – obviously she'd mistaken my tears for kisses – we pulled each other down on the little turret bed amongst the swaying branches and *fucked and fucked the whole damned night, skin, blood, bone and breast and all*, as Annabel in good old Anglo-SaXon language would say. ('SiX letters *beginning* with 'f' this time, from L. *futo*, 'to have conneXion with a woman' – Oh well.')

Father Xmas entering the Nursery at twilight?

Little Red Riding Hood in bed with the Wolf?

Like all good Freudian Xmas presents, the best dreams always unwrap themselves.

Ta tête sur m/a nuque pèse, tes canines
entaillent m/a chair au plus sensible, [. . .] j/e sens tes
poils toucher m/es fesses à hauteur de ton clitoris,

tu m/e grimpes, tu m//arraches la peau des griffes de
tes quattre pattes, [. . .] il vient un moment où
tout enfiévrée tu m/e prends sur ton dos m/a louve
m/es bras autour de ton cou m/es seins m/on ventre
appuyés à ta fourrure m/es jambes t'enserrant les
flancs m/on sexe sautant contre tes reins, tu te mets
à galoper.

Monique/Wittig: *Le Corps Lesbien*.

It was the Missing Fourteenth Piece. The lost phallus of the
embalmed Osiris, my foot. Isis making love to the body of the dead.
The very same paperback with the phantom white cat cover I had
seen sticking from the rucksack along with PB's 'Champavert,
Contes Immoraux' when I went up to put the HWB in her bed.

Another's voice, hélas, maybe, but at last, at last, like Miss X
herself that time with Nobody in the little secret flat behind the
Musée de Cluny, I, Mary/Wolfe, had given tongue . . . given
tongue *a tergo* on another she-wolf's back! (not that I'd really *want*
to write like that).

**PS. Annabel and I are living together for seven months of
the year now**, by the way.

Just like Amanda Carbuckle and Miss Hilbert. (What became of
her, I wonder? Devoured by that new word-processor in the Study,
no doubt.) **Just like Bill and Mary Wolfe**. Just like . . . Well, just
like an ordinary relationship, damn it. Walks in the countryside,
coming down to breakfast like something the dog's brought back
from the cornfield, writing my *real* novel while she prepares me my
goats' yoghurts and vegetable stew (but I thought you said you
lived alone and used a walking-frame, now, Mary?), changing her
post-modernist library books at Boots, and picking up poor
Mowgli together from the vet's.

As George Sand said (now *there's* a useful pseudonym), and Paul
Valéry after her, the only thing in life worth having is that which is
contrary to life itself. Friendship, memory, art, love . . .

Da, da, da, da.

The gaudy, blabbing, and remorseful day
Is crept into the bosom of the sea,
And now loud-howling wolves arouse the jades
That drag the tragic melancholy night;

Who with their drowsy, slow, and flagging wings
Clip dead men's graves, and from their misty jaws
Breathe foul contagious darkness in the air.
(Shakespeare – *Henry the SiXth* – who else?)

'Why mathematics, Lou? Isn't that a bit remote?'

Despite Pin's hysterical anXiety phobias about flying (perhaps like the shape-shifting Melusine or that foXy thing we heard barking in the field by the cottage, she fears she'll turn into a bird and fly away for good), she and I and Annabel were on a plane together (Pan Airways). Let's just say near Taormina on the Plain of Catania, known to the Greeks as the Laestrygonian or Cannibal Fields and thought by some to be the source of the StyX.

Flying to Sicily to see the tomb, of course.

You knew I would.

I told you we literary lycos have to follow things right through to the bitter end and even farther, digging up our own graves, sirens howling, frantically seeking the source of the source. And besides, don't they say the murderer always goes back? Look at our ancient werewolf, Seth.

It was the Easter break, or, if you like, the vernal EquinoX again.

For Pin and Annabel anyway. Leaving Bill with my half share of the housework now as well as his own, I wrote all the time in those days – my Tragedy book – if only to kill off the need to write at all. (Patience, Mary. Not yet, not yet.)

'Well, it may seem odd,' I replied as calmly as possible given the horripilant eXperience of being millions of feet up in thin air (you flying-foXes can speak for yourselves, we wolves can't *stand* having our feet more than a few inches off the ground, you know)

' . . . it may seem odd, but ever since reading the first part of all this aloud, I've been groping about for some kind of *Theory* (careful Mary – is this the place?) which, less concrete than a pebble, but in some ways more reliable, would suddenly bring the whole Novel into focus with a bang by accounting for the marvellous process of the cure itself. And by "cure" – transference or metamorphosis if you prefer . . .' (Annabel's hackles had begun to rise again predictably all along my spine)

'I . . . simply mean being able to forget Miss X completely along with "IT" ' (the plane gave a lurch preparing for landing near the cemetery, a bit like *Treasure Hunt* on TV – Pin need not have worried: I have been known from the corner of an eye)

. . . 'and being able to *choose* my own identity perhaps for the very first time in my life' . . . (and here confident enough by then to risk a ghoulish stereotype, I squeezed Annabel's left hunker salaciously like a voyeuristic 'male' reader just between the top of her buttoned gardening boots and gray flannel skirt. It's not the difference between the seXes, but the difference between individual beings that counts, as she knows.)

They both looked blank as a virgin page.

Pin with her eyes tight shut into the bargain (F *par dessus le marché*, 'over the marketplace'), clutching her safety-belt like grim death, poor fool. (Along with 'PB', I was clutching mine too, so I should know.)

She was *still* hot on the trail of finding me a suitable *nom de plume*, by the way. Something which would suitably eXhibit the meaning of the Novel while safeguarding the family honour, as we said. Never mind the gruesome Murder of Miss (and Mrs) X, perhaps she feared *she'd* be the last Wolfe shot in Britain yet. 'Oh, and Lou,' she had just reminded me with a somewhat sarcastic wink, 'you could always put on the fly-leaf "the characters in this novel are all purely fictional", needless to say.'

'It's to do with variables and invariants,' I continued gravely with an eye to keeping our minds off this other you-know-what, noisily backfiring on me even as I spoke. (I always feel personally responsible for the safety of bicycles, wheelchairs, aeroplanes, walking-frames and things.)

'Having, unlike Dad, developed a near phobia about algebra at School (Miss Hilbert and the Carbuncle, needless to say), at last I've begun to understand that if **X** is a constant variable representing the unknown (all those different things I made her stand for over the years), then I, Mary Wolfe (call me '**Y**' if you like) provided the controls. My own projecting process was the constant invariant ($\mathbf{X} = \mathbf{Y}$).'

Pin yawned like a tomb, though it could be lack of oxygen, and Annabel looked decidedly pained as if she'd smelt a whiff of false 'universal consciousness' again. (No good eXpecting sheepish acquiescence in these things. You have to eXperience them at first hand, remembering accordingly to treat the Other as an unknown quantity in the process of learning . . . neither fish, fowl nor cloven hoof . . . living anomaly like yourself.)

'Then, armed with this basic notion of transformation . . . psychological transformation I mean, of course . . . *what is to prevent me from eventually hijacking the projective or selective principles* ("**Z**"), and, always along the same abscissa (aXis of symmetry??) making "her", Miss "**Y**" (a gift has a reciprocal debt, after all), feed back different lucky stones to me in turn . . .? (**Z (Y) = X**)' ('Mary Wolfe's mathematics leaves much to be desired': if only Miss Hilbert could have seen me now, perhaps she'd have wanted to live with *me* too!)

Never mind a flying-foX (Annabel's Gothic fruit-bat accusation obviously still smarts), they were looking at me by this time as if I were a total lunatic, Nietzsche's madman come down from the mountains dressed like a wolf in a mulberry suit.

The Imagination, was what I meant in a way, I suppose, though put like that, it looks, as it sounded then, so tame and uneXciting. More like a sack of italicised old grain in a musty potting-shed than a golden panther's skin etc. dancing in the wind . . .

'Seriously though,' (as if it all wasn't earlier) 'this could apply to *all* our mental life . . . like a kind of constant, do-it-yourself therapy modelled on the interactive nature of eXperience without the dangerous Poppy Morpheme of Religion to confuse the brain and block the eXploratory freedom of creative desire.'

Pegasus gave another violent, backfiring cough eXactly like a plane about to blow up.

'Yes. How's this . . . **the theory of the Xiasmus or self-devouring criss-X** . . . a universal principle for creative change and refleXive, self-eXculpating liberation from the petrified myths of enmity, dominance and self-fearing homophobic aggression, set in action in my case (here's the true rub at last) **by the self-devouring criss-X of WRITING ITSELF!**' (One up on the *OediPUS(s) compleXXXX* any day since capable of cutting the Gordian knot by accounting for its *own* two-way metamorphosis into the bargain. We literary lycanthropes have X-ray eyes it seems, bent on penetrating substances normally totally opaque and impervious to light. No wonder *I* didn't need the analyst.)

'Xt, Lou,' cried Pin urgently. (I thought for one precious split second she'd heard what I said and was having some rejuvenating post-metaph**Y**sical crisis or something.)

' "M" for Mary is really "W" upside down! It stung me like a wasp between the eyes when the plane did a somersault just now.'

I didn't say, so as not to hurt her feelings, but I'd seen it already, along with 'God/Dog', 'Pan/Nap', 'PS/SP', 'Wolf/Fowl' (well, nearly), 'EXIT, IT/EX' and, hélas, the close structural affinity between my brilliant and totally self-taught Theory of 'Xiasmic metamorphosis' just now and Pascal's lack-sap fail-safe wager of the eXistence of immortal life. ('No harm in believing, Mary. Nothing to prove things either way.') *Structural* affinity only though, thank god. **The meAt of the wager was very different indeed, as I was soon to have confirmed in a VERY BIG WAY.**

But before I could eXpound my previous argument any further we were all gritting our variably sized fangs – Wolfgang Amadeus – for the crucial moment of landing, a little way up the brilliant snake of the coast. All eXcept Annabel who adores risks. *Amor fati*. Overcome the sheep inside yourself. *There's* the true gamb(ol)ling goat in our midst.

By now we were entering the actual cemetery, Annabel smoking heavily as usual and Pin and I surreptitiously licking Neapolitan ice-cream from the beach while looking about anXiously for the right piece of wall. Funny if we couldn't find it after coming all this way! (Not that it would matter for the other two . . . mainly here just for the ride on my back, so to speak. By a strange coincidence, the same rented villa where Miss X so 'nobly' took Miss P on *her* Easter holidays, all those many full moons ago.)

One of those fascinating but hideously cluttered cemeteries full of massive crucifiXes (don't remind me), portly angels and pious marble doves . . . the coffins presumably sealed up in those deep, sinister walls on all four sides of us bristling with millions of little name plaques. ('That's how they bury them out there, Lou, you know.')

Pine trees, though.

Even more shaggy, rich and resinous than the ones back home. Creature of the forests, I took to them at once.

'Entre les pins palpite, entre les tombes . . .': pine trees pulsing over the Temple roof of the shimmering sea, resplendent bitch guarding its flock of white stone sheep . . . isn't there a famous poem on the theme . . .? Can't for the life of me think who wrote it, though.

(Albeit, thanks to *Miss X*, a hundredfold sharper than it was in my youth, my phenomenal memory seemed to have turned blunt as a carving-knife ever since entering the cemetery . . . there where, as if miraculously to compensate, all siX other senses, taste in particular, suddenly became as keen and sharp-toothed as the wolves of superstition, if not the winds of Man's ingratitude.)

Sicily. If not where burning Sappho loved and sang, then at least fabled seat of the Festival of '*I Morti*', centred on the very Rock from which Demeter is alleged to have cast herself to reach Persephone in the Shades below.

On many of the sepulchres at this time of year you find stalks of wheat tied with little red *and* green bows, an ancient ceremony going right back to the ancient vegetation rites of Adonis, well Osiris then . . . that crucial X-ing point in human history when, eschewing a mild, lone life of lettuces, pine needles and poisonous ivy, Man left all fours and took to hunting in savage, carnivorous packs, slaughtering and roasting, if not boiling his innocent prey (the cornfield – don't remind me – I feel so ashamed) . . .

. . . while on the evening of jolly old Good Friday, a waXen effigy of the dead Xt looking like a dead fish (well, it would, wouldn't it?) is carried aloft by the wailing priests (no women *here*, thank god), on a cart adorned with lemons, jessamine, dog violets, Pascal roses (in spring, Mary?), goose-grass, barleycorn, old agrimony, heliotrope, sun-spurge, pomegranates, asphodels, . . . you name it . . . in fact just about everything but my lovely, for ever absent, yellow sea lupins (*lupinus lupinum*) from Dungeness. Perhaps I should have brought a bunch with me for Miss X. Never mind . . . a few bits of wolf's bane knit together with ivy, and lamb's tongues and the stalks of viper's bugloss will have to do instead. (Horned poppy can apparently cause delirium, by the way. Boiling up the roots in mistake for sea-holly, a poor man once mistook his own chamber pot for a crock of gold. That fatal confusion between talent and desire . . .)

Hyacinth though too, Mary. Don't forget the hyacinth, that beauteous purple flower of joy and woe born – hélas – from her very blood.

Everyone then laments mournfully until midnight – talk about *Totem and Taboo* – when, as the clock strikes twelve (what else?), the Bishop appears in his quilted nightdress (I thought of our own less indirect Jack the Ripper back home) and, having first rapidly adorned himself with the sign of the X, sorry, + a quick flick of the right indeX finger up to the forehead, down to 'Messer Gaster', then to the left shoulder, then to the right – announces in all its paradoXical strangeness (well it would be, wouldn't it? cart before the fish as always in these crypto-metaphorico matters), *sum qui sum*, the ResurreXion itself: 'Xt is risen, He (sic) is risen indeed', climAXE of the most gruesome Pot-Boiler of them all, followed ('We have seen His disfigurement and now we are healed') by a burst of tautological fireworks throughout the town. What a +

Miss X had to bear herself, though, albeit worth its weight in gold and humbly rotated through forty-five degrees.

(I'm horribly scared of fireworks myself. Ever since that fatal November 5th when Sigmund ran off in a kind of Dionysian fit at the sight of a catherine-wheel and got killed by the lorry you know where. Oh and it turned out at the autopsy that agoraphobia isn't a psychological illness at all, by the way, but simply a tiny flaw, missing piece or dysfunction in the brain through either a bout of whOOping cough or having missed out on learning to crawl at the appropriate stage. So much for Freud's Theory of AnXiety as a vital defence at the demands of the libido setting repression in motion and, unlike the Wolf Man's animal phobia – *he* never integrated the Primal Scene, poor lamb – without conversion symptoms of any kind other than imagining herself a Man.)

We began to read the names aloud.

Nothing yet. Mainly only Marias and Giovannis. (Nobody to teach us Italian at School. Only a few lines of *Paradise Lost* with up and coming Miss Twee who, ever since I'd heard of her uneXpected climb up the ladder to replace Miss P as Vice Mistress, I'd begun to look down on that little bit more. Self-fulfilling power of the label again. Thrones should be empty or not at all.)

Some treasure hunt, this!

We were hot on the scent now like Cerberus, alias Anubis, himself, though with no more clues to guide us than that little poorly XeroXed black and white photograph Mother received years ago from Mrs FoX-cum-Salmon. ('Look, Pin, isn't this the corner of that railing over there . . .?' It was not.)

And so on, interminably, in the boiling, dry heat of midday (in spring, Mary? Yes, dear Reader, in spring).

I was alone when I found it, needless to say.

No thief's accomplice necessary now.

Pin and Annabel had given up the hunt by then and were already loping off together towards the town. Arm in arm, I noticed, though sometimes turning to look back warily in my direction . . . in case I started howling fearfully and digging her up or something, I shouldn't be surprised . . . running by with a leg on my shoulder like the murderous brother in *The Duchess of Malfi* again. And what with Easter always coming just after full moon . . . the time when we lupey, yellow sea-dogs need to roam abroad.

Not that there's any question of moonlight now.

Boiling sunshine just as I said, blazing like the Cooking-Pot of Justice itself.

And all this time nothing but the drone of the cicadas, Byron's 'people of the pine' (L. *cicada*, 'an insect with homopterous or uniform, as opposed to heteropterous, wings') . . . a shrill, dry, precise sound, on and on as if bent on scratching the silence with a pine needle . . . scratching the emptiness, scraping up the memories (don't remind me), ticking away like a jammed, twelve-inch gramophone record of 'His Master's Voice' as, waiting there in the bedroom in my pinky-red caftan listening to Schubert's 'The Trout' . . .

Here it is at last, though.

A simple plaque with the date and:

MISS X / AD ASTRA

just as Pin said, with, ghostly palimpsest in my mind's eye down in the left-hand corner, the secret nickname, 'PASCAL', just to add a phantom dose of salt to the wounds – not that it matters any more – by proving she had used it with Miss P too.

I went up sheepishly (we wolves are really *all* like that on the inside) and scraped half-heartedly at the massive stone over the entrance. More to enjoy the cool touch beneath my fingernails as I did during my dogged graveyard vigils neXt to The Pagoda than to . . .

Oh, I don't know. Why *did* I go to all this trouble to bring you here, after all? Certainly not *this* time to rip off my clothes, though goodness knows it's hot enough now. This squeaky, pseudo-Realism, too. Annabel was right. Unable to sound grave and glowing even now. Half saccadic lambaste, half eXhausted caprice. *Still* thrice crowing wolf at the midnight hour . . .

Yes, I was/am beginning to feel thoroughly eXhausted and giddy by then/now and felt/feel I must sit/lie down a year/moment in the shade. Under the table (tombs), under the lamp (shade), under the pines a little/long way off, but where, leaving my new rucksack, no, handbag again by then balanced on the entrance stone (crocodile-skin but only mock, of course), I could/can still stare back at the plaque itself, incised on my eyelids like an indelible badge (a NO SMOKING notice in the Ladies' Loo can sometimes get fiXed in the same way if you stare long enough, seared on the eyeball like a brand of fire), together with its sneaky/shady soubriquet.

('Et l'amertume est douce et l'esprit clair': who *did* write that famous 'cemetery' poem? Would I keep seeking his or her name if I didn't unconsciously already know?)

Annabel and Pin must have long since arrived back in the villa for a cup of Postum or Earl Grey tea by then. Laughing together like hyenas . . . laughing like Miss X and Miss P after my manic bike ride up the lane on Lady Macbeth, I shouldn't be surprised.

> That my foul knife see not the wound it makes,
> Nor heaven peep through the blanket of the dark . . .

(She was another of us in a way.)

How long did I crouch there waiting so faithfully like Greyfriar's Bobby by his Master's tomb? Xt only knows. (Careful, Mary. Here of all places. The marble crosses, the pious doves. The tooth of the living worm of pain waiting and listening still beneath the table tops.)

Why did I wait there?

Ditto only knows.

'*If I ever change towards you, promise to keep on knocking, my love.*'

Could it be for the sake of that once terrible prior decree even yet?

Miss X, please ring and wait for ever and ever.

'HEADMISTRESS PLEASE KNOCK.'

Could she hear me in there? '*Walls have ears, Mary, and you never know.*'

Knuckle, knuckle. Toc. Toc.

Who's the wolfkin, who's the fat cat, nibbling away at my little flat,

Ringing away at my little bell to share my wolfish marriage bed?

Mary.

Mary who?

Mary Wolfe.

Come up, my dear.

No thank you, Miss X. The grave's a fine . . .

But if it won't hurt your feelings, huff, puff, I'd rather not.

'All that weird modern literature, Mary. Where are its *values*, I ask you?'

'Precisely in its *lack* of fiXed values, Miss X. Writing is a form of eXorcism or CATharsis in touch with the unknown, you see, my lamb – a gigantic refleX of the unconscious (not that the sublime can be confused with mere orgasm), which, by eXposing the wager of its own tautological, meAtaphorical, dialectical . . .

But here, from the tomb itself, nothing but the unmistakable sound of silence . . . tumultuous, sepulchral, mulberry-coloured, omphalitic silence (well, there would be, wouldn't there?), fulfilling its SphinX-like, algebraic function to the last.

As stone-deaf now in death as she had turned stone-hearted in living, Miss X had missed her chance for me again.

No ears to *those* walls, Mary, my love.

That's it, though, isn't it, dear Reader, Writer, or whoever we are?

Imagination aware of itself! That precious criss-X in the living eye of the wager, which, by providing a glimpse of its own feed-back, knows itself the source of that very same infinity it seeks to fiX and tame outside, 'below' or 'above'.

Fail-safe wager if you like – better be hanged for a goat as well as a sheep – but not for the eXistence of 'God' and 'Eternal Life'.

Wrong for the right reasons like Pascal, Miss X as usual had got things upside down and inside out.

Hers was not the voice in the Wilderness.

She was not the source of the debt of living second life I came here to repay with my silly literary wreath of absent flowers.

By now I begin to feel a slight breeze on my face.

Strange, really, in such intense, dry heat.

Can Zeus have a howling storm up his nightshirt, or, failing that, at least a thundershower of gold to penetrate the chamber instead of me? . . . He who at least had the decency to make love to Callisto disguised as a WO-MAN. Wolfish Artemis, in fact. Not that . . .

A warm, bluish light too, and the tallest of the great pine trees begins to sigh and gently creak if not moan, lone, groan, bathed in the rich glow like a flying birch or golden sycamore, a single, premature evening star in its topmost branches and its ivy-covered thyrsus, usually straight as a mast on the ship of Odysseus, slowly bending down towards me like a sharp lead pencil as if it might even snap right off . . .

L'heure bleue.

Air itself an eXtension of sight . . .

. . . And all this though there seems to be no wind at all now, I realise . . . only the almond eyes and warm, sweet breath of something, passing, passing, like a vibrant shadow over the pine trees, over the table tombs, over my unsuspecting – well almost unsuspecting – head . . .

But what is this?

Who says a watch-pot never barks?

With eXquisite timing and Racinian relevance . . . almost as if to substantiate the claims of the very Theory I've just eXpounded . . . not to mention an unmistakable noise of tearing, grinding, snoring, no, *waking* from snoring (Homer's real Cyclops, Mount Etna, remember, is just up the road from here in the flesh), *the Great Stone is obviously being torn from the entrance* under the pressure of some violent CATastrophe, finally to rip it open with a last mighty hiccup: handbag, homemade ivy-wreath, falsely identifying name plaque, eXcluded middle, and all.

Yes, no doubt about it. Stylistic ornaments kicked violently aside for a moment (pseudo-Realism, my foot!), the Great Stone Lid of the Great Stone Watch-Pot is being rolled carefully and yet flamboyantly aside or asunder . . .

And there, dressed in loose black slacks and what looks a bit like my own white angora sweater (I thought for one taXing moment it might be myself), tottering slightly on her surely painfully cloven feet in the sharp stilettos (no decadent cigar now like Annabel, though, I'm relieved to notice), eyes kindly cast down at first as if to pretend not to notice my embarrassment, her left hand (wrapped in a small, white bandage, for some reason) pointing mysteriously upwards like the hand of St Anne in the famous Leonardo cartoon (the *Virgin and Child with St Anne and the infant St John*, you must know it), young St X and Capricorn miraculously restored to life (the child Horus?) and clinging like Romulus and Remus somewhere on her person, auburn hair rippling like a radiant Gold Fleece in the gentle, but still clear evening light, there stands who else but

the *other* Miss X!

the New Tutor!

not the first Miss X at all!

– giving me, just as she did that day after the sheepskin rug affair in OXford, an unmistakably humorous wink, followed by a critical but (joy, oh joy), still decidedly encouraging smile. (What else is a Novel but a form of Essay, seeking a mark till the very tomb, I ask myself more freely now?)

The *other* Miss X! The New Tutor!

Greatest literary Xiasmus of them all!

She who first set me on the road to be myself, as you know . . . biting for ever now with her blessing the precious hand that fully fed. (Yes, forget the maternal vulture Freud surely totally mistakenly found hidden in the swirling skirts of a further version of the painting: I myself, together with thousands of hungry intellectual Mary Wolves like me, must have caused the bandaged hand, I'm afraid.)

11 a.m. Coffee. MISS X AND MARY WOLFE
SATURDAY 14th FEBRUARY, 1959

Feast of Lupercus! Valentine's Day!

I had returned to the point of transition, the point of Xiasmus, the point of metamorphosis . . . the point when Miss X, the *first* Miss X, I mean, so nearly failed to pass the Torch, the very same Torch – here the only *true* pelican – which flared so joyfully before me now. '*Pierre de touche*, Mary. Got your French notebook? . . .

It was the *other* kind of touchstone: Imagination. Love and Learning all in one. That rare being who contains our meAtamorphoses without in the process turning to stone or being tempted to gobble us up in return . . .

Imagination. Mon seul désir. My, halcyon's nest, my joy, my sorrow, my source of empathy, my science, my freedom, my first and only truly sighted, truly reciprocal Lighthouse Lamp.

Now it was I who had seen a wolf (and after I'd seen her first this time, too)!

. . . One of those moments far too difficult to dare to describe in mere words (then spare us, Mary) . . . **like listening to the Mozart Requiem** (his *own* in Mozart's case) on the car radio that time with Bill outside Hey Presto's Supermarket (well, Safeways, then, I think it's changed hands and gone organic – careful, Mary –), and seeing, passing before us in their millions (millions, Mary? well, hundreds and thousands, then), fat, thin, old, young, male, female, each, yes, each tenderly unique and intensely physical, individual person, the same yet different, different yet the same (no mere 'X's here, you see, that's the whole point of it) . . . **or like looking at the Leonardo cartoon itself** that time in London with Annabel and dear Mowgli – those wondrously balanced and entwined, no, adjacent, purely adjacent laps and sublimely blissful smiles admired by Freud so that even the notion of sublimation . . .

If I had howled my eyes out that night by the River . . . tears of abandonment, tears of loneliness, tears of wretched, shameful jealousy . . . now my only tears were those of incredulous recognition . . . the tears of Admetus seeing again his dear Alcestis,

213

not that, in this case . . . but now, this time, restored for ever . . .
tears of gratitude, tears of silent, gormless rapture, scalding the
very paving stones of Troy. (Well, gormless on the outside,
perhaps. Inside, unlike that previous cathartic moment in the
cornfield, my mind was perfectly lucid and clear . . .: that love
which *cannot* speak its name simply because of too much joy.)

On the marsh the grasses blow and blow
And I shall be happy, I know and I know . . .

Didn't I tell you? Didn't I really always know?

The tallest of the great pine trees was rustling impatiently again by
now . . . rustling and singing . . . almost, you might say, ringing . . .
white cats in its branches (you pull off their tails as a cure for
vertigo), sweet pagods hung with curfew bells, tiny, clattering
hooves like a sleigh on a roof-top (at Easter, Mary?) . . . sound itself
taking off like a creaking cello concerto, drunk and intoXicated
with the lambent joy of the moonlight (I must have stayed out here
far longer than I thought), while all along the side of the path we'd
tried to cut with the scythe that morning (but I thought that was
back at the cottage, Mary?), the long whispering grasses – reeds,
grasses, bulrushes, make up your mind, dear – trembled and bent
like living ninepins, down but then up again, swathes of white
parsley (*Saint* Anne's Lace, proffered Mother hopefully) and
trembling, feather-bed goose-grass, pricking up mad March ears as
we passed, until . . . but hark!

. . . It is the wingèd guardians faint calling
'Ere that thread of life,
Dark skein across the still pale sky,
Weaves stronger till at last, from overhead,
Sweet air swirls round her senses
And the richness of that ancient sound,
At once full-bellied and ethereal,
Reaches her heart . . .

(Pin's second poem, written on that special Xmas Eve together
back at The Unicorn, kept till now a total secret, and though I
found myself stifling a yawn as I heard it – what is anXiety but
eXcitation without oXygen? – worth a hundred pot-boilers any
day) . . . As if from nowhere, the far north, the Arctic wastes, the

great, glittering snow-fields, land of Sibelius, Grieg, Prokofiev, the Back of the Heavenly Wind itself perhaps . . . honking and whiffling, skein after skein of them, their feathered scissor-blades stretched like a great V-shaped pine needle of living bodies in unison across the whole garden (so it *is* the garden now, then?), ancient image of desire: the geese, the geese, the blue, blue geese (L. *anser*), perpetual wild watch-dogs chasing thin air.

EXtasy, EXcelsior, EXanimo, EXucontian, EXcalibur! Thirst made source!

It was Pan, I know it. (But I thought you said . . .?)

Pan of the many shapes and disguises like Proteus.

Pan, the New Tutor, friend of Dionysus and Apollo both.

Pan the joyful one with his wild (but still controlled and reasonable, surely?) love of music (literature too, Mary, don't forget love of literature – isn't that what this is all about in a way?) and dance, dance, dance (oh yes, with her own auburn hair that time, flying, flying, words have their movement, too, dance, dance, dance) . . .

Yes, Pan, the great Pan, with his reed-fashioned pipes.

Pan, the assuager of ancient guilt and remorse.

Pan the true shepherd, goatherd, then, half beast, half man, born on Mt Lycaeus in Arcadia (lucky Devil) of Zeus by Callisto, Callisto by Zeus, then, if not Zeus by a woodpecker ('pecker up, Mary! . . .'), some say a nightingale, some say a cuckoo (stag's horns, Mary, got your green uniform?) and some, like my tattered old *Dictionary of Myth* (VIa, Prize for Classics signed you-know-who) say Amaltheia, the goat nymph, honoured in turn, when time and circumstance were right, as the constellation Capricorn . . .

Pan, alias Lupercus, Lord of the Harvest if not Lupercalia (didn't I tell you?), corn goat, corn wolf, corn goat in white sheep's fleece, seducer in turn of chaste Pitys of the pine tree and Selene-cum-Artemis, goddess of the moon, in turn in love with Keats's Endymion, asleep for ever on the mountain slopes . . .

Pan, yes, Pan, the drowsy faun or cat-napping Satyr (must be some mistake with her alert and so lucid), the breeze of his own warm breath cool on his fleece now, the uneXpressed flames of Mt Etna but a touch of obscure rose there in the background, asleep and dreaming of Mallarméan nymphs in the tufted slumbers of this very same Sicilian afternoon sun (my crime to have divided two such mysterious Xes, there where one alone now, only one) . . .

Pan of the sudden, sacred fear in the wild, wild woods or the pattering forest, calling the wolves to stand and dance in the cornfields, when all of a sudden – hark, nyX, night, chaos – words no longer mean as she patiently taught them, fall in panic, and 'IT' alone, but joyous now, hallowed, the Queen held before me, scatters piercing-sweet chaos, chaos and ruin to the order of Pentheus, fearful yet buoyant, skims like a dragonfly over the blue, blue empty spaces, comfort in terror, close of the day now, pure fading light now, alone now not upright, over the tombstones, over the citadels, nods the shimmering mountain pine . . .

Pan, the Great Pan, not dead after all, then, father (some say brother) of red-faced Silenus, tutor in turn of the great Dionysus: Dionysus Zagreus, Dionysus the Goat God, born (didn't I tell you?) from the rapture of the Satyrs that time in the Wilderness, and rising from the bulrushes, reeds in the reed bed, then (hélas, poor SyrinX), like the would-be child phoeniX of every arid, Novelistic quill . . .

Oh, not the cruel, savage Dionysus of the Bacchic orgies that time by the cup-cupboard – mere wolfish underbelly of our Father Apollo watched salaciously by the tyrant, Pentheus (see there, those wild women, savage, anonymous, call them women, tearing to pieces with uneXpressed fingernails his helpless body perched aloft on its pine tree, and she so moral beyond moral, caring, humorous, diligent, wise) – nor yet the Dionysus of my would-be tragic sacrifice of a goat in His name in the cornfield (yes, I'm quite sure now, sobering thought), but Dionysus Child of the Double Door, most terrible and yet most gentle to us eXtraordinary mortals here above Him in our *heavenly* emptiness, cut from the thigh of Zeus the Father (neither seX nor gender are natural categories anyway according to Annabel), and reconstructed, like whispering SyrinX, lost for ever, but does it matter – all her hollowed cost and pain – from the sweet, purple blood of the hya . . . no, pomegranate, murmurous two-way food of our belovèd daughter, Persephone, seized while picking in these very stone meadows, all her bitter-sweet Sicilian flowers . . .

Honey-fed Dionysus, married, some say, to Demeter, reared like a girl (you see, that eXplains it) and later, upright and alone, a ram, who rescued Ariadne – easier to suffer than to comfort and be strong – from her cruel abandonment on the isle of NaXos (shades of Taormina) by the very same ungrateful Theseus, husband of Phèdre, whose life she saved, not to mention his own dear lost Mother, Semele, from her underground omphalos (Mrs X, don't remind me), consumed by a thunderbolt when she insisted on looking his father full in the thigh . . .

Dionysus of Inspiration (Gr. *eXtasis*?), He whom *true* Reason ignores at its peril, with His terrible thyrsus of twisted pine (that rippling flight of animal whiteness, blue, blue whiteness, then, is geese still, you notice, Dear Reader, not swans) or, better still, **Imagination, Queen of Faculties Herself . . . in fact, where we came in, not really Dionysus, Pan or Demeter at all!** Many the transformations of the gods.

(Some confusion of laps and limbs here, Mary, let alone cultural genders, generations and so on. Maybe dear Annabel was right and we *do* need a terrifying New Rhetoric after all, born in my case back and anew from my own mysterious struggle to unite two different worlds and poured like dry rain from my trumped up flute . . . Is it up to us so-called lacking ones to disguise the new god of Women, Wine and Song in the mere sheep's clothing of the Good Shepherd Eros? Is rest in chafing restlessness not far more drear

Than to be crush'd, in striving to uprear
Love's standard on the battlements of song?

Almost crushed to pieces now like Romulus and Remus under the belly of the She-wolf, let alone Odysseus under the belly of the Ram, I felt the great shaggy body with its sweet-smelling breath, snub nose and all-tickling goat's beard (a bit like Bill's, now I come to think of it) adjacent to my own leaf-green lap in the moonlight, and, again quite unlike that guilty time writhing on my tripod in the stubble like a truncated python, mouthpiece of Apollo, was not ashamed or androgynous or only half human at all.

Had I not felt for one dazzlingly clear instant of rapturous panic ('The handbell, Mary. She wants the handbell'), but, with her help again this time, for ever and ever, the perfect fusion, no, cohabitation, of two distinct selves, Public and Private, thought and emotion, wave and particle, Self and Other, Man and Beast (**male and female? no, of course not, Mary, that's nothing to do with it**, as I've been telling you throughout this Novel), finite and infinite all in one?

As the Emperor of China finds for his pains in my equally tattered old Hans Xtian Andersen (IIa English, before her time), no creaking, trumped-up, mechanical nightingale, however bedecked with gold and sapphire, is half so sweet as the bird in the woods.

O Sicilian shores. Did I love a dream? But no. **It was real**. Joy of the cornfields all along.

Drunk on the glow of my fabulous tears, alone and upright now as a rod, couple, farewell! I go to see the shadows we become.

In uneXpected ways the gods perform. Many a thing past hope have they fulfilled before too long.

Imagination, Queen of Faculties, without which Morality itself . . .!

No wonder poor Miss X, the first Miss X, I mean, had chased and then abandoned me, burning her fingers when they touched the inner flame.

Even there in the broom cupboard under the stairs with her tongue in my mouth and her hand groping down, confusing the Other with the Self, *that's* what she wanted for her own lonely cooking-pot! That's what she was after all along!

There was a poem, of course. Back at the villa within the hour. 'Between two Mirrors or Frost in the Park' (in March, Mary?), entombed with the rest in the Black Tin BoX, beginning somewhat grandiloquently:

> Splendour holds tears of you. However slowly I begin
> To shovel random drifts of snow,
> The outline of the garden springs
> Quite suddenly translated by the frost
> Into the particles of long discovery,

and ending, a few hundreds of strained octosyllables later:

> It is not failure to forget, nor failure to go on.
> Perfectly loved, you shall be set
> Slow in the future velvet of the dark
> With a clear reverence. And yet
> Your fine hands gesturing alive
> In small kind rings of knowledge and advice
> Will never touch and never know
> This detailed tenderness of snow
> Where trees shine delicately dark
> And where my joy of you has sprung
> Through the soiled tunnels of the sun
> Into the great white splendour of the park.

. . . a poem in which (still always that primitive contrast of hot and cold, pure and impure, even now, you notice), the intense, Sicilian heat of the little maritime cemetery has become mysteriously confused with the snow that Xmas Eve of my very last visit to the old School building. 'Snow in June', as Pin had so judiciously said.

She at least, the New Tutor, had forgiven my temporary fictional acceptance of pain, of emptiness, of loss. (Ah, Mary Wolfe, what reversals *there*.)

'You *did* invent that bit about the murder in the kitchen, Lou,' Pin went on eagerly, though I could see she was worried all the same.

'The bit about climbing up the pine tree and staring in at the window too. Unlike walnut trees, mature pines don't *have* any lower branches, as you very well know.'

We were back in the plane on the return journey to Heathrow by now and carrying on the conversation virtually where we left off. For some reason I hadn't felt like telling them what had happened back there in the cemetery. In case they confused imagination with mere fancy, I suppose. The *true* secrets start when there's nothing to hide . . .

'Seriously though . . . All this "literary fantasy" stuff. Aren't you afraid that at the end of it all, they'll charge you with . . . oh, I don't know . . . wishful thinking, thin air? Inventing your own Freudian unconscious if you like . . . getting the cart to pull the horse, as you're always whining on about yourself . . .'

The image of poor Sigmund on one of her reluctant walks to the town crawled slowly before me on all fours – well, it would be, wouldn't it? – tail clamped in a rigid, anoreXic curve between her back legs (no more false pregnancies, though, you notice) loose, black skin wrinkled round for ever reproachful eyes as she strained back obstinately from the direction of advance, presumably the terrifying supermarket again to get vegetarian sausages for lunch.

' . . . The reason *I* never want to write that kind of . . .'

'Certainly not,' I crowed like a thief's accomplice before she could finish, proud to have the chance to break from covert and be openly rather than crypto-didactic at last. To please *and* teach, didn't Racine say?

And besides . . . the plane.

Relapsing into Patriarchy and false Reason – don't we all? – I *still* needed sanctimoniously to produce some kind of trump card, if not metacritical stone paperweight – the ultimate Rhine Gold? You can tell why Wagner became a Xtian – to control their feelings before the whole thing backfired and it was for ever too late.

(Annabel was passionately immersed all this time in another of

M/W's best-selling Lesbian Feminist novels but, just like that time with Bill in the cottage, I knew she was listening all the same.)

'It's all very well for Annabel to try to pass the buck like that' (the 'PB' note with my birthday card) 'and say that only psychoanalysis can cut the Gordian Knot. But what you *all* don't realise . . .' (I was addressing the other passengers too by this time. A free public diatribe in the Forum of the clouds, why not? – marvellous clouds with rose-flushed edges chasing each other over the bottomless abyss, though how on earth I can manage all this infinite space . . .)

' . . . is that **it's only Writing in the first place which can** . . .' (The plane was lurching violently again now, and, raising my voice to full, vibrating wolf-whistle above the bull-like snorting of the engine, I clutched 'PB' with even more compulsive superstition than before. Isn't that what a touchstone, alias lap-dog's for?

'Well, put it like this. **What if Literature itself is a form of conscious latah?**' (Coughing violently now although I don't smoke. For some reason everyone seemed to be listening intently, even Pin who asked the question, so I'd have to be quick and, despite acute vertigo again at so much blue sky, pluck up courage to jump through the gap.)

'You know, that self-induced state of trance I often mentioned earlier in conneXion with so called primitive tribes who imagine they have changed into wolves or something and rush about devouring human flesh . . .' (I was feeling more and more savagely irritated by now at having to repeat myself for the benefit of all the nefarious passengers unable to profit from my careful definitions before they came in. That and a strange arching and elongating sensation all along my backbone – at least I still had one! – which made me feel as if an eXtreme effort were required to keep myself in human shape. Smiling self-consciously too by now, lips pulled back in a yellowing, Kafkaesque grimace – must get some bicarbonate of soda for my few remaining front teeth; no time for Wolfgang Amadeus of late.)

'**Even if I did invent the Murder, in other words** . . .' (let them still wonder about climbing the pine tree to surprise Callisto bathing naked like that) ' . . . creating, if you like,' (a bit like Sigmund's false pregnancies, come to think of it) 'my own self-conscious seXual identity, sorry, literary myth . . . **well, the ritual of Writing is not, any more than the ritual of latah, a mere one-way diagram, but something which helps to release the X-factor or unknown** . . . something unavailable in the system before and which, since, unlike Religion, Literature is potentially aware of itself . . .'

'Oh for Xt's sake, Lou,' snapped Pin suddenly, groping ferociously in her OXfam bag for a Mars. (Gives you such a fright when they interrupt like that when you think you've got them eating from the palm of your hand. Only true sister under the skin, Pin herself, though. I did not invent her.)

'OK, OK. Keep your hair on. Only a few more deliberately deadly-dull paragraphs to go.' (Things seemed to be hotting up all round us now and I was getting more and more prickly, elongated and incandescent, flicking my pink-rimmed reading-glasses on and off as I spoke and rubbing 'PB' like a magic amulet, signifying crystal of very Phobia itself. A double rainbow just above us, too. Obviously the crock of gold was on its way, and let's hope not merely a chamber-pot.)

'What I'm *trying* to say . . .' (and sometimes the build-up to these things *is* the message, something Philosophers never understand) '. . . is that 'IT' could only disappear back into the desert or, in my case, up the mountains to that wild glen in Scotland with Pin, Mother, Annabel or Bill, **when Writing had given nothingness a name** . . .' (Yes, that's it. The crunch at last. From this side of the signifying bar at least I can see what she means now about the delay.)

'**EX/IT, IT/EX:** that same self-devouring Xiasmus or criss-X I was whiffling . . . no, sorry, that's the geese . . . waffling on about earlier in the cemetery, where, by gaining a glimpse of its own feedback . . . the nothingness, then, of its own empty centre – **the fiction of identity and identity of fiction, yet again, if you like** – the mind is free to accept itself: that which stands still by changing shape, free to run in the mountains at last. **Seek and ye hath already found (Pascal).** The talking-cure I suppose, in a way?' (I looked appealingly at a red-faced businessman with a huge, pear-shaped stomach just across the aisle, glowering lasciviously over the top of a copy of *Playboy*: treacherous 'bunny girl' eXploited supine on top. Hélas, they who bind us do not speak our language, as Lacan, no, Leonardo da Vinci once said.)

Even as I talked, I felt just that precious fraction suspicious of myself, however.

Surely I must have turned back to the scene of the crime for some more honourable purpose than the mere personal therapy of a howl amongst friends . . . some further need which, in retracing, or *appearing* to retrace my own footsteps in Public through the very same shaggy dog story that gave them birth? (one remembers *because* one is cured, after all) . . .

But, of course.

Myth! (Preferably the Greek and so long as they knew what they were doing.)

The communal resources of the tribe!

Herne the Hunter

The Hamatsa

The Witch Doctor

The TriXter

The Healer

The HeXe

. . . bringing back for others into the Marketplace the secret of taming the very same fear of eXcessive hunger (suppressed anger in my case according to Annabel) which . . .

The Shaman

The Magpie

The Shape-Shifter

The *Bricoleur*

The Dancer

The PhoeniX

. . . or, if you must, the Literary Lycanthrope . . . concentrating and displaying her fragmentary trophies like the courtship ritual of some strange, human guinea-fowl (Freudian slip, I was thinking of money still: boiling the pot for the coming of winter) and going on learning from them in turn.

Courtship rituals, did I say? (I had forgotten my home audience completely now and was off on a further wild blue-goose chase of my own.)

Yes. Not to put too fine a point on it, **Annabel herself and the single, magic touch to release me from the monstrous myths of the inaccessible . . .** source of Tragedy, source of the Gods, source of just such Theories of Art and SeX and Death as I find myself still nervously eXpounding even now . . .

Annabel herself and the single magic touch . . . though, truth to tell, sometimes I almost feel I **invented her too**, critical tooth within my own head . . . all but myself and, of course, Miss X . . . and that **Writing is the only true bird in the bush** to keep us on the toes of metamorphosis.

Is there no end to the foXy tricks of desire without imagination to hold it in check? Can the geese never roost on the lake in the meadow? **Will the Wolf cry Wolf till it's devoured the Sun?** Is there, thank goodness, *no* resting-place?

None at all, Mary, just as we said.

We were flying over the Sea now (talk about Icarus and the fabled Aegean, though, of course, no one did).

. . . Everyone else looking reasonably normal and human eXcept yours truly, lurking suspiciously on all fours near the rear-side wing, which I happened to notice was covered in vines and glossy strands of ivy as if Dionysus Himself were on board (with the lust for immortality characteristic of the ephebe, could I have swallowed even the New Tutor too?), and, indeed, so cramped up now that my vertebral column felt eXcruciatingly bristling – must be the doomsday, sorry, greenhouse effect – and well nigh on fire (a bit like poor Dad, and the first Miss X after Dungeness crammed down under the front seat of the car) . . . almost as if I might have slipped a floppy disc simply by sitting there so long.

Toothache, too, to make things worse. An eXceeding sharp pain as if a sabre-toothed dolphin (Wolfgang Amadeus, Wolfgang Amadeus) were trying to bite my upper lip, let alone write a requiem, just by that line of whiskers on the left-hand side of my mouth. (Not that at my age, there's any risk of turning into a grandmother now)

. . . When suddenly, with absolutely no warning at all (perhaps I'd hijacked it or something, though in that case, so as not to hurt our feelings, I should surely have sent us all a kind message in advance?), the plane must have eXploded into at least fourteen pieces, blown to bits anyway like Hippolyte's ill-fated horsedrawn chariot and – never mind all the other poor guilty passengers – all three of us were **killed on the spot**.

So much for my lucky Philosopher's Stone, *Solve et Coagula!*, smashed to smithereens along with the rest (I never really understood all that Jungian alchemy stuff), and, were he not crouching here smugly still on my desk with all the mysterious endurance of the inanimate object refusing dissolution, gone to shed crocodile tears in the Nile along with OXy you-know-what.

'X = Y', my foot!

Unlike similarity – '*like* wolves' ('*comme* les loups') – total identity is no relationship at all.

Total identity is death!

Now **do you see the Writer is always separate from the Work?**

223

Just before 'IT' happened though, or rather *as* 'IT' happened (like appearing to wake just a fraction before your alarm clock and never quite knowing if it's simply a delayed reaction or not), glancing out towards the near-side wing of the plane (what else?), **I had frightened myself clean out of my skin to see what looked indubitably like a huge, hooded black bird** with ass's ears like those of poor Midas, **advancing towards us with wolfish, impetuous beak** . . . vast, drowsy wings flapping slowly and ineXorably – oh the patient, pagan souls of my N. American Indian Ancestors – vulturous, self-anointing lips outstretched to speak like the plaintive lips of Alcyone flashing as a kingfisher to join CeyX, her dead lover (I thought again for a moment of Freud's hidden vulture) . . . **and**, too late, hélas, for poor old Pin, but jazzy, alliterative, Xiasmic, self-devouring, just as she suggested (mustn't hurt her feelings), **screaming my perfect *nom de plume* as it passed.**

I leave you, dear Vampire, to work out what it is for yourself. Indeed, if you fail *your* Imagination just at the last, *you* have only to steal a glance at the sheepskin jacket of this Book – thief's accomplice now yourself – to see it shine out smug and clear as the thirsty stars.

A wolf must die in its own skin, as George Sand, no, George Herbert, apparently said.

As for me, I'm a **Real Wolf**, *canis lupus* now at last.

Speak of the wolf and the wolf appears: you knew I would be, all along . . .

A wolf, a real wolf, running, running (lack of oXygen, *now* they tell me), breathing freely at last, at last . . . through the plains, through the deserts, through the sweet-smelling pine forests, down that private track at the back of the old cemetery, along the sinuous edge of my cornfield, through the wild, purple glens, through the glittering snow-fields . . . my sharp ears flattened, the wind ruffling or smoothing my long grey fur and eXciting the sensitive, white bristles round my nose and mouth, my tail held in nearly a full circle between my back legs and lining my lean belly with its primeval curve.

No one can accuse *me* of not having the courage of my own nomenclature, of not living eXistence *jusqu'au bout*.

The rocks, the streams, the trembling goose-grass, the bright leaf-green moss used to staunch wounds in the First World War . . . I love them all. I know each hillock, each hummock, each hollow . . .

each strange, luminous sea loch, each beach, each barley-field, each eXtraordinary pebble, each hairy weft and wold.

The sun is on my spine now. My savage claws are sheathed, almost delicate, padding lightly in my characteristically swinging trot, my tongue – oh, that infamous red tongue of mine – hanging soft and quivering from the corner of my mouth.

I can be gentle too, you see. I care for my young. For them and for the sick and lame amongst us I regurgitate my spoils. You like to think that redeems me in some way. I know when to lie down and present my neck like a unicorn to the dominant partner (though that admittedly is not without its interpretational problems, turning my muzzle away so as not to provoke with fear of biting when I might have simply liked to lick and play).

I lie alone or with my faithful, carefully chosen, repeat faithful, carefully chosen mate in the dens or burrows we have stolen and enlarged together, homes of red rabbits, badgers, pole cats, gluttons, weasels, lynX, minXX ('*vison*, Mary. Got your French notebook?') and sometimes even the crafty foXXX, whom some think a distant relative of mine (totally mistakenly, of course). We curl around each other head to tail. I lick our tender, burning flanks. If and when time and season are right, we make love, L. *more ferarum* (well it would be, wouldn't it), admittedly usually with the so-called opposite seX, imagination not eXactly being our favourite cup of barley mead, or if you must, our desert well.

My pups lick and play with the soft pink teats hidden deep in my grey fur (no choice in my case, but to ring the changes I sometimes rear human orphans as well: Romulus and Remus, Kipling's Mowgli, the Wild Boy of Aveyron and, though I usually keep *his* name a secret, Oedipus of the swollen feet, abandoned on a hillside by his parents in his case – and look what still happened – long, long ago. My, the appetite of the orphan child! My, those sharp teeth guzzling vigorously at my sevenfold dugs even when they're fully grown and should be suckling from cows like mature werewolves on their own! There's really nothing you can do but wait, wait, patiently wait until that blissful day when they stand on all four feet and set out to found Rome.)

Then off again once more, running, running, always running, running for *her* sake, movement itself, perhaps, gaunt, grey ghost along the thin, grey ridges, wandering (L. *erro*) through the deserts, through the forests – oh those eXquisite, sweet-smelling pine forests – through the glens, through the plains, through the glittering snow-fields, down that private track at the back of the old cemetery, past the cackling geese (eXcuse me a second) at the foot of the golf course . . . I who was once a *Man* in another life: Lycaon himself, perhaps, straight from the fresh-cut pine-tree pages of my siXth form School prize Ovid, a gleam in my eye and my jaws flecked with blood, driven by my wolfish appetite (well I would be, wouldn't I, being a wolf? None of that terrible metaphorical slippage now – '*entre chien et loup*, Mary. Got your French notebook?' – which plagued me in another life.)

No point in even *trying* to convey here my sense of smell, a million, million times more sharp and compleX than your own (I'm not joking).

My glowing, amber eyes (a bit like Annabel's, come to think of it) are keener, too, than even those of the proverbial vulture, Horus-headed falcon, avenging nightingale or hawk (magpie, jay, raven, vulture, crow – genus *corvidae* – they're all the same. Wolves on wings, croaking and vying for every wish-bone.)

I see the bird wheel and drop far, far off down the mountain. But what am I saying 'the bird'? . . . The lamb, the sheep, the goat, the foX-cum-salmon, the stag, the moose, the wildebeest, Hannibal's elephants over the Alps, the first Miss X herself, given half the chance. We can hunt alone or in packs like Hitler's U-boats (not that . . .), a hundred of us fitting eXactly into a single set of prints made by the friend in front of us, then spreading out and organising who does what. 'For the strength of the Pack is the Wolf, and the strength of the Wolf is the Pack.' Why, sometimes running for miles and miles on my febrile, dancing paws, faster, even, than the freckled fingers on a modern word-processor with a billion bites, I round up a whole herd disguised in sheepdog's clothing (we wolves have our own sick puns and jokes too, you notice, the lure in the service of a greater need, as Jacques Lacan said) – trotting, dancing, shuddering, squatting, waiting, forever patiently, doggedly waiting, waiting, until one lame or sick one (stragglers also have their ruses) drops eXhausted and at last I pounce as you knew I would.

With specially fitted incisors like mine, *I* don't need to write a carnivorous pot-boiler.

Those and my iron-jaws are enough.

I prefer to disembowel my prey *living* (don't worry, Mother, they hardly feel a thing, dying almost at once in a state of severe shock), my white teeth ripping the warm, red entrails and crunching the bones until they sing. Dead flesh sometimes too, though, I admit. The dead horse, the laughing jackal – they too have their little jokes – the dead, dead duck. I have been known to return to the carcass, or even – though only when forced to keep the Man from the door– the human graveyard, there to gorge myself like my faithful ole fellow coyotes, baby-snatching dingoes (not really), laughing hyaenas, wild dogs.

It's our nature, you see. Robbers and Ravagers all.

Can the vulture *really* change her plumage? Can the She-wolf change her skin even with the help of a jazzy pseudonym?

We predators keep the balance, after all. EXiled from the future, we need your love.

Well, it's better than eating human beings alive. That's just a cruel, anthropomorphic myth devised as an eXcuse to make us all eXtinct, **we who are basically eXcessively shy**, as St Petrus, St Peter, then, and St Andrew, our patron saints, well knew, sending us to punish with our special cicatriX only those who eat meat on their special feast days, only those who 'seven times never kill Man' . . .

Friends, Chickens, Citizens, Sheep, Goats, Children, Readers, Hypocrites, Writers, Lovers, male *and* female Patriarchs, beware my gentle, padding footsteps, bind me to the mast by the tip of my grey tail lest I should rush into the Marketplace with the violence of a werewolf and devour your fair daughters in their cradles (woe to the sheep whose judge is a wolf) or tear you to pieces on the spot (another of my risky little self-deprecatory jokes, of course – it's only you who *think* that I would), or, failing that, lest, standing on my hind legs like a Female Novelist (if you can't beat 'em, join 'em), unleashing the hounds of my imaginative wrath, **rave, rave, rave** like the ancient prophets (I'm thinking, of course, of the abominable Book of Leviticus) against everything oppressive and anti-blasphemous, yes, **anti**-blasphemous under the Sun . . . against Religion, against the Club, against the very . . .

(Careful, Mary, lamb. What if the wolf . . .? **But I *am* the Wolf now, Auntie. I can rave and rave now as much as I like. Dies Irae. Trumpet and cello from the mouth of the lion. The Mozart Requiem at last.**)

. . . that terrible anger (Mozart's is compassionate, didn't she say?), which, once identified in its deepest burrows, must be controlled, eXorcised, reharnessed, transformed, rechannelled, lest, like Actaeon's dogs failing to recognise their own Master's Voice . . . **'Actaeon! Nobody! Miss X! Wolf! Wolf!'** . . . it turns and tears you limb from husk (Actaeon, G. *aXth*, 'bruised grain or

227

corn', hence part of the great cycle of Dionysus, Demeter, Isis, and John Barley-corn) . . . lest in trying to eXtirpate that which is divisive, repressive, power-mad, you become yourself no more than a raving . . . where we came in – though *I* mean, of course, MAN.

We wolves have three sources of learning after all. Our ancestors, our parents, our own eXperience. Shy, compleX, intensely social *and* lone (there, you see!), I use them all. I am myself. Not frightened any more of my own infinite appetite, but only of **you**, dear Reader, **you, you, you!** . . .

You who never spare me with your shepherds and your dogs.

You who in your smart, foXy uniforms pursue me in the darkest forests, across the plains, through the deserts, down that private track at the back of the old cemetery – 'trespassers will be persecuted' – round by the cackling etc., etc., through the glens, through the seas, through the Arctic snow-fields, even to the heart of the Wilderness . . . with your jibes, your guns, your poisons, your lycanthropic shepherds and your treacherous dogs . . . those spies, those emissaries of the Devil, those cowering agoraphobic sycophants on leads, Murderers of Murderers – give a dog a bad name – my own family blood . . .

You who alone stigmatise, eXtirpate, erase, omit . . . the Other, the different, that which 'pollutes'.

You who alone with your savage, book-burning rites, rampant as an ulcerous skin disease, my foot, torture and hound and maim and kill aware of the nature of suffering itself . . .

YOU who would even rather imagine yourself a wolf (Man to Wolfe and Wolfe to Man) than stand on your own two legs and look your own unknown identity full in the eye, that sacred flame at the heart of the Temple (I'm joking again, there is no Temple – life *is* the flame that must destroy the Temple) with its power to transform the crimes of the past . . .

You who strangle the Joy at its birth, Pan, the Great Pan and the Planet itself, given half the chance.

You who are the poison and the wolf's bane of my life.

Learn to brook my lamb-soul yet . . . I who alone (pace Dionysius-Zagreus) am innocent of the Wolf of Death.

But now, lone wolf to the bitter end (who says the last wolf in Britain has been shot?), here I am climbing to the highest grey rock in the silence of the mountains (for the very last time, perhaps – who knows when *that* is?), up to that great grey boulder eXactly shaped at last in my own grey image, my symbol, my cypher, my unique embodiment, my ultimate meAtaphor, and there, lifting up my primitive neck with its characteristic ruff (often confused with hackles), my keen eyes closed now in a kind of eXstatic compulsion like Miss X that time at the top of the staircase, or, if you prefer, Leconte de Lisle's great mountain condor, my short, pointed ears pricked a moment against the huge crimson globe of the sun, my lips pulled back the way all dog lips do, my long tongue vibrating against my anthropine teeth – Wolfgang Amadeus – as the great ululation boils up and escapes along my throat from my stone-filled belly, I let out at last, at last, quoting Nobody now but my own primitive ancestors, my special wolf's howl:

Wow wow wow oooooooo OOOOOOO oooooooo WOW!

A howl full of snowfields and deserts and mountain tops.

The howl of a wolf's own unique self-identity, evoking the soul of the ancient wolves.

The howl of MetamorphOsis.

The howl of a wolf **crying wolf** in the Wilderness.

The howl of Nature against itself, against all those false things THEY say WE are.

You knew I would.

You too, like Miss X, have been doggedly waiting. Hours, weeks, months, years even, waiting, waiting, to eXpress, to eXpel, to eXorcise, to give tongue at last.

Actaeon! Miss X! Xtine Crow! Mary Wolfe, Woolf, Wolf!

A howl hidden too deep beneath the ice-fields ever to escape from a mere literary work, ever to be interpreted eXactly correctly in its strange, confused voice.

Of course I have other languages too.

I bark, I whimper, I bay, I yap. I pass on to my children my special seasonal songs. I know how to speak with the marvellous organ of my whole living body, the position of my neck and ears and the movement and curve of my tail or the laughing motion of my lips when at play. I scent the rocks with my special signatures of urine, fierce or moderate according to the direction of the prevailing wind, the type of person I eXpect to read me, and a thousand other subtle things which only an eXtra special listener like yourself . . . (you see, we are learning to trust each other at the eleventh hour, now that we understand each other's similar differences and special needs, now that you know I'm not out to kill you, nor you me (?).)

No matter, though. It is always my howl you will remember and misinterpret . . . that same ancient howl which for centuries and centuries you have heard in your burrows and on your beaches, by your firesides, in your carefully dug earth-houses, in your Iron Age forts above the lapping sea lochs . . . in the moss, amongst the stones, ah, stones, in the supermarkets, on the motorways, in the courts and quadrangles (though that's a bit more difficult), reminding you of ancient guilts and fears . . . reminding you of long lost suns . . .

You wept for seven years.
The oceans swelled with your grieving.
And then, one silent evening, that howl, high and wide
As an ancient oak tree, echoing round the hollow hills.
It fills and empties me too like a bowl.
I am fused with it, ankylosed like a bone to its vigorous, living
                                                        death-wings,
Sweeping our family like tender leaves in its torrents
Monstrous leviathan flailing in the waters of its own raging
                                                        heartache.
The howl of injustice, loss, waste, oppression.
Ariadne. NaXos. Philomela. Procne. Niobe. Mother. Annabel.
                                                Bill. My sister.
That evening your pain had entered the world.
I shall remember it for the rest of my life.

. . . The howl of the great She-Wolf of Grief itself, rocked in the ancient arms of the universe, 'Lacrymosa', 'Dies illa', 'Ai, Ai', 'hélas, hélas', head back, mouth open, rocking, rocking, head forward now, then back again, stretching up, bowing, stretching, rocking, that age-old rhythm, heartbeats, footsteps over the deserts – gathering itself up slowly, the beginning of the Mozart, 'Requiem aeternis', remember, but no, not yet again, the unbearable, unsayable – proud, too, compassionate, gentle, disbelieving, powerless(?), terrible, for all those who have lost that which never, never . . . for the captives, for the conquered 'et bien d'autres encore'!
. . . that same ancient sound which, once your own ears have heard it, can never again be walled up or bricked over without the mask in its turn gaping open like a wound . . .
(Actually, it isn't a howl of grief at all, in my case – pecker up even here, Mary, 'must keep positive' – but a moan without pain, a

song without music like the wind, the wind, the *heavenly* wind, a compleX social ritual like Writing designed, as she said, to transmit the esoteric secrets of its own metamorphosis in finite, eXoteric form.)

I provide the food for literature and myth. Ovid, Homer, Webster, Mary Wolfe, Perrault, Baudelaire, Daudet, Kipling, The Three Little Pigs, La Fontaine, Leconte de Lisle, Petrus Borel, Alfred de Vigny, Sigmund Freud, Jacques Lacan, Jack the Ripper, Little Red Riding Hood – though she, of course, was not a Novelist – and many, many more.

I climb up walnut trees and enter your dreams.

I stare in at windows with my sad, loving eyes.

I fish in frozen rivers with my warm, furry tail.

I appear at your door like the cry of starvation.

Cruel to be kind and kind to be cruel, begging you dumbly to ask me to follow, Voice of the New Rhetoric standing on its own hind legs . . . **I am the scapegoat for your monstrous fear of the Imagination, that which given half a whisker of its own free head and denouncing the resting-place of bigotry, fear and belief**, will never cease to learn and transform till doomsday or the Twilight of the Gods, when, released by the Norns at last from my chain to the North Pole under the great ash tree, you have me turn like a heliotrope and swallow our Father/Mother, the Sun.

Change! Infinity! The unique! The unknown!

Rave, rave against the prior decree! . . . The unknown identity within the finite, Pascal's wager in reverse, not like anything or anybody else and which *is* therefore everything and everybody else! . . . that it didn't always have to be the same as before! startling into life again that strange inner creature, neither foX, nor bird, nor snake, nor wolf, who has slumbered so long, so lost, in its caverns, waiting, only waiting, if only to wake again, back and anew again, to sense again the living path of the dragon, lost and refound again . . . the moment, the opening, that pathway to joy . . .

Change! The X-factor! The unknown! The nameless heavenly Wind. The 'sum qui sum!' The precious X-over in the eye of the pin(e)-needle to catch the fruits of your own feed-back! Freedom to imagine yourself imagining yourself a Wolf and, in so doing, at last cut the Gordian Knot!

Zen and above all not Zen! Lesson of the empty Pagoda itself! Give up the path once you can no longer make it your own!

Sever the cord, cut loose, destroy your own god! Fear nothing but the fear of losing, through fear of movement, change and loss, the bright inner sword (sword, Mary?) to cleave the brambles choking the stream, source of the Other in the self . . . promise of water, promise of wealth here on the doorstep all along!

(It's true, though, isn't it, what they say about Fairy Tales? If the hero has only three true options when faced with CATastrophe: to forgive and take tea with the Wolf, to slay the Wolf, or to be eaten by the Wolf while lying asleep, possibly to be cut free from his/her stomach later on, then I, Mary Wolfe, had chosen all seven lives: the Witch, the Wolf's Bane *and* the Gingerbread.)

And so, dear Reader, the Happy Ending after all.

The other Miss X. Imagination, Queen of moral Faculties yet again. The Wolf in the dersert whose same eyes (Gk. *homos*) you fear as your life. Clue 'X' in the treasure hunt, the precious unknown identity under all our School hats! *Pierre de touche* of just about everything under the Sun including the precious identity of fiction itself.

> A travers les déserts courez comme les loups;
> Faites votre destin, âmes désordonnées,
> Et fuyez l'infini que vous portez en vous!

I'M THE WOLF WOMAN NOW. I can die in my own skin.

For the wrong reasons, Baudelaire was right.

Infinite Joy *is* appetite, the true resurreXion in *this* second life.

I gave up my 'Tragedy' book in the end, by the way. (Pecker up, Mary. Must keep positive!)

Ever since I discovered 'tragedy' isn't necessarily derived from the Greek *tragos* meaning a 'goat' after all, but from a similar-sounding word for 'spelt' (L. *spelta*), a gruff, if not husky, form of barley-corn.

'Miss X' is my 'Tragedy' book, you might say.

And besides . . . better be hanged for a goat than a lamb . . . have you never tried crying wolf just for fun? 'Miss X', 'my seX', 'CeyX', 'say X': supposing the whole thing was simply some intoXicated ole lycanthropic pun?

'Do you have a boy-friend?' asked the analyst almost right away at the first and last interview.

'Certainly not,' I replied sharply, 'and nor do I want one, if that's what you think.'

Only in the final few seconds, driven no doubt by the severity of IT to trust this new prophet despite myself, did I deign to reveal that I had, all the same, known the flames of true passion, true, reciprocated, yes, reciprocated passion, passion for an older person, a Person of Authority, who just happened to be nearly three times my own age, not to mention the same seX as myself.

Apart from Baudelaire's crafty poem about the forbidden fruits of Lesbos – women as ravenous wolves in the deserts – placed in a separate section of our edition of *Les Fleurs du Mal* and relegated with other 'Condemned Pieces' to the very end of the book, all I had heard or read even then on the subject was that queer, twisted novel, *The Well of Loneliness*, by Radclyffe Hall, its language oozing with the very concepts it purports to condemn. (At least, with Baudelaire, it's a Sin, not a disease, and the Devil far superior in artistic know-how and love of infinity to God, the Father, pipe and slippers in his Bourgeois armchair.)

On guard now for the slightest sign of prurience or pity – by their fruits shall ye know them – did I sense a moment's minute hesitation, a flicker of eXtra interest on the bland, SphinX-like face?

If so it vanished at once behind those sinister dark glasses – more a visor than two separate lenses – bunched like a single, blind eye in the middle of his forehead. (Like Racine's Phèdre, I too shunned the light in those days. Fair enough, I thought. Fair enough.)

'And what is her name?' he proceeded smoothly on receipt of this dramatic, last-minute avowal, pencil poised rapaciously above the virgin page.

'**Miss X**,' I replied like a shot. '**She shall be known as Miss X**,' and, to his chiding protestations ('Everything in this room is, of course, strictly confidential'), refused to budge one Greek iota or jot.

Even within these professional ramparts ('Walls have ears,

Mary, and you never know'), I, Mary Wolfe, long since abandoned without mercy, would keep my promise of total discretion, my tongue tight-knit to the roof of its cavern, my lips as tight-sealed as her tomb below.

Indeed, only now, all these many years later, Miss X herself sealed up in a wall ('That's how they bury them out there, Lou, you know'), do I feel at last I can tell our strange story, stitch together its scattered pieces, transform the living fictions of the past into truth. Who knows but that, free at last from fear of betrayal and removal from office – lying tongues more savage than the very nails of the Bacchae – she, Miss X herself, would not have begged me to tell it, final act of undying devotion releasing her poor soul at last from its prison, shouting it from the rooftops for all to know?

If it is revenge, my love, this wicked third person, heating the stone to boil the water, pecking and devouring your poor corpse to the bone, let it at least be for the crime of the turnskin (L. *versipellis*, 'turnpelt', 'turnskin'), not for the pain of illicit desire.

Were we not, you and I, goats in the sheepfold, sisters of rebellion under the skin? Did we not, after all, follow the same star?

I never went back – to the analyst, I mean.

Writing itself can sometimes eXorcise Love.